Raves for the Previous Valdemar Anthologies:

"Fans of Lackey's epic Valdemar series will devour this superb anthology. Of the thirteen stories included, there is no weak link— an attribute exceedingly rare in collections of this sort. Highly recommended."
—The Barnes and Noble Review

"This high-quality anthology mixes pieces by experienced authors and enthusiastic fans of editor Lackey's Valdemar. Valdemar fandom, especially, will revel in this sterling example of what such a mixture of fans' and pros' work can be. Engrossing even for newcomers to Valdemar."
—*Booklist*

"Josepha Sherman, Tanya Huff, Mickey Zucker Reichert, and Michelle West have quite good stories, and there's another by Lackey herself. Familiarity with the series helps but is not a prerequisite to enjoying this book."
—*Science Fiction Chronicle*

"Each tale adheres to the Lackey laws of the realm yet provides each author's personal stamp on the story. Well written and fun, Valdemarites will especially appreciate the magic of this book."
—*The Midwest Book Review*

"The sixth collection set in Lackey's world of Valdemar presents stories of Heralds and their telepathic horselike Companions and of Bards and Healers, and provides glimpses of the many other aspects of a setting that has a large and avid readership. The fifteen original tales in this volume will appeal to series fans."
—*Library Journal*

Choices

TITLES BY MERCEDES LACKEY
available from DAW Books:

THE NOVELS OF VALDEMAR:

THE HERALDS OF VALDEMAR
ARROWS OF THE QUEEN
ARROW'S FLIGHT
ARROW'S FALL

THE LAST HERALD-MAGE
MAGIC'S PAWN
MAGIC'S PROMISE
MAGIC'S PRICE

THE MAGE WINDS
WINDS OF FATE
WINDS OF CHANGE
WINDS OF FURY

THE MAGE STORMS
STORM WARNING
STORM RISING
STORM BREAKING

VOWS AND HONOR
THE OATHBOUND
OATHBREAKERS
OATHBLOOD

THE COLLEGIUM CHRONICLES
FOUNDATION
INTRIGUES
CHANGES
REDOUBT
BASTION

THE HERALD SPY
CLOSER TO HOME
CLOSER TO THE HEART
CLOSER TO THE CHEST

FAMILY SPIES
THE HILLS HAVE SPIES

BY THE SWORD
BRIGHTLY BURNING
TAKE A THIEF

EXILE'S HONOR
EXILE'S VALOR

VALDEMAR ANTHOLOGIES:
SWORD OF ICE
SUN IN GLORY
CROSSROADS
MOVING TARGETS
CHANGING THE WORLD
FINDING THE WAY
UNDER THE VALE
NO TRUE WAY
CRUCIBLE
TEMPEST
PATHWAYS
CHOICES

Written with **LARRY DIXON**:

THE MAGE WARS
THE BLACK GRYPHON
THE WHITE GRYPHON
THE SILVER GRYPHON

DARIAN'S TALE
OWLFLIGHT
OWLSIGHT
OWLKNIGHT

OTHER NOVELS:

GWENHWYFAR
THE BLACK SWAN

THE DRAGON JOUSTERS
JOUST
ALTA
SANCTUARY
AERIE

THE ELEMENTAL MASTERS
THE SERPENT'S SHADOW
THE GATES OF SLEEP
PHOENIX AND ASHES
THE WIZARD OF LONDON
RESERVED FOR THE CAT
UNNATURAL ISSUE
HOME FROM THE SEA
STEADFAST
BLOOD RED
FROM A HIGH TOWER
A STUDY IN SABLE
A SCANDAL IN BATTERSEA
THE BARTERED BRIDES

Anthologies:
ELEMENTAL MAGIC
ELEMENTARY

And don't miss THE VALDEMAR COMPANION
edited by John Helfers and Denise Little

Choices

All-New Tales of Valdemar

Edited by
Mercedes Lackey

DAW BOOKS, INC.
DONALD A. WOLLHEIM, FOUNDER
375 Hudson Street, New York NY 10014
ELIZABETH R. WOLLHEIM
SHEILA E. GILBERT
PUBLISHERS
www.dawbooks.com

Cover art by Jody Lee.

Cover design by G-Force Design.

DAW Book Collectors No. 1809.

Published by DAW Books, Inc.
375 Hudson Street, New York, NY 10014.

First Printing, November 2018
1 2 3 4 5 6 7 8 9

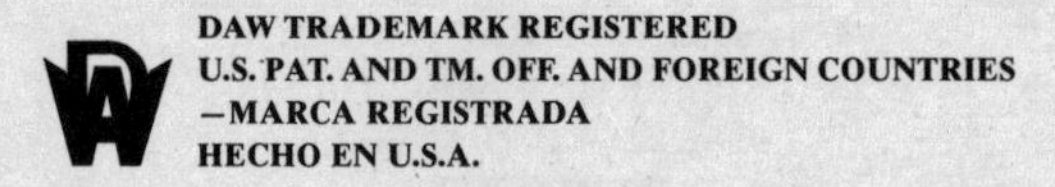

PRINTED IN THE U.S.A.

Contents

With Sorrow and Joy
Phaedra Weldon 1

Of Crows and Karsites
Kristin Schwengel 22

Feathers in Deed
Jennifer Brozek 41

The Letter of the Law
Angela Penrose 55

Who We'll Become
Dayle A. Dermatis 76

Unceasing Consequences
Elizabeth A. Vaughan 88

Beyond Common Sense, She Persisted
Janny Wurts 115

Moving On
Diana L. Paxson 136

The Right Place
Louisa Swann 153

A Siege of Cranes
Elisabeth Waters 174

Cloud Born
Michele Lang 186

Letters from Home
Brigid Collins 209

Friendship's Gift
Anthea Sharp 229

Enduring, Confusing, Perfect, and Strong
Ron Collins 244

The Once and Future Box
Fiona Patton 265

Acceptable Losses
Stephanie Shaver 285

Weight of a Hundred Eyes
Dylan Birtolo 310

Woman's Need Calls Me
Mercedes Lackey 327

About the Authors 353

About the Editor 360

With Sorrow And Joy

Phaedra Weldon

"A year."

Herald Uli kept his tone as even and emotionless as possible, coached by his Companion's soothing voice in his mind. But he was failing to keep his composure, even as he felt the burn of tears behind his eyes. In his rooms at the Collegium, he could express how he felt, acknowledge his sadness and loss with grief and proper mourning. But not here. Not in the hold of the Norton family, the place of his birth outside Westmark.

"Uli—" His Uncle Osric began as he stepped forward. He, Uli, and Uli's older brother, Cyrus, all stood in the hold's great hall, a place where the Norton family had gathered since bringing their family's woodcraft from Hardorn to Valdemar. The interior had been built with the famous Norton oak, walls stained and oiled through the decades, standing as testament to the family's craftsmanship. Ceiling to floor tapestries adorned three of the walls, depicting the arrival of the Nortons, the harvesting of trees, and the annual replanting begun by the first Father after the first winter.

It was all there. The history of Uli's family. And it was under his ancestors' gaze that he had just learned his estranged father, the man who had cursed him for being Chosen by a "magic horse," had dismissed him as no longer being a part of the family . . . of their Hold.

Uli held up his hand, aware that he stood out among his family, dressed in his Herald Whites. He'd donned a clean set at a nearby Waystation on his way from the Collegium. Just returned from a two-year Circuit, Uli had rested enough to satisfy the Healer before answering an urgent summons home. He had secretly hoped the message, though not signed by his father, had come from Cade Norton so that he and his middle child could hopefully . . . mend fences.

But that was never going to happen.

"Uli," Cyrus said, his rough, callused hands on his hips. "Are you crying? You'd think after eight years in that fancy school, you'd at least learn how to be a man."

:It seems Cyrus is still angry,: Sillvrenniel spoke with an almost scolding tone. She had been stabled away from the rest of the Norton horses and now ran in the field amid the tall, strong trees of the north.

:He will always be angry,: Uli thought back. *:Cyrus will never forgive me for leaving.:*

:I do not think that is where this anger is coming from.:

:Oh?:

Her voice took on a mothering tone. *:Dry those eyes and pay attention. It is important.:*

His uncle and brother were watching him. He was sure they'd noticed the faraway look in his eyes as he spoke to Sillvrenniel. "Tears are an expression of emotion, Brother. You have known of our father's death for a year. And yet I have just learned of the tragedy upon walking into this room. Surely when you heard, you shed at least one tear for the man who raised you? Protected you?"

Uli had struck a nerve, and he knew it when he looked into Cyrus' eyes. They narrowed as Cyrus lowered his hands to his sides and balled them into fists.

"That's enough," Osric said, his hands up as he moved between the two of them. "Arguments have no place here. Not now." He turned to Uli. "It is good to see you well, Uli. Though you do look tired. It is there, behind your eyes. I heard you've been on what they refer to as a Circuit?"

"Yes, Uncle. An apprenticeship." He and Osric had always been close, even when Uli's own father had looked at his son with disgust. Osric had always seemed to know when the two had argued and had sought out Uli to comfort him, making excuses for his own brother's behavior. Osric had been the one to escort a much younger Uli to Haven after Sillvrenniel had Chosen him, claiming to be proud there was a Herald in the Norton line. "I was paired with Herald Cerys for the last year of the Circuit. We traveled around the east, close to the border."

"Is this Cerys a woman or a man?" Cyrus said.

"Herald Cerys is a woman," Uli said, but did not look at Cyrus. "She is gifted with Farsight, which works well with my own gift."

Osric clapped his hands together. "Then the reports that you have found stolen items are true?"

Uli hesitated. "I wasn't aware there were reports."

"I have always kept an eye on you, Uli." Osric crossed his arms over his chest.

Uli smiled and blinked back tears. "You were always more of a father to me."

Cyrus snorted. "So we're back to that, are we? Father never loved me enough."

"Cyrus," Osric looked his nephew. "That's enough."

To Uli's surprise, his brother didn't say another word. Cyrus had always been outspoken and verbally abusive since he could put words together. To see him actually stop talking because their uncle commanded him came as a surprise. Things had changed in the Norton Hold.

"Uli, I kept up with you because I wanted to know how you were doing. What you were doing. And where you were." Osric dipped his head and raised his shoulders.

"Unfortunately . . . on occasion I lost track of you. Heralds are good at disappearing when they need to."

That much was true. And while traveling together, he and Cerys had made a few enemies and found it necessary to veer off their chosen path to protect themselves and their Companions. "Why didn't you send word when he died?"

"I did," Osric said. "But there was no response. So after three days of mourning, it was time to put your father to rest. He's in the chapel crypt if you would like to pay your respects. But first, I must discuss with you the reason you are here."

"Uncle—" Cyrus said abruptly.

"You can go, Cyrus. Now."

Uli looked at his brother and saw the blaze in Cyrus' eyes as he glanced at Osric. Cyrus bowed to his uncle, then shot a withering glance at Uli and stalked out of the room, slamming the door upon his exit.

"I see my brother's temper hasn't changed," Uli muttered.

"I'm afraid not." Osric motioned to the fire at the other end of the hall, and the two walked over and sat at a bench. Two women brought out a flagon of water and cups, a bowl of cheese and grapes, and a loaf of hot bread. Osric poured water and then gestured for Uli to break bread. "Will you be wearing those clothes the whole time you're here?"

"Only on official Herald business," Uli didn't have to force a smile. He was among the many Heralds who thought the Whites a bit too . . . ostentatious. As well as absurdly visible. It was the equivalent of wearing a target. "Uncle," he paused after breaking the bread in half. He really didn't have an appetite. "Why didn't you keep sending me messages?"

"I don't understand."

"Once the first message about Father's death failed to reach me, why not send more? Why wait for a year before bringing me home?"

"Things aren't as . . ." He set a cup in front of Uli. "It's not that simple, dear boy. Your father's death was sudden, and it destabilized the business for a while. You remember the Ohbokhens?"

"Yes, one of the other woodcrafters near Delcaire. I remember father mentioning they were here before the Nortons came."

"Aye. Before his death, Cade shared something with me. Master Sorenson found his physical inventory didn't match what the accounting reported. He showed Cade and together the two of them did a physical audit. When they were done, Cade said half a year's wood and the equivalent in income were missing, even though the records said otherwise."

"Who was doing the bookkeeping?"

"Cyrus."

Uli's eyes widened.

Osric continued, "Sorenson noticed the discrepancy because several large orders couldn't be fulfilled. The ledgers said we had enough wood, but that wasn't the case. The merchants were angry, and they took their business to Stanis Ohbokhen."

Uli put his hands on the table. "Did father confront Cyrus?"

"Cade died two days later." Osric shook his head. "I'm sure you didn't know this, but your father didn't leave Cyrus in charge of the company, Uli. He left it to Eda to run."

Eda. Uli's younger sister. "Eda?" He looked around. "Where is Eda? How come she's not here?"

"She hasn't been here in over a month."

"What—" Uli searched his uncle's face. "What's going on, Uncle? Why isn't Eda here if Father left the business to her? And why hasn't someone confronted Cyrus about the loss?"

"Because after your father died, Eda managed to build the business back up again, and we regained our reputation. But then a month ago we uncovered evidence that Eda had been selling that wood to Stanis Ohbokhen and pocketing the money. The Healer also kept evidence of Cade's murder from the public. But I knew of it, and so did Cyrus. Eda killed your father because he found out what she was doing and threatened to disown her."

Uli slowly stood and stepped away from the bench. "You said Father died. You didn't say he was killed."

"Uli—this is why I requested you come home. This is why I need you as a Herald."

"I don't believe you—Eda would never have hurt Father."

"We have evidence that she poisoned him, Uli. When she was confronted, she fled, and we haven't been able to find her since." Osric stood and also stepped away from the bench. "Herald Uli, I request you find Eda Norton and bring her back to Norton Hold to stand trial for the murder of your father, Cade Norton."

:You need to calm down.:

"How can I calm down?" Uli paced back and forth on the soft dirt before his Companion. After asking his uncle for some time, he went straight to Sillvrenniel, where she stood waiting by the fence. He slipped under the taut wire and remained with her while his mind rallied in defense of his sister. "This is impossible. How can they actually believe Eda would kill our father?"

:You have told me on many occasions that you do not know your sister:, Sillvrenniel said as she gracefully settled down on the ground and crossed her front legs. Her bright iridescent eyes watched him as he moved back and forth. *:She was only eight when I Chose you, my love. She had yet to grow into her own.:*

"My father would never have given over the business to her if he didn't trust her." Uli stopped pacing as a thought occurred to him. "Which means there was something about Cyrus he *didn't* trust. Was it the discrepancy in the books?"

:Now you are finally sounding like a Herald. You can be told a thing, but there is also merit in discovering the truth on your own.:

"You sound like one of my teachers." Uli smiled at his Companion as he knelt on the grass before her. He leaned his shoulder into her neck as she brought her magnificent head around to cradle him.

:I am one of your teachers. And you are one of mine. You will grieve for your father, but not today. First you must locate your sister. But you have to know the details before you can search for her.:

"Osric says they discovered her treachery a month ago. The Healer withheld evidence my father was poisoned, which I assume he knew at my father's death?"

:Do you see the first question?:

:The first question?: Uli gave a short sigh. So often Sill would guide him this way during their travels together. He and Cerys would inevitably become inundated with the emotions of those wanting the Heralds' help, and the path forward would grow murky. Sill would be the voice to lead them out of that swamp of despair. "Why did it take them eleven months to find this evidence? What lead them to believe it was Eda?"

:I think you have the start of where you need to go.:

He stood and brushed moist dirt and grass from his pants. "I do. Can you get word to Tirithiel that I could use Cerys' help in locating my sister?"

:I will give it my best, my love. But for now, learn what you can before you give your uncle your answer. Because once you find your sister, she will be condemned to death.:

"You don't believe she'll get a fair trial?"

Sill tilted her head to the side and caught Uli in her beautiful eyes. *:Do you?:*

Uli knew he needed to talk to the one who found the evidence Osric claimed they had against his sister. He didn't want to ask Osric because he was sure his uncle would take that as Uli accepting the assignment of finding Eda.

Before he was Chosen, Uli had worked in the larger of the lumber yards, sweeping sawdust and oiling the blades used to cut the wood. But that had been eight years ago. He wasn't sure if he would see familiar faces. Perhaps it would be simpler to start in town with the Healer.

While on Circuit, he had grown accustomed to the attention his Whites garnered him when he and Cerys entered a town. In fact, he sometimes enjoyed the awe and goodwill the uniform afforded him. But here in his home town, he wasn't as accepted. The looks and stares bothered him, but he kept up his Herald duties and smiled, even helped a few people with their tasks on his way to the Apothecary.

Among the things he loved most about Westmark were its cobblestone streets and red brick buildings. The Apothecary sat on the corner near the town's center. Uli knocked on the door several times, but when there was no answer, he stepped inside. He was assaulted by the scents of chemicals and herbs, some familiar, some not.

"Heyla," he called out. "Is Master Caragi about?"

When there was still no answer, Uli stepped inside. The hairs on the back of his neck stood on end. Something felt wrong.

:Uli—:

There was something in Sill's tone that alarmed Uli. *:What is it?:*

:Cerys found Eda.:

:Where is she? What town?:

:She's here.:

The opening of the apothecary door behind him broke the communication. Sillvrenniel's tone put him on guard, so he ducked down behind the table and peered through the bench legs at two pairs of leather boots. They moved together, stopping and starting.

Then, "I thought you said he came in here?"

"He did. I saw him with me own eyes. You can't miss that white suit."

Uli moved as quick and quiet as he could to the other side of the counter. He crept along the floor to the other side and caught sight of their boots again, not daring to stand straight just yet. Not until he knew who these two were or why they were hunting a Herald.

"So we're supposed to do what? Kill him?"

"No," the other voice said as they moved. "We take him and let bigger heads sort it out."

What? Bigger heads? Sort what?

A hand came from his right shoulder and clamped over his mouth as a blade flashed in front of his eyes. "Why do they dress you in those clothes?" A familiar voice whispered next to his ear.

Eda! He put his own hand on hers and pulled hers from his lips. "If you don't want them to keep looking, let me go."

"You're not thinking of showing yourself, are you?"

He turned and looked at a hooded figure and just saw her features shadowed beneath the cowl. "No . . . but I need to distract those two."

"How?"

He put his finger to his lips and looked out again. The two strangers were on the far right. Uli rose from behind the counter and with his hand outstretched, touched the large, wooden shelf beside them with his Gift and pulled the entire thing over on top of them.

He turned back to his sister as the two intruders struggled to get out from beneath the heavy shelf. "Is there a back way out?"

"You . . . how did you do that?"

"No time. Let's go," Uli grabbed her hand and the two of them moved through the curtain—

And Uli tripped over something. He crashed into a table that sent all manner of books and glass bottles into the floor. Cursing under his breath, he turned to see what he tripped over—

"He's back there! Stop him!"

"I'm stuck!"

Eda reached out and grabbed Uli's arm. "We have to go now!"

But Uli was staring down at Caragi's body. He lay face-down, the hilt of a knife protruding from his back. His eyes tracked back to the knife his sister held in her hand. It was the same type of blade, if not the sister, to the one in Caragi's back.

"I didn't do that," she hissed as one of the men burst through the curtain. She ducked, spun around, and leg swiped him, knocking him on his backside. Once their assailant was down, she popped up, grabbed Uli's wrist, and dragged him out the back.

There were shouts behind them, and a bell rang. The two of them ran into an alley and then turned left, then right, and then right again. Uli was a little confused directionally as they came out behind a tavern.

:To the left, then run straight. I'll meet you there.:

"Come on." Grabbing Eda's wrist, he pulled her with him as he followed Sill's instructions. As they reached the end of the alley, his Companion stepped into view. Eda pulled back and wrenched her wrist free of his grasp. Sill moved a bit and tried to inch around so Eda could get on.

Eda stepped back. "Get out of here, Uli. I just wanted to let you know I didn't kill Father. And I didn't kill Caragi. But I know who did. I saw him do it."

"Who?"

"I saw them go down that alley!"

:Young lady, I suggest you get on my back so I can spirit you out of here.:

Uli grabbed Eda's wrist and pulled her onto Sill's back behind him. The Companion took off down the opposite alley, made several turns and twists until they were outside the city and close to the Norton Hold.

Eda said in his ear, "You're in danger, Uli. But not from me."

"Wait, Sill," Uli said as she came to a stop near one of the Hold's secret entrances.

"I'd forgotten about the secret passageways," Eda said. "Good thing you remembered. I don't think Osric or Cyrus ever knew about them."

He looked back at Eda. "I didn't know about Father—"

"I know. He insisted you not be bothered with the death."

"Who?"

"Osric."

Uli frowned. "But he said he did try to reach me."

"He didn't."

Uli dismounted and helped Eda dismount as well. "What happened? I need to know the truth." He quickly relayed to her everything Osric and Cyrus had said in their meeting with him.

"It's all a lie, Uli. A lie to frame me and Cyrus. Osric killed our father. And he knows I have proof."

As a Herald, Uli had heard tales of familial as well as courtly machinations for power. These stories were so often the glue that held together the nobles as well as the court. But he had never thought to hear of such betrayal in his own home—and certainly not from his own uncle.

He didn't want to believe Osric was capable of such treachery. Eda *must* be wrong. When he'd believed his father thought him a failure, it was Osric who had lifted him up from despair. It was Osric who had written to him while he was at the Collegium. It was always Osric who had assured him that his place was in Haven, and not at home.

It was Osric . . . who had kept him in the dark.

Uli felt as if the foundation of his existence were being eroded away and he was left on an island, a single survivor in the middle of isolation.

:Calm yourself, dear one,: Sillvrenniel's voice in his mind dismissed the festering storm. *:You do not need*

my council to tell you that your sister speaks the truth. Beneath your trust and fortitude you have known, all along, that something was amiss. Though you never spoke it aloud, it has been forever in your thoughts. Remember what I said of being told a thing? It is time to know it.:

"Uli?" Eda put a hand on her brother's arm.

Uli hadn't realized he was holding onto Sillvrenniel's flank, and that his Companion had moved closer to support him. He looked at his sister. "You have proof of what Osric did?"

"Yes."

"Why haven't you used it? Let me see it. I can help."

"He tried to kill me when he realized I had that proof. I hid it, and I haven't been able to get back inside the Hold to get to it. I ran when he tried to kill me, and I've been hiding all this time." She smiled weakly. "Osric didn't send for you . . . I did."

Uli searched her face. "You . . . *you* sent the missive?"

"Yes. I was able to speak to Healer Caragi. He kept quiet about father's death because he knew Osric did it, but he was afraid. When I finally confronted him, he told me he had proof that Osric administered the poison. He told me to come back today, and he'd give it to me."

"But you found him dead."

"Yes. I saw you come inside, and I knew they'd come after you. Osric doesn't want you discovering the truth. You're a Herald." She put her hand on his. "Your life and that of your horse are in danger, Uli. You have to flee."

:We need to go, my love. There are horses coming down this road.:

Uli made a quick decision. "Where is the proof you need?"

"I hid it in father's study. Cyrus has the key now, and I'm sure Osric has one as well."

"I need to talk to Cyrus—"

"No!" Eda reached for him. "You can't do that! He believes everything Uncle Osric says. He thinks I killed our father."

Uli shook his head, remembering the interaction between Cyrus and Osric. "I don't think he's as devoted to Osric as you believe. Eda, we're a family. We're going to have to work together to beat Osric at this and clear your reputation, as well as Cyrus'." He winked at her. "Trust me. And trust your brother."

"Then I'm coming with you."

"Eda—"

:You need to work together as a family, my love.: Sill nudged his cheek with her nose just before she turned and ran into the woods. *:I will be nearby.:*

Uli led Eda to the secret door. Once inside they carefully made their way to the passageway in the estate and the library where he and Eda had found the door as children. He motioned her to hang back as he stepped out into the hall.

Almost immediately, he was confronted by his brother, flanked by two of the Hold's guardsmen.

"You stay right there!" Cyrus pointed his finger at Uli. "I need a word with you."

"And I, you," Uli countered as he straightened his shoulders and called upon all of his Herald training. He'd never confronted his brother before; he had always backed away from him. Until now. The sudden change in Uli's demeanor didn't go unnoticed by Cyrus, who drew up a bit. "While Father was alive, did he ever allow you to look at the books?"

"Yes," Cyrus frowned. "Why?"

"Did you *look* at them? I am asking if you *understood* them."

"I'm not an imbecile, Uli. I can read and write, and I understand how a business works." Cyrus crossed his arms over his chest. "It was just . . . Father never trusted me as much as he did you or Eda."

"Father didn't trust me. I left the family." Saying this out loud brought back hurtful memories for Uli. Memories of how his father's words turned his joy at being Chosen into a horrible betrayal against the Norton family.

Cyrus stared at Uli, and a strange silence formed between them. Uli wasn't sure what else to ask, or how to communicate with his brother. There had been so much distance between them, even as children. And now his brother believed he had to face him with armed guards?

Finally, Cyrus waved the guards away and waited until they were gone from the hall before he said, "He never stopped trusting you, Uli. You were going to be a Herald. Heralds are the most trusted in Valdemar."

Uli narrowed his eyes. "But when I left, Father disowned me—"

"I know . . . I heard him." Cyrus looked uncomfortable, and Uli expected him to stop talking. But he didn't. "I was there, just outside the door, the day you left. I was jealous that you were leaving. You weren't going to have to work in the forests and yard anymore. You were leaving this place, and you had a magic horse."

"Sill's not a magic horse."

"So you always say," Cyrus gave a short sigh. "What I'm trying to say is, you left right after that, and I was too stunned at what Father had said to do anything. As young as I was, I believed leaving was the same thing as being banished or disowned. I'd never heard Father speak so harshly to you. Not long after that, Eda asked if she could be included in the day to day, and Father agreed. She didn't hear what he'd said to you, and she thought she would see you again soon.

"But I knew better. I sort of . . . assumed to leave meant to be without a family. And that depressed me. I started drinking because I didn't want to do this, Uli. But I felt I had no choice. And I screwed up. A lot. And then Osric took me under his wing when you were no longer around."

"He told you that you needed to replace Eda and me, didn't he?"

"In so many words." Cyrus rubbed at his face. "And after a while, I started hating Eda for gaining Father's devotion. It wasn't until after he died that I started to understand something."

"What?"

"That Osric was a snake. The moment he said Eda was responsible for father's death, I stopped trusting him."

A noise at the end of the hall made Cyrus draw his knife. Uli was instantly on guard and his mind sought out Sillvrenniel. She was near.

Cyrus stepped closer to the wall and dropped his voice. "Were you in town earlier? With Eda?"

Uli hesitated. "Yes."

He looked at Uli. "Why were you asking me about the business?"

"I need to see father's office." He put up a hand before Cyrus could protest. "Eda said there was proof there. Proof that shows Osric killed Father."

Cyrus' eyes widened. "And she never told me?"

Uli arched his brow. "Are you really surprised? You were Osric's puppet."

"*Was*," Cyrus said. "I started paying attention to what he was doing. I started following him, and saw him meeting with Stanis Ohbokhen a few times. I never knew what they talked about, and I got the feeling that last time, the other night before you got here, that Osric knew I was there."

"That follows with what Eda suspects. We need to get into father's office, Cyrus. Can you get us in there?" At that moment the library door opened, and Eda stepped out.

Brother and sister faced each other. Uli stood to the side, ready to Fetch weapons away from the two of them if needed. Cyrus still held his knife, but Eda faced him unarmed.

Finally, Cyrus lowered his knife and slipped it into its leather sheath at his hip. He then removed his brown cloak and placed it over Uli's shoulders. "Need to cover those robes, brother. Let's go."

"Why are we sneaking around?" Uli asked as Cyrus stopped in front of a door near the cellar and unlocked it with a metal key.

"Because Osric is looking for you," Cyrus said. "I overheard him tell some of the stable boys to corral your horse. That worried me."

"I'm afraid if anyone tries to hold Sillvrenniel, they'll get a nasty surprise."

The three of them stepped inside, and Cyrus locked the door behind them.

Uli remembered this place. It was always his father's room. There was a fireplace, a table with two benches, a wash basin and cabinets along one side.

Eda immediately went to the fireplace, the ash long cold with neglect. Uli was sure there hadn't been a fire since his father died.

He watched as Eda stepped to the side of the stone and pressed one of them. It snapped out and she removed it. After passing the stone to Cyrus, she stuck her hand in and retrieved a metal box. Uli and Cyrus followed her to the table where she opened it and the three of them examined the papers inside.

"These are bills of sale," Cyrus said. "To a name I don't recognize."

Uli picked up one of the bills. "Goram Marog? Is that a person or a place?" He looked closer at the bill in his hand, then at the ones in the stack. "And why does it say Ohbokhen at the bottom of each one? Who bought the lumber? Marog or Ohbokhen?"

Eda said, "That's what father was tracking because he tried to match up the missing lumber with the payments and couldn't. He confronted Stanis about it, threatened to request a Herald if he didn't tell him who Morag was. This happened the night before he died. I didn't learn till after father died that Goram Marog is the name of a collector in Declaire."

"Collector?" Uli asked.

Cyrus took a step back. "He collects gambling debts. Merchants hire him to get their bills paid." He looked at his brother and sister. "Okay, yeah, I had some debt, and I had to pay him. But nothing recently."

"But why would a debt collector purchase lumber from us?" Uli said.

"He didn't," said a deep voice from the door.

All three of them turned to see Osric standing inside the room, a key in his hand. He had a man standing on either side of him, each with a sword in hand. Uli recognized them from the apothecary shop.

"I've been looking for those receipts ever since Cade died. I assumed he'd told one of you. I thought it would have been Uli." He looked at Uli and shook his head.

Uli removed his brother's cloak. "I think I'm starting to see the truth now," he said as he folded the cloak and set it on the table. "You accumulated a lot of gambling debt in Declaire, didn't you, Uncle Osric? So much that this Goram Marog came looking for you. You had to think fast. So you made a deal with Stanis to sell him Norton lumber. You pocketed the money and then paid Morag off."

"You stole from Father?" Cyrus stared at Osric.

"He also stole from Stanis," Eda said as she stood by Cyrus. "You created those receipts not only to keep track of what was taken from the lumber yard but also what was paid out. And then you used their existence to threaten Stanis and his reputation. Selling Norton lumber under his own name?"

Uli moved to the right as his sister spoke. He was listening, but he was also watching his uncle and the two men. He didn't think it was coincidence they were all in the same room together. *:Sill?:*

:I am being hunted. Just a moment.:

:What?:

Osric began a long, slow clap. "I am impressed. Not so much with you, Eda, but with Cyrus. I always assumed he wasn't as gifted as you." He looked at Uli. "Or Uli. Come out from behind them, Herald. I don't like you lurking in the background."

Uli stepped forward, just in front of his brother and sister. "Why are you hunting my Companion?"

"Ah . . . I forgot you can talk to the magic horse. Now that you three know how Cade died and why, you can't leave this room alive. So I've planted suspicions around town that Eda had returned and had kidnapped her brother Uli. She forced him to bring her back here, where she would be joined by her brother Cyrus, and the two of them would be caught removing those receipts—receipts they created for just the reasons you gave, Eda. Stanis is ready to back me up that it was the two of you who stole from your father and then killed him to cover it up. And as for poor Uli—" Osric gave Uli a sad face. "—he tried to be the heroic Herald, but he failed as he and his horse were killed by his siblings. A tragic tale."

He stepped forward and held out his hand. "I'll take those receipts now."

:Sill?:

:All is well. I'm afraid Osric hired men with bad aim. They're sleeping now. Will you disarm Osric?:

:Yes. But doesn't he know what my gift is?:

:Does he?:

Something felt wrong as he used his ability to Fetch the two mens' swords to him. Once they were in his hands, Cyrus attacked one guard while Eda threw a knife at the other. Both men went down together.

"Uli, look out!"

He hadn't been paying attention to Osric as Cyrus lunged at Uli. His brother tackled him to the floor as Eda yelled out. Something cracked in the air as the door was broken down. Uli managed to squirm out from under his brother as Sill came through the doorway. She reared up in front of Osric as he screamed and threw up his arms. Eda grabbed the metal box and slammed it into the back of his head. Osric fell beside his two unconscious guards.

Uli looked at his brother and saw the knife sticking out of Cyrus' back. Osric had tried to throw the knife at Uli, but Cyrus had stopped it with his body.

"Cyrus!" Uli shook his brother, but he wasn't moving.

:Quiet, my love. Cyrus will be okay if you stop shaking him like that.:

Eda moved to her brothers' side as people started flooding into the room. One of them was Master Sorenson. He took one look at the scene, looked at Uli, and barked orders for a Healer to be brought as soon as possible. Eda put her arms around Uli's shoulders and hugged him tight.

It took most of a day to sort out what happened. Everyone took the word of a Herald without question. Osric and his men were arrested and taken away, and Uli took possession of the receipts as evidence of his uncle's treachery. A day later, he and Eda and Sorenson came to Cyrus' room when they learned he was awake and filled him in on what had happened.

"So everything worked out," Cyrus said.

"Yes. But you don't look happy," Uli said.

Cyrus pushed himself up in his bed and asked if he could speak to Uli alone. The others left the room and closed the door.

"What is it?" Uli asked.

"See that box over the mantel? Bring it here."

Uli did as his brother asked.

"Open it."

He did. Inside was a single letter addressed to Uli. It was in his father's handwriting.

"That letter is how I knew how Father really felt about you. I found it in his room after he died. He'd kept it under his mattress, on the side where our mother once lay. I knew it was private, but after what he'd said to you that day, and how it affected me, I wanted to know what he wrote. And I decided that if it was bad, I'd destroy it, and you'd never know. That way he couldn't hurt you anymore."

Uli swallowed as he stared at the letter, afraid to take it out of the box. "You didn't destroy it."

"No. Because you need to read it, Uli. You need to know exactly how father felt. Those are his words." He smiled at Uli. "Take it. Go be with your Companion and . . ." Cyrus blinked a few times. Uli realized his brother was trying to hold back tears. "And don't be afraid to cry, Uli. Don't ever be afraid again."

Herald Uli Norton took the letter from the box with shaking hands, left the home of his birth and with his Companion at his side, walked to the business his family built.

And there he sat on the floor of his father's office, cradled beside Sill, and read.

My dearest Uli,

This moment is when I am happiest your mother insisted I learn to craft my own letters, because these are words and thoughts I cannot leave to another's hand.

First and foremost, I love you. I am proud of you. And though my actions that day were that of a cruel father, I feel I must explain myself. Only to you.

It is not you that I am angry at, nor your brother or sister, but at myself. In you I saw the possibilities of the Norton name, of the business continuing with an honest son at the helm.

And I saw a way out for myself. I inherited my talent for wood from my own father, and it was decided long ago that continuing the wood-working tradition was the best way to provide for my family. But it was never what I dreamed of as my future. I wanted to travel, to see the world, experience life—but there was always family, and duty, and business. I thought . . . I hoped, with you in charge of the business, I could finally see the world. I had always wanted to see those places the Bards sing of, especially the Pelagiris Forest, and my greatest of dreams, to see a Firebird.

I admit, in shame now, that when you were Chosen, I was filled with anger. And disappointment. But not in you, my Uli, but in knowing I would not see the world as you would as a Herald. I was jealous.

I hope that when I pass from this world, you will see these words, for though your mother would insist I send this hours after it is finished, I am still a man with faults. And I am ashamed of how I treated you. I hope you will understand, Uli, that I do love you, that I want only the best for you.

And that I am proud of you. Above all else, if you do not believe the former, believe that statement after I am gone.

Be the best Herald you can be, Uli.

I love you.

Cade Norton.

PS: Try to see a Firebird as you travel, and when you do, think of me.

The years of fear, and anger and disappointment melted as Uli let the letter fall from his fingers and leaned into his Companion as he wept with sorrow . . . and joy.

Of Crows and Karsites

Kristin Schwengel

"I'm bored," Rinton announced, gazing up at the near-cloudless blue sky from the grassy clearing he was lying in. The days were shortening, but a sunny day like this kept the autumn chill from the air.

Linx raised his head from the mountain-fed spring and stared at his Chosen, water dripping from his muzzle. *:You do know, don't you, that among certain peoples, 'May your life be interesting' is a very potent curse?:*

"We're nearly finished with this Circuit, and there's been nothing beyond the most minor of disputes to settle among the locals. You'd hardly know we're on the border at all. We haven't even had particularly foul weather, and certainly no brigands." Rinton ran one hand through his dark hair, the short strands standing nearly straight up. It wasn't that he wanted something bad to happen, but this was his first Circuit near Karse, and he had somehow expected that the mere location would change what he did as a Herald.

:It is a small, remote portion of the border. The mountains take care of a lot of disputes on their own. And you know that Selenay and the Heraldic Circle would never have sent a relatively green Herald out here—even if he does have a knack for languages and was personally tutored in Karsite by Weaponsmaster Alberich—if her advisors hadn't been able to assure her

that it was likely to be a, well, boring Circuit.: The Companion ambled over and nudged his Chosen, icy droplets spattering his Whites. *:But if we want to make the next Waystation before dark, we need to get moving.:*

Rinton sighed, then stood, carefully folding the blanket he had been lying on—it was acceptable for a Herald to appear on Circuit in battle- or blood-stained Whites, but grass stains from idle lolling in an empty clearing? Never.

Reattaching the bedroll to his packs, he mounted. "No time like the present, eh, Linx?"

What answer the Companion might have given was silenced as a wave of . . . something . . . swept over them. Fear, anxiety, distress, all crowded into their minds, threatening to overwhelm any other thoughts. Linx shook his head against it, and belatedly Rinton put up a Mindshield. His only Gift was Animal Mindspeech, and he had become sloppy about maintaining shields when out on Circuit.

"What was that?"

:Empathic projection. And a strong one. From the south and a bit to the west. Not so far as the Holderlands:

Rinton turned to the south and raked a hand through his hair again. Karse.

"Some sort of new weapon they're trying? To fill unshielded Valdemarans with fear?" He nudged the Companion, who started down the road at a ground-eating trot. This was what he had hoped for: something different. Wherever this projection was coming from, they needed to find it. And stop it, if they could. And if not, get as much information about it as possible so the Queen and the Council could deal with it.

Linx shook his head. *:Karse hates all the Gifted, but I would think most especially the Empaths. It's such a vague Gift, I can't see them thinking to attempt such a thing. Weaponsmaster Alberich would know more, but I don't think they value Empathy at all.:* A pause stretched between them. *:And I think it would destroy an Empath to be used in that way.:*

"But don't they have Healers, acting on the Sunlord's behalf?" Rinton frowned, shifting his lanky frame to match Linx's smooth gait. "Healers are Empaths, too, and they are not shattered by working in Karse. Their responsibility is always to Heal those in need."

:Our knowledge of how they use their Healers is . . . uncertain. From what the Weaponsmaster says, most of what they have are herb- and knife-healers, not much in the way of what we call true Healing. Most Karsites simply say something about the Sunlord's blessings and that's the end of it. But I'll leave that to the priests to argue.:

Linx's stride lengthened. *:We have more important things to think about. No Waystation for us tonight, I think. We should make it to the Border nearest whatever it is by dark, to explore tomorrow.:*

Linx objected, of course, but Rinton left his Companion in the thickest woods, close to the Valdemar border, before his early morning scouting. The terrain looked rougher farther into the trees, and even with a Companion's preternatural sure-footedness, he didn't want to risk a hoof getting caught in rocks or an animal hole.

"Besides, if anything happens to me, you'll have a better chance to get back from here—and if there's another projection that has any harmful effects, you might be out of range." He gave a crooked grin. "You've always said my mind's the weakest in Valdemar, so I'm the best choice to get close to whatever it is."

Linx shook his head, bridle rings rattling, then pressed his broad forehead against Rinton's chest. *:You know I never mean it. Be careful.:*

Rinton nodded, suddenly unable to trust his voice. In their years together, he'd never heard such a vulnerable note in his Companion's mind-voice. He touched his own forehead to Linx's neck, to calm both of them, before turning and slipping between the trees, heading in the direction the projections were coming from. The waves of feeling had continued as they had ridden yesterday and again this morning, but since that first surge they had been weaker, somehow muted. All, however, had carried the same emotional tone: fear and distress.

Rinton moved as quickly as he could, picking his way through the rocks and brush. There was, in fact, a narrow track, just wide enough for a simple cart, but he chose to follow it hidden in the trees alongside. Around here, any traveler without a wagon or horse would be local, so anyone he might encounter would be immediately suspicious of him. He had changed from his Whites into drab traveler's gear, but a stranger afoot in a remote area like this would still stand out.

It took him several candlemarks to work through the undergrowth to where he could see the buildings marking the end of the trade road. The town itself was just a tiny village, enclosed by a high wooden palisade, which surprised him. To spend the effort and resources to erect protective walls around such a small community suggested either a great level of fear or a great need to shield something of high value. He narrowed his eyes, wishing he dared get a little closer. From this range, the tops of the walls looked rough and uneven, as though put up in haste.

Keeping the same distance, Rinton worked a little way around the hamlet, enough to see that the palisade completely surrounded it except for the gateway to the road. He saw no signs of activity other than smoke rising from a few of the buildings, heard no sounds other than the natural noises of the forest as he passed through. Not even a gate guard stood outside the wooden wall. Something in this small village was very wrong, and he had no idea how to find out what without exposing himself to potential danger.

Finally, he sidled back to the thicker woods and

hurried to where he had left Linx, his mind proposing ever more fantastical solutions.

:You've been thinking about this the whole time, how to learn more. You've got an idea, haven't you?: Rinton had shared just what he had observed through Mindspeech, keeping his other thoughts to himself as he backtracked to his Companion.

"You're not the only one who can dredge up bits of distant cultures and the forgotten past. I'm thinking of the siege tactics of Dread Varang." Though many people thought of them as mere stories to entertain the littles, the legends of Varang the bandit captain held kernels of truth. "Particularly the birds."

The Companion was quiet for a moment as he sifted his own memories; then his blue eyes held Rinton's. *:Absolutely not.:*

Rinton blinked under the intensity of that gaze until he realized what Linx was thinking. "No, not tying burning twigs to their tails to set the town on fire—what kind of Animal-Mindspeaking Herald do you take me for? I just want to use one as a messenger. There are a lot of crows around, and some crows are smart enough to really understand what I want. If I send out a questioning Mindcall, I can try to get one to carry a note to someone inside. If I'm lucky, I'll get one smart enough to give me clues about what's going on beforehand."

:And we'd better do it quickly. The morning is gone already, and the less time we spend on this side of the border, the happier we'll all be.:

:?: Rinton pitched his call to the level that registered in his mind as "bird" and watched the dark silhouettes that perched along the topmost eaves of the town, barely visible over the palisade. Almost as soon as he had sent his call, the largest shape lifted its head, followed by a few of the others. A moment later, the large bird launched

itself into the air with a hoarse caw, flying unerringly in his direction.

:It looks like your idea might work.: Since everything around the village had remained quiet and unthreatening, Linx had insisted on joining him at the edge where the forest thinned. How a large white horse could remain unobserved was beyond Rinton's understanding, but time and again the Companions had shown themselves more skilled at hiding in plain sight than any number of the common sneak thieves that worked the seedier areas of Haven.

The crow, at least half again as large as the ones Rinton was used to, landed on a nearby branch and tilted its head to look at the two of them.

:?: It replied to Rinton. Linx nodded a little, indicating that he, too, was listening.

:Need help.: Rinton had long ago learned that it was best to keep things very simple until he knew the relative intelligence of the animal he addressed. There was no point in exhausting his Gift trying to explain complex concepts to a creature incapable of grasping them.

Another head-tilt. *:Hurt? Need food? Need nest? Need mate? Kiyan help.:*

Rinton blinked. "The bird has a better understanding than I could have hoped," he murmured to Linx. *:The people in the buildings. Why does no one come in or out?:*

:Red-robe worried. Girl frightened. People frightened.:

Rinton almost groaned. "So, there's a Sunpriest in residence, and his phrasing suggests that the Empath's projections have the whole town paralyzed with fear."

:Which would explain the rather hastily erected palisade. I wonder . . . : Linx's Mindvoice trailed off, leaving Rinton unclear on what exactly he was wondering.

:Is the red-robe kind?: It was the best way he could think of to ask about the Sunpriest's role in the village.

:Leaves seed for Kiyan, feeds meat to cat.:

"Well, that at least is promising. A kindly rural Sunpriest might not take quite so dim a view of Gifts, or of Valdemarans even, as those of the cities. Maybe Kiyan should carry my note straight to the Sunpriest."

:Lurking around the periphery of the town isn't going to gain us anything but lost time. If the Empath is a young girl, we need to get her out of the town and into Valdemar for her own safety, and we need contact inside to make it possible.:

:Will you carry something to the red-robe for me?:

The bird bobbed its head vigorously, his enthusiasm comical. *:Kiyan help mind-friend!:* Both Rinton and Linx winced at the volume of the bird's mind-voice.

Rinton turned to Linx and dug around in one of his saddlebags for a carefully oilskin-wrapped bundle, which he opened to reveal a sheaf of paper sandwiched between two writing boards, a quill, and a tiny tube of ink. Cutting a small strip off one of the sheets, he sharpened the quill with his dagger and dipped it in the ink, then paused. "How much should I reveal?"

:At this point, absolute truth. From here I can get you safely back across the border if armed Karsites come out of the palisade gate. And if we want a Sunpriest to trust us with one of his flock, we should show the same trust in him.:

Rinton nodded, then began to write, carefully translating into Karsite. "I wish there were a word in Karsite for 'Herald,' or something other than White Demon," he grumbled. "It seems inadequate to say that I am Valdemaran, and my Companion and I want to help with the Gifted One who feels fear."

:Any Sunpriest worth his robe can fill in the blanks from that.:

Waving the scrap of paper to dry the last of the ink, Rinton eyed Kiyan, who had closely watched the writing. He folded the paper, but Linx nudged him before he began to roll it up.

:Put some of my tail-hairs into the paper. That more than anything else will show that you are truthful.:

Rinton moved to his Companion's hindquarters and ran his hand through the glimmering strands, taking the few loose hairs that clung to his fingers and coiling them together before tucking them into the folds of the paper. Rolling it tightly, he pulled a short length of red cord from the writing kit and tied a secure knot around the tiny roll.

Before he could even address Kiyan, the bird had hopped over to land on the rock he had used as a makeshift writing desk and reached out one claw for the paper.

:Kiyan take to red-robe. Mind-friend share eyes?: He tilted his head to Rinton, who blinked.

:This is not an ordinary crow, Chosen. I was wondering about him, and now I'm certain that he's one of the special Hawkbrother birds, like those mentioned in the Chronicles of Vanyel's time, although how he got over the Comb from the Pelagirs is beyond me. They were somehow . . . Gifted, and far more intelligent than any normal bird. He's offering for you to link your mind with his, to see through his eyes.:

"I've only done that with you, Linx, and only to see if I could do it. To join my thoughts to a strange bird seems foolhardy. There's no telling what might happen if I get lost or distracted. But to be able to actually see the Sunpriest, and how he reacts . . ." Rinton let his voice trail off, realizing how foolish his protests were. No matter how nervous he might be about sharing even a small portion of his mind with someone other than his Companion, the potential gain was far too great to miss. And Linx would be right next to him.

:Yes, thank you, Kiyan. I would like to share eyes.: Staring into the bottomless black of the crow's pupils, he slowed his breathing and drifted into a light trance, enough that he could shift his mind to align it with the

bird's, as he had with Linx, until he suddenly saw himself, eyes closed. He struggled to prevent the disorientation from breaking his connection with Kiyan and nodded slightly.

The crow correctly interpreted the gesture, and his view changed as the bird launched from the rock into the air and with steady wingbeats took his mind-passenger through the forest until they soared over the small village.

Rinton's stomach lurched as Kiyan dropped out of the air, angling for a tiny open window on the side of one of the largest buildings. The painted solar disc over the front door proclaimed this the local "Temple" of Vkandis Sunlord. Rinton had barely time to recognize that detail before the bird darted through the window and into what appeared to be a small study. A gray-haired Sunpriest sat at a desk, drumming his fingers against the table, ignoring the open book in front of him, until Kiyan landed next to him, beak open and, Rinton assumed, cawing for attention.

The Sunpriest's lips moved, his weathered face welcoming, despite the clear worry lines that creased his brow. Those lines deepened as he noticed the bird holding out the paper, and he tentatively held out his hand to receive it.

Rinton watched as the man untied and unrolled the paper, pausing in shock as the silvery coil of horsehair fell to the desk. The Sunpriest picked up the strands, rubbing them between his fingers with a stunned expression, as though to convince himself that they were real, then rapidly unfolded the note and scanned the written lines. He exhaled heavily, and Rinton had no doubt that there was clear relief in his face, before he turned the paper over and reached for his own quill and ink.

When Kiyan had taken the reply from the Sunpriest's hand and launched himself out of the window, Rinton separated his mind from the bird's. Coming out of his light trance, he felt Linx's solid presence behind him, supporting and protecting him. He kept his eyes closed, preparing himself for the disorientation of seeing once again through human senses, without the strange sharpness and precision the crow's eyes had given him.

A harsh caw, followed by a jubilant Mindcall, shook him fully back to the present. *:Mind-friend! Kiyan brings from red-robe!:*

"He keeps using that phrase. I wonder what he means by it," he murmured to Linx.

:I think, Chosen, that the crow has, for lack of a better word, Chosen you as well.: The Companion's Mindvoice was full of laughter. *:The Hawkbrother birds are apparently very special, although nothing like a Companion. I shall have to get used to sharing you.:*

Rinton's eyes flew open with surprise, then closed again as he examined his own mind and found a faint thread weaving a connection between himself and the crow. It was a pale shadow of the brilliant cord that bound his mind and heart with Linx's, but it was undeniably there.

"Well. That's unexpected," he finally managed. "How am I going to explain him to the Heraldic Circle?"

:I expect that it won't be nearly so difficult as you imagine it to be. And depending on what we find here, it may be a minor issue indeed.:

The Sunpriest's note was short, but Rinton read his concern even in those few words. *"I can no longer protect Mirideh. Black-robes are coming in a day or two, and nights will not be safe. I will hang a red cloth over the palisade—meet me there."*

"I can only assume he means me to meet him as soon as possible. You should wait here; it's about as close as you can get without running the risk of being seen." He reached up a hand to scratch behind Linx's ears. "I will not let you take any chances. Just because their Sunpriest is willing to work with a White Demon doesn't mean that panicky villagers won't try to turn anything large and white into a pincushion."

His Companion lowered his head in silent acknowledgement.

"And we have no idea how the Empath will respond to me, or to you. Better to have just one of us at first."

Linx's head came back up. *:I don't think you're strong enough to impose a Mindshield on her, but I might be able to, through you. You'd have to be touching her, though, until you bring her close enough that I can see her.:*

Rinton's eyes widened. "That . . . would be immensely helpful. I was going to try to do it myself, but if she resisted, I know I couldn't maintain it."

:Just . . . be careful.:

Rinton nodded, then turned and slipped between the trees, skirting around the edges of the thicker woods to try to see the red cloth the Sunpriest would be using as a signal. Kiyan hopped from branch to branch, following him closely. He was nearly to the opposite side of the palisade when his eye was caught by a flicker of movement, and he saw a square of color, no larger than a handkerchief, hanging along the side.

:Hmph. I suppose any fabric would count as a "cloth," but he's lucky that there's a bit of a breeze today, or I'd never have noticed it.: He was so accustomed to speaking aloud to Linx that projecting Mindspeech to his Companion felt strange, even though it shouldn't have been any more unusual than talking to Kiyan or any of the pets up at the Collegium.

:Well, part of the point is to not be noticed by the villagers, either.:

Even though the Companion couldn't see him, Rinton nodded, then studied the trees and terrain leading up to the back of the palisade. There were at least some stands of trees that he could use for cover as he moved, and the cloth hung a few feet from a low scrubby briar. Taking a deep breath to calm his jangling nerves, he began working his way forward.

The nearer he got to the palisade, the more signs Rinton saw of how hastily it had been erected. Many of the posts weren't even securely anchored into the ground, simply lashed to others. As a defense, it would fail utterly before the weakest intruder. Against what did the villagers think this would protect them? His stomach roiled in anticipation before each movement, his senses turning every whisper of wind in branch into the whistle of an arrow past his head.

:Mind your shields, Chosen!: The sharp edge in Linx's voice cut through the strain, and he strengthened the protections that had begun to slip. Almost at once, the fear and nausea eased, and he realized with a bit of chagrin that he had nearly succumbed to the Empath's continued projections. Now that his shields were up, he could feel the peaking distress as something clearly outside of himself, and he turned his attention back to his stealthy progress.

The bit of red fabric, it turned out, had been wedged into one of the numerous gaps between the unevenly shaped logs. The last stretch was the most unnerving for Rinton, for it meant he would have to completely leave the cover of the trees. As he was about to spring forward, he heard caws from overhead, the local birds greeting Kiyan, and nearly smacked his forehead over his stupidity. All along, he had been accompanied by the perfect means to gauge his danger.

:Kiyan? Does anyone watch from inside?: A burst of movement sped skyward from the nearby branch where the crow had landed, and he watched the bird climb, then soar briefly out of view over the palisade before returning to sight.

:Red-robe and girl.: Kiyan settled onto the top of one of the palisade posts, preening himself.

Making himself as small as possible, in case the bird's keen vision had missed something, Rinton darted across the final length of open ground, squeezing between the scraggly shrub and the palisade.

His breathing hadn't even settled to normal when one of the posts near him moved, bowing outward with its neighbors like a makeshift door. The red-robed Sunpriest he had seen through Kiyan's eyes poked his head out to study him.

"You sent the note with the bird?" The Sunpriest jerked his head upward to indicate Kiyan on the post nearby.

"Yes, Honored Father. I am Rinton." The Karsite language felt awkward to his tongue, but the other nodded, so his accent must be passable. He said a silent thanks to the Weaponsmaster for the hours of stilted conversations while cleaning and repairing leather practice armor.

"You are—" the Sunpriest paused, as though searching for a word, "—a White Rider? You do not wear white." He looked pointedly at Rinton's dull gray-brown traveling gear.

Rinton blinked at the courtesy of the Sunpriest in calling him something other than a White Demon. "One of my kind in white inside Karse does not live long," he replied with a smile, and the small joke was met with a thin answering smile.

"I am called Fides," the Sunpriest continued. "My granddaughter Mirideh is the Gifted one, and the black-robes are coming soon, and this time she will be taken to the Fires. I can no longer hide her. I've even tried to use a mind-numbing herb, but she's too strong for it. You must take her with you. She understands this and is ready to go."

"She will not be able to return—" Rinton began, but Fides cut him off.

"But she will live, which she will not if she stays—"

A clarion sound drifted to them on the breeze, and unmistakable fear washed over the Sunpriest's face.

"The sunhorns. The black-robes are nearer than I thought. You must hurry. Mirideh!" He gestured and pushed a little harder on the wood, and a slim girl of about twelve summers slipped through the widened opening, her brown eyes huge and dark with fright, a small bundle clasped to her chest.

Rinton reached out and caught her arm, feeling Linx's presence strengthening his own protections as the Companion worked through their bond to place a Mindshield around the girl. A smile of sheer relief blossomed over her face.

"Thank you," she whispered. "The voices, the feelings . . . they're gone." She looked over at Fides, who smiled as well.

"You have done what I could not. My training could only help me protect myself, but not others."

Rinton filed what they said into his memory, certain that the Queen and the Circle would be interested in what it suggested about the Sunpriests. But then the strange horn sound reached them again, and Fides reached out to grasp Mirideh's hands.

"The Sunlord hold you and keep you in his arms, little one," he said, a tear tracking down his face.

"And you, grandmother."

Rinton gaped, and he felt Linx's shock as well. A woman Sunpriest? Was that not anathema? He studied the short-haired Sunpriest, now recognizing that what he took for a close-shaven chin was in fact beardless, that the worried lines on the face disguised surprisingly delicate cheekbones.

Fides took a moment to grin at his shock. "Most of the villagers are either related to me, and thus protect my disguise, or are too young to remember when I was Fidesa, old Berthelm's assistant. After Berthelm's death, I took over the rites and rituals. The Sunlord has always granted me the blessings I have asked on their behalf, and the village trusts that. Besides, there is change coming, even to Karse, and sooner than those in Sunhame think." Her voice dropped lower on the last sentence, ringing with a strange resonance.

Before Rinton could ask what that meant, a third echo of the horn sounded, and Fides—Fidesa—released Mirideh's hands. "You must go, before the black-robes send out their demons to catch you. Even your white horse will be hard-pressed to race with them. Go with Vkandis' blessing."

"My thanks to you," Rinton managed. "Mirideh will be well-cared for, I promise." He reached out to grasp the Sunpriest's hand, then turned and guided the girl away from the only home she had ever known.

That third sounding of the horn had seemed suddenly too near the village, and Fidesa's worry over it infected Rinton and the now-shielded Mirideh. Hand in hand they scurried through the woods, not even trying to conceal their passing, until they reached the clearing where Linx waited, one silvery hoof pawing impatiently at the ground. Kiyan had flown dark and silent overhead, circling high up.

:How near are the newcomers?: If they were in immediate proximity on the road, Kiyan would see them.

:Not close. Horses stopped. Black-robe stands. Guards watch.:

Rinton was not comforted. As he and the girl had run through the forest, the late autumn sun had been sinking steadily, and the implications of the Sunpriest's note were not lost on him.

"Black-robes are coming, and the nights will not be safe." Even a poor student of the Chronicles would remember the tales of the horrors of the night-demons that chased anyone out after dark in Karse. With barely a pause, he lifted the awed Mirideh onto Linx's back, pulling himself into the saddle behind her.

"It is a good thing we are both skinny," he murmured to her, and he was pleased to hear a faint giggle. With Linx protecting her mind from outside distress, she was calm, and she seemed to have inherited a healthy dose of her redoubtable grandmother's practical nature. Despite her strong projections of the past days, now no panic came from her—although surely her Gift told her that he meant her no harm.

"Hold tightly, little one. We fly." At the words, though they had been spoken in Karsite, Linx leaped forward.

In almost the same moment, the strange horns sounded again, and this time the blast held a different note—a distinct warning and threat. In the fading light, Kiyan spiraled overhead, then his flight took the same arrow-straight path to the north as Linx's pounding hooves.

:Mind-friend, hurry! Something comes!: It was harder for Rinton to read the bird's mind-voice than Linx's, but it was clear that the crow had no word to describe what came. And whatever it was, even aloft the bird feared it.

Somehow, the Companion found an even faster stride, and Rinton flattened himself as much as possible over his back, one arm wrapped around the young girl, who clung to the pommel with one hand and Linx's mane with the other. A detached part of his mind marveled at her current lack of fear, and he wondered if Linx had taken a stronger control of her mind so that their flight would be easier.

:Yes, I have,: his Companion replied shortly before he could articulate the thought. *:You have been trained to stay on my back at a gallop. She has never been on a horse before.:* Then, silence other than the pounding of hooves and a new, strange whistling behind them.

Fear crept up on Rinton, a different fear from Mirideh's inadvertent projections, although like them, it came from outside of him. This dark dread clawed at his shields, fraying the very protections he set against it, as fatigue weakened him.

:Hold on, Chosen.: Linx's Mindvoice was sharper

now, and he could tell that the Companion, too, felt that otherworldly fear. In the fading light, he could only marvel that Linx could see at all, much less run with such headlong speed, leaping obstacles and maintaining his footing on the other side. Even for a Herald, it was a harrowing ride, and it took all of Rinton's concentration to hold up his own shredding shields and keep himself and the girl on Linx's back. The dark terror kept growing, the strange whistling louder and closer, the silence other than the whistle and Linx's hoofbeats more deafening, until he half-expected to feel claws in his back to match the claws raking at his shields. In desperation, he closed his eyes against the darkness, clinging to the girl and to his Companion, dread threatening to swallow him whole as Linx raced towards the border.

To his mind's eye, his Companion had always had a luminous glow to him, but now Linx shone like a blazing star. Even with his eyes tightly shut, Rinton could see the terrain ahead of them just by the Companion's own radiance, could see faint lines threading ahead of them to pick out safe passage, where silvery hooves could find purchase to drive them forward ever faster. With this strange new vision, Rinton dared not turn to "look" behind them, fearing the shape the darkness might take if he saw it now. Instead, he drew from Linx's strength to bolster his shields, to hold them against the terror that pursued them.

There were no signposts, no markers in the forest to show where, precisely, they crossed into Valdemar, and yet they all knew the moment they did so. The horror behind them checked suddenly, as though it ran into a wall where they passed unhindered. The strange whistling peaked into an angry keening. A burning malevolence filled with fury and frustration washed over them, sharp threat still clawing toward their shields, and then it cut off into sudden silence.

Kiyan cawed once, not a warning, nor yet a triumph,

but with a note of relief. Linx's breakneck gallop slowed to a canter, then a trot, then a much more sedate walk as he cooled himself off.

:A rough camp again tonight, I'm afraid,: he said. *:I would wish better for the young one.:*

Startled from his thoughts by the reminder of Mirideh, Rinton straightened from his hunched position, loosening his grip on the girl to support her lightly.

"It is a poor welcome, little one, to Valdemar. But here you will be safe."

"What will happen to me?" Her worry was clear, even with Linx's shields preventing her from projecting.

Rinton's hand swept through his hair as he always did when frustrated. *:It's a good question, Linx. I don't even know for sure.:*

:We will take her to Haven, of course. She needs training in Empathy and shielding, at the very least. And, unless I miss my guess, she might be a Mind-healer, too. We were going to be meeting up with our replacements shortly anyway; we'll just meet them at a different spot on the Circuit.:

"We will go first to the city of Haven, to find those who can care for you. And you will learn, too, how to protect your mind, as Linx is doing for you now. But tonight we camp, and tomorrow we travel."

Mirideh nodded, leaning her head drowsily against his shoulder as the exhaustion of their flight caught up with her.

It is a good enough explanation for now, Rinton thought. Tonight, the three of them—*no, four,* Rinton reminded himself as Kiyan swooped down to land on his shoulder—would sleep under the stars. The morning would be time enough to explain more to the young Karsite, to guide her into her new life. It would be a while, he expected, before she would understand that her Gift, which caused such fear and turmoil in Karse, would be welcomed and, if Linx was right, celebrated in Valdemar. Empaths and Healers were uncommon enough, but Mindhealers were downright rare.

Besides, since Weaponsmaster Alberich's Choosing, no Herald at least had used the old saw "nothing comes out of Karse but brigands and bad weather." Perhaps young Mirideh would further help change Valdemaran minds about their southern neighbors. If, as Fidesa had said, change was coming to Karse, eventually it would also come to Valdemar.

And, as always, the Heralds would be there to meet it.

Feathers in Deed

Jennifer Brozek

:What do you think he'll be like?: Hadara asked as they traveled the trade route through Rethwellan on their way to Bolthaven. *:Old?:*

Kitha gave a quizzical whistle, then shrugged before answering in Animal Mindspeech. *:Probably mysterious and wise. With white hair. Magic always shows in the hair. Right?:*

They were an unusual pair: a blind gryphon of a tawny mottled color with white crest feathers walking next to a half-Shin'a'in Change-Child who had the stature of a ten-year-old and the weight of a toddler.

They'd spent weeks walking, flying, and gliding from the Dhorisha Plains to where they were now—just outside Bolthaven. The reactions to them along the way had been mixed and wary, though no one had outright attacked them. Strange beings traveled the trade roads since the Mage Storms. It was still fresh in everyone's memory. As long as Kitha kept herself hooded and showed the mostly human side of her face, all was well.

The gryphon was a marvel to see, and no stranger knew Hadara was blind. She wasn't when she used Kitha's eyes to see. And when the gryphon spoke for the Change-Child who wore the leathers and markings of the Shin'a'in, they didn't need to see that she'd been warped by the last Mage Storms and melded with a hawk. The wild magic had stolen Kitha's voice, her stature, and half of her face, but it hadn't touched her determination or will.

:It depends on the Mage, doesn't it? Tayledras Mages always go silver. It's part of their nature.:

:I suppose.: Kitha glanced up at her lifebonded companion. She didn't need to know what the gryphon was feeling or thinking to know that she was worried. The gryphon's feathers drooped, her steps were slower than normal, and her head was down.

They both worried about the same things. They worried that the vaunted White Winds Mage wouldn't be able to fix either of their magical ills. Worried more that if he could, it would sever the lifebond they had. It was through Hadara that the outside world could understand Kitha. Not even Mindspeech touched her. Only Animal Mindspeech. It was through the lifebond that Hadara could share Kitha's eyes and regain some semblance of sight. At least, that was their mutual understanding.

Not that Hadara always used Kitha's eyes. They'd both decided that that would be a bad idea. Blind or not, the gryphon was still competent. She didn't need to become dependent on the Shin'a'in courier. Her other senses and gifts were still sharp.

Just below the crest of a hill, Hadara stopped and listened.

:C'mon you giant birdbrain. Stop dragging your feet. We're going to see the Mage, like it or not.:

"Hussshh," Hadara said. "Liisssten."

Kitha tilted her head and listened. There, in the distance, a cry of distress. They both hurried to the crest of the hill.

Kitha turned her hawk eye towards the commotion and focused in to see as if she were there on the sidelines. Four people in a fight. A tall man in a tunic of the Bolthaven colors of blue, gray, and white seemed to be protecting a young woman in light-colored robes from a man and a woman in the rough brown clothing and leathers of bandits.

The protector took a double attack in the form of a dagger to the stomach and a couple of hard knocks to the face. He went to his knees and was clouted on the head with a dagger pommel.

:Keep your eyes on them.: Hadara backed up a couple of steps, then took a running leap off the hill. She unfurled her wings and glided at the group in a silence belied by her size.

Kitha, following at a slower pace, pulled her sight back a little to give Hadara a better view of her targets. She didn't know what the gryphon was going to do, but she bet it was going to be painful. Both of them eyed the male bandit as the more dangerous of the pair.

Even as Hadara glided in like an avenging angel, with Kitha sprinting behind her, the woman—*a Mage!*—was not helpless. She'd put some distance between her and her foes and brought up her hands. With them, a wall of flying debris—leaves, twigs, dirt, and small rocks—came up to form a moving barrier that blocked both thrown daggers and the bandits who tried to reach her.

Then Hadara was there, punching the man with a clenched claw. Fist struck temple and the man crumpled. Hadara wheeled and set down, giving a scream of challenge.

Kitha, running full at them with her cloak flying, answered with her own smaller challenge.

The woman bandit saw the tide had turned, reached into a pouch, and threw something to the ground. The world exploded in light and sound.

The Mage cried out and covered her face, dropping her protective wall. Hadara reared back, clawing at the air. For her, it was like being blinded once more and deafened at the same time. Kitha, still a distance away, was spared the worst of it. She blinked away tears as her ears rung.

When the noise and light faded away, the bandit woman was nowhere to be seen.

:Calm, Hadara. I'm here. It's okay.: Kitha skidded to a stop and caught sight of something strange. The downed bandit. There was a shimmer around his silver belt buckle, then the buckle was gone. Fetched away. It seemed the woman bandit had a gift beyond the skill of fighting.

The young woman Mage, hardly more than a teenager, blinked through watery eyes at the gryphon and the Change-Child. She didn't flee, but she looked afraid and ready to continue the fight.

Kitha took a look at the Mage's downed companion and knew she didn't have time to soothe nerves. She hurried to his side and pressed a taloned hand to the worse of the bleeding wounds and dug into her pouch for a bandage.

The Mage moved in to protect the man.

Hadara stepped up. "It'sss all rrright."

The woman looked as though she wanted to flee again. She stopped as she saw Kitha pressing a bandage to the man's wound.

:Ask her if she has any healing skills,: Kitha demanded.

"Can you hhheal?"

The Mage did not respond.

Hadara shook her head. *:I can't hear myself. Not really. That explosion . . . :*

:Wonderful. You can't see. I can't speak, and none of us can hear.: Kitha peered at the Mage, who watched with a keen and wary eye. She crooked a single finger to beckon the Mage closer. When she complied, Kitha moved in a slow, clear motion to grasp her by the wrist and pulled the woman's hand to the bandage.

The Mage understood and pressed her hand down to stanch the wound.

With the water she had left, Kitha cleaned her hands, then dug into her pack for needle and thread. The woman blanched and shook her head as Kitha held it up. Kitha made an impatient whistle.

"Hhoold the flessshh togetherrr forrr herrr," Hadara said, trying to help as she kept watch.

The Mage threw a startled glance at the gryphon. "I can hear?" she asked, experimenting. "I can hear. Thank the Winds, I can hear."

Kitha nodded and pointed to the wound.

"Yes. Of course. I'm Teralyn." She shifted the bandage and the man's shirt, then held the slashed flesh together. "This is Braden. Thank you for helping us."

Nodding again, Kitha mended the wound as best she could. She examined Braden and did what she could for the other wounds. As they turned him over to look at his back, they all saw the black dagger with a curved handle. It had a smooth edge and polished black horn for the grip. Well made, it didn't look like something a common bandit would have.

Kitha whistled low and took it. She offered it to Teralyn.

Teralyn shook her head. "They both had daggers like that."

Kitha shrugged and stuck it in her pack. *:Introduce us?:* she asked Hadara.

The gryphon fluffed up. "I am Hadarrrra of k'Leysss-sha Vale. This is my companion Kitha ssshena Tale'sssedrrrrin."

Teralyn stood and gave a small bow. "I'm Teralyn of Bolthaven, apprentice to the Mage Quenten." As she spoke, her hands moved in a series of complex gestures.

Surprised, Kitha caught several of the words even as Hadara repeated them in Animal Mindspeech for her. *The silent language?* Kitha signed.

"Yes, my brother cannot hear or speak. You know it?" Teralyn spoke aloud as she continued to sign.

A little. Kitha signed then gestured to Hadara. *:Tell her?:*

"Kitha wassss recccently afflicted. Sssshe is learning." Hadara opened her mouth in a wide grin. "We ccould talk morrre on the way to Bolthaven?"

Teralyn looked around, worried. "I'd like that. Please though, let me build a travois for Braden first."

"I must admit, the group of you made quite a sight arriving with my apprentice and her companion." Across from Hadara and Kitha, Quenten sat behind a time-worn desk filled with papers, scroll cases, writing implements, and several things that could either be knickknacks or magical artifacts. Kitha couldn't tell. The office itself had once been a meeting room, and was big enough to hold a dozen people with ease. She suspected he held lectures in here.

The Mage was a lean man with a quick smile, wrinkles around the eyes, and red hair shot through with gray. Between the wrinkles and the smile, it was impossible to say if he was thirty or seventy or somewhere in between. Despite this, he radiated a sense of calm power and poise that only came with experience and knowledge.

Kitha shrugged as she watched Quenten with interest and trepidation. Hadara felt both of their worry and fluffed her feathers as she resettled herself again.

"In any case, thank you for assisting my apprentice. There have been dark rumors lately about a growing . . ." He cut off his own train of thought with an abrupt slash of his hand and shake of his head. "I will think on that later: the missing buckle and the dagger you've given me. Now, the two of you have come to see me for another reason." Quenten spoke like a man who already knew what was happening.

"Ourrr maladiessss." Hadara turned her head to display her cloudy eyes as Kitha pulled back her hood to display her half-hawk face. "Both werrree magic borrrrn."

Kitha whistled once and held up a finger. Then she dug into her pouch for the letter written by Jerda shena Tale'sedrin and handed it to the master Mage. It introduced the pair and explained in succinct words what the two of them wanted to know: Could either of their problems—Hadara's blindness and Kitha's physical mutation—be fixed by magic? It explained the magical trap that Hadara had fallen into and the fact that Kitha had been warped in a Mage Storm. It also explained that the pair was lifebonded.

Quenten's eyebrows raised as he mouthed the words "Lifebonded." He looked at Kitha's Shin'a'in clothing, recognizing it for what it was. Glancing between the two, he asked, "How long have you known each other?"

"About fourrr monthsss," Hadara responded before adding, "I wasss blinded about nine monthsss ago. Sssshe was caught in one of the lasssst Mage Ssstorr-rms, about five monthsss ago."

"And you didn't know each other before then?"

Both Hadara and Kitha shook their heads.

Quenten put the letter on the desk. He rose and walked around it to stand before them. "What do you fear?"

Success, Kitha signed. After a moment, she added, *Failure.*

Quenten nodded to Kitha. It was clear he knew something of the silent language. He turned to Hadara. "And you?"

"The brrreaking of the bond."

The Mage rubbed his chin as he muttered to himself. Then he raised his head. "You both fear this?"

They nodded.

"And both fear that I might not be able to do anything to help you?"

Again they nodded.

"But you still want to see what I can do?"

"Yesss," Hadara said as Kitha signed the same word.

"My question for you two is this." Quenten paced like a professor giving a lecture. "If I cannot help you, what will you do?"

Courier, Kitha signed.

"We will continue asss we arrre and continue our plan to be a courrrierrr pairrr."

Quenten glanced between them. "And if I succeed?"

Courier, Kitha signed again.

"The sssaame." The gryphon gave the Mage a head tilt and an open-mouthed smile. "We will be courrri-errrss."

"I see." Quenten shrugged. "That makes my job a little easier. I'll need to examine both of you and do some research. In the meantime, Teralyn will show you where you can stay. Also, my apprentice has offered to teach you, Kitha, all she knows of the silent language while you are here. In thanks for rescuing her."

Kitha signed, *Thank you*.

The stable was warm, private, and enclosed. After months on the road and camping in the rough, a straw bed with a roof was a luxury. Teralyn had headed off into town to get provisions for the pair. While Kitha could eat mice and the like with ease, she could still eat cooked meat, and craved something warm that she hadn't had to catch.

Neither Kitha nor Hadara spoke after Teralyn left. The two of them retreated into their own private thoughts. Despite this, they both could tell what the other was feeling: a chaotic mixture of worry and hope.

Kitha pulled out the small mirror she'd been given and stared at her reflection. Taken separately, each half of her face was beautiful in its own way. From one side, her human face was smaller than she remembered, and the profile of her nose was wrong, but it was still a human face. The other half was humanoid hawk with feathers and the beginnings of a beak. It was pretty in its own way. Different, yes. But not unattractive. Looking straight on though, her face was two halves that didn't make a whole.

Could I live like this for the rest of my life? she wondered.

:Yes.: She answered in Animal Mindspeech. It wasn't a lie, but it was a reluctant admission. *:I could. I would.:*

Hadara shifted. *:Could, would, what?:*

Kitha returned the mirror to her pack and moved over to Hadara. She flopped herself down next to the gryphon and settled into her feathers. *:We don't have to do this. I don't have to be fixed. I've been changed, yes. But I can adapt. Can you? Are you willing to?:*

It took a long time for Hadara to answer. *:I miss the light. I miss seeing . . . but with you, I don't have to. It's not like my own lost sight, but I can see. At the same time, it's almost harder—shifting from darkness to your light. Could I do this, remain blind? Could I adapt? Of course I could. I did for months before I met you. But if there's a chance for me to regain my sight, I want to try.:*

It wasn't the answer Kitha wanted, but it was the answer she'd expected. *:What about us?:*

Hadara's answer was immediate. *:I would remain in darkness forever before I would give up our connection.:*

Kitha relaxed. She hadn't realized how tense she'd become. *:Me, too.:*

"We will adapt to whatever Quenten sssays." Hadara preened the feathers and hair on Kitha's head. "We don't hhhave to do anything."

Kitha whistled her acknowledgement. Hope was a hell of an emotion.

After two days in the stable, Teralyn convinced Hadara and Kitha that Bolthaven really was a haven for the strange and unusual, and that Kitha would not be looked down upon. It was a town supporting a Mage school. That meant the population was used to elementals in the pantry, strange sightings, and escaped experiments. All would be well.

A day later, Kitha decided to test this and agreed to meet her mentor in town for the day's silent language lesson. In truth, she felt closed in. She needed to get out and see what there was to see. While Hadara worried, she was willing to let Kitha go, as long as she promised not to leave the walls of the town.

It was the right thing to do. Kitha kept her hood raised at first. Then, as no one said anything in the marketplace and barely acknowledged her strangeness, she'd gone into a tavern for food.

Even now, as she walked down the street toward the meeting place, Kitha marveled at the barkeep's simple, "Huh. That's a hell of a magic mistake. Hope you get it fixed soon. What'll be? The special's lamb."

It made Bolthaven the ideal place after so many wary and scared strangers.

Something caught Kitha's attention: The sound of a scuffle in the alleyway next to the building she was to meet Teralyn at. She turned her hawk senses in that direction and listened, blocking out as much of the normal town noise as she could to hone in on the thing that didn't sound right.

"—where the black dagger is, or so help me I'll slit your throat."

"I don't know. I swear it!"

Both voices were feminine. One a stranger. One she knew. Kitha crept into the alley, using all her training to hide in the shadows. Peeking around a cart, she saw the bandit woman press Teralyn against the wall, a black dagger at her throat.

"Who has it? That Change-Child girl? Your master?"

Teralyn gritted her teeth, then clamped her mouth shut.

Kitha gave a frantic call to Hadara, but the gryphon didn't respond. There was a feeling of sudden urgency from her friend, but nothing concrete. She was on her own. Change-Child or not, Kitha was still Shin'a'in trained. She pulled her dagger as she unclipped her cloak, letting the fabric slump to the ground in a soft whoosh. She wouldn't be caught up in its folds.

"Answer me, or I'll kill you where you stand." The bandit pressed the dagger into Teralyn's flesh.

"I can't answer you if I'm dead."

"I'll kill them all, one by one until I get that dagger back. You, your master, the gryphon, the Change-Child, and anyone else who gets in my way. Now tell me where it is!"

Kitha narrowed her eyes, tensed, then sprinted at the woman. With a leap, she crashed into her back, hoping Teralyn wouldn't be too hurt in the process.

The bandit reared back and spun around and around, trying to dislodge Kitha as she punched at her. Kitha clung on like the *hertasi* of song. She wrapped her legs around the bandit in the parody of a piggyback ride. Then, bypassing the woman's attacks, Kitha slit her throat.

The bandit gave a gurgling cry, dropped her dagger, and threw Kitha from her. As she did, Teralyn summoned the wind and pressed the woman against the opposite side of the alleyway.

The woman jerked, gagging, as she still tried to fight. She flicked a hand at the fallen dagger. Having seen the woman's gifted skill in the last battle, Kitha knocked aside the dagger Fetched at Teralyn. She threw her own at the bandit. Already weakened and beset by the wind, the woman was unable to keep Kitha's dagger, pushed by Teralyn's spell, from plunging into her chest. After that, it was a matter of waiting until the woman stopped moving. As they watched, her silver belt buckle shimmered and disappeared.

Bleeding, Teralyn lowered her hands, dropping her

dead foe with a thump, and sank to the ground. Kitha hunkered next to her. Teralyn grasped Kitha's shoulder. "Thank you."

She nodded.

They both looked up at the distant sound of a frantic, blind gryphon crashing through the marketplace, shouting, "Cloak and Daggerrr! Wherrre is the Cloak and Daggerrrr?"

It was days later when Quenten summoned them back to his office. He gave them a kind smile as they came in like schoolchildren who'd been caught doing something forbidden. "It's not that bad, my friends. Not at all. Well, it's not all good either. Come in and brace yourselves."

Returning to the same spots they had before, Kitha felt like she was going to throw up until she heard the Mage's next words.

"I've done some research. According to all known lore, lifebonds cannot be broken. Yours wasn't created because both of you were affected by magic. A lifebond is soul deep. If neither of you had been blinded nor caught up in a Mage Storm, and you met, you would still have the same connection you have now. As far as I can tell, curing you will not break your lifebond."

Both Hadara and Kitha relaxed into this new knowledge. "Good newsss indeed," Hadara murmured as Kitha whistled her agreement.

Quenten crossed his arms and leaned against the edge of his desk. "That's the good news. I have bad news and other news."

Bad news first, Kitha signed. She had gotten much better at the silent language under Teralyn's tutelage. Even Hadara had learned some of it, though neither of them could fathom a situation where they would be able to see each other, but not communicate via Animal Mindspeech.

:He can't help us,: Hadara sent to Kitha as Quenten spoke.

"I don't have the skills to cure, or even attempt to undo, what the magic had done to either of you. Hadara, yours would be the simpler of the two, I think, as it only affects your sight. But, the magical trap was old and powerful." He turned to Kitha, "You are much more complicated. The magic, the melding of your body and the hawk's body, is systemic."

Hadara and Kitha nodded in unison.

"But . . ." Quenten held up a hand. "There are Healer Adepts in Haven who might have the skill to help you. I have heard things . . ." He gestured to Kitha. "If not get your voice back, perhaps to allow you to have the whole of your face again. I don't know. I do think the healers in Haven are your best bet."

He stopped, allowing them a scant few seconds to absorb the good, the bad, and the possible. "Now, you both said you wanted to be couriers no matter what. As it so happens, I have a job that needs a courier . . . and an escort. If you are interested?"

Kitha gave him an open-handed gesture to continue.

"That dagger you brought me, along with witnessing of the disappearance of the belt buckles, makes me believe that there is a new evil rising. Dark Mages are organizing under the name of Silence Breakers. I believe it might be a reference to when Ma'ar fought Urtho, the Mage of Silence . . ." Quenten stopped at the blank looks. "More information than you need."

He gathered his thoughts. "I need the thorn—that's the dagger—taken to the Mage Council of Valdemar, along with a missive and my apprentice, Teralyn. She is one of the first to be attacked during the day. The first in Bolthaven proper that we know of. We don't know if she was a target of opportunity, a specific target, or attacked because she is a White Winds Mage.

The Silence Breakers know of you three. With the magical Fetching of the belt buckles, I believe they are still trying to hide. This may make all of you targets. Thus, I am sending you to an old friend of mine, Kerowyn . . . what?" Quenten furrowed his brow at their mutual grins.

Relative of mine, Kitha signed.

"Well, that makes it easier. Of course, you don't look like you used to. Had you two met?"

Kitha shook her head.

"You'll still need a letter of introduction and Teralyn along. I'll ask Kerowyn, or someone she trusts, to meet you in Sweetsprings and escort you into Haven itself. While gryphons are seen more and more . . ." He spread his hands wide.

"We underrrrsssstand," Hadara said.

Quenten moved around the desk and sat in his chair. "I'll perform a sending to both the Skybolts and to a Mage friend in Haven so you'll be expected. I imagine you should arrive by the end of Fall." He squared his shoulders. "Now, my courier friends, what will it cost me to have you escort my apprentice, along with a possibly dangerous artifact, to Haven?"

At a loss for words, Hadara blinked a couple of times. *:Uh, Kitha . . . ?:*

Kitha rubbed her hands together. *:Speak for me?:*

:Of course.:

The Letter of the Law

Angela Penrose

The narrow road of packed gray dirt finally passed through the mouth of the cut—a tight opening that had been chiseled out to the width of a farm wagon some centuries past—and Herald Josswyn felt as though he could breathe again. A thin wind ran down the cut, the only pass between the North Trade Road and the Tolm Valley, but somehow the soaring granite walls had seemed to suck away all the air while he and his Companion, Dashell, had passed through.

Joss had a decent time sense and knew it was only midafternoon, but the western end of the Tolm was already shadowed, giving the impression of evenfall. The spreading vista of tough, scrubby grass spotted with the occasional clump of low, gray-green shrubbery, was far preferable to the tight granite walls, but the landscape still looked bleak and empty in the dim light.

:This time of year, the sheep will be in the eastern pasture,: Dash commented. *:No need to be imagining boojums.:*

:I'm not imagining anything,: Joss retorted. *:It's just not my favorite place to visit.:*

:Especially after riding through the cut.: Dash's mental voice had a note of sympathy. He was familiar with Joss's preference for open, airy spaces.

:That doesn't help, no.: Riding through the cut and places like it took more courage than he'd ever admit to anyone but Dash. But even aside from the unpleasant transit, the Tolm wasn't a friendly place to outsiders. This particular stop on Circuit was more about keeping contact and showing willingness than anything else; the Tolmen hadn't actually brought a problem to a visiting Herald in longer than Joss had been in Whites.

Dash said, *:The sooner we get there the sooner we can leave,:* and he shifted from a walk to a canter. Joss agreed, and in less than a candlemark, they were passing farmsteads, and Baron Tolm's manor appeared in the distance.

The smaller farmhouses were built of sod, which was cheap and plentiful in the valley, warm in the winter and cool in the summer—if one didn't mind living in a dirt house. The better-off farmers and more prosperous crafters built of stone set in earthen mortar. All the roofs were sod over rafters, no matter what the walls were built of. Some of the more enterprising families had herbs or even shallow-rooted vegetables like greens growing on their rooftops.

The houses were built low—none more than a single story—and wide. Each one had a fenced yard behind it, the width of the house and one hundred paces deep. More vegetables grew in the yards, and some had berry bushes. Here and there, a sheep grazed in one of the yards, the few not in pasture with the others.

The only other thing all the houses had in common was that they showed no sign of human habitation. Unlike the sod roofs, that was unusual, and Joss felt his scalp start to prickle.

Relax, he thought to himself, careful not to let it spill over to Dash. *It's nothing, you're just still spooked from riding with walls pressing on your shoulders for half a day. Relax . . .*

:Likely there's a festival of some sort in town,: he said. *:A wedding perhaps? Something that drew everyone from home.:*

:Likely,: Dash agreed. From his tone, Joss could tell he wasn't fooling his Companion for a moment, but he appreciated Dash's discretion in not mentioning it.

By the time they rode through the gap in the earthen wall that surrounded the Baron's Town—which had no other name—Joss was feeling more like himself. They'd left the shadow of the mountains behind, and the warmth of the sun drove the chill from his bones. And noise drifting on the breeze told him he'd been correct about there being some kind of gathering ahead. Something solemn.

Dash had switched into what Joss called "sneak mode." Companions' hooves usually chimed like bells when they walked, but they could be amazingly stealthy if they wanted to.

:Not sneaking, precisely,: said Dash. *:But if they're in the middle of something important, we'd rather not interrupt.:* Joss agreed.

They rode past shuttered shops and empty lanes to the center of town, where the plaza in front of the Temple to the Tolmen gods was packed with folk standing quietly. Everyone wore what Joss recognized as their best clothes: dark greens and dull blues and the occasional brownish gold among the more common black and brown and beige—sheep colors. The men wore their hair in long braids, while the women wore their hair loose, long for the maidens and shorn above the shoulder for the matrons. Joss could tell the sex and marital status of everyone within sight because their backs were to him, facing a dais upon which was set a tall wooden chair.

It wasn't quite a throne, but it clearly had pretentions. From the elevation of his seat on Dash's back, Joss could see that the man on the chair wasn't Baron

Tolm, but his son, Lord Gaulvan. Next to him stood a crier, reading from a scroll he held in front of him, high enough to read but low enough not to block his voice.

"From Talvan the Carpenter, one keg of nails. From Grun the Baker, a dozen loaves of barley bread. From Soben the Smith, one keg of nails. From Poren the Cobbler, four pairs of lambskin slippers. From Durn the Potter, sixteen plates or eight mugs, glazed. From Von the Turner, a dozen long tool handles."

The crier rolled up his scroll, then looked out at the assembly and said, "From all others, the Baron claims the best beast. Bring the animals to Reeve Colvin before next market day. Thus commands the Baron."

He stepped back next to the Baron's chair and looked down at his feet. That was apparently the signal for the crowd to disperse. The susurrus was too low and contained too many voices for Joss to hear what any particular person was saying, but the tone was hard and grim.

:Tax day?: suggested Dash. *:Nobody is happy on tax day.:*

:Perhaps,: said Joss. *:Although this is an odd way to do it, out in public before everyone. Tax collectors usually visit folk one at a time.:*

:The Tolmen do many things differently,: Dash pointed out.

:True.:

Joss waited for the crowd to clear. Folk passing by glanced up at him, some eyeing Dash for a few moments before looking away. When most of the people had dispersed, he saw that twenty or so were crowded around the dais, apparently speaking with the Baron. He and Dash approached at a careful walk.

"But, sir, we've a fine laying hen," one woman was saying as he came into earshot. "Surely that would do. She gives nice, big eggs. Last month, one had two yolks!"

"Your best fowl is the rooster," said the man in the Baron's chair. "I'll not be cheated of my right, and I'll not be dickered with." Lord Gaulvan stood, and all the common folk at the dais shuffled back a step or two. "If you must argue, argue with the reeve." He turned and left, jumping down off the back of the thigh-high dais with the spry ease of a man in his twenties, despite having some few more years than Joss, who was forty-eight.

Joss had Dash maneuver around the small crowd and trot up next to Gaulvan. When Gaulvan looked up and paused, Joss slid out of Dash's saddle as gracefully as he could after some hours in it, and made a short bow.

"Good evening, Lord Tolm. I hope the day finds you well?"

"It's that time again, eh?" asked Tolm, giving Joss a sharp look. "Well enough, I suppose. My father passed away some four days agone."

That was news. "I am sorry for your loss," said Joss. "I'll convey the news to the Queen, and I'm sure she'll send her own condolences."

"If she must." Tolm shrugged and resumed walking.

Joss secured Dash's reins to the saddle and followed, knowing his Companion would keep up with them. "He had a good, long life," said Joss, looking for something to say about someone he hardly knew. "He was a good man, and fair."

That got him another sharp look, but only for a moment. "It was quick, at least. Died in his bed. His man found him. Better than lingering."

"Very true," said Joss.

Topics of conversation apparently exhausted, Joss said, "I'll leave you to your business, then," gave a short bow, and remounted Dash. Tolm grunted and waved him off.

:What say we ride out to the end of the valley?: said Joss. *:We can camp, you can commune with the sheep, then we can turn round tomorrow and ride back out.:*

:If 'communing' with the brainless fluffs is so fascinating to you, perhaps I'll drive a few sheep into your tent?: said Dash, his mind-voice sweet and teasing.

:Just a suggestion,: Joss teased back. *:Thought you might be sick of my company after all this time.:*

:I am,: Dash snarked. *:But even you're preferable to a sheep.:*

:Good to know.:

Back down in the plaza, a score or so folk still lingered, scattered into clusters, their heads close and their postures alternately hunched with worry or stiff with indignation.

It might've been general upset over the transfer of power to a new baron. Any change had the potential to be for the worse, and some folk fretted over any new thought that blew by on the wind. The local barons had a good deal of power over their folk, and especially in a community as isolated as the Tolmen, there was room for no little abuse—or just ham-fisted incompetence from a lord who'd yet to grow into his duties—before help could come.

Joss didn't think that was the problem, though.

The old Baron had been over eighty the last time Joss had come on Circuit, and that had been four years ago. The new Baron was over fifty and had been sharing duties with his aging father for at least thirty years.

Some nobles' heirs spent their lives in Haven or some other large town, spending their fathers' coin on wine, gambling, and commercially acquired affection until they came into their inheritance. That wasn't the case with Gaulvan Tolm.

:Why not ask them?: suggested Dash.

:If it were anyone else. . . . :

:At least they're not Holderkin.:

Joss snorted. *:No, true. But anyone except them.:*

Still, he'd learned to take a snub long ago, so Joss gave a knee signal for Dash to trot over to a clump of four folk who weren't huddled quite as tightly as some of the others.

He dismounted while still a few strides away, to be

polite, and said, "Good afternoon. My condolences on the loss of your Baron. He was a good man."

The four, two grown women, a young man, and a girl nearing womanhood, exchanged quick glances, then nodded to him.

"Our thanks, Herald," said one of the women, her short hair silver-brown and curly. "He did be a good man, a good lord. A fair lord. We'll that miss him."

A tense silence grew for a few moments, then just as Joss began to say, "Might there be anything—?" the young girl blurted, "May'p he be helping us!"

The other woman, whose hair was darker brown and limp, glared down at the girl and snapped, "Hush, Bruny!"

Joss glanced at them and spread his hands with a shallow bow. "If you've a problem, I'll try to help. It's what I'm here for."

The girl bounced on her heels a time or two but stayed silent, looking at the women and the young man, who, Joss figured, were likely her mother and brother, plus a neighbor or an aunt or some such.

"There's naught to be doing," said the darker woman, her voice low and resigned. "It be the law. The old Baron did be softer with it, but it be the law and there's no denying it. N'even a Herald won't go agin' the law." She gave him a hard look, as though daring him to contradict her.

"No, you're right. I'll not go against the law," Joss allowed. "But sometimes a solid law has a postern gate through it or 'round the back, if you know where to look."

More looks went back and forth; the two women communicated with silent head tilts and raised eyebrows that had Joss convinced they had to be sisters.

Finally the curly-haired one said, "Ask. If he kin card it out smooth, so to the good. If not, it be hurting none."

"It be hurting us if the new Baron do be riled, and yon Herald rides away with us left behind!" protested the darker woman.

"If there's nothing I can do, I'll say nothing to the Baron," said Joss. "What can it hurt to explain?"

More looks and eyebrow quirks, then the darker woman shrugged with one shoulder. "I be telling then. But we be walking, getting home before dark."

Joss agreed and tucked Dash's reins onto the saddle so he could follow without tripping while Joss walked with the Tolmen. The curly-haired woman said, "I be Adrun, and this be Agrun, my little sister. Her Ulren and her Bruny."

"Well met," said Joss. "I'm Herald Josswyn and my companion is Dashell." Dash gave a little whinny and nodded his head when the Tolmen turned round to look.

Bruny stared, wide-eyed and giggled when Dash winked at her.

"If you like, you may walk with Dash," said Joss. "He likes meeting new people."

"Can I talk to him? Her? Him?" she asked, her eyes going even wider. They were brown eyes, bright with wonder.

"Him," said Joss. "And yes, you can. He can't answer back with words, unless you can Mindspeak. But if you ask questions, he can nod and shake his head."

She made a squealy noise only young girls meeting a Companion—or a particularly cute kitten or puppy—seem able to make and skipped back to walk next to Dash.

:If she chatters my ear off, I'll blame you,: said Dash. But Joss could hear the humor in it, so he just smirked over his shoulder at his Companion.

They headed east, the rest of the way through the small town, past a carpenter's yard and a bakery giving off wonderfully savory smells into the air. They paused and Adrun went inside, returning with a clay pot wrapped in layers of thick rag.

"Supper," she said to Joss. "Tis only bean pottage, but you be welcome to sup with us, may'p you've a mind."

"Thank you, but I should not," said Joss with another bow, hoping not to give offense. "If I'm to help you, it would be best if there's no appearance of bribery, however slight. We have our own provisions, and I'll sleep on the common."

"As you be liking," said Adrun with a nod.

They passed through another, smaller, opening in the earthen wall and walked on down the track through rough meadows. More low buildings, stone and sod, clustered near town, thinning out as they moved farther away.

"So," said Adrun, "the old Baron be passed, and Lord Gaulvan, he be the new Baron now."

Agrun gave her sister a sharp look and took up the tale. "That did be four days agone. The day after that one, my Ulden passed. My husband, he did be."

"I'm very sorry," said Joss. "That must have been hard."

"It did be hard. Do be hard," Agrun said, looking away.

"It would be less hard if he'd passed some days earlier," said her sister.

"Adrun!" Agrun glared and drove a bony elbow into her sister's ribs.

"It be hard but true!" Adrun glared right back, moving out of elbow range. "If he'd passed while the old Baron still lived, we'd not be looking at starving come winter!"

"May'p so, but it be cruel to think and more cruel to say."

Before the sisters could settle into their brangle, Joss said, "So the new Baron is doing things differently?"

"Yay, he be," said Agrun. "He be claiming best beast of all the farm families. N'any be spared."

"We only be having the one ram," blurted Ulren, looking away from his mother and aunt. "It be na right!"

"Ulren, hush!" His mother scowled at him, but he scowled right back.

"I'll not! I be the man of the hearth now! I should say! I should be the one to be fixing it!" He stood with his back straight, but his knuckles were clenched white; Joss could tell the thought of "fixing it"—which doubtless would require bringing a protest to the Baron, or at least his reeve—was rather terrifying to the boy.

"Until you be having a wife, you be not man of anything," his mother retorted. She looked away from Ulren as though that settled things, and she said to Joss, "He do be saying true, however much he be sassing. We be having shares of eighteen sheep. It be paying rent on the house, but no more. Bouncer be a fine ram. Studding be nigh only trade we be having. If the Baron does be claiming him as best beast, it'll be leaving us with nothing."

Joss remembered the "best beast" rule from his law classes at Collegium. It was a law the Tolmen had brought with them from wherever place they'd left centuries ago. When a head of household died, his liege lord could claim the household's best beast as a sort of inheritance tax.

"And the old Baron would've overlooked the best beast law?"

"Yay," said Agrun with a nod. "If a household be in a hard way, he did be choosing another beast. Or even be forgetting entire. One of the ewes would be fine eating for the Baron's household for some days, or would add a fine wooler to the Baron's flock, but Lord Gaulvan is being a hard man, now he sits in the chair. We've a cousin Adrun could live with, she be a hard worker, but we three be too much."

"Surely your neighbors wouldn't let you starve?"

her voice low, she asked, "Do you think may'p I could be learning to be a Bard? If I could be going to Haven some way?"

"You could always try," said Joss, thinking about it. It might not be a bad idea, if he could arrange safe passage for the girl, someone to look after her on the trip. If she were accepted at Bardic, it'd be one less child for her mother to feed and clothe. For that matter, if Bruny got through training, she could eventually send a bit of coin home.

It's not a solution entire, he thought to himself, *but sometimes solutions to problems come bit by bit.*

"Do you know any especially happy songs?" he asked Bruny. "Or even any very sad ones?"

"Oh, yay," she said. "Be you wanting a song?"

"Yes, if you please. Sing me something from your heart."

She cocked her head at him, then set down her jugs in the water and stood straight. She launched into a bouncy, rollicking song about a young he-lamb who'd tired of being a sheep, so he tried to fly like a bird, and swim like a fish, and burrow like a worm, coming to humorous grief each time. Joss couldn't help but laugh, Bruny's mirthful pleasure in the song threading into his very bones as he listened.

She had the Gift, he was sure of it. It wasn't *that* funny a song, but her singing it made it so.

"You've the Bardic Gift, Bruny," he said when she finished. "The masters at the Collegium would be very pleased to have you."

"Be it true?" Her eyes went as wide as her smile. "You'll not be saying it to make a child happy? I be not a child, you know, and be not needing such coddles!"

"It's true, I promise. I'll speak with your mother, and do what I can to see you safely to Haven, if she agrees."

"Oh, thankee!" Bruny splashed over to him and squeezed him tight enough to nearly crush his ribs.

When they finished filling the jugs, he offered to take two of them from her, but she refused, saying she was used to the weight, and it was much harder without the yoke. She stepped smartly for home, and Joss had to stretch his legs to keep up with her, even unburdened.

Bruny's happy burbling completely confused her mother, but Joss broke in gently and explained.

"It's a Gift, Agrun. Like my Mindspeech. A kind of magic. The Bardic Gift is valued highly in Haven, and she'd have good schooling, at no cost to you. They'd see to her needs and prepare her to be a Bard. It's a good trade." The Bardic Masters would doubtless be horrified to hear their craft called such, but he thought Agrun would understand it in those terms.

"And people be truly . . . singing? For their work?" she asked, clearly dubious.

"Yes. Many people do. With her Gift, Bruny could be a Bard," he repeated. "Minstrels can have a hard life, but a Gifted Bard will never go wanting. Once she's through her schooling, she could send home a coin now and again."

"It would be lessening the burden," said Adrun. "If they'll be feeding her and such."

"My daughter be no burden!" snapped Agrun.

"We all be burdens," Adrun snapped right back. "That be why you be pushing me to live with Cousin Tern, because I be a burden once Bouncer be gone. I know it, and I be not too proud to own it. If these Bard folk be willing to keep Bruny, that be one step farther from starving you and Ulren will be."

Agrun glared, looking as though she wanted to deny it all, but clearly she couldn't. She huffed out a breath and gave her daughter a sharp stare. "You be wanting this?"

"Yay, mam! Please?"

Agrun stared out the one small window for a few moments, then her shoulders slumped, just a little. "Then yay," she said. "If the Herald can arrange it."

"Thankee, mam!" Bruny bounced over and hugged her mother, much as she'd hugged Joss, but for longer. Agrun murmured something to her, and she murmured something back. Joss couldn't hear what they were saying, but he was happy something was working out.

Joss excused himself from the family and rode Dash back into town, in search of the reeve. He had an office at the manor, and over Joss's objections, he shooed two farmers out of it to receive Joss with no waiting. Courtesy aside, though, he had no good news for Agrun and her family.

When Joss had explained the problem, the man, Reeve Bordren, could only spread his hands and shrug. "I be that regretful, Herald," he said. "But the Baron did be making himself plain. I do be feeling for Adrun, she's being a good woman, and her husband was being a hard worker and is missed. But still, the Baron insists on best beast. He says it be only once in a generation, and he'll be having it."

"Would he take two ewes, if I could persuade Agrun of it?" Joss asked. "Surely two fine, healthy beasts would be worth more than the one?"

Reeve Bordren shook his head. "Nay, the ram be that valuable. Good coin from his stud. He'll never agree."

Joss swallowed down objections, thinking furiously. "When is market day, then?" He had some thought that the sisters could perhaps persuade some number of their neighbors to breed their ewes before the ram was surrendered, at least giving them a bit of savings.

But the Reeve's answer dashed those hopes, too. "It be two days nigh, Herald."

So much for that thought.

He took his leave of the man and left the office.

:It's the Baron, then,: he said to Dash. *:I have to try. Maybe he'll be a bit more yielding in private than he can afford to be in front of all his folk..:*

:Maybe,: said Dash, but Joss could tell he was dubious.

So was Joss, but he had to try. People had surprised him before.

A question to a servant found the Baron in his own office, writing a letter. The place was shabby but clean, with good light coming in the wide window, and a good shelf of books to one side on the same wall, where no direct light could fade their covers.

The Baron looked up at Joss's entrance and said, "Herald," then waited.

Joss made a bow, then straightened and said, "I'd like to speak with you about one of the families of the valley."

Tolm scowled at him and sat up straighter. "If any've come crying to you, it'll do them no good."

"Surely it does you no good to have any of your people starving? The loss of workers, or the burden of caring for folk who could care for themselves if you'd only be flexible—"

"The law says a death duty is owed," said Tolm. "Without law, we're no better than the barbarians. None are exempt from the law, not me, not you, and not any of the folk. The law has ruled this valley since our forefathers settled it, and it's led us true. If I make an exception for one household, everyone with a complaint will expect an exception made for them as well, and we'll fall into chaos."

"With respect, your father made exceptions," Joss pointed out. "Your father tempered law with compassion, and things went well under his rule."

"I am *not* my father." Tolm's voice turned harsh and his stare hard. "And I'll thank you to mind your business. We pay our taxes and obey the Queen's law, as well as our own. I would think a Herald would appreciate law-abiding folk wanting to remain such."

"As you say," said Joss. Clearly there was nothing to be gained by arguing, so he bowed himself out and left.

:That one should have been a lawyer,: said Dash as Joss strode through the manor toward the back door.

:As fond of he is of the law,: Joss said, agreeing. *:I agree that the rule of law has to apply to everyone, but there's room for human judgement, and mercy. The law applies to everyone, yes, but—:*

He cut himself off, staring at a thought that'd popped into his head.

:What?:

:I think I have it.: Joss grinned at nothing and jogged out the door.

On market day, Joss went into town with Agrun and her family. Ulren, fresh-scrubbed and pale faced, led Bouncer the ram by a rope knotted around the animal's neck. Bouncer wasn't pleased by the arrangement, and the women of the family chivvied him along with their staves whenever he tried to buck or jerk the rope out of Ulren's hand.

They lined up with the other folk waiting to pay their death duty to the reeve, who was sitting behind a small trestle table in the plaza. Baron Tolm sat in his great chair beside the reeve, and half a dozen helpers bustled about, collecting duty from the folk as they paid, stowing it in boxes and baskets, stacking it to one side, or leading it away, as appropriate.

Agrun looked alternately stern, hopeful, and terrified. Adrun's hands clenched and squeezed each other, although her face stayed blank.

Bruny was as well-scrubbed as Ulren, and she wore her best dress, of fine pale wool with dancing leaves embroidered around the neck and hem in green-dyed wool. She had a thin, braided rope of pale wool in her curly brown hair, wound from the nape of her neck up to the top of her head and tied in a bow.

When the reeve called for Agrun, she stepped forward, her jaw clenched. She led Bruny forward by the wrist, then stopped and bowed, hauling Bruny down with her.

"Reeve Bordren," she said, her voice loud enough

for everyone within twenty paces to hear, "I be bringing my best beast, as the law be saying. This be my daughter, Abrun."

She let go Bruny's wrist and put her hand to the small of Bruny's back, giving her a gentle push. Bruny took a step forward, her eyes wide and fixed on the Baron.

The reeve stared at Bruny, at Agrun, at Joss, then at Bruny again, then turned to look at the Baron for direction.

Baron Tolm glared at Joss. "Herald Joss," he said, his voice louder than Agrun's and twice as hard. "If you think I'll take possession of a young girl like an animal, you're much mistaken. Perhaps such pandering ways are common in Haven, but here in the Tolm we are decent people."

Joss stepped forward and made a deep bow. "I intend nothing of the sort, my lord. You're correct—such a thing would be despicable. But Agrun has agreed to present her daughter Abrun to serve in your household. She has the Bardic Gift—it's a kind of magic and is much valued." Which he was sure the Baron knew; he'd been fostered with a noble family in Haven as a boy. But Joss was also playing for the crowd. "Many great houses have their own Bards, and there are many at court."

He stepped up beside Bruny and put a hand on her shoulder. "Sing for the Baron, Bruny. Show him." He gave her shoulder a squeeze, and she gave him a trembling smile.

She knew all the folk in the plaza, and they'd discussed what was to happen, but still, her nerves were understandable.

The Baron scowled and opened his mouth, but Bruny hurried to begin, and once she'd started singing, the Baron seemed to no longer have the will to interrupt. She sang the lamb song again, and within a line or two, everyone Joss could see was smiling and nodding and tapping their feet. By the time she finished, the atmosphere about the plaza had lightened, and the day seemed happier.

Joss whispered, "You did beautifully, Bruny." and gave her shoulder another squeeze.

He straightened, and looked Lord Tolm straight in the eye. "She has *magic,"* he repeated. "All here felt it. Her Gift lets her make folks who hear her feel what she feels when she sings. She can cheer the despairing, calm the angry, hearten the fearful. She is unique in this valley and is much to be valued. She is clearly Mistress Agrun's 'best beast.' The ram is here as well, in case you would prefer him. He is clearly Mistress Agrun's *second-best* beast, but if you prefer to accept him, that is, of course, up to you."

Baron Tolm clearly saw the trap closing around him. The gathered folk were nodding, agreeing with Joss. And if the Baron chose Agrun's "second-best beast," then he'd not be able to insist on everyone else's first best.

He gave Joss a look that said he'd like to murder him, but he stood from his chair and said, "Clearly I must agree with you."

:Clearly he must,: thought Joss, keeping a smirk off his face, but letting Dash pick it up.

"I accept the girl Abrun into my household. She'll serve at my court."

Such as it was. The Barons Tolm had less of a court and more of a largish family, but the form of it was what mattered. Joss bowed to the Baron and urged Bruny forward. She gave him a doubtful look, then looked to her mother.

Agrun set her jaw and nodded, shooing Bruny away toward the men helping the reeve. Bruny nodded and went where she was directed, standing next to a keg of nails and in front of a bolt of woven wool, wrapped in clean rags and sitting on a crate of something else.

Agrun's family bowed and withdrew a few paces away, staying to watch. The line moved forward, and the reeve collected death duty from each household in turn. Most went on about their business, but some stayed to see what might happen next.

When the last family handed over a rooster in a cage and withdrew, the reeve stood and said, "The duty has been collected. Our business is concluded."

Before anyone could leave, or the Baron could stand, Joss stepped forward and said, "Begging the reeve's pardon, but the death duty has not all been collected."

Baron Tolm rose from his chair and stalked over to glare straight at Joss. "I've put up with your nonsense, but we're through now. You'll leave before you outstay your welcome."

"The letter of the law must be upheld," said Joss, staring straight back at the Baron. "Your lord father died recently. As his liege, Queen Selenay is also owed a death duty."

The baron jerked backward just a bit, startled. "That is not a kingdom law," he protested.

"We are here in the Tolm Valley," said Joss. "And the law of the Tolm rules. By the law of the Tolm, the Queen is due a duty."

Tolm humphed and nodded. "Fine, fine. What would you have?"

Joss gave him a sweet smile. "Your 'best beast' is clearly the girl Abrun. Her Majesty values Gifted folk very highly, and it would please her to see to Abrun's care and training. I'll escort her to Haven, to the Bardic Collegium, where she'll be taught to control her Gift. She'll make a fine Bard one day, and she will surely sing of the beauties of her home and the benevolence of her Baron."

Tolm snorted and raised an eyebrow at Joss. "You've already won, Herald," he muttered. "Don't drown me in butter." He took a step back and said more loudly, "If the Queen would like Abrun as a death duty, then she may have her with my blessing. The law applies to all. None are exempt, not even me."

Joss gave him a full court bow and said, "I give you the Queen's thanks in advance. I'll take my leave now and will escort Abrun to her schooling."

"Do so," said the Baron. "Quickly."

They exchanged pointed looks before Joss withdrew. He only hoped it was a good few years before he rode this particular Circuit again.

Bruny had dashed back to her family and was managing to bounce up and down while hugging her mother and crying. Agrun looked over Bruny's head at Joss as he approached.

"I not be knowing if I wish to thank you or strangle you, Herald," she said, her voice tight.

"It'll be hard," said Joss. "I remember when I left my family to go to Haven. I was homesick, but I was excited too. Bruny will do well and will be fine."

"Yay, I be knowing. My head be knowing. My heart be protesting. But you did be saving our family, and for that my head and my heart both be thanking you."

"You're very welcome," said Joss with a smile and another bow.

:Letter of the law,: said Dash from where he waited at the edge of the plaza. *:Baron Tolm is the one who insisted the law applied to everyone, including him.:*

:To everyone,: said Joss. *:Even him.:*

Who We'll Become

Dayle A. Dermatis

We sing to bring light to the darkness
We sing to welcome the sun
We sing of family and loved ones
We sing of a new year begun . . .

The traditional Midwinter song filled the great hall of Traynemarch Reach's manor, the children's voices imperfect but heartfelt, the melody soaring up to the high, dark rafters and swirling around the listeners. It mingled with the fire blazing in the stone hearth draped with ivy and holly and fragrant pine boughs.

The longest night, the shortest day, and the Midwinter Feast that brought family and friends together.

Syrriah had missed the last two years' celebration at Traynemarch Reach, her old home. This homecoming was bittersweet. The familiar song brought sparkling tears to her eyes.

Three years ago, she had been the Lady of Traynemarch Reach, and she and her husband were preparing to pass their roles on to Syrriah's sister and brother-in-law. A wintery river and a collapsed bridge in need of repair had changed everything. Of course Syrriah's husband had helped the villagers. The resulting chill he suffered grew worse—and then deadly.

Everything changed six months later, when the jangle of bells announced the arrival of a Companion.

Not a Companion ridden by one of Syrriah's four children, who had all already been Chosen.

A Companion for Syrriah.

This was the first time she'd been back home since that bewildering but ultimately rewarding day. Not a day went by when Syrriah wasn't astounded by her relationship with Cefylla.

Right now, despite the warmth of the fire in the hearth, the beautiful singing (which included her two youngest, Benlan and Natalli), and her family around her, Syrriah half-wished she were in the barn with Cefylla.

She heard a snort in her mind. *:Hardly,:* Cefylla said. *:It's a nice sentiment, but I rather think you'll enjoy your feast over my warm mash.:*

Syrriah bit back a laugh. *:There is that,:* she admitted. The long, white-cloth-covered table was laden with deep blue ceramic dishes and pitchers. The traditional foods: tender roast mutton and crispy-skinned duck, carrots and parsnips in a creamy dill sauce, small seed cakes decorated with suns made out of dried flower petals. Sweet summer wine, vinted especially for this feast. Between everything, dark blue candles representing the midwinter night sky, each flame a call to the rising sun at dawn.

She should have felt at home; after all, she'd been the Lady here for more than twenty years. But in the relatively short time she'd been away, the Collegium, Cefylla, the Heralds . . . they'd become her life.

Plus, Riann, her sister (for whom Syrriah had named her oldest daughter), well, she did things differently. When Riann and her husband had stepped up to run the manor and holdings, Syrriah had offered her advice and assistance, but only if they asked. She respected and trusted them both.

And, certainly, the changes were not of any great

import. If Riann preferred that everyone wait until after the feast to open the cloth-wrapped gifts that sat above each dinner plate, that was her choice, even if it went against tradition and made the younger children fidget. (Riann's youngest kept reaching out and touching the fabric wrapping with a forefinger. Each time, his older sister nudged him, and he shoved the finger in his mouth. The food on his plate was largely untouched.)

The curtains covering the tall, stone-framed windows were different: Riann's preferred greens and blues to Syrriah's reds and golds. Syrriah would probably have a bruise on her left hip before she left, because the furniture in the main hall had been rearranged, and she could never remember to skirt that one chair.

Indeed, the new arrangement gave fresh life to the room, and Syrriah hadn't thought about colors since she went to the Collegium—other than the colors the various Trainees and Heralds wore. She was glad Riann and her husband had made Traynemarch Reach their own. And she'd heard nothing but good things about their stewardship of the holdings.

It just all took some getting used to, this familiar-but-not.

Waking up this morning had been strange as well. At the Collegium, there was always the chatter of student voices in the halls in the morning, or outside her window as Heralds and Trainees returned from spending time with their Companions at the stable. Here, she could hear the crackle and snap of the icicles hanging from the eaves just outside. Plus, the room may have looked like Traynemarch Reach, but it wasn't the one she'd spent more than twenty years waking up in.

Her clothing was yet another matter.

She'd looked forward to wearing her old gowns, which she'd left behind, rather than her Trainee gray tunic and loose pants and boots. She'd missed choosing what to wear each day.

Her gowns, however, no longer fitted her the same. She'd always been an active woman, but her training at the Collegium, including a newfound affinity for archery, had reshaped her. Her gowns were looser in some places but tighter than others, such as her shoulders and arms. She had to be careful not to raise her arms too high, or she might tear out a seam.

She felt constricted by that, and the heavy skirts, and was already longing for the simple comfort of her Trainee Grays.

She might have been able to brush off all of that if it hadn't been for one final thing:

She felt completely useless.

Oh, she'd struggled with that before being Chosen, but being Chosen had given her a new purpose—and that new life. Here, she was even more strongly reminded that she had no function at Traynemarch Reach.

"You're looking rather serious for a celebration," Riann, next to her, said with a gentle nudge of her elbow. Her voice was light, but Syrriah saw the concern in her blue eyes.

Syrriah's Gift of Empathy had broken free during her training at the Collegium, and she wouldn't have been surprised to discover such a talent could run in a family to a lesser degree. Riann had always been kind and caring, as well as organized and intelligent, which was why Syrriah and Brant had chosen her to take over the manor.

Syrriah felt guilty for worrying Riann. As hostess, her sister had far more important things to worry about.

As the final notes of the song faded, she smiled and squeezed Riann's hand.

"I'm fine," she said, and it wasn't entirely a lie. She was glad to be with her family, no matter how unsettling the changes were.

Or how useless she felt.

:You're quite useful,: Cefylla gravely informed her. *:In*

fact, if you're through eating, I could use a good brushing.:

We honor those who have passed on
We honor the year now gone by
We banish the darkness with kindness
We rejoice when new dawn greets the sky . . .

The next day, the sun indeed did rise, with the day bright and clear, giving a sense of warmth even in the chill of the season. An auspicious start to the Midwinter Festival.

Syrriah's old riding gear proved more comfortable than her gowns, and her mood lightened as she rode on Cefylla alongside Riann and her husband, the rest of the household following behind along with a packhorse laden with gifts. The chill in the air, the laughter and banter rising on visible, mistlike breath, the joy of the season. Hooves crunching on packed snow. Sweet smoke from chimneys. The glitter of the river in the distance; the fallow fields slumbering in preparation for spring planting.

As they rode through the village, Syrriah noticed which houses had new decorations and which had added a room or a new fence. Lives had continued, just as hers had.

They were joined by other riders, as well as by families walking as they headed out the other side of the village. Eventually they came to the crossroads where the monthly market was held, drawing merchants from several nearby towns and villages.

The Midwinter Fair market, however, was a special event indeed.

People wore new clothing they'd been gifted, coats and hats and scarves. Children ran about, shrieking and laughing. The fair was a time to celebrate children, too, so shopkeepers had sweets or small toys to hand out.

In the center of the marketplace was a white-painted gazebo from which announcements were made and news was shared. Today, it was draped with pine boughs and silver-and-blue ribbons, and a small group of musicians with lute and drum and shawm performed traditional songs. Syrriah put coins in the basket they'd set out, and the lute player nodded and winked his thanks.

They left Cefylla and the horses at the public stable, and Lord and Lady Trayne, and their children, began the annual procession around the market, handing out small gifts and tokens. At first Syrriah accompanied them, but eventually she fell back, spending more time perusing the market wares.

At the Collegium, she lived in a small room, and her necessities were provided for: clothing, food, and so forth. She had little space for personal items, and she had brought things from home that were special to her, including a portrait of Brant, with a lock of each of her children's hair tucked under the glass.

She was busy enough at the Collegium with her studies and training that leisurely shopping had also become a thing of the past. Now, she indulged in fingering some fine linen, a dark red chevron pattern shot through with gold. She sniffed the flowery perfumes and soaps, the jars of teas. She admired sheep fleeces and tanned leather and furs. Cheeses, wine, flour, and hops.

She knew many of the merchants, although there were always some who came and went. Some curtsied or bowed—even though she no longer ran Traynemarch Reach, there was still memory and respect, and she was delighted to greet them all and learn how they had fared since her departure.

Eventually she came to the stall of one of her favorite artisans, a man everyone called Carver because of his incredible woodworking skills.

She breathed in the sweet smell of wood shavings, undercut with the cider he had in a pot on the small stove at the back of the stall. Heat from the stove took an edge off the day's chill.

By the front of the stall sat a basket filled with gifts for the children who came by, obviously made from pieces left over from other projects. Rings for fat baby fingers to grasp, dolls, blunt swords, blocks with letters on them.

She was greeted not by Carver but by his son, Eron.

The hair at Eron's brow had receded since the last time she'd seen him, but, then, her own hair had new strands of silver shot through it. He was just as tall, just as wiry, with the same long-fingered, capable hands cross-hatched with pale scars from his work.

Both he and his sister, Vaice, were skilled woodworkers in their own right. Some said even more talented—including Carver himself.

"Lady Trayne," he greeted her, his voice hearty and his brown eyes smiling. Then, with a small shake of his head: "I'm sorry—*Herald*. How are you?"

"I'm well, Eron. But please, I'm not a Herald yet. You can call me Herald Trainee, but here, now, I'd prefer Syrriah."

"'Tis strange to call you that, I confess, after all the years of you and your lord in the manor."

"My title may be different, but I've not changed," she said.

"Ah, but haven't we all?" he said, echoing her thoughts.

He offered her a cup of cider, which she gratefully accepted. Made from her favorite local apples, it was tart, warm, and laced with cinnamon and cloves.

Every piece Carver created was unique, a fact in which he took great pride. (Unless, of course, he made a set; then each part was indistinguishable from the next.) Every piece was solidly crafted, too. The cradle she had purchased almost twenty years ago had served her four babies well, before she had passed it on to Riann.

His skill was known throughout Valdemar, even

though he could make only a small number of large pieces each year.

She asked Eron about his father and learned that Carver had recently passed the business on to Eron and Vaice. He was still carving small things, but he didn't have the energy for larger pieces anymore.

Eron showed her the headboard he was carving for a wedding, and Vaice's latest project, a set of anniversary cups, the names of the couple's children spiraling along the bowl of each. The work on both was exquisite.

But underlying his words, masked by his smile, was a thread of unhappiness. Something troubled him. Syrriah tamped down on her Gift, not wanting to intrude. She was not the lady of the manor; she was not quite a friend. If it was something he wished her to know about, he would tell her.

She was just about to leave when Vaice ducked under the awning to the merchant stall.

Vaice was as tall as her brother and father, with the same wiry strength. Her light brown hair was plaited, the braids wrapped around her head to keep it out of the way while she worked.

They both must be nearing thirty now, Syrriah realized, no longer children at all, even though it was easy to still think of them that way.

As soon as Vaice entered, Eron's sense of being troubled flared.

"I was hoping to speak with you, actually," Vaice said to Syrriah after sketching a brief curtsy. "I was wondering when you planned to return to Haven."

"In a little more than a weeks' time," Syrriah said. "It will depend on the weather; I'll leave earlier if necessary."

Vaice bit her lip, clearly avoiding looking at her brother. "Would you . . . would you and your Companion be willing to let me ride with you? If I wouldn't slow you down, I mean."

"Surely you can wait until spring . . ." Eron said.

"I'm not changing my mind, so waiting won't make a difference," Vaice said.

Syrriah was a mother of four. She didn't need Empathy to hear the stubbornness in Vaice's voice, and see it in her squared shoulders and the jut of her jaw.

"Maybe this is something you can help us with," Eron said, turning to Syrriah. "Give us your advice, based on your training."

Syrriah's training wasn't complete, but before she could point that out, Vaice said, "I'd be interested in hearing what you have to say. Especially if it means convincing my brother it makes no sense to be stuck in the past."

"We've been given a legacy," Eron said. "It's our job to uphold it—not destroy it."

It was clear they'd been having this argument for some time. They barely even seemed to hear each other's words.

The job of a Herald included diplomacy and negotiating skills. Syrriah wasn't a Herald yet, but as lady of the manor, she'd needed similar abilities.

Besides, this was a family dispute, not a situation in service to the Monarch.

She could pull Riann away from the Midwinter Fair—it was an issue that could very much affect the Major holdings, as the business brought wealth and commerce to Traynemarch Reach—or she could see if she could help.

"I'm willing to listen and give my opinion," she said. "But not as a Herald; I'm still a Trainee. As . . . an unbiased ear."

Vaice motioned her to a set of chairs in the corner. They were serviceable, solid, with clean lines. The grain of the wood gleamed with polish and felt incredibly smooth. There wouldn't be a splinter to be found. They had a quiet beauty and what Syrriah thought of as the Carver quality . . . although they bore none of the intricate carving she'd expected.

A moment later, she learned why.

Vaice went first. "I have been studying economics and business," she said. "My father made a good living for our family with his work, but now there are two of us, with two families. When Eron and I began helping Father, our output increased, but it has decreased, obviously, since he retired."

"We could bring in an apprentice," Eron said.

"Apprentices still need to be housed, and clothed, and fed," she countered. "And there's no guarantee they'd ever get to the skill level needed, or that they wouldn't leave to start their own business."

"You make good points," Syrriah said. "I'm guessing you have a solution?"

Vaice held out her hand. "You're sitting on them," she said. "We can make simpler items much faster—and we can hire people to help with the basic work. Set up work stations, even. So, for example, one person is turning spindles, another person is doing something else. We would make sure the quality was just as high as it is now, but be able to produce more. Plus, it would widen our customer base. So many people can't afford what we make, and these items would be priced cheaper."

Syrriah was knowledgeable enough to have helped with the books at Traynemarch Reach, but this was something she'd never considered. It made a great deal of sense.

"Eron?" she said.

He leaned back in his seat, arms across his chest, even as his body language betrayed that he didn't want to be sitting on this particular chair.

"Our business is known for the individual pieces my father, and then we, have crafted. He created a legacy from nothing, a heritage that we can't turn our backs on. It would devastate him."

He sighed. "But Vaice is right about the money, and I don't have an easy solution. We can look for a different supplier for lumber, but we'd have to be certain the quality wouldn't change. I don't want to charge more for what we make, but . . ."

Vaice nodded. "We probably could command more, but I don't think the higher prices would cover the fewer orders."

"You both agree that quality is paramount," Syrriah said.

They both nodded.

She ran her hand along the silken-smooth arm of her chair. Could the solution be as easy as it seemed?

"It's true," she said, "that your father's business has always been known for the unique pieces he made, the gorgeously intricate carving and design. But I think that the other component was, as you both agree, quality."

She considered her next words. "Beauty can be found in many forms," she said. "In the intricate work of that headboard or those goblets, but also in the lines and the flow of these chairs. The cradle your father made for me has held many babies over many years, and I know this chair is solid and will last generations as well. And as you said, Vaice, there is a benefit to creating less expensive pieces so more people can enjoy the quality and beauty of the work."

"Thank you," Vaice said.

"However," Syrriah went on, "it's also true that the Carver name is known for intricate, unique pieces, and there will always be people who want those as well. My suggestion is that you divide the business into two businesses, both operating under the same name to remind buyers of the underlying quality, but clearly distinct in what products each business offers. Traditional methods on one side, new experiments on the other."

She felt a weight lift from her chest, leaving behind an almost giddy feeling. She didn't want to laugh at the looks on their faces, however, as their expressions turned from stubborn to dawning realization and shared consideration.

"I think . . ." Eron said. "I think that might just work."

"I think it might," Vaice agreed. "We'll have to figure out the details, of course."

Syrriah tried to sneak out while they were talking, but they caught her before she left, thanking her profusely and trying to press a gift into her hands. In the end she relented and took toys from the basket for her niece and nephew.

Then, her step lighter than it had been, she went to find her family.

We sing away the old year, and welcome the new
We sing of the past, and the winter so cold
We open ourselves to who we'll become
We sing of the future and the secrets it holds.

The bells on the bridles of three steeds—Cefylla, and Natalli and Benlan's Companions—jangled in the sunshine, a counterpart to the honks of the snow geese flying overhead. The weather had held, cold but bright, and Syrriah had enjoyed every moment with her family before she had to leave.

Just as she would enjoy every moment back at the Collegium.

Going home reminded her of all she had loved, and still loved.

It had also reminded her that she was a different person now, and she had more to love and experience and learn.

Counseling Vaice and Eron had shown her that she did have at least a strong foundation of fairness and mediation to build upon as she completed her studies and became a full-fledged Herald.

:You see, my dove? I knew I Chose well.:

Syrriah leaned forward, hugging Cefylla's neck. *:Thank you, dearheart.:*

They rode together toward Syrriah's bright future.

Unceasing Consequences

Elizabeth Vaughan

Dearest Father,

Please understand that I am grateful to the Trine for the blessings I have received. The honor of being made the Lady of Sandbriar and swearing fealty to Queen Selenay was beyond my wildest hopes.

We have come through the winter, but there is still a struggle to restore the land and the economy of this holding. While my coffers are sparse, everyone here is willing to work and work hard. But every problem of the land and the people are mine, and everyone looks to me for answers.

And there are many, many problems.

"Mold," Lady Cera of Sandbriar stared at the black spots with dismay.

"That's a problem, yes?" One of the women clustered around the table asked.

"Yes," Cera said, trying not to sound disheartened. Her audience consisted entirely of women, old and young, clustered about one of the long dining tables, which was piled high with wild kandace flowers.

"They're all like that." One of the younger ones pointed out.

"All the dishes?" Cera asked, and this time she could hear her own dismay.

They'd had ten pans filled with tallow and then had carefully pressed the flowers into it, to allow the essence to be drawn into the fat. They had let them set for a few days and then replaced the old blossoms with fresh, repeating over and over until the fat was saturated.

Enfleurage, her mother had called it and had made it seem so easy. At least, this was how Cera remembered her mother doing it. But her mother's pans had never molded.

"All of them," the women pulled flowers out and showed her the spots. She could smell it too. Under the sweet scent of the flowers was a clinging, musty odor.

"Well, we've never done this before, so we're bound to make mistakes." Cera tried to sound confident.

Bella, one of the older women, nodded her agreement.

"So, we'll try again," Cera said. "As far as I know, we are doing everything right. I remember my mother's stillroom off the larder, and her working to press the flowers in." Cera looked up with a rueful smile. "As best I remember. I paid as much attention as some of you pay to learning new stitches."

Some of the young ones giggled, hands over their mouths as the older ones rolled their eyes.

"But I think I remember enough," Cera continued. "Let's scrape this batch out and use it to make soap. We'll wash the pans, start with fresh tallow and flowers, and see what we see." Cera handed the pan to Belle. "If we can make it work, it makes a wonderful oil for stiff joints and body pains."

"It smells too sweet to be a healer's tonic." One of the women laughed as they pressed closer to the table and got to work. Cera stepped back and let them.

"And the other method?" Bella asked. "The hot method?"

"We heat the flowers in the fat," Cera said. "Stir and

stir and then strain and boil again with new blooms. The hot method is quicker, but the oil is not as strong."

Bella nodded. "We could lay in a supply of that before the blooms fade and the sun beats down on us."

"Worth doing," Cera agreed. "I'll write to my father and see what he remembers of my mother's methods."

"You'll find a way to solve this." Bella said.

Cera gave her a nod of confidence she did not feel and left the hall. With the discovery of fields of wild kandace, she knew she had a source of funds for Sandbriar. The dried leaves made a healing tea, and the seeds were valued as well. But if they could make and sell the oil, there was real profit to be made. Profit that could go into buying breeding stock and restore Sandbriar to what it had been before the Tedrel Wars had drained it dry.

Drained it of resources—and of healthy men and women. Another pressing problem.

That was the thing, in truth. For every problem was hers, Lady Cera of Sandbriar's problem. To face, to deal with, to solve. And while she didn't mind so much, there was a weight to each one that added up over time. Also, her people looked to her, depended on her.

She scolded herself for complaining, even if just to herself. Because, still and all, it was not a bad thing. To be in control as opposed to being controlled.

With a sense of guilt, she said a swift prayer of thanks to the Trine as she mounted the stairs to her Seneschal's chambers. It might not be proper to give thanks for the death of an abusive husband through his own greed and stupidity. Cera did it anyway, for as a result she was Lady of Sandbriar, and none could tell her nay.

She was free to do as she pleased, no longer constrained in dress or manner, no longer expected to sit by the fire and sew and await her husband's return. She shuddered at the memory as she smoothed her plain work shirt over her trews, made of good solid homespun. Practical, warm, and so much more comfortable than formal garb. Perfect for working in the barns with the sheep. That afternoon she planned to learn more about the *chirras* Withren had brought with him.

The halls were quiet as she walked them and climbed the final set of stairs to Athelnor's office. The manor house was all old stone and wood and solidly built. She loved the gleam of the polish on the wooden doors and the thick rugs on the floors. A bit worn, true enough, but it was hers.

Even after almost a year, she still didn't quite believe it.

She opened the door to her Seneschal's office to find Athelnor leaning on the large table, with his grandson Gareth to one side and Withren Ashkevon on the other. The table was covered in large maps, and their faces were covered in frowns.

Cera had a sinking feeling, but she smiled anyway. "Well?" she asked "What have you learned?"

"It's worse than we thought," Athelnor raised a shaking hand to his forehead. "Lady, I–"

"Athelnor." Cera moved into the room and closed the door behind her. "Let's sit before we talk. I've a need for some hot tea before you hand me another problem."

Withren raised his head at that and gave Athelnor a worried look. Withren had recently brought men and *chirras* from the north to find new homes in these southern lands. He'd proposed the idea of sending out a force of men and women to aid with the spring planting and survey what remained in the settlements, farmsteads, and villages of Sandbriar. It had worked well, with more crops being planted by combining their strength and energy with that of the local farmers.

Athelnor took Cera's arm, and she lent him her strength as they slowly headed to the chairs by the fire. Carefully positioning himself before the chair, Athelnor plopped down with a relieved sigh.

There was a kettle by the fire, and Cera served them both. Withren limped over to stand by the mantel, and Gareth sat cross-legged on the floor.

"So?" Cera settled back in her chair. "Tell me."

"The reports are a mix of good and bad," Withren said quietly. "The good is that crops are being planted and fields are being reclaimed from weeds. Feral livestock are being rounded up. Firewood is being cut and set to dry for next winter. With a good growing season and a bit of luck, we'll not starve."

Cera felt a bit of weight come off her shoulders, but she knew better than to relax. "And the bad?"

"So many lost in the war," Athelnor said. "So much knowledge and skill."

"There is a great need for skilled workers among the settlements, farmsteads, and villages. Some have been abandoned altogether, some are in need of repairs." Withren shook his head. "You've only two blacksmiths, barely enough to keep plows mended and the horses shod. The pottery and tannery are abandoned, and all the brewing is being done by individual households."

"Ager knows brewing," Athelnor raised his head.

"That's not something I can ask of him," Cera frowned. "Not after—"

"For Sandbriar, he could try," Athelnor insisted.

Withren raised an eyebrow, but Cera shook her head, not wanting to discuss Ager's problem with drink. She tried to lighten the mood. "But crops are going in?"

"Aye, that's working well." Withren smiled. "We can reform the teams in the fall and have them go from field to field, harvesting together to get more done and faster."

"The blacksmiths have taken apprentices," Gareth added. "Some of my friends expressed an interest, and that was all it took."

"But it takes time to train a good blacksmith," Athelnor fretted. "What will we do in the meantime?"

"Any farmer worth his oats knows tricks to keep things going," Withren soothed him. "You can't always leave the fields to see to a broken plow. And the abandoned farmsteads supply us with spares as well as harnesses and leather for repairs."

"Good leather takes time to make—months, a year, even if one knows how to treat the skins," Athelnor fretted. "And if the farmsteads are abandoned, you will need to name new holders." He turned to blink at Cera. "And there are those who might want to reclaim their lands. You'll need to sort out their rights as well." He shook his head, his worry clear. "There's bound to be arguments over that."

The weight of it all pressed her down. Of course it was her responsibility. "Well, that's not today." She reminded them and herself with her words. "I'll need advice about who to select." Cera thought about it. "From you and the others. And about your men, Withren. With due respect, they've not been here long enough for us to know their mettle."

Withren shrugged. "Some are better workers than others, and some better followers than leaders."

"There's a place for all." Cera said firmly. "And we will find it."

"But not without troubles—" Athelnor started, but a knock on the door stopped him.

The door opened to reveal Marga, Athelnor's wife, with Emerson the tapestry weaver hovering behind her, clutching some drawings.

Emerson had appeared on her doorstep as a suitor a few months ago, although that had been his father's plan, not his. His plan was to weave tapestries, another investment she had made with the promise of real returns.

"Your pardon," Marga smiled. "But Emerson needs a few strong backs to help set up his loom."

Emerson pushed past her, looking down at the papers in his hands. "For the new tapestry panel," he started in his rapid-fire way. "I need help setting the warp threads. It's tricky because—" He came to an abrupt halt, seeing Withren. "Oh. I—"

Withren straightened, his cheeks also turning red. Clearing his throat, he avoided looking at Emerson, but he shrugged. "I'd be happy to assist."

"Me too," Gareth jumped from the floor, clearly eager to escape.

Emerson only had eyes for Withren. "Would you? I don't want to be any trouble. I am sure you have more important—"

"No, really," Withren insisted. "I'd be happy to help—"

They both blushed again, stumbling over each other's words.

Gareth caught Cera's gaze and rolled his eyes.

Cera resisted the urge to laugh. "We are done here for now."

"Er," Emerson nodded. "This way," he said and headed out the door. Withren waited for Emerson to turn before limping toward the door. Gareth followed.

"They're *still* dancing around one another?" Athelnor grumbled after the door was shut.

"Oh, yes," Marga laughed. "It's adorable."

"Time was, a young man knew what he wanted, he spoke up." Athelnor scoffed. "I knew what I wanted and went after it."

Marga gave him a look. "It took you hours to ask me for that dance."

"But I knew what I wanted," Athelnor caught up her hand and held it to his cheek. "And I did ask."

"You did," Marga leaned down and kissed his forehead. "Now, speaking of dancing . . ."

Cera sighed.

"No more of that, Lady." Marga folded her arms over her chest. "You've invitations to send for the Midsummer Fair. Your mourning period will be well over, and you might as well invite all and sundry instead of waiting for them to straggle in."

"A general invitation. To the Fair." Athelnor stressed. "No need to be more specific than that."

"I'll leave the list," Marga said firmly. "You should get them out soonest, so they have plenty of time to travel."

Cera gave her a glum look, but there was no sympathy to be had. True enough, suitors would be coming. She reminded herself that under the laws of Valdemar, she had the right to reject any or all, if that was her mind.

"Which reminds me." Marga drew a blanket from the back of Athelnor's chair and shook it out. "Gareth needs dance lessons."

Cera allowed herself a grin. Gareth would be horrified.

Marga fussed over Athelnor, tucking the blanket over his legs. "Are you warm enough?" she asked, taking his mug. "Would you like me to bring you another blanket?"

"Quit your clucking," Athelnor mock-scowled at his wife. "I'm fine, I'm fine."

It was Marga's turn to roll her eyes, but then she grew serious. "There's another matter. The Queen's Bread."

"Bread?" Cera asked.

"By the Queen's Command, all children must be taught reading, writing, and ciphering during the morning hours until proficient. Any who arrive on time are fed a good breakfast, at the Queen's expense."

"Truly?" Cera blinked, a bit surprised. "At no cost to the families?"

"At no cost." Athelnor sat up straighter. "Are you saying we haven't provided—"

"We have," Marga said firmly. "As best we could, given the need for any hands to work. But the time is coming when we need to be a bit more formal in the teaching and make sure the children are learning." She shook her head. "There are those that think it a waste of time."

"Teachers who need be paid and rooms for them to use." Athelnor slumped down. "Aye, it's a credit against the taxes, but we must come up with the coin."

"We will," Cera said soothingly, with a confidence she didn't feel. "We will."

"But how?" Athelnor glared at her. "You need coin, and brewing cider is a way to get it fairly quickly. You need be talking to Ager. There was a brewery near—"

Marga sucked in a breath.

"I know, I know," Athelnor slumped back down. "But he's got skills, skills we need."

"We need his skills with *chirras* more," Cera chided him gently.

"Lady . . ." Athelnor sat forward, but Cera placed her hand over his on the arm of the chair.

"I'll speak with him," she said. "Any aid he can give is welcome. But he's sworn off drink, and I will not force him back to that life or endanger him in any way."

"Of course not," Athelnor nodded. "But he could brew without—"

A knock at the door and Young Meroth popped his head in. "Lady Cera, you're needed in the barns. Da sent me to fetch you."

"What's wrong?" Cera asked.

"It's about the *chirras*."

Nothing else could have made her feet fly so fast to the barns. She left Young Meroth in the dust, running down corridors and stairs and bursting out into the sunlit yards. The barns weren't far from the manor house, but she was breathing hard when she plunged through the large open doors into the shaded interior.

The cooler air was still and filled with the reassuring scents of animals and hay. All seemed well enough at first glance. But the *chirras* were all clustered together in one corner, shifting nervously, their ears flat. Empty wool sacks lay off to one side. Voices were trying to sooth, but the animals shied when approached.

"What's wrong?" Cera gasped.

Men and *chirras* all turned to look at her as she stood, heaving breaths.

"What's wrong?" Old Meroth groused from his stool by the door, his three elderly sheep dogs at his feet. Even with his right arm lifeless and the sag to the side of his face, he still ruled the yard. "They've never been sheared, that's what's wrong. You go near them with the shears, and the durn things spook like yer a damned wolf!"

Young Meroth trotted up, right behind her. "Sorry, Lady, I would have told ya, but you took off like an arrow." There was admiration in his voice.

Ager was standing there, with shearing clippers in his hand, looking as confused as she was feeling.

The *chirras* shifted again, clustered together, their ears down, eyeing Ager.

Jatare, one of the men that had come with Withren, spoke up. "I tell ya, we don't shear 'em. They shed some in the summer, but we don't shear 'em. Comb 'em out, sure, when we're loadin 'em, to make sure there's no burrs or mats under the straps. They're pack animals, Lady." he said apologetically. "Up north, that is."

Cera bit her lip. "So what is the problem? Doesn't anyone remember how?" she blurted.

"Aye," Ager snorted. "It's not in the 'how,' it's in the doing."

"There's two ways," Old Meroth announced. "The high and the low. High, they stand there. Low, ya wrestle them down and get them on their side."

Jatare's eyes widened. "You don't want to wrestle 'em down, ya might hurt their necks. They ain't used t'that."

"But don't they need to be sheared?" Cera asked.

"Nay," Jatare shook his head. "They shed, sure. In the springtime, leavin' bits of fur on the stall walls and along the fences. Birds take'em for nests, and such."

"Ours were used to being shorn, and we need to get that wool off for the summer heat to come." Ager rubbed his face.

Old Meroth spoke up. "I'll be doing it."

They all looked at him.

He gestured with his cane. "I'll be telling Young Meroth there what needs be doing. And I'll mind he leaves an inch behind or thereabouts. Too close to the skin, and they'll sunburn."

Young Meroth looked none too pleased.

"Sunburn?" Jatare's eyes went wide.

"Aye," Ager said. "Things are different here in the south, to be sure."

Cera moved slowly toward the animals, glad to see their ears perk with curiosity. She reached for the nearest, and gently stroked over the coarse outer coat. The *chirra*'s ears both perked up, and it leaned into her hand. Her fingers sank in, feeling the other two layers of its pelt, each progressively softer. "You comb them?" she asked.

"Aye," Jatare said. "Just before we load 'em. They get a burr, or a load that's too heavy, and they plop down and refuse to budge."

"Then that's where we start," Cera said. "We can get them used to being combed, then start slowly to shear small patches."

Ager looked doubtful. "The first fleeces aren't going to be of much use."

Cera sighed. "True enough, but I'd rather we train them and us to get used to it instead of it being a struggle. The heat's not due yet, right?"

"Aye," Old Meroth spoke up. "Not till well after the midsummer."

Ager nodded. "You're right, Lady. We'll go slow and get them to accept it. We've time." He gestured to Jatare. "You say you comb them out for burrs? Show us how you do that, and we will work from there."

"Save what wool you can," Cera said as she moved off to let them work.

Ager stepped toward Cera. "It may be a few years before you get the wool you want from them, Lady."

"Worth waiting for," Cera said. Another expense to maintain the herd to be sure, one that would not see a return for some time to come. She hesitated, a bit sick at heart, but not willing to put off the conversation. "Could I talk to you a moment? Outside?"

"Aye," Ager said.

They walked out into the sunshine, and Cera led him around the corner of the barn.

"Ager, I—" Cera stopped unsure of where to start. Ager stared at her with open curiosity. He stood there, lean and fit, a far different man from the drunkard who had come at her months ago.

Cera firmed her shoulders and forced the words out. "Ager, I have heard tell of the quality of your cider. It could be a source of revenue for Sandbriar. The brewery has been neglected, and I need to ask your aid. I know the season is a way off, but I need to know now to make plans if . . ." she let her voice trail off as a shadow came over his face.

"Lady, I've not touched cider or ale since that day." Ager's voice cracked. "Water, tea, it's all I've been having."

"I know," Cera said. "I would not ask but for Sandbriar."

Ager looked out over the fields. "There's not a day—not an hour goes by that I don't crave it. I can still taste it, still remember the feeling as it slid down my throat and took my cares away. I see others leaving half-full glasses on the table, and I want to point out what's there and that they should finish it. Or I should."

Cera looked down, embarrassed for him and for herself.

"But then I take a breath," Ager said. "I look in

Alena's eyes and see her smile, and I remind myself of why I do it. To stand tall and straight, to earn her respect. To earn my own back again."

"Ager, I would not risk you." Cera felt miserable for even mentioning it. "Would not risk your life."

Ager nodded. "I thank you, Lady of Sandbriar. We both know the need. But I will be honest and say that I would not trust myself with a bottle on the table, much less in a brewery."

"That's that then. Besides," Cera tried to smile. "I need you for the *chirras*. Who better to nurture my herd?"

He gave her a lopsided smile. "Not the drunk I was." He stood straighter. "But Lady, if you find someone who wishes to brew, I'll give advice and my secret recipes. Over a hot cup of tea."

"Done," Cera said and held out her hand to shake his.

Ager took her hand and bowed over it. "Lady," he said, with a smile. "I'd best be getting back to the *chirras*." He tilted his head. "You're a good shearer, Lady, or so I have been told. Care to join us?"

She was tempted, so tempted, but shook her head. "I've letters to write."

Ager nodded, and they parted at the barn doors, he for the animals and she for her writing desk. Cera sighed at the unfairness of it all as she returned to the manor house.

She assured Athelnor as to the well-being of the *chirras*. "Thanks be," he said, and held up a stack of letters. "These came with the latest caravan from Rethwellan." he said. "And here is Marga's list."

She took the letters eagerly; the list less so. "I'll work in here," she said. "These will take a while." More because she'd find excuses not to do it if she was alone in her chambers.

Athelnor nodded, cleared space on his desk, and offered writing materials. She pulled a chair close and settled in.

"Marga will send up our noon meals," Athelnor reminded her, then turned back to his work on the manor books.

Cera nodded absently as she sorted through the letters. There was one from her father, and she saved that pleasure for last. One in a hand she did not recognize and the other from Apothecary Reinwald. She opened that with great hope.

Reinwald expressed pleasure in hearing from her and rejoiced in her good fortune. He wrote that he would take all the dried wild kandace and seeds that she could provide and trust her on the quality. Cera flushed at his faith in her skills, but then her eyebrows rose at the price he named. It was better than she'd dared hope.

He also mentioned oils and syrup, with offers of even more coin for those items. Syrup? You could make a syrup? She frowned, having no memory of that in her mother's stillroom. She'd write to her father immediately. Perhaps he would remember details.

Her mind on syrups, Cera picked up the next missive and opened it. Expensive paper and written in a clear, strong hand, but not one she recognized.

But her heart leaped into her throat.

It was from her father-in-law, Lord Thelkenpothonar, Sinmonkelrath's father.

It was addressed to her with no titles, no honorifics. The beautiful clear script carried words of hate and loathing, demanding to know how it was that his son, her husband, was dead of a 'hunting accident,' and her, now, a landed lady at the bequest of the foreign Queen, and one wonders how that came about.

Cera flushed hot at the implications, guilty at that bit, for it was true enough. She'd never written, never found the words. She'd never had a relationship with Lord Thelken beyond the basic wedding ceremonies. How then to tell him his son was a traitor and an oathbreaker?

Lord Thelken went on, accusing her of withholding the truth. He'd had no news, no information from her, and only the formal notice from the Rethwellan Court. He'd demanded more from her father, but—

Cera went cold, dropped the letter, and tore into her father's note, her heart racing in sudden fear.

It had been written hastily, to be sent swiftly. Hopefully with the same caravan as Lord Thelken's.

He came by with fire in his eye and smoke pouring from his ears, demanding more information from me than I had. What you do not know, and what he may not tell you, is of the death of his eldest son from a fever. Such a waste and a pity, for the lad was a fair young man. I asked Lord Thelken into the garden, served him jasmine tea, and listened as he poured out his anger.

The knot in Cera's chest relaxed. Her father and his jasmine tea.

I suspect there is that which you have not put in words, nor should you. But a trusted messenger might be wise. The Lord's anger needs to go somewhere, and the truth, however painful, is still the truth.

Cera looked up from the letter, glancing at Athelnor, but he'd not noticed her upset. She took a deep, slow breath and let it out just as slowly.

She'd never shared the truth with any but Helgara, the Herald who rode the Circuit in Sandbriar. Her handmaiden, Alena, knew, for she had served Cera since before her marriage and had been with her when she'd been told of Prince Karathanelan's attack on Queen Selenay, and Sinmonkelrath's part in the conspiracy.

But the truth of Sinmon's death had been hushed up by the Crown of Valdemar, and to Cera's best knowledge, by the Crown of Rethwellan as well. "Hunting accident" had been the agreed upon phrase, and it had not been questioned.

As to Lord Thelken's demands for information, she dare not write such a missive. Never mind that her gut churned at the very idea of putting those words to paper. She'd sworn an oath of loyalty to Queen Selenay and to Valdemar, and she would not betray those oaths. But there was wisdom in her father's words.

Cera was at a loss. How best to deal with Lord Thelken's pain without violating her promises? She stared into the fire for a time, thinking.

She couldn't send a messenger. She wouldn't risk Alena to Lord Thelken's wrath, nor would she tell any other who could make the journey. It needed to come from someone Lord Thelken could not lash out at, for he certainly would.

She looked at her father's letter again. If Sinmon's elder brother was dead, that meant that Lord Thelken had no male heir. There were daughters, but for one of Lord Thelken's status, that would not suit.

Her heart hurt for the man. He hadn't ever been harsh with her, and losing both his sons must have caused him terrible pain. But as sympathetic as she might be, she would not risk a letter.

Herald Helgara and her Companion Stonas were due soon on their Circuit. Perhaps they could let someone at Haven know of the problem and pass word to the Rethwellan Court.

In any case, passing the task to Helgara was all she could do. All she was willing to do.

A knock, and the door opened to reveal Alena and a tray. Cera smiled at her handmaiden.

Who promptly scowled at her, stomped into the room, and dropped the tray on the table, sending the dishes rattling.

"Here, now—" Athelnor protested, but Alena had already turned on Cera, eyes flashing.

"You had no right!" she protested. "No right to ask

that of him. He's had a hard enough time of it, and I fear for him every day, that he'll slip between my fingers. To ask him to brew, to drink, that's not—"

"Alena—" Cera stood to confront her.

"You had *no right*—" Alena repeated, but Cera cut her off.

"Alena," Cera forced her voice low and steady. "You are right, but you are also wrong. If we want Sandbriar to grow, to thrive, I must ask. Must ask my people to make sacrifices."

Alena froze, dropped her gaze, her hands clutched together. "Yes, mi'lady."

"Ager told me he can't brew. Can't be around a bottle. So that is the end of that." Cera tried to soften the blow. "I will not endanger him, Alena. But I had to ask. He did say he was willing to give advice and share his old recipes. I will not ask for more than that, I promise."

Alena raised her eyes then, the anger gone. "It's just that . . . he has come to mean so much to me. And I fear—"

Cera moved forward and opened her arms. Alena stepped in, and they embraced, two friends facing hard truths together.

Alena broke away first and wiped her eyes. "The embroiderers in the solar, they've asked to speak to you this afternoon. After your meal."

"What's not spilled," Athelnor groused.

"I'll bring fresh," Alena promised.

"It's fine," Cera looked over the tray. "Rattled, but nothing spilled." She smiled at Alena.

"I'll come to them as soon as we've eaten."

"Yes, Lady." Alena curtsyed, and closed the door as she left.

Cera stared after her for a moment.

Athelnor started to help himself to the tray. "It isn't always easy, you know, to be the Lady of Sandbriar. To put the needs of the land and your people first. It calls for hard choices and lonely decisions."

Cera sat back in her chair. "So I am learning."

"I'm proud of you, Lady." Athelnor said, gesturing to some of the bread. "Now eat. Then you need to start on those invitations."

Cera sighed.

She managed to get a few done between bites of food and sips of tea. But then she decided that was enough, and she escaped Athelnor's eagle eye to head for the solar.

The room was buzzing with the women and young girls, all learning the complicated embroidery and lace-making. Cera already had a market for their work in Rethwellan, and there had been demands from Haven as well. But there were bolts of brightly colored cloth on the tables when Cera walked in, and girls on chairs, plain broadcloth patterns pinned to their clothes.

"What's this?" Cera asked as she walked into the bright room. Alena stepped in behind her and closed the door.

The chatter and the giggling stopped.

Bella stepped forward. "Lady, there's cloth been stored here before the Tedrel Wars, and we all had a thought. For the dance, you see—" Bella seemed uncomfortable.

"Gowns," one of the young ones exclaimed, and suddenly they were all talking at once, showing her bolts of cloth and holding them up to themselves.

"It's frivolous, we know," Bella spoke over the noise. "And there's time before the Midsummer Fair for us to make dresses for all. But we thought there'd be no harm."

In truth, the cloth could be sold. But then she thought of her father and his joy at something so simple as jasmine tea.

"No harm at all," Cera said. Here was a problem easily solved. "No better use for all that material, and a joyful one."

"For you too, Lady." Alena said.

"For me?" Cera hesitated. "No, there's nothing wrong with—"

Alena gave her a push, and suddenly the young ones were getting her out of her shirt and trews, and Cera found herself up on a stool in a simple shift with all the women talking at once, and patterns being pinned to her form. Others climbed up on the table and started pulling her hair from its braid and piling it up on her head.

Cera laughed, and gave in. "No, no, not that low," she insisted as they pinned the bodice.

"Beggin' your pardon, Lady, but you need some 'oomph,'" Bella exclaimed.

"Not that much 'oomph,'" Cera scolded, pulling the pattern up farther on her chest. There was a great deal of laughter all around.

"It's a fine thing," Alena finally said, and the women pulled back and admired their work. "Just look."

There was a mirror on the wall, an ancient thing, clouded with time. But still bright enough that Cera could turn and see her reflection.

She didn't know herself.

These months, spent in new freedoms. No longer sitting at the fireside, waiting on her abusive lord. She'd been out and about in the fields, seeing to her herds and her lands. She was slimmer now, tanned and healthy.

She smiled at her reflection and it smiled back, confident and strong.

"It's well, Lady?" Alena asked.

Cera looked around at all of them, smiling. "Yes, it's very well." She covered her bosom with her hands. "But no 'oomph'!"

Alena and the other ladies chortled, but they agreed.

* * *

Days later, Cera was in the field with Withren and others, happily learning to comb a *chirra*, when she heard someone calling her name.

She looked up to find Marga—*Marga,* of all people—running through the grass toward them, winded and upset.

"Marga!" Cera dropped her combs and reached out to steady the older woman. "What–"

Marga gripped Cera's arms hard. "Emerson," she gasped.

"What happened?" Withren demanded.

Marga swallowed, and took a shuddering breath. "Emerson's father, Lord Cition. He's here. He found Emerson at the loom and—" She shook her head. "Come, come quickly."

Cera started, then turned back. "Withren–"

"Go," he gritted, already limping after her. "I'll get there."

Cera took off, with Marga right next to her. She headed for the front doors, but Marga grabbed her arm and steered her toward the kitchens.

"Lord Cition, he's of an old family," Marga forced out the words. "You need to wash and–"

Cera allowed herself to be pulled along, and they burst through the kitchen garden door to find a small army of her women waiting there.

"Off," Bella commanded, and Cera found herself stripping, pulling off tunic and trews. One woman knelt to unlace her boots, another brought water and soap.

Marga collapsed on a nearby bench, breathing hard. Cera could hear a loud and angry voice through the door to the hall. "What's happening?"

"Wash," Bella commanded, already reaching for Cera's braids.

One of the woman was peeking through the door to the Hall. "The steward's trying to interfere, but the old man just keeps yelling. Poor Emerson looks like a beaten dog."

Bella was combing Cera's hair, twisting it in a knot on top of her head.

"It's my fault, lady," one of the younger girls whispered as Cera dried her face and hands. "He came in and asked for Emerson, and I took him to the weavin' room. I didn't think—"

"Dress," Bella's commanded. Cera was wrestled into one of her old dresses that had been hung in her clothes press. Rethwellan style, but too good for work-a-day clothes.

"Shoes," one hissed, and Cera toed off her boots and let them slip on her dress shoes. The roaring continued beyond the door. She could just make out Athelnor trying to intervene.

Marga staggered to her feet. "There's a tradition among the nobles," she said quickly. "One doesn't just show up uninvited and unannounced. It's considered very rude. You sent him an invitation to the Festival, but to show up this way, and this early, is not acceptable."

Cera nodded, tucking the last stray hairs behind her ears.

"Let's have a look at ya," Bella said, and they all stepped back, nodding their approval.

Cera lifted her chin, drew a deep breath, walked to the wooden door, and with only the slightest hesitation threw it open hard enough so that it banged against the wall. "What is the meaning of this?"

The slam echoed into the room. Some of her people were crowded at the far end of the room. Four men stood before the hearth. Three turned to look at her: Athelnor, looking relieved. Gareth, looking furious. A large, stocky man, sweating and red-faced, sweat pressing his sparse hair to his head, looking fit to be tied.

Emerson didn't look up. He stood there, head down, looking utterly defeated.

An all-to-familiar-feeling rose in Cera's breast. But now, here, in this time and this place, it was kindling to her anger. She stepped forward into the silence and narrowed her eyes. "Who are you, sirrah, to berate my people in such a manner?"

Lord Cition reared back as if stung. "Sirrah? I am Lord Cition, Emerson's father, and I demand–"

"How do I know that?" Cera demanded. She advanced on Cition, locking eyes with him. "You claim to be a Lord of Valdemar, but you appear uninvited, unannounced, and barge into my manor without so much as a by-your-leave?"

"I–" Cition took a step back, looking about him as he if realizing his own rudeness. He deflated slightly. "I admit–" He glared at Emerson. "I was concerned for my son."

"Lady Cera," Athelnor spoke. "May I present Lord Cition." He cleared his throat. "I can attest to his identity."

Lord Cition went purple.

Cera looked at the stocky, sweating man before her, and a calm came over her. She'd a flash of memory, of her father dealing with an angry customer. The angrier he'd become, the calmer her father got. "*Kill with sweetened cream*," he always said. So she folded her hands before her, and nodded to the man. "Lord Cition, welcome to my lands and within my walls. You have traveled far. Let me offer you some refreshment."

Lord Cition pulled a handkerchief and mopped his face. "That would be welcome." He admitted in an apologetic tone.

Cera gave him a polite half-smile, then lifted her voice. "If you would all return to your duties, please. Emerson, we will summon you after I have spoken to Lord Cition." She didn't give Cition a chance to protest but stepped closer and put her hand on the older man's arm. "Gareth, if you would see to refreshment? In Athelnor's office." She fixed Lord Cition with a steady eye. "There's a nice breeze there when the windows are open. This way, Lord Cition." She didn't make it a question.

Lord Cition took her arm with a nod. "My thanks, Lady."

"How did you find the roads?" she made polite conversation as they mounted the stairs up to Athelnor's office. Lord Cition was puffing a bit when she gestured him to the most comfortable chair in the room. She threw the shutters wide as Athelnor settled behind his desk, and then she settled herself in the chair beside Cition's.

Cera smiled at him, letting a bit more warmth into it, and waited.

Lord Cition blew out a breath. "Lady Cera, I must offer an apology," he started. "We'd no word from Emerson, no letters, just your invitation to your Festival. Then I come to discover that he'd taken the loom and was here under false pretenses, and, well . . ." He shifted uneasily in his chair. "My anger overwhelmed the best of my courtesy."

Cera gave him a slow nod. "Worries for a child stick deep, do they not?"

"They do," Cition eased back in his chair. "Emerson's a good lad, mind you, but a constant worry. Worry about him making his way in this world doing women's work. Always drawing and talking about colors and dyes. His mother worried herself sick when I sent him here. Now I come to find out the lad lied to me—" Lord Cition shook his head, his expression pained.

A rattle of dishes and a knock on the door. "Come," Cera called. Gareth entered with a tray and a murderous expression.

Cera blinked. "Thank you, Gareth. On the desk, please." She rose to pour. Gareth bowed and then went to stand by the door. She shot him a warning glance as she pressed a mug of cool ale into Cition's hands.

Cition sighed. "I fear our family has not made the best of impressions on you, Lady Cera, and for that I am sorry."

Cera offered a mug to Athelnor, but he waved her away with a silent nod toward Cition. So she poured her own mug and settled back in her chair. "Nothing could be farther from the truth," she responded firmly. "The foodstuffs you sent with Emerson were goddess-sent, and we blessed you for it. And Emerson was honest with me," Cera continued. "From the beginning. There was no pretense."

"Well, at least there is that." Cition took a grateful gulp.

"I don't think his interests lie with me," Cera said as delicately as she could. One never knew how a parent would react or how much they knew.

"Aye, that too." Cition grimaced. "His mother laid into me about that as well. But I'd hoped perhaps—" he stared into his mug. "Well, these are not your troubles, Lady. Emerson will return home with me. If you'll lend me a wagon, we'll load up the loom and his weavings. My apologies for all of this."

Gareth stirred by the door, and Cera glared at him even as she spoke to Cition. "Emerson came here for the opportunities that Sandbriar could offer. There are prospects for lands and hearths left cold by the war."

"Aye," Lord Cition nodded. "We were all tested, but Sandbriar bore the brunt."

"And there is the matter of the debt," Cera continued.

"Debt?" Cition looked at her over his mug.

"Emerson is under formal contract with me to create a tapestry for my halls when he is finished with his grandmother's," Cera kept her voice cool as she lied. "There has been a debt incurred for room and board and sundries. One that I expect to be repaid, in the form of a tapestry."

Lord Cition's eyes narrowed. "This is so? You would require the work? Not coin?"

"Yes," Cera said. "Gareth, if you would fetch Emerson?"

Gareth slipped out the door.

Lord Cition gave her an appraising look. "I heard tell you were a merchant's daughter before being awarded these lands. It would appear that you have a merchant's soul."

Athelnor coughed. Cera just gave Lord Cition a slow, sweet smile.

Lord Cition quirked his lips. "And I'm thinking that's not an insult to you."

"No, Lord Cition," Cera smiled wider. "It is not."

The door cracked open, and Emerson slid in, his face at once both timid and hopeful. Cera caught a glimpse of many bodies in the hall.

"Lady Cera. Father." Emerson gave a slight bow to both of them.

"Is this true, lad?" Lord Cition asked. "You've contracted your services to Lady Cera."

"Y-y-yes, Father." Emerson straightened up, and his voice took on a defiant tone. "I didn't want to deceive you—" his voice cracked, "—but you wouldn't even let me set up the loom."

"Well . . ." Lord Cition sat back in his chair. "What's done is done. You must honor your agreements, I've always told you that. Even if I think Lady Cera will not do well by this. Still, you do well by her, yes?"

"Yes, Father." Emerson's face still held a hint of fear, but his smile was brilliant. "Thank you, Father."

"Just write to your mother, lad." Lord Cition said gruffly. "She worries so."

"Yes, Father. Thank you, Father. Lady Cera." Emerson bowed and slipped out, pulling the door behind him. Cera could hear muffled cheers beyond.

"Please, Lord Cition, stay the night before you journey back." she offered.

"I will, and thank you." Cition picked his mug back up. "I think we might have other things to discuss, Lady. Who knows what opportunities lay between our lands. But please, if you would," the lord sighed in resignation. "Make sure he writes his mother?"

"I will." Cera smiled. "I have some experience with that."

To Lady Cera of Sandbriar, in the Kingdom of Valdemar

Dearest Daughter,

Forgive me, child, but I know little of your mother's stillroom methods, the Trine rest her soul in peace. I doubt that Reinwald will share his trade secrets. Perhaps you could write to the Healers' Collegium in Haven? One hears wondrous things about their skills.

Have no fear for my safety, child. For all of Lord Thelkenpothonar's wealth and lands, he is a poor man, deflated, angry, and sore of heart. I encourage him to visit, to drink tea in my gardens, and I listen to his woes. I also remind him of the strength there is to be found in our womenfolk.

I am sorry to hear of your troubles. I would remind you of something your wise mother would say whenever we faced obstacles or felt overwhelmed.

'No matter what tears are shed, no matter what trials are faced, some things stay the same. There will always be day and night, stars and sky, hope

and rest. There will always be compassion, always be friendship, and always, always, love."*

I've enclosed some packets of jasmine tea. Mind that you take the time to drink a cup or two and enjoy a quiet moment.

Be well, beloved Daughter,
Your Father

---

* *(paraphrased from the last paragraph of* The Black Gryphon *by Mercedes Lackey & Larry Dixon)*

Beyond Common Sense, She Persisted

Janny Wurts

Chased to the ragged edge, three surviving Companions, two Heralds, and Kaysa rode through the outer gate and entered the city of Haven. The confined clatter of hooves hammered through the alarmed challenge of the posted guards. Answering their urgent questions, Lara confirmed the horror of Jess's death. She reported Arif's deep wound, bleeding yet through a field bandage. Repeatedly tracked and assaulted by Change-Beasts, Kaysa and she had been lucky to suffer no worse than bruises and scrapes.

Kaysa herself was no fighter. Before the Mage Storm beset her village and led her to rescue a stricken Companion, her livelihood as the weaver's daughter had been spinning yarns by touch. Unprepared, blind since birth, she had weathered the harrowing journey from the Pelagiris Forest. Nights of tense watch broken often by ambush had forced their desperate flight off the road. Kaysa had clung to Lark's tangled mane as they fled, scarcely able to stay astride to bear warning to Valdemar's Queen. For an unknown enemy had felled two brave Heralds, with one Companion killed outright and the other left too deranged to communicate.

"We were tracked by dark spells set into the bloodstains left on Lark's saddlecloth," Lara explained. Her gesture cautioned the gate guard. "In that bundle, yes. Be careful! Heralds are susceptible! The lethal taint's been kept constantly wrapped after Kaysa's sensitivity fingered the cause."

But there was another, somewhat weaker, lure. The strikes had lessened but not ceased. Ensorceled Change-Beasts had hounded them through the open country far beyond the forest verge.

Kaysa was too tired to think. Though the unresolved threat risked Valdemar's peace, she could barely sort through the barrage of raw noise to maintain her orientation. Oily smoke clogged her nostrils. Lit torches suggested the hour was well after nightfall. Echoes bouncing down emptied streets went unmuffled by the bustle of late going traffic. Jostled by armed riders as the guard attached an escort for added protection, Kaysa was folded into the party sent on a swift course toward the palace. A messenger galloped ahead to roust council officials and Healers from sleep.

Exhaustion flattened the thrill of success, that against all odds, Kaysa's critical role had salvaged the Heralds' mission. Weariness stifled her curiosity, even as Haven's exotic scents enriched every drawn breath. Kaysa sampled the fragrance of baked bread and acrid dust; of cured meat, empty beer barrels, and reeking dye vats. Past the lower town, tinged by lingering traces of a rich lady's perfume, the sharper acoustics suggested the buildings on each side rose higher. The dew dampness of foliage and a nightingale's song winnowed from a walled garden.

Kaysa was too numbed to interpret for nuance. Battling distortion from sleep-deprived senses and dizzied by surges of faintness, she scarcely noted the guard who braced her upright as their cavalcade swept through the entrance to the palace. The jolt as Lark halted nearly tumbled her from the saddle.

Kindly hands crowded around to steady her as Kaysa dismounted, stumbling amid a barrage of concerned exclamations. Led indoors, shepherded through strange corridors to a closed hall, a person clothed in the swish of fine silk set her down in a cushioned seat. She mustered frayed wits while more people arrived, also clad in expensive clothes and the fragrance of refined soap. Chairs scraped. A delicate hinge creaked, likely from an opened lap desk by the distinctive musk of goose quill pens and the acrid whiff of an uncapped inkwell. Presented with a readied scribe and surrounded by hints snagged from hushed conversations, Kaysa gathered she was facing an assembly of Haven's experienced Mages.

Then their questions began. They analyzed everything, in particular the freak storm that struck her remote village on the day she had found the lost Herald's injured Companion snagged in a wrecked tangle of splintered trees. Kaysa answered from a blind girl's perspective. She explained again how the likely effect of dark sorcery in the bloodied saddlecloth had attracted the Change-Beasts that killed Jess and hurt Arif. The uncanny susceptibility aimed to harm the Queen's Heralds—Kaysa recounted the horrific details until sleeplessness impaired her faculties.

Eyes drooping, shaken awake by someone's grip on her wrist, she arose and shuffled where she was prompted. Without the stick left strapped to her saddlebags, her weary feet stumbled over the edges of carpets and tripped on the stairs. Doors opened ahead and closed at her heels. More strangers' voices exclaimed and gave orders, until finally just one quiet helper remained. Kaysa fumbled through the assistance that removed her soiled clothes. But the polite thanks she intended went unspoken. The moment her sore body sank into the blissful comfort of a clean bed, dreamless sleep overcame her awareness.

Kaysa wakened to warmth. Sunlight striped her cheek from an open casement. Hungry and stiff, she shoved upright amidst the cotton-thick stillness of solitude. *I reached Haven*, she acknowledged, amazed.

Lara and Arif were not with her. Groping failed to locate the stick careful habit would have propped by the mattress. Alone in a strange room, Kaysa pushed off a coverlet finer than any at home. Sliding out of bed, she gasped as her toes sank into a soft carpet.

The missing stick hampered her tentative movements. Kaysa stood in place and clicked her tongue, reliant upon ambient echoes to detect obstacles in her path. Her impaired effort had managed two steps when a knock sounded at the entry.

"Who's there?"

"Tassie," a girl's voice responded. "May I come in?" The latch clicked, and an eddy riffled the air as the door cracked open. "You didn't hear the bells. I've waited until you awakened."

Kaysa frowned. "Bells?"

The draft signaled Tassie's breezy entrance. "The dawn bell, of course, and summons for breakfast. The housekeeper said you might be too weary to rouse. I'm sent to attend your needs. Since you fell asleep ahead of the soup tray, you're probably famished!"

But Kaysa disregarded her growling stomach. "Where's Lara? Is Arif all right? What about Lark? He's suffered damage from a brush with dark magic, and I should be with him."

"Whoa! Hold up." Tassie chuckled. "The Collegium's offered you a student's place in recompense for your brave service. Lara's with the Queen, closeted in council. They and the Mages are weighing the disturbance in the Pelagiris Forest." The girl's chatter continued to a thump, then the drag of a bulky object across the floor. "Your saddlebag's here. The Healers have Arif dosed to the eyeballs with jervain. His wound's expected to knit, given time, and Lark's hurt is a matter for wiser heads than yours or mine."

Steps approached, followed by a breathless grunt as

the lifted pack bumped against Kaysa's chest. "Get yourself dressed. After we find you something to eat, I'll show you about."

Kaysa sorted her clothing by touch and donned trousers and a fresh blouse while Tassie tidied the rumpled bed, still energetically talking. "You needn't worry. During your stay, you're invited to attend classes with the students until the way's safe to send you back to your family."

"I don't want to go home," Kaysa objected. Dismayed that lost weight had loosened her waistband, she asked after the belt left with last night's trousers and also her missing stick.

Tassie broke off her scatterbrained musing. "Oh! I'm sorry. Right here." Realizing her error when Kaysa groped, she exclaimed, "Dear me! You can't see the hook. Your walking stick's leaning in the corner."

Tassie retrieved both items and resumed her chatter, "You can't return to Ropewynd just yet. The way through the Pelagiris Forest is suspect until Tarron's fate has been determined." Still gushing, she clasped Kaysa's forearm. "About your course of study, don't worry! The dean's scheduled an interview tomorrow to see which classes suit your capabilities. Afterward, you'll be issued new clothing, color matched to your assigned school. The dean's kind, and your blindness won't matter a whit! Many train here with a disability."

Kaysa clutched her stick and politely let Tassie guide her. She was hungry. Enough not to bristle at unwanted assistance or stall for what might seem ungrateful questions.

The kitchen at the Collegium kept food available between mealtimes. Given a piled plate of seed rolls, fresh fruit, and cheese, Kaysa ate. Tassie kept her company and followed up with an inquiry after her friends.

The Healers refused her request to see Arif.

"He's resting and better off not disturbed." Tassie

qualified, apologetic. "Herald Lara's in conference with the Mages, discussing strategy with the Queen's guard captain. The session's ongoing until they've found the best way to defeat this assault by dark magic."

At least Haven's council confronted the hostile act seriously. Kaysa expressed her relief, reassured she would be called for at need. Meanwhile, she burned to know whether Lark's sorry plight had been remedied.

Finished with her cleaned plate, Kaysa ventured, "Might we visit the stables?"

"Great idea!" A brisk jostle as Tassie bounded from her seat. Her enthusiasm pulled Kaysa along. "The grooms who tend the Companions always hear what's up before anybody. The walk is short. We'll take the afternoon to investigate."

Outside the Collegium, Kaysa slowed down. Established habit positioned her against the buildings, with Tassie on her flank at streetside. The tap of her stick in front of each step tested for hazardous footing. The flagstone paving was level and swept. The texture of the echoes bounced back told her when they passed recessed doorways, or stone walls, or side alleys that breathed the chill of deep shade. Necessity had taught her to be a quick study in unfamiliar surroundings. She memorized the particulars of their route, soaking in each subtle cue. The dank fust of a storm drain, the lush whiff of greensward, then the light buffet of wind at the left turn where the ground dipped, before she mounted a gradual uphill slope. An internal map drawn from sensory impressions would allow her to retrace her own way, later on.

Yet the massive size of the stables at Haven soon challenged her roadwise confidence. Beyond the access street's rattle of carts, Kaysa passed a stout gate into a broad courtyard bustling with activity. Rakes scraped. Grooms chattered. Hooves clopped. The eddied breezes wore the pungent scents of oiled leather, warm animals, and hay. Young voices greeted Tassie by name, then fell to shy whispers.

Kaysa caught scraps of muffled admiration: "*—must be that blind girl who saved Tarron's Companion—*" and, "*—her warning spared Arif and Lara from evil sorcery and crazed Change-Beasts—*" then, "*—sadly, too late for poor Jess.*"

Kaysa demurred, wrenched by renewed sorrow. Her warning had roused their beset camp, just barely. "In fact," she corrected, "Jess's heroic stand bought our narrow chance to escape."

Tassie squeezed her hand. "A memorial commemorates all fallen Heralds to honor their sacrifice in the Queen's service. Anyone present as a living witness may speak for their memory in tribute."

Steered from the sun's warmth into a shaded aisle lined with box stalls, Kaysa entered a calm refuge filled by the munching of contented animals and the rustles of hooves in fresh beds of straw. Fragrant with the melange of old beams and rope halters, the great stable surrounded her presence with booming reverberation. Water splashed into a pail to her left. Counting steps, she traversed a space large enough to cram most of Ropewynd's cottages under one roof.

Grooms and staff hustled about their duties, the brisk patter of feet stitched through the squeaky wheels of muck barrows and handcarts laden with fodder. Kaysa noted the clang of the blacksmith's hammer, and the wheezing bellows that wafted the acrid tang of hot metal and coals from the forge. So much to take in! She eagerly sampled each sound and smell while Tassie described the individual animals, from the warhorses and carriage teams to the hardy *chirra* harnessed as pack beasts. Through the movements of the massive beasts, she acknowledged the head butts of the resident cats, sorted the secretive rustles of rats and the bleats of the collared goats kept to soothe the breeding stallions.

A lisping boy found her a stash of treats. Entranced by the velvety muzzles plucking sweets from her palm, Kaysa dared a further inquiry. "How's Lark, do you know?"

"The Companion forsaken by Tarron's demise?" The lad sighed. "Brave creature! He's suffered terribly. Though the healers are doing their best, he might never regain his natural mind."

"What happens if he doesn't recover?" Kaysa asked, fighting tears.

Steadied by Tassie's arm, she endured the boy's piping summary. "His shoes will be pulled for rest, I expect. Then turnout in the Companion's Field, if a comfortable retirement's the best can be done. He'll live peacefully with the mares and foals and the other unbonded Companions."

Lark might never select another Chosen. Saddened, Kaysa buried her disappointment. Fortune might yet enable her dream, if not through Lark, then perhaps with another Companion.

Low spirits masked, she finished the tour through the stables. Sunset brought a return to the Collegium for supper. Tassie took her into the crowded dining hall with the students. Amid deafening noise, everyone seemed friendly. But Tarron's loss left a hole in the Heralds' ranks, and Jess's lively humor was missed. All admired the courage of Lara and Arif. Kaysa flushed under the praise for her role in bearing the news back to Haven.

"The Mages are studying that saddlecloth cautiously," one boy ran on with respect. "Dangerous spellcraft, they say, to inflict a perverse influence on a Herald on contact." His nervous conclusion confirmed the horror that Tarron's ruin had been unclean. Kaysa's bravery was acknowledged by others, while the student Mages whispered in dread, then debated in speculation.

Kaysa had nothing further to contribute. Silent through their animated discussion of which methods were best to locate and disarm such a murderous enemy, she felt useless. Turned out, like Tarron's broken Companion, as though kindness alone could humor her through the lack of a position based on her merits. Lessons in the Collegium seemed a dull prospect. After the meaningful thrill of service with the Heralds on the open road, the thought of spinning yarn in her sleepy village curdled her spirit. Kaysa could not bear to let a meaningful future pass her by unfulfilled.

Tassie noticed her stifled unease. "You'll enjoy your time here, you'll see. Who knows where the dean will place you? Musical training requires no sight. Valdemar's had famous Bards who were blind. They were welcomed and gained respectful employment wherever they wished."

Kaysa smiled, too wretched to admit she could not sing a true note. Her father's laughter still stung for her one lame attempt to hum tunes at the spinning wheel. *"Your tone is flat as a honking goose,"* Mama had teased. Since her brothers had mimicked the noise with seemingly endless mockery, Tassie's reassurance fell short. A sightless girl could not scribe or keep records. Book learning for Kaysa always meant somebody else must read her lessons aloud. No loyal subject of Valdemar would burden the Collegium during this crisis! Not while an evil Mage in the Pelagiris Forest sought to corrupt Heralds for a wicked purpose.

Kaysa wrestled with her venomous doubts long after Tassie said goodbye for the night. Washed up and tucked into bed, she lay wakeful, too well aware that she held little worldly experience. Luck and brash impulse had brought her this far. Lara's insistence that she take pride in the victory of winning through while under mortal danger was not enough. No longer sheltered, Kaysa measured her shortcomings. Good sense insisted that the wisdom of Haven's counsel was best equipped henceforward to shoulder the dangerous cause.

Nonetheless, Kaysa ached for her insignificance. Ropewynd's simple lifestyle had little use for a privileged education. Beyond scribing dye recipes and the straightforward accounting that balanced the ledgers and weighed up raw yarn, knowledge added nothing to the grind of workaday chores: the milking, the butchering, sowing and threshing, the tireless cutting and splitting of wood for the stove. The smith's tinkering and the family's profession of twining cord and dyed yarn were the only crafts in the village. Kaysa tossed, tormented by her feelings of worthlessness.

Her anxious sensitivity to hearing, touch, and smell lent no advantage to the pursuit of higher learning. Kaysa resented being patronized. Only pretense awaited once the dean discovered she possessed no worthy endowment to train. Sent home to carding wool in the loft, she might never be free of her overprotected background again.

Only Gran's advice encouraged her passionate desire for independence. *"If you don't risk the knocks in life for yourself, the choices of others will limit your days. Safety will tame every dream that you have, until you destroy your free spirit."*

Kaysa must act tonight to determine her destiny. Tomorrow would be too late. Before the distinctive clothing of an assigned school marked her as a Collegium student, her plain country garments would let her blend in. The bold moment to shelter with the servants in the stables must be seized straightaway.

Kaysa slipped out of bed and dressed quickly. Stick in hand, undeterred by the dark that would hamper anyone sighted, she steered herself through the Collegium's corridors with the confidence gained on the open road. She counted the doors and descended the stairwell by touch. The smell of baking bread, and the late, muffled talk from the kitchen marked her turn toward the outside door.

Mouse quiet, she ducked into the side alleys to avoid the steps of passersby. Caution let her through the gate to the stables. She slipped inside where, in a nook behind the hayloft ladder, she slept until nearly dawn.

Before birdsong at sunrise, she woke to the clang of buckets and the rustles of the sleepy staff, who set about measuring oats and forking fresh fodder. Kaysa crept into the open, just one more shadowy figure tending to chores. She picked her way down the row of stalls. Shortly, her stick tapped a box filled with brushes, comb, and a hoof pick. She snatched the equipment, slipped through the nearest half door, then propped her stick in a corner and set to work on the animal quartered inside.

Nobody noticed one more busy groom. A faked limp masked her reliance on the stick, and a chatterbox boy who assumed she was new showed her where to fetch the breakfast baskets sent from the kitchen. Afternoon found her tucked into a dim corner in one of the tack rooms. Amid the small group detailed to oil bridles and scrub saddle cloths, she learned by touch how to polish the bells worn by the Heralds' Companions. Nobody remarked upon her lack of sight. Listening, she found the stables employed the deaf and a backcountry girl who was mute.

The Master of Horse criticized no one who wasn't shirking or lazy. Quiet amid the bustling grooms, Kaysa applied herself with singular will. She could prove herself worthy! Immersed in her work, determined one day to be trusted to attend the Companions, she missed the abrupt stillness until too late.

A deliberate tread advanced down the aisle outside. Someone of authority, she deduced in dismay as the industry of the staff faltered around her. She ducked her head, frozen. Perhaps her delinquent presence would be overlooked.

But the boy at her elbow poked her in the ribs. "The Queens's Own!" he whispered, astonished. "Looks like he's here to see you!"

Kaysa's face flamed. Her impulsive plan left her nowhere to hide. Now the foremost Herald in all the realm had been sent to rebuke her wayward behavior. Mortified, she braced for a scolding.

But the Herald met her embarrassment with mild reproof. "When you left your room, Kaysa, no one knew where you'd gone. The dean was concerned when you didn't show for your interview. Did you think the realm of Valdemar is ungrateful? Or are you unbearably homesick?"

"Neither." Kaysa swallowed. "Truthfully, I'd rather make myself useful tending the animals here." She pleaded with fate that her heart did not show that access to the Companions meant more than everything else.

The pause stretched while she burned red under the interest of the bystanding grooms and the Herald's piercing regard.

Out of pity, perhaps, he chose not to humiliate her. "If you're certain, Kaysa, do as you like. The Queen wishes only to make your stay rewarding. If academic instruction doesn't suit you, I'll make disposition with the Master of Horse. Your room at the Collegium stays assigned to you, meantime, along with meals with the students. Inform the dean if you change your mind. You may tire of menial tasks well before we've subdued the threat lurking in the Pelagiris Forest."

Struck by the timbre of dismay that marred the man's otherwise mellow temperament, Kaysa blurted, "Were the Mages unable to track down the source of the bane from the residue in Lark's saddlecloth?"

"They tried." The Queen's Herald sighed with heavy regret. "But their effort triggered an embedded safeguard placed against outside magic. The fabric burst into flame and destroyed the bloodstain that preserved the evidence."

A crushing defeat, bound to delay the full explanation of Tarron's mysterious demise. Kaysa shivered. Jess and his Companion had lost their lives for that precious lead, delivered to Haven at terrible risk. This brutal setback would devastate Lara and Arif, left grieving with no telltale trace left in hand.

"Still, forewarned is forearmed," the Herald allowed in commiseration. "The next foray sent to investigate will take a trained Mage, along with additional guards. They'll carry word back to your parents as well. Rest assured, you'll stay under the Queen's protection. See the dean for any needs that arise until we've secured the road for your safe return."

Kaysa related her grateful thanks, overwhelmed with relief. She had asserted her independence. Seize the day, keep on reaching, and fortune might open the way for her secret ambition to become Chosen.

Kaysa applied herself without reserve. She groomed horses, brushed their coats to slick silk, and gently combed tangles from manes and tails. Her careful, slow movement and sensitive touch quieted the excitable foals and won over the most stubborn *chirra*. Moreover, her natural penchant for listening and the practiced interpretation of nuances earned favorable notice from the Master of Horse. His appreciation of her redoubled the day he discovered her knack for settling quarrels.

"How did you know which of my grooms was the bully?" he inquired, amazed, while she knelt drying the tears of a nobleman's child muddied from a fall in a puddle.

"Easy." Kaysa shrugged. "I listened for the braggart." The boys' brash intonation had exposed the culprit whose shove tripped young Jordie up from behind. "To my ear, arrogance has a smug ring that marks a liar's evasion."

"Well, there's a vital asset for keeping the peace."

The Master of Horse chuckled, quite pleased. "Kindly help Jordie saddle his pony before he's late for his lesson."

Shortly thereafter, he called upon Kaysa to weigh who was responsible for the loose *chirra* that raided the grain bin and later, again, to finger which lad deserved scolding for neglecting to unload the hay cart. Before the week passed, her place was accepted without further question.

"You never complain for yourself," the Master of Horse observed while she bent over her latest assignment to oil harnesses on a damp afternoon. "An even temperament's a virtue not to be wasted. Let's put your quality to better use caring for the newly bonded Companions."

"Truly?" Kaysa embraced that trust with a dazzling smile. "Might I also see Lark?"

"You've certainly earned the privilege to ask." The Master of Horse plucked the polishing rag from her grasp. "What are you waiting for? Off you go!"

Kaysa snatched up her stick, brimming over with happiness. She tapped her way down the aisle, ducked outside, and splashed through the rain in the puddled yard to the specialized wing that housed the Companions. There, no latches fastened the doors. A rear gate in the loose boxes opened into a clipped meadow for grazing, backed by the hedge that bounded the Companion's Field and the secluded Grove at its center.

Kaysa approached the woman in charge for assignment and asked whether Lark had recovered.

"Not fully," the elderly mistress lamented, "though the Healers did all they could. A pity, since he posed the best link we had left to discover what overcame Tarron. Turnout with the herd in the Companion's Field has caused some improvement. He's regained his Mindspeech, but he still has no memory of whatever horror befell him. Shock left his mind blank until the moment you rescued him from that deadfall in the Pelagiris Forest."

"Poor Lark. I'm sorry." Crushed by more than grief, Kaysa nursed disappointment. Hope flagged that return of the Companion's Mindspeech might enable the bond to make her Lark's Chosen.

"Well, it's thanks to you we have him back at all." The mistress patted her shoulder and brightened. "Tomorrow, when the weather clears, you may visit Lark for yourself. Meantime, there's work. You come from a yarn loft, perhaps you can braid?"

"Easily," Kaysa responded. "How many strands? I can weave most patterns by touch."

"Excellent!" The mistress steered her ahead. "We're always short of experienced hands. A state delegation's scheduled to depart. The two Heralds assigned will require blue ribbons woven into their Companions' manes."

That task finished the day. As Kaysa left for her quarters at dusk, the Master of Horse fell in stride at her shoulder. "Your transfer went well? Good. You were sorely missed."

"The brawl out by the smithy, perchance?" Kaysa tested the slope with her stick and adjusted her downward step.

"Oh, yes." A sigh followed. "Two lads took to fisticuffs. Longtime friends, who could guess? Bloodied their faces before we separated them. I sent the older one home to cool down. The younger won't say what started the fight. Have you a moment? Maybe we'd sort out the root of the problem if you gave the story a hearing."

"Sure. No trouble at all." Kaysa valued her chance to be useful, though her acute senses were nothing extraordinary. Most likely, blindness made her seem unassuming to others. Lads shared their confidence more freely with someone who wasn't a formal official.

The boy sat through the interview, words slurred by

his swollen lip. Between sniffles, his terse answers lashed out like a person tied in a knot. Kaysa marked his aggressive tone, spiked through by sullen resentment. The argument had started in the forge by the scrap barrel, which seemed odd. The smith had no shortage of leftover steel. His Shin'a'in generosity often fashioned sundry pins for the asking, and he mended worn pots for the goodwives.

Cued by that peculiarity, Kaysa asked after the source of contention.

"T'was a used nail," the lad confessed, defensive. "Nor do I have it. Turn out Mic's pockets, not mine."

Clothing sighed nearby as the Master of Horse unfolded crossed arms. "Then Mic will be asked to turn over the disputed item tomorrow. Thanks to Kaysa, you're excused to go home. Be sure you soak that split lip in cold water."

Kaysa picked her way to the Collegium through the drizzle and sat down to a welcome hot supper. Around her, the Herald Trainees discussed the delegation appointed to return to the Pelagiris Forest. The recovery of Lark's abandoned saddle posed the logical next step in the thwarted investigation. Kaysa's account had described the bloodstains left ingrained in the claw scarred leather. The last clue left from Tarron's demise, the gear might still retain a residue for reliable scrying if weather had not ruined the evidence.

"Lara's going," said the older girl about to graduate. "She volunteered in Jess's memory. Arif was insistent, too, but the Queen refused to risk him with a recent wound. Two more Heralds and an experienced Mage will accompany her. Even so, Lara shoulders a dangerous assignment, no matter she's taking four of the Guard for extra protection."

While the talk bent toward particulars and speculation, Kaysa pushed her supper plate aside. More than anyone else, she grasped the mission's high stakes. Direct contact with the stains in a saddlecloth that had been washed repeatedly posed a dire threat to a Herald. Their flight to Haven had been harried by Change-Beasts, even carrying the perilous artifact heavily wrapped. Only Kaysa had handled Lark's gear with impunity. More, her sensitivity had detected the presence of hostile pursuit before anyone else.

Yet nobody thought to approach her for help. Even Lara, who would face the lethal threat yet again. Worse, if she failed, or if the jettisoned saddle was lost to recovery, Valdemar's investigators must return to Ropewynd to seek Tarron's cold trail at the source.

Kaysa tossed through a restless night. Concern drove her to rise at predawn. She hurried to the stable before breakfast. Birdsong heralded daybreak at the Companion's Field, where she paused for her visit with Lark. Fierce hope sparked her excitement. How she longed on this day to be Chosen! If a Companion bonded with her, she might claim a place with the party sent after the essential trace of dark magic.

But Lark was not among the herd of mares and foals crowded in for their morning grain. The unbonded Companions kept their distance, too, which nearly broke Kaysa's heart. Her dejected step dragged to the tap of her stick as she turned away. Quiet as shadow she crept into the stable for her assigned duties.

Disturbed shouts and the chinking clatter of hooves echoed down the Companion's aisle from the smithy. An unknown Herald confronted the Shin'a'in farrier, who snapped in his regional accent, "Hold her still! If I can't set that nail, your Companion will cast off her loose shoe. A split hoof and lameness will delay your mission far worse than a moment taken to tighten a clinch."

"Then why won't she stand for you?" the Chosen yelled back.

Lara's exasperation heightened the fracas. "We'll

have Change-Beasts dogging our trail, mark my word! We must clear the city gate by sunrise if we're to reach shelter by dark."

The dissonant fury jarred Kaysa's ears. Lara's patience had never sounded so frayed, even amid the frustrating difficulties imposed by her blindness. Did no one else recognize something amiss? Chilled by fear, Kaysa hastened ahead, while the ongoing crisis spun out of hand.

The taint of dark magecraft that afflicted the Heralds and their Companions transferred through objects charged by contact with Tarron's spilled blood. What *else* had Lark brought to Haven that had been on him during the assault?

Kaysa gasped as the puzzle piece clicked into place.

Too slow to push through the turmoil, she cried, "Stop! Where's the Mage?"

Suppose Lark had *stepped in* pooled blood during Tarron's demise? His shoes were pulled off when he had been turned out! *Everything* made sense if a residual influence had poisoned the scrap iron forged into nails.

Lark's instincts *always* had reacted, first, even when the ill effects stifled his Mindspeech. His restlessness matched this Companion, today, who refused to stand fast to be shod. Kaysa risked a bruising collision and ran. "Get the Mage in here, *now!*"

Terrified, Kaysa crashed into the bystanders. Heedless, she elbowed packed bodies aside. Underneath the Companion's furious snorts and the rattle of terrified hooves, through the chink of the fateful loose shoe, she could hear: *the ugly, skin-crawling note that was wrong, underlying the quarreling voices!*

She waited for nothing. Guided by the chiming bells on the reins, she crashed into the Companion's warm hide. Whuffed air from flared nostrils fanned over her skin. Kaysa grabbed hold. Frantic hands wrapped in the bridle, she pleaded through tears to the Heralds,

"For your life's sake, stand back! Fetch the Mage!" Consumed by the urgency of her message, she shrugged off all efforts to drag her away. "Listen up! If that nail's been tainted by the same spell that hurt Lark, you Heralds could be endangered!"

"Goddess of the Four Winds!" swore the farrier, stunned. "You think an active curse stems from one of Lark's discarded shoes?"

"Pulled yesterday," the apprentice lad exclaimed. "Of course! We tossed the used iron into the scrap bin."

"Which explains why those Change-Beasts kept tracking us," Lara reasoned through her rattled shock.

"Yes!" Kaysa stroked the Companion's neck to calm her trembling. Hindsight also connected last evening's inexplicable fist fight.

"Fetch gloves," she suggested to the Shin'a'in smith. "That nail must be drawn and safely wrapped for the Mages to study." This pass, the dread sorcery's origin would not elude them. Unlike the volatile saddlecloth, spell-marked steel would not burn to blank cinders.

The dean's study in the Collegium wore the scents of books and ink, and the fragrance of flowers eddied in from the garden past the open window. Kaysa perched in a cushioned chair, folded hands gripped in her lap.

"Valdemar owes you a tremendous debt," acknowledged the woman seated behind the broad desk. In the resonant voice of a portly frame, she continued, "Your unique perception enabled our Mages to thwart a wicked plot to subvert our Heralds. While I know you aspired to becoming Chosen, you understand the Companions always know best. They are a mystery gifted to the realm, and their vision is unsurpassed. Surely you realize, had you been a Herald, the malign sorcery's influence would have destroyed you?"

Kaysa sighed. "The thought occurred to me, yes. Lark probably knew I'd serve the realm best as I am."

Wood creaked as the dean resettled her bulk.

"You've earned a place here for life but, I think, doing more of importance than stable chores."

Kaysa drew a quick breath to protest. She loved nothing better than tending Companions! But the dean's firm counsel interrupted.

"Hear me out, Kaysa. The Herald Trainees seated with you at mealtimes claim you've absorbed their discussions enough to argue a few fine points of the law. Did they tell you they must draw that knowledge from memory?"

Kaysa blushed. Obviously, the Heralds executed the realm's justice far and wide, in small towns and villages beyond access to the Collegium's library. Apparently her inability to read a book posed a groundless impediment.

"I know from the Master of Horse, and from the record of the entrenched dispute you once settled between angry neighbors in Beckley that you've a knack for exposing falsehoods. Suppose you studied with the Herald Trainees for employment? Many cases need a skilled advocate gifted with the art of compromise."

Kaysa stirred to a thrill of excitement. "One day I might ride alongside the Heralds?"

"Sometimes." The dean chuckled. "For difficult hearings and for specialized diplomacy, yes. While in Haven, you'd also have time to help with the Companions."

Kaysa's face heated. "How foolish of me to have fretted for nothing." The interview she had ducked out to avoid in fact might have determined her avocation much sooner.

But the dean leaned forward in warm sympathy and squeezed her clenched fingers. "Perhaps, Kaysa. But some people prefer to decide for themselves. If more folk followed their hearts, as you have, they might discover fulfillment on their own."

So it came to pass that Kaysa made her livelihood in the royal court. While life did not offer her the grand role, or bestow the Choosing she dearly coveted, Bards sang of her courage, and great honor accompanied her many accomplishments as an arbitrator.

History recorded that after Leareth was destroyed, no Mage ever subverted a Herald of Valdemar. Yet, to this day, the granddams of Ropewynd say different, and their tale, that one tried, tells the truth.

Moving On

Diana L. Paxson

It was the morning after Midsummer, and the group of Trainees whom Deira had unexpectedly aided with a spell to protect Haven from Karsite magic had gathered at the rooms where she lived and did her weaving, still babbling with relief from the stress of the last few days.

"Our magic with the yarn and the gods-eyes certainly did *something*—" said her daughter Selaine, setting a steaming teapot on the laden table. "When I walked down from the Healers' Hall, I saw more smiles."

As Deira gazed at the young people, she found her own lips curving. "Beyond some cheerful decoration and healthy exercise?" she asked, filling cups and passing them along.

"And a grand subject for my next song!" said fourteen-year-old Donni with a grin.

"It was certainly the last thing I expected to be doing when we came here from Evenleigh," Deira replied.

"I don't think any of us could have imagined our lives here," said Garvin, an apprentice Healer a little older than the others. "But choices are like that. You think you know what you are choosing, but then life happens, and you move on—" He shrugged.

"Some of us are Chosen instead," murmured Lisandra. Rumor had it she would be changing her Trainee Grays to Herald's Whites very soon.

"But you accepted," said Garvin, "because of other choices you had made before."

"How far back do you go to find out where it all began?" asked Donni.

Deira sighed. How far would she, with twice as many years to remember, have to go to understand the choices that had brought her here?

"For my mother and me," said Selaine, "it began when Master Arbolan the Healer came to Evenleigh."

Summer was ending, and the last of the season's heat lay heavy across the southeastern lands of Valdemar. Deira dipped water from the bowl to moisten the flax she was drawing from the cloud of fibers on the distaff, sending a welcome spatter of drops across her lap. The regular reach and twist of the fingers as she fed the fibers onto the wheel and the rhythmic tap of the foot that kept it spinning required a minimum of effort, but she could feel perspiration soaking the thin cloth of her shift. She glanced through the window, open to catch whatever breeze might waft up from the river, but last night's rain had saturated the earth without cooling the air.

Beyond the green pastures she could see the blur of gray marking the village of Evenleigh's new stone wall. In this weather, even the creatures that sometimes attacked it were sheltering in the shady forests of the Pelagir Hills. The enemies they faced now—molds that rotted wood and leather and fevers that laid men low—cared nothing for walls.

The rug that was her current project hung half-woven on the standing loom. Praise from Herald Garaval, who had helped the village destroy the spider-monster that had attacked them the year before, had brought her orders from nobles in Haven. The money was welcome, but today was too hot to even think about working with wool. *Might as well have used my own sweat*, she thought ruefully, *to sleek the flax down.*

The opening of the front door set the loose fibers on the distaff fluttering. Deira looked up as her daughter Selaine came into the big central room and set the empty egg basket down. The girl turned first to the cage where the dove whose broken leg she had splinted was recovering, checked it, then sank into the wicker chair by the empty hearth. Her cheeks were flushed with the heat, her fair hair darkened to old gold where it clung to her brow.

Deira lifted her foot from the pedal and the wheel stuttered to a stop. In front of the window hung a pot filled with mint tea, its coarse earthenware surface beaded with droplets. She poured some into a mug and offered it to the girl. "Drink—it will revive you."

Selaine nodded. "I felt like a roast in the oven, penned 'tween those new walls." Their cottage, with the big central room that held the looms and the loft where they slept, stood on a rise a little way outside of town, surrounded by fields. The old oak tree in the dooryard provided some welcome shade.

"Three more children lie sick," she went on, "and no—I didna go near!" she added before her mother could respond.

"Nor will you!" Deira said sharply, the image of the bright-faced girl before her replaced by pictures of Selaine raving with fever, then lying stark and still.

For a moment the girl looked rebellious. Then she shrugged. "Perhaps there'll be no need. We've had no word from the Healers' Temple in Freetown, but a wandering Healer is come. His name is Master Abolon, trained in Haven, they say!"

Deira tensed at the worshipful tone. When she first realized that her daughter had the Fetching Gift, she had feared a Companion might one day show up at their door. But it was the Healers' Collegium, not the

Heralds', that was most likely to take Selaine away from her. After they had defeated the spider-monster, her daughter had chosen to stay in Evenleigh and had informally apprenticed herself to Mistress Hanna, a stout widow famed as the best herbalist for miles around. What the old woman did not grow in her garden by the river, she gathered wild, and the girl had become her shadow. Was Selaine tempted now to change her mind?

"I wonder if they know about this illness at the Collegium?" Deira strove for a neutral tone. It was an odd sort of fever, brought by a little family fleeing westward from the wars that had made a waste of Valdemar's borderlands, in which a cough that might be a summer cold turned to a high fever and delirium.

"They must!" Selaine said enthusiastically. "Master Abolon will know what's to do."

"Indeed, and we will leave such matters to those who are trained to deal with them," her mother replied.

When next Selaine delivered eggs, Deira went with her. She said it was because she needed some new needles, but they both knew she meant to buy enough supplies to wait out the plague safe at home.

At first the village looked as usual. The main road led past half-timbered houses to the market square, bordered by shops on two sides and by the smithy and the inn on the others. But a second glance showed her signs of trouble—trash lying in the street, a whitewashed wall that had been abandoned half-done.

Mistress Bernalise, who sold everything from cookpots and brooms to the ribbons and laces brought by wandering peddlers from Haven and places more distant still, was only too happy to bring them up to date on the news.

"Have ye heard? Two more have died—" she announced with a kind of lugubrious cheer. "Marol's middle girl and his old gran'fer as well. An' now I hear Headman Bartom's cook is ill."

"Not just a child's disease, then," Deira sighed. "What does this Master Abolon say?" She could feel Selaine tense, listening. The girl had ceased to pester her to talk to the Healer about letting her help, but every motion proclaimed her interest.

"Well, ye can ask him yourself, Mistress—" Bernalise gestured across the square, "for doesn't the man himself come to the inn for his noon meal each and every day?"

Selaine pressed closer, and Deira sighed, this time with resignation. She wondered if her daughter's ability to focus came from her father, the Herald Aldren, whom she had loved so long ago. It was said that Heralds defied all obstacles to achieve their goals.

Tucking the purchases into a hemp bag, they headed for the market square. The headman was standing on the raised platform at its center, his red face running with perspiration. As they neared, Deira caught his words.

"—'tis an epidemic, and we must fight it together! But gods be thanked for the chance that has brought us Master Abolon, a Healer trained at the Collegium in Haven itself, to guide us through this perilous time."

"Not chance—" said the Healer as he joined the Headman on the platform. "Chance it would be if I lived soft in Haven and simply happened to come this way. But I left the capital of a purpose seven years ago to ride the back roads, to serve folk who have never seen those who have such training as I was privileged to receive."

He must once have been a very good-looking man. The years had weathered his face, but his voice, gentle and low, would have gained him a fortune as a Bard. It had certainly convinced Selaine, who was gazing at him wide-eyed. His clothing spoke of past prosperity. Despite the heat, over his frayed linen shirt he wore a loose-sleeved robe of fine green wool, gone shiny in places with long wear. Its borders had been damasked with a garland of healing herbs that still bore remnants of tarnished gold. The man himself looked to be on the down-side of middle age, graying hair colored an unlikely rust color, as if he was trying to defy time as well as poverty.

"Speak to us, Master!" cried the Headman. "Tell us what we must do!"

"First, we must isolate the sufferers," Abolon replied. "Build a shelter for the sick here in the square so the illness cannot jump from them to those who are still healthy. In this warm weather they will do better in the fresh air. I will show those who volunteer to nurse them how to protect themselves."

That makes sense, thought Deira. It hardly mattered whether he had rejected an easy life in Haven to serve the people or had been forced to flee to the countryside by some scandal. If Abolon had no miracle cure for the sick of Evenleigh, at least he brought a soothing voice and another pair of hands to help the herbmistress nurse those who were ill.

"Is there no cure?" came an anxious voice from the crowd.

"I know of one herb that may help," the Healer replied. "It grows only in the Forest of Sorrows. We call it All-heal. Added to a brew of common healing herbs, it gives them power over even the strongest diseases, if activated by the proper spell. I have a small bag, and if you will gather the other herbs to make up the medicine, we will brew the potion. In Haven there is only one apothecary who stocks it. It is hard to come by, and his price is high, so we will hope we can stop the plague with what I have."

"Bring the herbs to me at the Weaver's cottage on the hill," Deira spoke up. "I will scrub out the great cauldrons I use to dye wool, and my daughter and I can brew up as much as you need."

* * *

"You offered to boil the herbs to keep me away from town!"

Deira sighed. Since the beginning of her daughter's adolescence, she had become all too familiar with that accusing tone. The sun made a golden aureole of Selaine's hair, but her face had darkened like a cloudy sky the closer they got to home. Now the thatched roof of their cottage showed above the apple trees at the top of the hill, and Deira braced herself for the storm.

"You'll keep me stirring the pot till everyone is cured or dead, and I'll never get to find out how Master Abolon drives the disease demons away!"

Deira opened her mouth, then shut it. Selaine had read her motives exactly. There was no point in trying to reply. The girl had clearly been working up to this since they left the village, and her mother could not have gotten a word in if she had tried.

"When will ye stop trying to protect me! I'm a woman grown!" Selaine whirled, blocking the path, and Deira realized they stood eye-to-eye.

"You are seventeen." Deira said flatly.

Lively as a young filly, with legs still a little long for her torso and breasts barely grown, Selaine promised to achieve her father's height and lean build. *Not like me,* thought Deira, considering her generous bosom and equally generous hips. Weaving kept her upper body strong, but the days when she could walk all day and dance all night were long past. *It might be wise,* she thought as they started up the path to the cottage, *to get some exercise that would improve my wind.*

"You were no older when you had t' flee Westerbridge, pregnant with me!" retorted Selaine.

"Aye, and I had to grow up too fast. I wanted something better for you."

"Heralds get Chosen younger still—"

"And then spend five years training at the Collegium."

"Then let me *train!*" her daughter exclaimed. "Master

Abolon is from *Haven*! When will I have such an opportunity again?"

"That's not what you said when Herald Aldren offered to escort you to the Collegium last year—" Deira began.

"Then, I was still a child," Selaine said loftily. "Now I'm old enough to *do* something *useful*! You can't keep me wrapped in wool rovings for the rest of my life!"

I can try . . . thought Deira. "Brewing herbs will be useful," she said aloud. "I am trying to protect both of us, can't you understand?"

"I want to be a Healer . . ." Selaine said grimly. "Risking sickness is part of the job."

Someday . . . thought Deira, striding ahead. *But not yet! Not now!*

"White willow, waybraed, chamomile, weal-wort, elder . . ." Selaine's murmur blended soothingly with the burble of simmering liquid and the crackling fire as she sorted the herbs the villagers had brought in. "But why is sweetseal on the list? To make it taste better, maybe?"

You certainly couldn't tell from the smell of the potion, thought Deira. As wind shifted the steam, she felt a warning tickle in her throat and turned away from the cauldron, pulling up the neck of her shift to catch her cough.

The labor was mind-numbing, but the constantly shifting patterns in the cauldron exercised a strange fascination. When the steam lifted, the spiraling currents pulsed with a dark sheen. *I must be becoming accustomed to the heat,* she thought, for despite the fire and the weather, her forehead was quite dry.

"Around, around, the spell is bound . . ." Deira sang as she did sometimes at the loom. The tasks were more alike than she would have imagined. In both brewing and weaving, unlike elements were mingled to create a harmonious whole. But she was growing bored with the patterns that were all the folk in the village wanted. If she looked long enough into the seething liquid what would she see?

She leaned over the cauldron, her gaze following the swirl of chaff from the dried herbs. It spiraled inward . . . downward . . . "Around . . ." she whispered, and found herself coughing again.

"Mother!" Selaine gripped her arm and piloted her to the wicker chair. "'Tis the third time you've coughed this past hour. Drink this!" The tea in the mug the girl handed her was hot. As she drank, it soothed tissues scraped raw.

"Thanks," Deira said hoarsely. "The reek of those herbs catches in the throat. If the smell is any indicator, it should be a powerful brew."

"Stay right there!" snapped Selaine as Deira started to rise. "I'll take a turn at the cauldron. You need to rest for a while."

I'll sit for a few minutes . . . here where the air is clear. She settled back against the cushion, breathing very carefully to keep that annoying tickle at bay. A faint throbbing at her temples threatened a headache, but her lips twitched with amusement as she remembered how authoritative her child had looked, marching her to the chair.

Like a real Healer, she thought as her eyes closed.

When Deira woke, she was on her bed, and she was cold. Darkness had fallen. She plucked at the blanket, and suddenly Selaine was there, tucking the folds back around her. In the lamplight she could see beads of perspiration on her daughter's brow. Deira wanted to ask if the weather had changed, but the light hurt her eyes, so she shut them.

After that, periods of confusion alternated with glimpses of her daughter's set face, then a period of jolting movement until she slid into darkness once more.

The next time she was aware, her wandering gaze fixed on the shifting pattern of light and shadow on the striped cloth suspended above her. *I wove that . . .* She turned her head a little and realized she was lying on a straw mattress beneath a roughly stitched canopy made from miscellaneous pieces of cloth attached to ropes stretched from posts at the sides of the square to the great oak tree.

This is the market square at Evenleigh. Slowly the thoughts came, with a vague memory of arguing about the journey. *Selaine is getting to work with Master Abolon after all.*

Deira floundered in a sea of delirium, struggling to cling to the occasional islands of clarity. She remembered Master Abolon praying over her with fanatic fervor, Selaine kneeling with rapt attention by his side. She was still trying to recall if she had seen Healers do that before when the world faded out once more. The next time, she noted that though his voice vibrated through the ground, she felt no flow of energy, and her daughter looked less adoring.

And then came a day when the babble of many voices roused her. From her bed she could see the platform in the center of the square. Master Abolon stood before it, displaying a green velvet bag.

"This is the last of the All-heal!" He up-ended the bag and a fine powder sifted into the cauldron. "I had hoped to get more from the Healers at the Temple in Freetown, but they have none to spare—"

"But so many are still sick!" The villagers who had been doing the nursing cried out as Abolon gave the bag a last shake and tossed it aside. "What will we do?"

"Give me a good horse, and I will ride to Haven. The potion in the cauldron should last until I return. But the herb is rare and expensive—I will need as much coin as you have . . ."

Metal clinked as the village folk lined up to drop

coins into a basket, Selaine among them. Deira glimpsed a glint of gold, and tears stung her eyes as she realized her daughter was giving up her greatest treasure, the coin struck to celebrate the coronation of King Sendar that had been a gift from Herald Garaval. She tried to remember when the Herald's Circuit would bring him back to Evenleigh, but the effort plunged consciousness into chaos once more.

"Lady Trine please be with me, Kerenal who helps Healers hear me . . ." the voice was thin with strain.

Deira opened her eyes. The play of light and leaf-shadow above her had been replaced by a warm flicker of lantern light. Selaine knelt at her side, the bag that had held Abolon's magic herb clutched like a talisman. There were dark circles under her eyes, and on her cheeks the shining trail of tears. Carefully she laid the bag on her mother's breast.

She thinks I am dying . . . The thought came slowly. *It might even be true.* Deira tried to summon the will to fight, but her chest was an agony, and she was too tired to even be afraid.

"There's no use in waving an empty bag, dearie." Mistress Hanna patted the girl's shoulder. "We must wait. She's in the Lady's hands now."

Selaine picked up the bag. "I thought . . . maybe some of the virtue of Master Abolon's herb might remain." She shook her head in frustration. "Are you sure that All-heal doesna grow in the Pelagirs? You said that in different lands the herbs can have other names—"

"It was already powdered, dearie. I cannot give any name to an herb I cannot see . . ."

"What about the taste?" Selaine thrust the bag into the older woman's hands. "You know all the plants—some bit of powder must be there—taste it and tell me!"

Hanna sighed, but she wet a finger and scraped it

along the lining, then touched it to her tongue. After a moment, her brows bent.

"Why are you frowning?"

"I don't understand," Hanna said slowly, "It tastes like chamomile!"

Selaine grabbed the bag, sniffed, and stared up at her mentor, eyes wide. "Maybe . . . maybe it is. But that would mean—" She surged to her feet.

"Hush, child! Don't disturb—"

"They have to know Master Abolon betrayed us!" The intensity of the adoration she had offered him rang in the anguish of her cry.

"And lose what little hope they have? If there was no magic in his medicine, it's their belief that is keeping our patients alive."

"And our money!" Selaine muttered as if she had not heard. "My golden king-coin! I want it back! I want *him* back, the cheat, to answer for his deceptions!"

She stretched, reaching, features furrowed in concentration, face flushing red. There was a small "*pop*." When her clenched fist opened, a golden coin spun out and rolled across the ground.

"I Fetched it . . ." The wonder in Selaine's voice changed to a desperate hope. "What else can I Fetch if I try?" She turned, staring as if she could see through Deira's flesh to the torment within.

"I see you, evil ones . . ." her whisper rose to a shout. "I summon you, evil wights who torment my mother now. I draw you forth and cast you out! Be gone, be gone, be gone!"

She leaned on the bed frame, gasping. "Listen to me, Mother," she said, still in that tone of command. "I see your lungs clear, your throat clean, your body cool . . ."

Selaine's prayers became a murmur on which Deira's consciousness focused as their intensity rose and fell. She twitched as an energy that was not quite physical frothed along each nerve. *Clean and cool . . .* she thought. *She is trying so hard . . . I have to try too . . .*

She took a deep breath and then another, surprised to find it did not hurt as much as it had before. She heard Selaine's voice falter, then other voices. She tried to rouse, but this time it was cool peace that carried consciousness away.

Morning light, filtered through the linen shade, cast a gentle illumination across her daughter's sleeping face. Deira found it strange to see it so, after having been accustomed to look up at the canopy for so long, but whatever magic Selaine's prayers had wrought had revived her enough to demand a chair. Since dawn she had kept vigil, alert for any sign of fever, but the tea Mistress Hanna had brewed for Selaine's headache had put the girl to sleep, and her skin was cool. Deira told herself it was the effort of Fetching, not the plague, that had felled the child. Perhaps the worst was over. There had been no new cases for two days, and most of those who had been brought to the square for nursing had either died or were recovering.

Was that a shift in the light, or had Selaine moved? The girl sighed. Then her eyes opened, blazing with joy as she saw her mother sitting there.

"You're well!"

"Not quite, but I am better," Deira replied, "better than you look right now. How do you feel?"

"Like a dishclout that's been wrung out and hung to dry—"

"I am not surprised. It seems you Fetched the disease demons away."

Selaine's eyes widened. "I don't remember . . ." Her gaze moved from her mother's face to the green bag and the gold coin that lay beside it and her face changed. "Master Abolon!"

Wonder was replaced by a reflection of her former fury, and as if the words had been a summons, they were echoed from outside. There seemed to be rather a lot of noise in the square for so early in the day. They heard a babble of excited voices, and hoofbeats, and the chime of silver bells.

"Master Abolon! How did you get back so soon?" came the cry.

"We found him in the forest," someone replied in a pleasant baritone, "Riding in circles and making no sense at all. We thought it best to bring him back here."

Selaine met her mother's eyes and began to smile. "It's Herald Garaval!"

"Master, did you get the herb?" asked Headman Bartom as people crowded under the canopy, Herald Garaval in the lead with Abolon, followed by a younger man in green.

"He did not and he cannot, for there is no such herb as 'All-heal,'" Mistress Hanna declared as she pushed toward them through the crowd. Her white coif hung in limp folds around her face, but her sturdy frame radiated indignation. She took up the green bag and waved it over her head. "The only herb in this pouch was chamomile!"

"I am a Healer from the Collegium," shouted Abolon as the blacksmith reached for him. "Keep your filthy hands off me!"

"He is not!" Mistress Hanna responded. "He is a swindler and a charlatan!"

As they reached the platform, Abolon lurched toward Selaine and was hauled back again. Scratched and dirty, with green robe torn and dyed hair askew, he did not look like a Master Healer now.

"You!" he exclaimed, focusing on the girl. "Witch, what have you done to me?"

"Silence!" Garaval's voice cut through the clamor. The babble faded as all turned to look at the girl.

Selaine's eyes widened. "I only wanted my coin!"

Deira laid a restraining hand on her arm. "I believe he was fleeing with the funds the village raised for medicine. My daughter has the Fetching Gift, but she is untrained. The coin came first—" she held it up. "Is it possible that her Gift has drawn this man and the rest of the money back as well?"

A shocked murmur swept through the crowd, and then a little nervous laughter.

"If that is so, I think I can release you." Herald Garaval stepped to Selaine's side. For a moment he looked at her, then set his palms to either side of her head. As she gave a sigh and fell back against her pillow, Abolon ceased his struggling.

"Selaine, I offered to take you to Haven once before," said Garaval. "I repeat that offer now. The Healers and the Heralds both will want to find out how you did this and teach you how to keep it under control."

Selaine cast an imploring glance at her mother.

"I agree. In fact, I insist," Deira replied. Best not to tell them how the girl had used her Gift to heal, if indeed that was what she had done. Seeing how exhausted her daughter still appeared, she suspected that Selaine could drain herself of life if she overused that power.

"But what of the man?" the Headman called, "and the herb he took our money to buy?"

"Is that what he was babbling about?" The Herald's companion, a slender fellow in a serviceable green robe, stepped forward. Deira looked from him to Abolon, wondering how she could ever have mistaken the man's tawdry splendor for an authentic Healer's gown.

"I am Healer Kernow from the Temple at Freetown. I know of no herb called 'All-heal,' nor any that might deserve that name," he went on. "But I have brought febrifuges and restoratives, and I will stay with you so long as there is need. I am sorry I could not come sooner—the man you sent was ill when he arrived, and it was only two days ago that we at the Temple learned of your situation. I am grateful to Herald Garaval for escorting me here."

"I'm glad I did," the Herald replied, "for it took the two of us to bring this fellow in, though I thought only that he was some madman displaced by the wars. What shall we do with him?"

Looking at her daughter's face, Deira realized that was the question. Selaine had retrieved her precious coin, but nothing could bring back her trust, or the faith of all those who had believed in the man.

"Make him tell us the truth!" said Headman Bartom.

Deira sighed. If trust was broken, she supposed that truth was the next best thing.

"He *said* he studied in Haven," said Selaine.

Garaval looked at his prisoner. "Is that true?" he asked. He began to whisper something they could not quite hear. There was a gasp from the people as the space around Abolon's head took on a blue glow.

"Did you train at the Collegium?"

"I did! I was one of the best students in my year." Abolon spoke defiantly, and though the glow flickered, it was still there. A murmur of doubt rippled through the crowd.

"And did you complete your training?" Deira asked then.

"I studied there for five years! I was first in my class!" Abolon cried, and still the blue glow remained.

"But you were not confirmed as Healer, were you?" the Herald said softly, a rather frightening focus in his gaze. "You were not given the right to wear that green robe . . . Answer me!" The glow intensified.

"I passed . . . the examinations . . ." Abolon fought for every word. "But they . . . wouldn't . . . they did . . . not . . ." He stopped, gasping, though his glare needed no words.

Garaval nodded. "I think your answer is clear. It takes more than knowledge to win the green robe. Character counts as well, and I judge that you have none. To Haven you will go, and your fate will be decided by the Healers there."

* * *

Deira sat by the window, open to receive the breeze that had begun as the sun went down. The weather still held fair, but the valley no longer felt like a kettle with the lid clamped on. Selaine was sorting clothes on the long table, muttering to herself.

"You know that at the Collegium you will be wearing a uniform most of the time. You won't need half those things," Deira observed.

"If they let me in . . ."

"After what you just showed you can do? Garaval would be failing in his duty if he did not insist you be trained! They will be delighted to see you!" she said bracingly.

"I hope so—" Selaine managed a smile.

Deira hesitated, "In a little while, I might come to the capital too. Not to keep an eye on you—" she added quickly. "You will live at the Collegium, and I am sure you will be kept busy there, but without you the cottage will be very lonely. I need a challenge, and the nobles will pay for work that is unique and unusual.

"I won't go with you now—" She gestured around the room, "I need to recover my strength, and it will take time to organize a move." She paused, searching for words. "And I think you will find it easier to settle in if I am not there."

She watched the play of expression across her daughter's face, understanding all the things Selaine would not, or could not say.

"You're *asking* me?"

"It is time for you to move on . . . and I think it is time for me as well," Deira replied, and she was rewarded by something she had not seen in months—her daughter's smile.

The Right Place

Louisa Swann

Petril crouched in the back corner of the last stall in the run-down stable, surrounded by mouse nests and owl droppings, and tried not to breathe.

Why, oh why, did I ever want to be a hero?

He actually thought he'd become that hero . . . sort of. He *had* risked life and limb battling evil, after all.

A high whinny sent his heart leaping into his throat. Petril could *feel* the baby's distress, but he didn't know what to do. All he knew was he couldn't get caught. If he got caught, there would be no one left to help his stall mates—a Shin'a'in mare and her foal. The ones he'd saved from kidnappers what seemed like a lifetime ago.

"Hush," he murmured, keeping his voice low. He reached up and stroked the foal's neck, trying to calm the little one down. Bella gave a low whicker, as if understanding the need for quiet.

Ya'd think someone who saved a Shin'a'in mare and her foal would be fed sweet pies and given soft beds ta sleep in and have Bards singin' 'is praises.

But . . . no. Ever since he'd left home over a month ago in the company of Fritz—an ancient carter with wrinkles as deep as Lake Evandim and eyes like black obsidian—things had been . . . different. There'd been an occasional meat pie, but mostly he'd been fed some sort of boiled meat he couldn't identify and could barely choke down.

His *bed* had been the hard ground beneath the cart with a worm-eaten wool blanket to wrap around him.

And there had been no Bard—or anyone else for that matter—singing his praises, not since leaving home, anyway. The only praises he'd received lately had been a nicker from the mare when he'd thrown her a flake of hay last night.

"I told you—that boy stole my horse. I'm here to reclaim both her and her foal."

The man who spoke not only sounded ugly, Petril knew from experience he *was* ugly—on the inside anyway, though his outside looked presentable enough. Ugly enough to beat innocent animals to a bloody pulp.

And now he was accusing Petril of being a thief?

Yer tha one wanted this, he reminded himself, resisting the urge to lift his head so he could see over the battered partition—slightly shorter than he was tall—separating Bella's stall from the next stall over. *Tha one what wanted ta see new lands and go adventurin'.*

So far, that *adventurin'* had involved shoveling manure and loading carts, leaving him feeling like a harpooned sturgeon after a long, desperate fight for its life by the time day was done. He barely had enough strength left to curl up in his blanket, and as soon as he did, it seemed it was time to get back up and do it all over again.

Petril was willing to work—work was a fact of life for fisherfolk. He'd been fixing nets and helping the womenfolk for as long as he could remember, and he was old enough—and strong enough—to harpoon his own sturgeon. With a little help from the other men.

No, work wasn't the problem. But he hadn't expected the man he'd been working for to up and disappear.

Leaving his eight-year-old *apprentice* behind.

In a strange city.

Without a word as to what Petril was to do with the mare and her foal (he'd named them Bella and Sunfish), or as to how he was going to get home.

Life had ended up more tangled than a fishnet after a storm.

He scanned the stall, struggling to find someplace to hide in the filth lining the floor along the partition walls to either side and along the back. He already knew the search was useless. Except for a small rat hole in the far corner (and yes, he'd made friends with the rats), there was nothing but dirty straw.

He'd tried to clean things up as best he could when they'd first arrived, but the straw he'd found to replace the filth he'd removed had scarcely been any better.

Petril drummed his fingers against his leg, frustrated at not being able to see exactly what was going on. He listened intently, straining to catch the sound of footsteps.

All he could hear were voices mumbling near the stable's front door. The voices raised.

"You want proof? I've brought a guard. Isn't that proof enough? Now take me to my horse."

Petril shivered. He would recognize that imperious voice anywhere.

He hazarded a quick look over the partition wall. A tall, lanky man with dark, shoulder-length hair stood in the wide door leading into the stable, cast into shadow by the sun riding high in the noonday sky.

And next to the Tall Man stood a man in fancy trousers and grand cloak.

Lord Fancy Pants.

The man who beat horses.

Another man, just as lean as the first but not as tall, stood slightly behind the others, looking like he'd rather not be there. The guard?

The stable owner, a brutish man with arms the size

of trees, held a hand toward Lord Fancy Pants the same way he had the night Fritz had rented the stall. "No going inside without payin'," he had said. A man big enough to make sure no one broke his "rule."

Petril sank back into the straw and tried to think.

The acrid stench of aging manure and overripe urine stung his nose and burned his eyes. He scrubbed them with his fists, suddenly feeling as young as his five-year-old sister. He hadn't been gone from home all that long, yet it felt like forever.

He'd never felt so lost. Or so alone.

All his life he'd dreamed of battling pirates and raiders to save his village, or maybe even becoming one of the king's spies (there were always spies in stories about kings and queens) and saving the world.

Not one of those dreams had involved hiding in a dirty stable trying not to get thrown in prison or killed. He glanced at the rear door—on the far side of the building.

All ye have ta do is run faster than an osprey on the stoop, stay quieter than an owl on the hunt, and be braver than a . . . a Herald in battle. Easy-peasy, blue gill breezy, Petril told himself.

He swallowed a snort. He could be quiet—he'd practiced sneaking up on his sisters and brothers, even his da, over and over until he could move without making a sound—but that kind of stealth required slow, careful movements. Every time he'd tried to move both quickly *and* quietly, he'd made more noise than a kiddie learning to swim.

Ye cain't even save yerself, he grumbled. *How ye 'spect ta save the world?*

He didn't need to worry about the world right now, though. Bella and Sunfish were the ones needing saving.

An owl hooted softly overhead. The mare nudged Petril's arm with her nose, as if trying to tell him something.

He'd shared pain with that mare. Shared her terror and her fury.

He'd thought all that behind them, but it appeared Fate had something else in store.

"I've got ta git help," Petril said, the words practically sticking in his throat. He didn't want to leave the mare and foal behind, didn't want to venture out of the relative safety of the stable into the confusion that called itself a city.

They'd passed through large villages as the carter traveled from Lake Evendim to Haven, but nothing had prepared Petril for what the old man called "the hustle and bustle of city types." When they'd first arrived, Petril had been so overwhelmed by the people and noise, he'd wanted to run screaming back home. He had lived through violent thunderstorms and fierce snows. Those were but a whisper in the dark compared to the tumult that had greeted them.

At least things quieted down at night—a mite. Instead of crickets and hooting owls and gently lapping waves, there were mumbling voices of those who never slept, the clank of guards' weapons as they made their rounds, raucous laughter from nearby inns, stomping animals in the stable itself, and sudden cries of those unlucky enough to be caught by the ones who did their dirty deeds beneath the cover of night—

"I know you're in here, boy."

Petril jerked upright.

"Come on out, boy," Lord Fancy Pants continued. "No one's going to harm you. We'll clear up this little *misunderstanding* and you can go home." The words echoed through the building.

Home.

The man sounded reasonable, in both word and tone, but Petril knew better. A baited hook was still a hook, no matter how tasty the bait.

The owl hooted again. Bella shuffled restlessly, and

the foal let loose another whinny. Sunfish knew something was wrong. So did Bella.

Could they tell he was scared?

She probably smells my fear, Petril realized. *Just as she smelled the ones who'd kidnapped her.*

As they'd traveled, he'd found out that Bella was not only smart, she had a memory as long as a sturgeon's. If a sturgeon ever survived an encounter with a harpoon, that fish would *never* come near another boat.

Not only had Lord Fancy Pants kidnapped the mare, he'd whipped her bloody and caged her foal.

No, Bella wouldn't forget.

Neither would Petril.

Bella stomped a rear hoof and Petril bolted to his feet, remembering at the last minute to keep his head low. Sitting next to an angry mare was asking to get tromped into fish food.

His stomach felt like a dozen fingerlings were trapped inside, struggling to get out. He couldn't stay here. He needed to get help.

Memories swam through his mind, the sound of cracking whips and heavy blows. The scream of frightened horses. Pain exploding through his head when Lord Fancy Pants bludgeoned Bella with something he'd called a "blackjack."

Lord Fancy Pants wasn't here to help anyone. Petril knew it. Bella knew it. Even little Sunfish sensed that evil was about.

Alarm fluttered in Petril's mind. Not the blind panic he'd felt the first time he'd experienced another animal's pain. This was more of an alertness as something—the owl?—prepared itself to flee.

He didn't know why or how he felt the animals' emotions. At first, he'd only felt pain or fear, the kind of emotions he'd shared with Bella while trying to save her. During the trip, however, he'd been able to sense when the foal got into what Petril's mum would call "an impish mood."

He had practiced, trying to control how and when he sensed the animals' emotions. He'd focused thoughts at Bella so intently, he'd given himself a headache. Once he'd even ended up with a bloody nose, though that was probably because he'd run headfirst into a tree. He'd been so focused on trying to "communicate" with the mare, he'd walked right off the path and had come nose to trunk with a leafy elm big enough to wrap his arms around.

He was pretty sure the tree hadn't felt a thing. His nose, however, had gushed like a stream during spring melt.

Again, that sense of alert awareness washed through his mind, bringing his focus back to the troubles at hand. Petril steadied himself on his feet. If the owl flew low enough, caused enough of a distraction, maybe he could get away. He imagined running like lightning, ducking out the back door, and vanishing like a bat in the night.

"Jus' do what he says," Petril whispered to Bella. "Don' git yerself hurt none. I'll git hep and git back here afore ye can sneeze."

Bella snorted as if to prove him wrong, but Petril didn't have time to chide her for it. He caught a glimpse of the owl as it swooped from the rafters.

A moment later, Lord Fancy Pants let out a howl that made the hair on Petril's arms stand on end.

Now!

He bolted from the stall, keeping his head down as he ran as fast as he could toward the back door.

He hazarded a glance down the main aisle as he ran and almost tripped over his own feet when he saw the owl digging sharp talons into Lord Fancy Pants' hair. The owl flapped hard and soared away, carrying tufts of brown with him.

Lord Fancy Pants clapped a hand to his head. He must've caught sight of Petril at the same time. "There he is! Don't let him get away!"

Petril tucked his chin to his chest and made his legs move faster. He was a deer, bounding through the woods, trying to escape the arrow headed his way.

The door loomed before him, larger than he'd remembered. He put both hands forward, intending to shove through it, then remembered the latch. He slid to a stop, grabbed the latch and yanked on it.

The latch didn't move.

Petril's mouth suddenly felt drier than a cleaning stone left in the sun. He pried at the latch handle, glancing frantically at the men headed toward him, guard in the lead. The guard's lean face wore an exasperated expression. Was the man frustrated because he'd been called on to chase down a boy?

The latch finally popped open with a loud *clack*. Petril shoved through the door and slammed it shut, then raced down the alley between buildings, ducking to the left, then the right, keeping his moves as unpredictable as a scared rabbit.

A turn to the right dumped him into a square stuffed with people and wagons and critters of all kinds, from donkeys to horses to animals he'd never seen before. A haze of dust drifted around the people, carrying with it the stench of sweat and ripe animal dung.

Petril froze, trying to figure out which way to run. He got a quick impression of surprise followed by curiosity and turned to find himself looking up at a creature almost as tall as Bella, with a shaggy coat and the face of a . . . rabbit? The creature tilted its head to one side, then the other as if trying to figure out exactly what *he* was.

Footsteps pounded in the alley he'd just left.

"Got ta run!" Petril told the creature and took off into the crowd, not caring which direction he went.

He wasn't small for his age, but he wasn't all that tall either. It would be hard to find him in between all these people.

Wouldn't it?

He slowed to catch his breath when he reached the public fountain and found himself in line for a drink.

A mite o' water wouldn't hurt me none, he realized. He turned slowly as the line shifted forward, scanning the people as the crowd surged around them like a stream around a boulder.

He felt that sense of curiosity again and glanced back toward the rabbit-faced animal just as the crowd parted way.

Letting a guard with a face like a winter storm come through.

"Sorry," Petril muttered as he ducked behind the woman in front of him. "Beg pardon." He mumbled to another.

He stumbled over a basket filled with vegetables, then darted behind the fountain, crouching low so he wouldn't be seen. He duck-walked along the back side of the fountain until he reached a horse trough at the far end, then rose into a crouching run.

When he reached the end of the horse trough, Petril sat on his haunches and tried to see between the legs of the crowd. A woman who looked round enough to roll through the square sniffed at him and swished her skirts to one side as if afraid he might be contagious.

No one else seemed to notice him. Or maybe they'd just decided he wasn't worth their attention.

A break in traffic let him see the buildings on the far side of the square. What looked like an enormous inn stood directly in front of him, its door wide open as if to invite passersby.

Petril heard the rumbling wagon as it moved past the trough. Casting a look over his shoulder, he darted between the wheels and then under the wagon bed, managing to keep pace with the wagon. He forced himself to breathe the dust-laden air, fighting off the feeling that he was about to drown.

Jus' two more steps, he promised himself.

Ye'll be run over before ye can get shed o' the wheels, a little voice whispered in his mind.

No. He'd made it this far. He'd make it to . . .

Petril's gaze fastened on the door to the inn, still open and inviting. He took a deep breath, strangled on a cough, and dashed out from under the wagon.

He thought he heard someone shout as he ran, but didn't look back.

His thoughts spun and twisted like spider weaving a web as he frantically tried to come up with a plan.

Could report Fancy Pants to the guards . . . but the guards were already with Lord Fancy Pants.

Who could he turn to, then?

Who would be willing to help an eight-year-old boy from Lake Evendim?

A thought flashed through his mind as he ducked through the inn door, rolled under one table, then another, ignoring the curses shouted overhead, and dashed out the back door.

He found himself in another alley and turned right.

He had to find a hero, Petril thought suddenly. He *had* to find a Herald.

As if Fate had once again listened, Petril spotted a woman dressed in white sitting along a wall in a small square, a small metal box sitting beside her.

This square was quieter than the public square he'd just left. An inn—smaller than the one he'd raced through—sat on the other side of the wall. Flowers of varying colors danced among the bushes too regularly spaced to be natural.

He had to get her attention. Get her to listen to him. Petril chewed his lower lip as he thought about what he should say—

He froze, heart in his throat, and wondered if he'd ever breathe again. The idea swimming through his mind like a wall-eyed trout caught in a whirlpool was totally bonkers.

Try as he might, he couldn't come up with anything else.

If he didn't get someone's attention, someone who would actually be able to help, Bella and Sunfish would be taken away by Lord Fancy Pants and who knew what would happen to them then.

Petril studied the small metal box the Herald had set to one side. The woman seemed to be tinkering with something else, though Petril couldn't tell what it was.

What're ye waitin' on? Petril asked himself. *The sun won't set no quicker.*

He tried to remind himself that this was what he wanted—to be a hero.

But somehow what he was about to do didn't feel very heroic. It felt . . . desperate.

A faint scream echoed somewhere in the maze of his mind.

Sunfish.

Petril gritted his teeth and dashed forward. She turned toward him, surprise widening her eyes.

"Sorry," Petril mumbled as he snatched the box in one hand and shoved at the Herald with the other.

Then he took off as if the devil himself was chasing him.

Petril felt a rush of confusion, though he couldn't really tell if it was his own mind being confused at what he'd just done or the Herald or something else. He'd never really sensed feelings from a human before—at least he couldn't *remember* doing so. And there weren't any other animals around . . .

Except for the Herald's Companion.

Darkness crowded the edges of Petril's vision and he could swear his heart stopped dead as a rabbit's from fright. He didn't dare look back over his shoulder. Didn't dare look right or left.

Git yerself back to the stable, he reminded himself. *Bella and Sunfish're needin' ye.*

His da had once taken the boys—all six of them—to watch trout returning upstream to Lake Evendim. The trout fought their way up falls and around rocks in their struggle to return to the lake, leaping upward only to be washed back down, then leap upward again.

Petril pictured those fish now, tried to mimic their single-minded determination.

He had one goal right now, one purpose. To get the Herald back to the stable in time to stop Lord Fancy Pants from taking Bella and Sunfish away.

He tried not to think about what might happen once they got there. Tried not to think about how angry the Herald might be.

Tried not to think about the Companion thundering behind him.

He darted around one corner, then another—and found himself facing three windowless walls.

With no way out.

The alley behind him filled with an enormous dark shadow that slowly resolved itself, changing from dark to white as the afternoon sun glistened on pristine white hide. For a moment, the animal seemed to fill the entire opening, standing as tall as the buildings themselves.

Petril blinked and the horse—the *Companion*—suddenly looked . . . normal. Huge, yes, but not monstrously so.

"It's them 'orses," Petril gasped, holding his hands up as if he could stop the enormous white horse standing in front of him from biting or charging or stomping him into fish paste. He realized he was still clutching the metal box. "'ere, ye kin 'ave it back. Didna want ta take it, ye see. But I didna ken what else ta do. No one'll believe me, but them 'orses need yer hep. Ye 'ave ta get 'em away from that fancy-pants lord fore he does somethin' bad to 'em."

The anger he'd been feeling faded to something resembling irritation, then—amusement?—followed by concern.

The Companion snorted, showering him with dampness.

Petril rolled his eyes, but he didn't move. It looked like he wasn't going to be stomped into fish paste. Not yet.

"Ye 'ave ta hep me," he repeated. "We gotta save 'em. I done made Bella a promise."

The Companion visibly relaxed, shifting his hips from one side to the other and nodding his head as if in agreement.

"Ye should see what they done to 'er," Petril went on. He knew he was blathering now, but he couldn't seem to stop himself. "Lord Fancy Pants done whipped her bloody, and then whapped her a good'n on the head, and they locked Sunfish in a wagon—"

"Who whipped whom bloody, and who in the blazes is Sunfish?"

Petril gulped as the Herald squeezed past her Companion, a stern look creasing her round face. He found himself reminded of a full moon—if the moon were to frown instead of smile. He held out the box and gingerly stepped forward, ready to leap back if the Companion decided it was time for some stomping.

"Sunfish is Bella's baby," he said.

"And Bella is . . .?"

"Bella's the Shin'a'in mare I done rescued from those bandits," Petril declared, standing a little taller as he said it.

"You?" The Herald raised an eyebrow, though the frown had eased just a little. "You rescued a Shin'a'in mare?"

Petril nodded. "An' her little 'un. Had ta do it. Weren't no one else ta do it."

He studied the Herald's face. Did she believe him? Would she help?

The buildings seemed to sway—just a little—and he felt something . . . *prodding* . . . at his mind. Startled, he glanced at the Companion, and found himself drowning in sapphire blue eyes.

Instinctively, he pictured the mare and her foal, *remembered* what had happened to them before they came to Haven, their journey and the carter's disappearance.

Whatever he'd been feeling abruptly vanished, leaving Petril feeling as lost as a duckling without its mother. He glanced at the Herald, who had a distant look on her face. She blinked, then focused, the frown back on her face, but this time he didn't think she was frowning at him.

"Where are they?" she asked, her voice gone from angry to impatient.

"Tha . . . tha . . ." He swallowed hard and tried again. "Tha stable on tha other side o' the square. Beyond those other buildin's." He glanced at the walls surrounding him like a fish trap. "It's where I were headed 'fore I got turned around."

"There are four stables in the vicinity." She crossed her arms and glared at him. "Be more specific."

"Um . . ." Petril tried to think, but he had really and truly gotten himself lost, though he'd refused to admit it until now. He thought about the stable and the owner. "The owner's a big fella. Not really all that tall, but 'is arms is big as a tree."

Once again, the Herald got that distant look on her face. She nodded as if reaching some sort of decision. "Come on then. We'll take a look at old Ben's. He isn't the only man I know with arms that big, but he's the only one running a stable close by and the only one stupid enough to try to hide a Shin'a'in mare."

Relief washed over Petril so suddenly he thought his knees might collapse. She *believed* him. He gave the Companion a tiny smile.

The Companion nodded, the movement causing something on the bridle to jingle.

They believed him.

"Name's Petril," he said as he cautiously inched nearer the pair.

"Mira," the Herald said, turning and leading the way out of the tight alley. "And this is Bryn."

The Companion lowered his head as if bowing. Petril stared, then, realizing he was probably being rude, bowed his own head. "Pleased ta make yer acquaintance," he said stiffly.

He wasn't really sure if that was the right thing to say, but he'd heard the phrase several times when old Fritz had met someone new.

Again, he got the sense of amusement. Was it coming from the . . . Companion? The Companion nodded, and this time Petril could see amusement reflected in the sapphire blue eyes.

They managed to get out of the alley, the Companion backing gracefully while Petril followed. Mira led the way back through the square, skillfully dodging people hurrying to whatever destination they had in mind. She held up a hand, pausing as a brightly painted wagon drawn by four horses rumbled past, then hurried forward.

The Herald led the way down one street, then another and another. Just when Petril thought they might be going the wrong way, he spotted the front of a stable.

And standing outside, looking thunderous as a summer storm, stood Lord Fancy Pants himself.

"Tha's 'im," Petril whispered. He sensed something wrong, but couldn't figure out what. "Got ta check somethin'."

He raced forward, darting past Lord Fancy Pants and under the guard's outstretched arm. The owner shouted something as Petril raced by, but he didn't—couldn't—stop.

Petril slid to a stop outside Bella's stall and put his hands on his knees, trying to catch his breath and failing.

Bella stood perfectly still, head down, as if she could barely keep from collapsing.

Sunfish was nowhere in sight.

"Get that boy away from my horse," Lord Fancy Pants demanded as he strolled up behind Petril. "He's a horse thief. I want him arrested."

Mira walked up as if she hadn't a care in the world. The Companion wasn't with her.

"Wha'd they do ta ye?" Petril asked Bella, going down on his knees in front of the horse's head. He put his hands on her cheeks and tried to *feel* what she was feeling.

Nothing.

At first he thought he just wasn't connecting with her. He'd never really been able to control his ability to sense an animal's feelings, after all.

Then he realized that he *had* connected. He was feeling what she was feeling—nothing.

A memory teased at his mind, the memory of his oldest brother carried in from the boat, limp and unmoving. He'd grabbed hold of a nettlefish while clearing the net. Nettlefish were known for their poisonous sting. One poke could render a man unconscious for days, maybe even kill him.

"She were poisoned," Petril said, casting an accusing glare at Lord Fancy Pants. "Ye poisoned 'er, didn't ye?"

A lump rose in Petril's throat. Was Sunfish already dead, then? Was he too late?

He blinked hard against the burning in his eyes, refusing to cry like a blubbering widdle.

He'd been only four—helpless and confused—when his brother had died from the nettlefish poison.

He wouldn't let Bella die too.

"Where's 'er baby?" Petril demanded. "What you done wi' 'er baby?"

He could hear the Herald questioning Lord Fancy Pants and someone with a deeper, harsher voice.

Instinctively, he focused on the mare, trying to will his strength into hers. He could almost feel the poison running through her veins, black and deadly.

Bella's head dropped until her muzzle rested on the dirty straw. He could feel the connection slipping . . .

No.

Again working from instinct, by what he felt was *right*, Petril visualized that blackness turning to light.

His heart skipped a beat as the blackness seemed to lighten just a little.

Petril felt a presence at his back and then a slight pressure in his mind, not like a poke or a prod, more like someone had reached out to support him.

He focused harder, clenching his teeth so tight his jaws ached. He closed his eyes, held onto the connection he felt with the mare and *willed* the poison to change as Bella's head seemed to sag into his hands . . .

No, no, no, no . . .

Everything around him faded until he and Bella were all that existed . . .

Bella snorted, jerking her head out of his hands. Petril sensed the mare's anxiety as she whipped around, stamping frantically and whinnying loud enough to hurt his ears.

"Where's 'er baby?" Petril demanded again, struggling shakily to his feet. "She—"

"I've got him," Mira said. Light from outside backlit her stocky figure as she strode toward him, casting her Herald whites in an ethereal glow. Sunfish walked beside her, his long, awkward legs seeming to go all directions except straight ahead. He perked up as Bella whinnied again.

"Go on with you, then." Mira released the foal's halter and Sunfish bolted toward his mother.

Practically mowing down Petril in the process.

"Heyla to you, too," Petril murmured as mother and son rubbed noses. Petril scrubbed at his temples.

"Me 'ead feels like a beatin' rock after washin' day," he muttered to no one in particular.

:*Well done, lad*: said an unfamiliar voice.

Petril blinked and looked around, trying to figure out who had spoken. Probably all in his head—

:*That it is—all in your head,*: the voice said again, this time with a sense of amusement Petril recognized.

Petril stared at the Companion standing against the rear wall. "Ye talkin' ta me, 'orse? I . . . I mean . . . sir."

The sense of amusement turned into a chuckle, which felt even stranger.

"Wait," Petril said with a frown. "Yer laughin' at me!"

"Bryn isn't really laughing at you," Mira said. "He's laughing *with* you. And you should feel honored. Companions don't speak to just anyone."

Petril started to nod, but the movement sent a bolt of lightning searing through his skull. "Me head," he moaned. He sat in the straw, unable to stay on his feet.

:*There's a Healer on the way,*: Bryn said. :*Make sure you drink what he gives you—finish the entire cup—then get a good night's sleep. You'll feel better by morning.*:

"'ow do ye know?" Petril asked. He just wanted everyone to go away and leave him alone so he could curl up in a ball and die.

:*We "'orses" know more than you think,*: Bryn replied.

Petril heard the sarcasm in the Companion's voice but decided to ignore it. "Take care o' Bella. She's still feeling a bit weak."

:*They'll both be well cared for,*: Bryn assured him.

"They won't be staying here," Mira said at the same time. "We'll take them up to the Collegium, where they'll stay until someone figures out what to do."

"She's special." Petril managed to peer up at Mira with one eye half open. "She's Shin'a'in."

"As you've already said." Mira gave him a tight smile. "Please rest assured that Miss Bella and Master Sunfish are now in good hands."

Petril let his eyes close and tried to concentrate on his breathing. Sometimes he'd come home after a day spent working in the sun and his head would be pounding so hard he thought it would split. Mum always gave him something sweet to drink and sent him to bed, reminding him to focus on his breathing.

What the Healer gave Petril to drink was *not* sweet. He forced the drink down, wondering if someone was trying to poison *him*. But the pain dulled enough that he was able to protest when someone lifted him onto a horse's back.

"Lemme down," Petril demanded, though his voice sounded like it was coming through a thick fog. "Bella's still weak—"

:Bella's fine,: Bryn said. *:The Healer's seeing after her as well as Sunfish.:*

Petril cracked one eye open long enough to see a broad white neck bobbing gently before him. "You!" He gasped.

What was the punishment for riding someone else's Companion?

Mira laughed, the sound so full of merriment Petril couldn't help but chuckle in spite of his worry.

"Wha? It ain't yer hide thas lookin' ta be tanned."

"Bryn offered to carry you; otherwise, you wouldn't be up there." Mira patted his leg. "You're getting the hero's treatment, youngling. Take advantage of it while you can."

The hero's treatment.

Petril felt a small glow start deep inside, a glow that grew into a small fire despite his aching head. He realized that he liked having Bryn's presence in his head. There was something comforting about actually *communicating* with an animal instead of only feeling their emotions. And this *hero's treatment* was kind of nice.

He studied Mira out of the corner of his half-opened eye.

"'xactly 'ow does one git ta be a 'erald?" he wondered, then felt himself blush when he realized he'd said the words out loud.

"You're still a little young—" Mira started, but Bryn cut her off.

:The Healers and one or two of the Heralds will speak with you. I'm not quite certain what your Gift will turn out to be—you have shades of several Gifts hanging about you, the strongest being Empathy, with some Healing thrown in. You have options, lad. But more on that later.:

:*Options?*: Petril tried to think the word at Bryn, but the effort sent pain shooting through his skull again.

:That was foolish,: Bryn said. *:You have a lot to learn.:*

Petril gave up any attempt to communicate mentally or otherwise. He did have a lot to learn. After all, he was only eight, though his head made him feel like he was eighty.

He pictured himself riding up to his little village on a glistening white Companion. Mum and Da would be so surprised, so proud.

His brothers and sisters would be green with jealousy—

:Not so fast, lad. Hard to say yet whether or not you'll be Chosen. You might better serve as a Healer—: Bryn seemed to catch himself and stopped midsentence. *:Never mind. You get some rest now, young hero. You've had enough excitement for one day.:*

Young hero.

Being a hero was hard, Petril reminded himself. It wasn't all sweet pies and soft beds. But he still wanted to help people, just as he always had. Wanted to help animals, too, now that he knew that he could.

Da always said heroes were born outta need.

That's it, Petril decided. He could be the hero he wanted to be. He just had make sure he was there when he was needed.

In the right place.

At the right time.

A Siege of Cranes

Elisabeth Waters

Lena paced back and forth through the rooms assigned to her at the Palace. The dressmakers had—finally!—departed, and she had stripped down to a plain cotton shift. For a girl accustomed to the robes of a Novice of the Temple of Thenoth, Lord of the Beasts, clothing suitable for a highborn young lady in her first Season at Court was miserable.

"The costumes they were fitting on you really are lovely," commented the young woman who sat calmly in the main room as Lena crossed from her bedroom back to it.

"Costumes is exactly the right word, Sofia," Lena said. "And they aren't costumes I can move about safely in."

"What do you need to do in them beyond standing around looking pretty, walking in the gardens if it's not snowing too much, and dancing?" Sofia was something called a "flyer"—she, along with the rest of her family, had an act that involved swinging back and forth between moving bars high in the air. True, there was a net below them, but it was a long way down. Lena had met them the previous summer, when she had joined their traveling show. She and a Companion named Meri, along with a Herald Trainee and her Companion, had been pretending to be a trained horse act. In reality, of course, the "horses" had been training the girls. Lena had also learned to fly a bit; Sofia had taught her. She loved it; it was as close as she could physically come to flying like a bird. She could come much closer to it mentally, having Animal Mind-speech, but that wasn't the same thing at all.

"That's all the dressmakers *think* I need the costumes for," Lena agreed, "but they're overlooking one important fact. I also need to be able to run, hide, or both well enough to escape my suitors." She made a disgusted face. "Have you had the misfortune to encounter Lord Repulsive?"

Sofia blinked. "Not under that name, but I wouldn't rule it out. What does he look like?"

"The usual. Tall, blond, chiseled features, richly dressed, thinks the rest of the world exists to serve him . . ."

"That describes all the highborn I've seen lately except for the ones who have dark hair," Sofia commented. "Of course, it's hard to judge height if I'm up in the rigging, but there are a lot of them who look at me as if I were a delicacy at a Midwinter Feast. My father is very cross about it. That's why he's having two of my brothers escort me everywhere I go."

Lena frowned. "Is he really worried for your safety?"

Sofia shrugged. "You know my father."

Lena did, and "overprotective" was the first word that came to mind. "Strict" was the second. He had taken on the responsibility of chaperoning her last summer.

"I knew you were highborn—well, I did by the time we got to Haven, anyway," Sofia said, "but I hadn't realized what a prize you were until now."

"Sad, but true," Lena sighed. "Even before the King told me I couldn't avoid taking my part in the Season this time, I've been avoiding prospective in-laws for years. Sven-August's mother tried to get us together over a year ago. I had just turned sixteen, and *he* was thirteen. Fortunately, she doesn't like animals."

"What did you do to the poor woman?" Sofia asked, clearly ready to be amused.

"Not a thing," Lena said with her best innocent look. "Maia and I were staying in her house for a project we were working on, and Lady Efanya thought Maia was my maid instead of a fellow Novice. So I asked Maia if her friend Dexter would be willing to help me."

"And Dexter is . . ."

"A raccoon." Lena grinned impishly. "He's very good with hair, but when one of the servants came in while he was brushing mine, she screamed loudly enough to bring in not only the housekeeper but Lady Efanya as well. I'm afraid she was a bit shocked. Seeing with her own eyes how likely I was to have animals around me all the time made me much less attractive as a daughter-in-law. And Sven-August and I regard each other more as sister and brother than as potential spouses." She sighed. "I was actually managing pretty well until the King decided it was time for me to participate in the social season. Now I just feel like a fox with a pack of hounds after me."

"You've been fox hunting?" Sofia was incredulous. "I wouldn't think you'd enjoy that at all."

"I wouldn't enjoy it, and I haven't been. I don't intend to in the future, either," Lena said firmly. "Unfortunately, Lord Repulsive thinks he's a mighty hunter just because he can stay on a horse's back while his hounds kill a fox. The truth is he's a really bad shot. When he comes home with a deer, it's the servants with him who actually shot it."

"They must really despise him if they talk about it."

"Oh, *they* don't talk. Either they're scared of his father or they like their jobs—probably the former. What he doesn't realize is that I can understand his 'prize bitch' just fine, and he takes her nearly everywhere he goes."

* * *

By the end of her fifth week at Court, Lena had sorted her suitors into three categories: annoying, obnoxious, and repulsive. The ones in the annoying category weren't bad men; they simply had no interests in common with her. If she absolutely *had* to, Lena thought she could tolerate marrying one of them, but she prayed the King wouldn't ask it of her. *We're talking about the rest of my life, and that could be a long time. But maybe I could marry someone who absolutely loved to live at Court while I lived in the country.* The obnoxious ones were men she wouldn't marry under any circumstances.

Lord Repulsive was in a category of his own. She had expected to like him when they were first introduced, mostly because he had his dog with him. She thought that meant they had a love of animals in common. But the more time she spent time in his company, the less she listened to whatever he was bragging about—he had one subject, and it was himself—and the more she "talked" to his dog Greta. Even though Greta liked her master, watching her view of his actions made Lena's feelings change from boredom to disgust.

The most frightening things Greta witnessed were the reports of the courtship Lord Repulsive was giving to his father. As far as Lena knew—and she had made a point of talking to the Chronicler about all her suitors—the family was highborn, respected, well-off financially, and the father was on the King's Council. They didn't need her or her money, and listening to them talk about her made her feel like a trophy—before they started discussing tactics that made her feel like hunted prey and start sleeping in the clothing she had worn as a flyer. At least she could move in it, and it provided more protection than a night shift.

It was late, after a long evening of dancing and mindless conversation. Lena crawled into bed wanting nothing more than to stay off her feet until morning. She was starting to fall asleep when she "heard" Greta nearby.

It took Lena so long to realize that Greta and her master were approaching her bedroom that there wasn't time for her to escape through the hallway. Thanking all the gods that she had spent the summer doing acrobatics—and was dressed for them now—Lena ran to her window, dove out, landed with a forward roll to her feet, and ran for the Companion's Field.

If I get in among them, I can buy enough time to call for help. Even Repulsive won't dare harm a Companion. The first Companion she saw was Meri, who was coming toward her.

:Up!: Meri ordered her. After their "trick rider" act last summer, Lena didn't even have to think. She was on Meri's back, and Meri ran. She didn't slow down until they were outside the gate and into the streets of Haven. *:Where are we going?:* she asked, slowing down as she ghosted into the back alleys.

:Home,: Lena replied, fighting back sudden tears. *:Thank you for saving me.:*

:You're welcome,: Meri replied. She didn't ask where home was. She didn't have to.

Lena sighed with relief as they passed through the Temple gates, and the Peace of the God fell upon them. Even Meri seemed to appreciate it. Lena slid to the ground and led Meri into the stable.

:You should go change into your robes,: Meri suggested. *:The Prior would prefer that to what you are wearing now.:*

"I'll change after you have water," Lena replied aloud, not expecting anyone to be in the stable at this time of night.

"What?" a young man's voice came from the floor. Lena discovered that her expectations were wrong;

there was someone here. The reason was obvious: there was a basket with a litter of very young puppies, well cushioned by towels, next to him, and he held a puppy in his lap, hand-feeding it milk through a cloth teat.

When did we get these? wasn't a question; they couldn't be more than two days old. "Where did they come from?" she asked instead.

"A sack someone threw in the river." Firm lips tightened in a face that Lena found attractive in the light of the lantern hanging from a bracket next to him. He looked to be maybe five years older than she was, and a furrow between his brows suggested chronic pain. He was sitting propped against the side of a stall with his legs stretched out in front of him, and she noticed a wheeled chair sitting nearby. The puppy he was feeding fell asleep so suddenly that Lena could feel it, and he switched it for another one from the basket.

"Why did you tell your horse that you would change your clothing after you cared for her?" he asked, sounding amused. "Was she suggesting that you change before?" He looked at her short tunic and tight leggings. "Not that she wouldn't be right."

:Of course I'm right.:

"Yes, of course you are," Lena shot back. "Very well, if *both* of you are going to gang up on me, I'll go change." She ran to the quarters she shared with the other women who served at the Temple. It didn't take long to throw on Novice robes. She was back in the stable in less than ten minutes.

Meri stood right where she had left her, and Lena quickly got her a bucket of water. "Are you hungry?" she asked.

"Do you expect her to answer you?" the young man asked. "And where did you find a Novice's robe?"

"I'm sorry," Lena said. "I guess introductions are in order. I'm Lena. I live here—most of the time, at least. This is Meri. She's an unpartnered Companion who was kind enough to help me escape from an overzealous suitor."

"You had to run all the way down here in the middle of the night?" He looked at Meri, and added, "From Court?"

"Lord Repulsive is persistent," Lena said dryly. "He wants what he wants when he wants it, and he doesn't care a bit what anyone else might think—especially a mere woman. He thinks I should be honored that he wants me."

"I'm guessing you're not as honored as he thinks you should be."

"I'm just as highborn as he is, so no. It's not as if the animals I work with care who my ancestors were. And they're all dead, anyway." She sat across from him, picked up another nipple from the feeding kit, and asked, "Which puppy should be fed next? Are you doing them in some order?"

He looked nonplussed. "I'm afraid I've lost track. I'm mostly trying to figure out which one is awake and hungry."

"Right." Lena closed her eyes and reached out with her mind, followed by her hand. "This one is the hungriest."

"How can you tell?" he asked, as she filled the nipple with milk and started feeding the puppy.

"Animal Mindspeech. Unfortunately, it doesn't work with people, so I don't know your name."

"I'm sorry. Didn't I tell you?" She shook her head. "It's Keven. Lord Keven Crane, actually, not that it matters anymore."

"Crane?" Lena gasped.

Keven winced. "You were talking about my brother Ruven, weren't you? You're right. He *is* repulsive." He sighed. "Unfortunately, he comes by it honestly."

"Yes, I've met your father, too. He really seems to want me for a daughter-in-law. He and Ruven were talking about resorting to rape if I didn't agree to the marriage."

"They said that where you could hear them?" Keven sounded incredulous as well as horrified.

"Of course not. They were in your father's study at the house in Haven. Greta told me."

"My brother's dog?"

"The one he takes with him just about everywhere? Yes, that Greta. I get on much better with her than I do with your brother."

"Any sensible person would," Keven muttered.

"So how did you come to be here?" Lena asked. "I've been stuck at Court for the past two months, so I wasn't here when you came."

"They aren't gossiping at Court?"

"Not that I've heard." Lena said. She turned to look at Meri. "Any gossip in the Companion's Field?"

:No. And that's odd. There should be at least a little bit. I'll ask around.:

"Is there?" Keven asked.

"Nothing that Meri has heard." Lena shrugged. "So unless you're willing to tell me—"

"Riding accident," Keven said briefly. "The Healers say that I will walk again," he tilted his head to indicate the chair, "just not anytime soon. And they said I'd probably always have a limp, and that was enough for Father to want me out of sight. He didn't want anyone to think deformity ran in our family and spoil Repulsive's chance to make a good marriage." He gave her a somewhat twisted smile. "I think I like your name for him."

"I should think it more likely that he'd spoil *your* chances," Lena said. "Given a choice, I would definitely marry you."

"Really?" Keven looked surprised.

"Aside from your father, who is presumably blinded by pride in his son, does *anyone* like your brother better than they like you? Dogs? Horses? Servants? Neighbors?"

"He does have friends."

"He buys them lots of drinks," Lena pointed out. "I've seen that much. And I'd bet he pays for other things he wouldn't be buying in front of me."

Keven looked at her in confusion.

"Have you heard the phrase 'wine, women, and song'?"

"He doesn't like music much," Kevin remarked.

"I don't think he likes women much, either," Lena said tartly, "but I'm sure it doesn't stop him from buying their services for himself and his so-called friends."

"Of course he likes women!" Keven sounded horrified.

"I'm not saying he's *shay'a'chern*," Lena replied. "I'm saying that he likes women the way he likes food, rather than liking any of us as actual people. My friend Sofia complains that he looks at her as if she were a delicacy at a Midwinter Feast."

Keven looked down at the puppy in his lap, who had fallen asleep. He carefully put it back into the basket, and asked, "Which one needs to be fed next?"

Lena put her now-sleeping puppy in the basket and pulled out two more, handing one to him. "Here you go."

Keven took the puppy and started feeding it. "Do you really think my brother is going to try to rape you?"

"That's why I'm here now, instead of in my rooms in the palace." Lena shuddered. "I don't understand it. He doesn't care about me as a person, and I'm pretty sure he doesn't have debts that he needs my money to cover."

"He's greedy," Keven said. "He and Father both. They have plenty of money, but they always want *more*." He took a deep breath. "If, all gods forbid, he does manage to rape you, and you would rather marry me, I would be honored to marry you. If we consummate the marriage immediately, then if you do get pregnant you won't have to worry about who the baby's father is. We would probably never be able to tell the difference."

"I'd still have your father for a father-in-law, but at least I wouldn't have to live with him. You are willing to live here, are you not?"

"Within the Peace of the God?" Keven smiled faintly. "Yes, definitely. Even being crippled, I've felt much happier here than I did at home."

"I know what you mean," Lena said. "My home was horrible after my parents died, but even now I'd rather be here than anyplace else. It's just that as long as I'm not married, the King has to have me at Court so people don't claim he's keeping me unwed for his own purposes. The Queen told me that several of the men on his council have sons of an age suitable for me to marry, so there's a lot of pressure on him this year. That's why I haven't complained to him. That, and the fact that things I overheard through Animal Mind-speech are not considered sufficient evidence." She fell silent, and they continued feeding the puppies until all of them were full and sound asleep.

Lena took advantage of the silence to question all the animals awake within the Temple and ask them what they thought of Keven. From the owls in the rafters to the horses, mules, and dogs surfacing from asleep to half-awake as her mind touched theirs, there was general agreement. Keven was kind, patient (most of the time, except when his injuries frustrated him—and even then he didn't lash out at living creatures around him), and gentle. The animals trusted him. And if the animals trusted him . . .

I like him better than any of my suitors at Court. Even the ones who aren't attracted by my money—or my looks—don't share my interests. He likes animals and he's willing to live here, which is more important to me than anything else. He's highborn, so the nobles can't complain too much . . .

She took a deep breath. "Are you really willing to marry me?"

He looked down at his hands. "Yes, but there's something I should tell you first." He was silent for several seconds and then forced out the words. "My father disinherited me."

Lena blinked. "Why?"

"Because I'm a cripple."

"That's crazy," she said in astonishment, and then something occurred to her. "You know, that's actually a point in your favor."

"It is?"

"You can become part of my family instead of me become part of yours. I'm the last member of my family, so the King should approve. We can reestablish it. And your father still has Repulsive—" She grinned at him. "He said that's what he wants, so how can *he* complain?"

"He will, you know."

"Of course he will. But we don't have to be there to listen. If we ask the Prior to marry us in the morning, and then I send word to the King, your father can't even blame him."

"Will he blame the Prior?" Keven asked anxiously. "It would be a poor return for all his kindness to get him in trouble."

"Don't worry," Lena assured him. "I will make very certain that any blame falls on me instead of him. The Prior has been a much better father to me than my own ever was.

"But, really," she continued, "I don't anticipate any problems. I did as the King asked and participated in the Season, I'm marrying a suitable man from a highborn family, and we are reestablishing my family, which would otherwise die out, leaving a lot of land and money for people to squabble over. The King is more apt to be surprised that your father disinherited—" She broke off.

"What?"

"How many people actually *know* that your father disinherited you?"

Keven stopped to think. "I don't know. For all I know he's told people I'm dead, but if it's not gossip at Court . . ." He looked warily at her. "Why are you grinning like that?"

"I'm visualizing your father's face when the King thanks him for allowing you to leave his family to join mine. Especially if he does it publicly."

Both of them started laughing together.

Cloud Born

Michele Lang

Sparrow was weary of waiting.

A year and more had passed since she and her heartmate had encountered the pain of the Forest of Sorrows first hand. Funny how she and Cloudbrother had rushed to Haven with their little son, ready to warn the world of the threat growing in the north, and then their headlong flight had turned to a long vigil.

Somehow, the world had kept turning while they cooled their heels in Haven.

Now, Sparrow and her son Tis stayed at her older brother Keeth's house on Haven's outskirts, waiting for her heartmate, Cloudbrother, to return from the Heralds' Spring Council.

A Herald cannot act without the knowledge or the sanction of the Crown. Again and again, the Council of Heralds had assured Cloudbrother that they were considering the best way to address the dangers they all faced.

Once, Sparrow would have chafed at the delay. But motherhood had taught her patience. The world would reveal its secrets to her in its own sweet time.

Sparrow's big brother, Keeth, was in the Guards, and a fine, loveable dunderhead he was. He and his loud, teeming clan had welcomed her and her quiet, dark little son into their family bosom, to stay indefinitely if need be.

She loved Keeth dearly, but he gave her a headache, too. He and his mate had seven sons; all of them had joined the Guards too and had married, and not a one of them had left their home down the Hill yet. As a girl back in the tiny northern village of Longfall, Keeth had seemed like such a man of the world to her, traveling all the way to Haven to protect Valdemar by joining the Guards.

But so much had happened since Keeth had left. In the middle of all this noisy domesticity, Sparrow realized that over the years she had changed from an unsure, quiet farm girl into . . . somebody else. Keeth had now become the rooted one, the domesticated one.

She enjoyed the family cacophony. But Sparrow, hidden within the screeching flock of her brother's house, still looked forward now to the open road.

Sparrow sought quiet places in the meantime. She was sitting on the front porch steps, shelling peas on a cloudy afternoon. Tis was outside with her, where he wanted to be, playing in the damp and the drizzle. Oddly intense, he was digging with a stick in the soggy dirt of the empty road, making what looked like elaborate maps of an imaginary world.

And all at once, Cloudbrother and his Companion, Abilard, reappeared like a thunderclap of a vision. All at once, her heartmate was back, after a fortnight cloistered away with his Herald kin.

And he was furious.

His face was red to the roots of his silvery hair, his jaw clenched as he sat tall and slim on his Companion's back. Cloudbrother's eyelids, sealed shut by a childhood fever that had robbed him of conventional sight, hid the subtleties of his rage from her.

Sparrow's heartbeat pounded in her ears, a warning drum. "My love," she said, her voice sounding loud and strange to her from inside her own head. "It's so good to see you again. Two weeks seemed like two years. Tell me your news."

At the sound of her voice, Cloudbrother's features crumpled, and the rage fled out of his body like a banished demon. He went from fury to exhaustion in a single moment.

Sparrow ran down the steps to him then, and rested her hand on his knee as she leaned against Abilard's flank, half a hug. "Abilard, welcome as always. You both seem like your feathers are well ruffled."

:Much news for you, dear,: Abilard Spoke into her mind. *:Much mystery as well.:*

Before Sparrow could reply, Tis ran over on his sturdy toddler's legs.

"Mama, up!" he commanded, and Sparrow, his faithful servant, scooped him into her arms, and in one swinging movement mounted him in front of his daddy. Tis buried his grubby little fingers in Abilard's glorious mane, and Cloudbrother wrapped his arms around the boy in a full, open embrace.

Cloudbrother sighed. "After a year and more, at last the Council has made its decision. We're not going to Lake Evendim after all."

The news hit Sparrow like a physical blow. "Not going? What?"

Before they had fled, Cloudbrother had sworn an oath in the Forest of Sorrows to heal the strife up north in the waters of Lake Evendim. It meant his life to try . . . their surviving the encounter in the Forest had been a near thing. He had come to Haven to bend his knee and ask for permission to travel to the Lake region to face the danger, as Heralds do.

And, after a year of waiting, he had been denied.

His face was pinched with failure. "They refused to tell me why," he said. "All they would say was there is much afoot near Evendim, and I must pursue my quest elsewhere."

His fingers shook as he stroked his boy's tangled jet

hair. "I told them that I had sworn an oath . . . It didn't matter."

Sparrow swallowed hard. By now, Cloudbrother was used to exercising his power, to prevailing over hard odds. He had grown unaccustomed to the bitterness of falling short of the mark.

She reached for his hand and squeezed his fingers. "No, love, you speak too harshly. The Heralds on the Council care, of course they do. You swore an oath to ease the Forest's pain," she said slowly, reaching for another way even as she spoke the words aloud. "You did not swear as to the means. We know the answer is hidden in the depths of Evendim, you and I. But that doesn't mean the answer could not be found anywhere else."

Cloudbrother's lips trembled. "I know. But the Forest cried out for water. And healing. A little sprinkle here in Haven is nothing near enough to restore the balance in the North."

"So, I guess we'll have to look elsewhere? Maybe the answer is hiding right under all of our noses."

Cloudbrother smiled then, a grim little smile. "Oh, no, I'm not done with my news. The Council is sending me on a delicate mission now. One I am not permitted to postpone."

Sparrow stroked Abilard's velvet-soft flank, almost against her will, just to give her fingers something to do as she suffered alongside her heartmate. She sensed the tension lurking in the rolling muscles under the glossy white-silver of the Companion's coat.

Cloudbrother kissed the top of Tis's head. The little boy, shielded from his father's emotions, pulled on Abilard's mane, wiggled his stubby fingers to nest even deeper.

"They are sending me—us—to Iftel," he whispered, almost too quietly for Sparrow to hear. "I am to go as an ambassador, as part of a relief mission. They said I am welcome to take you both as well. To see if I can help with the terrible drought they are suffering in Iftel's interior."

Iftel!

Sparrow had only heard the word spoken aloud a couple of times in her entire life. Iftel. The hidden, walled-away land that had joined the alliance of nations but still hid its secrets from the outside world.

The name evoked in Sparrow faint and weird images of strange and distant scenes, too outlandish for her to imagine as real. Nobody in Valdemar really knew what happened beyond the barrier of Iftel's borders.

Something Cloudbrother had said penetrated through her fanciful images to bring her back to earth. Something important.

"Wait. Did you say . . . drought?" she asked, almost as an afterthought. The idea of traveling to Iftel seemed so ludicrous, the reason why seemed almost unimportant.

"Yes, drought," he repeated, louder now. "I told them everything, how the Forest needed water desperately to restore the balance. I told them we knew the secret was hidden in the depths of Lake Evendim. And they are sending us in the opposite direction, into the middle of a drought!"

Sparrow couldn't help it. She started to laugh.

"It is more than absurd," she said finally, through her laughter. It was the kind of laugh you couldn't hold back at a funeral, the laugh of somebody trying very hard not to cry. "It is amazing. It can't be a coincidence, sweetheart. It just can't. The Council is sending you there for some good reason we don't understand."

:Sparrow speaks true. The Council is nothing if not economical. If it can combine diplomacy with magery, the Council will do it,: Abilard said gently. *:Success is failure turned inside out, you know. You think you failed to convince them, dear Chosen. But it is clear to me that the Council believes you may serve our quest*

best in the East, not the West. With good fortune, we may heal the Forest even as we bring aid to our ally Iftel. There is often an economy in goodness.:

Cloudbrother tried to stay mad, Sparrow could see it. The fury kept him grounded, gave him energy. But at his bottom, he was more patient than Sparrow could ever be . . . he'd had much more practice in setback, in lack and in trouble too. He had learned to be patient as a child, learned to accept pain, sickness, and heartache young.

He knew better than even Abilard that what his Companion said was true. Often healing in one place can lead to healing in another. That was true inside a single body's heart, and it was true for the land as well. Any farmer's girl would know the same.

"They paid you a true compliment," Sparrow said. "A mission to Iftel. By the Mother! That is the stuff of legends, my love. And what hey, we can always visit Lake Evendim for a pleasure cruise someday. A little getaway, when all of this is done."

That coaxed a lopsided, more genuine smile out of him. "All right. I bow to fate. You have a way of finding treasure in the dust, Sparrow. If anybody, it's you who'll find fresh water and a secret balm in the middle of a drought. Can't hurt for us to try. We'll make it come out right somehow, even upside down and backward."

Sparrow sighed, letting her tension out and pure happiness in. "There you go, my love. Spoken like a true Herald."

She led Abilard to the back of her brother's big, ramshackle house so they all could tell Keeth and the family the big news. They were heading out, that very night, on a mission too secret for the family to know.

The journey took weeks. They started along the eastern trade route leading to Hardorn, pausing at the town of Trevale to stock up on supplies before turning north. After that, it was mostly sleeping at Herald Waystations along the way, until they reached true wine country.

The Vineyard Hills rose south of the Iftel border, terraced and crisscrossed with gnarled rows of grapevines snaking over the hill crests and separated by rows of trees and bushes acting as a windbreak. It was lush, voluptuous farmland, more fertile than Sparrow had ever encountered before.

She was used to the rocky, hilly country up north near the Forest of Sorrows, stony ground that bred farmers who were flinty and closed-off, like the land.

This was another kind of country. Their last few days in Valdemar, they stayed at a remote vineyard with winemakers who offered them a guest room, and by night the air was scented with lavender, rosemary, and grapes ripening on the vine.

But as they turned north from there, the landscape abruptly turned dry. The track they followed to the end metamorphosed from Haven mud, to rich earth, to dry dust. By the time they reached the Guards' outpost a day's ride from the Iftel border, the rolling hills they traversed were no longer green and russet with flowers, but brown and dead.

They reported to the captain of the Guard outpost at Norflam, to check in as was customary for diplomats on foreign missions preparing to leave Valdemar. Captain Russ received them in the anteroom, while Abilard waited in the swirling dust outside the door. The Captain was agog to learn of the purpose of their mission, and even more amazed by the sight of Thistle in the party.

The Captain didn't offer them a seat. And she ignored Cloudbrother to speak directly to Sparrow.

"You're going *where*?" she blurted without any kind of formal greeting. "And with that little lad? It's within my rights to hold you here for your own safety, you know."

Sparrow's face flushed as she cradled Tis closer on her left hip. "We're like you, ma'am. We go where we must for the good of Valdemar. And my little fellow travels easy . . . he's a regular man of the world now, wouldn't you say?"

The captain shifted uneasily in her rough wooden chair. "I never was much about the littles, to tell you true. I always thought they needed to be wrapped in silk and kept off the ground until they could walk for themselves."

"Maybe you got raised that way, but up in the Northern reaches we learn to stand on our two feet pretty young."

Captain Russ didn't have an answer to that. She turned her attention to Cloudbrother, his pale, expressionless face, his closed for good eyes.

But still she spoke to Sparrow. "How do you take care of them both, I want to know?"

Sparrow's jaw clenched. She took a sharp breath, then forced her voice to stay even and calm. "I don't take care of my heartmate, he takes care of me. He's a Herald—don't you recognize his Whites? His Companion, outside the door? I know they are dusty from the road, but I assure you they were both snowy white when we left Haven. The Crown itself chose Herald Cloudbrother for this mission. And he can talk too, you know. He hears just fine."

Captain Russ leaned way back in her chair, as if she wanted to put distance between Cloudbrother's handsome, pitted face and her own. "No offense, sir Herald, but if you can't see, how are you going to figure out what to do? I haven't been to Iftel, nohow, but posted way out here, you do hear the stories. You hear the rumors. The general gist is that it's boring, nothing to see. But . . . something's eerie about the whole place. Off. Wrong. With all due respect, sir, how you going to figure out the lay of the land, get your little wife and son out of there in case of trouble?"

Cloudbrother drew himself up to his full height, crossed his arms. "I'm a Herald. I've managed until now. And if the Council has chosen me for the job, I must be the Herald best suited for it."

"But . . ." the Captain squared her shoulders, cracked her thick knuckles. "You, well . . . you can't see!"

Cloudbrother smiled. "I see better than you, Captain. You're from the Ashkevron lands, I can tell by the lilt of your speech. This is your first posting, and you have been here less than two years."

Captain Russ half-rose from her chair, spluttering, then remembered herself and plopped back down again. "How—how do you know that? Some kind of sorcery?"

Sparrow's heartmate shrugged, grinned, and for a flashing moment he looked just like he did as a mischievous five-year-old boy, before the fever had robbed him of his ordinariness. "No. I just have my wits about me. I remember the post list from the year I graduated, over two years ago, and your name wasn't there. And there are many ways of seeing, besides the regular kind. No true way, Captain, remember. Only the way that works."

"Thank you for your welcome, Captain," Sparrow said. "If you wouldn't mind, I'd like to get my boy settled and our gear set to rights before we head off this morning."

Sparrow knew when to stop talking. She stood next to Cloudbrother, silent, as the Captain considered the three of them once again.

"I don't like it," she finally said. "I don't appreciate it. But I better accept it. You're free to leave, and may Vkandis Himself watch over you out there. Because I can't charge over the border and save you if there's trouble."

"I know, Captain," Cloudbrother said. "Thank you. We will manage."

Sparrow's heart thrilled with the mystery of the

journey and the danger of it. She was not a Herald, but she was sharing the quest of the man that she loved.

Their ride to the border was almost disturbingly uneventful. The dust rose up from the dry track they traveled, half-choking them on a blustery, blazingly sunny early summer day.

Tis napped fitfully as they rode, wrapped tightly against Sparrow's back. She figured that keeping him out of the way—and out of sight if possible—would make it easier at the border crossing.

She had expected a great stone wall, some physical marker of the boundary that separated the hidden land of Iftel from Valdemar. With a line of fearsome warriors guarding the top, lances pointed at them or something.

Perhaps a fortress-like barrier protected other stretches, but here there was nothing.

And yet both Abilard and Cloudbrother knew the moment they had reached the border.

Abilard drew to an abrupt stop. *:All at once, we are here,:* he announced in Sparrow's mind, and she was sure, in Cloudbrother's mind, too.

"Ah, Star-Eyed," Cloudbrother whispered, as if he didn't realize he was speaking aloud. "Watch over us, protect us in the land of your beloved."

Sparrow echoed his heartfelt prayer in her own mind, because now that they stood together at the border, she was filled with an enormous, formless anxiety, a cloud that mingled with the dust and half-choked her. She had never really expected to leave Longfall, and here she was on the edge of a virtually undiscovered world.

She squinted through the whirling, gritty dust to look across the border. Did she imagine it? There was perhaps a slight shimmer in the air, the way that hot air wavered and formed mirages of water near the horizon in summer.

But that was all that she could see. Sparrow loved a Herald, but she didn't possess any kind of Gift, so the properties of the barrier keeping them out of Iftel were invisible to her.

:The boundary is no longer absolute, but we come in the name of Valdemar. As representatives of another nation, we may not pass without Invitation,: Abilard Spoke. She had never heard such a note of awe and humility in the Companion's voice. *:This is the protection of the Sunlord Himself. Only by His will may we enter.:*

Sparrow craned her neck to peek over Cloudbrother's shoulder. All she could see was the dusty track continuing in front of them. If she squinted, way down the path she thought she saw a farmhouse or something of that sort.

And yet Cloudbrother and Abilard both insisted that they could not go one step more along the pathway to their destination. Sparrow slid off her mount to the ground; her sore muscles were grateful to stretch as she considered their situation. Thistle squirmed for a minute, then sighed and went back to sleep.

She walked forward, put a hand out.

And something *was* there. It was a force pushing back against her hand, invisible, not harmful to her yet completely unyielding. It didn't hurt her, it didn't come after her. But it wouldn't let her walk forward either.

In the far distance, a solitary figure slowly appeared, a small dot traveling on the path to meet them. As it grew closer, Sparrow could make out elaborate, festive robes, bright red and green embroidered with complex geometric patterns. The figure walked with pomp and dignity, like a priest.

The figure grew closer still, and Sparrow dimly made out the claws, the scales, the iridescent greenish skin. The creature looked like a *hertasi*, but so much taller, as tall as Sparrow herself.

"By the Mother," she murmured. "That . . . that must be a *tyrill*!"

She couldn't believe it. *Tyrills*, larger than the *hertasi* she knew in the Vale. Larger than her best friend in the world, the *hertasi* Rork, who took such tender care of her in the days after she had given birth to Thistle. Risen from the creative fingers of Urtho himself, the stuff of legends.

Walking . . . to meet them.

"Sparrow!" the creature called. "Sparrow!"

The *tyrill*'s accent was so thick that Sparrow didn't realize he was calling her name until she heard it several times more. The language was similar to that of Valdemar, a dialect of it, but it sounded ornate and musical, ancient.

It sounded like the language that Urtho must have spoken, long, long ago.

And this personage, speaking in the Ancient Tongue, was calling her name.

She didn't know what to do. Instinctively she dropped a small curtsy, because politeness and respect were a universal currency. It certainly couldn't hurt.

"Hello!" she said. "Yes, I am Sparrow. I come from the village of Longfall in the far north of Valdemar, and lately from k'Valdemar Vale. We come on mission from the Crown of Valdemar. Thank you for your welcome!"

"Ah, yes, Sparrow k'Valdemar, welcome, welcome. I know, I know. I am the Lord Ivinchi, welcome, welcome. My goodness, you are dusty, drab. I had heard that Heralds were fancy."

And Lord Ivinchi seemed disappointed indeed. "I am so sorry," Sparrow said quickly. "I get disgusted by the filth of the road myself, it is good to meet a kindred spirit. There's no way to get a body proper clean while traveling, not even if you manage to find a clear-running stream and a nice rock for beating out the laundry! But we all clean up nicely, I promise."

Lord Ivinchi brightened. "We shall see, my lady. Please, step forward."

"I would most love to, Lord. But, you see . . ."

Lord Ivinchi stretched to his full height, raised his clawed, bony arms up to the sun. "Nonsense, love. Step! Forward! By the light of Vykaendys, come!"

Sparrow's shoulder rolled with a gentle nudge, and she half-stumbled a step. She peeked backward to see the silver muzzle and the bright, cornflower blue eyes of Abilard looming directly in front of her face. His sweet, hot breath blew on the back of her neck.

:Go, we have found the perfect ally. Thanks to you, little mother. Go:

Even with Abilard encouraging her with his Mindspeech, she hesitated.

"I'm not a Herald, you know," she said uncertainly.

Lord Ivinchi clicked and clucked his disapproval of her indecision. "Of course, of course, but yes. I know, you do not come alone, but part of a Delegation." He rolled and trilled the word. "You are an emissary. We hope, of good fortune. Please, don't be afraid. Step forward now."

His kindness convinced her, and she passed through the barrier, which yielded slowly to her passage, like moving through thick jelly. Abilard walked a half-pace behind her, slipping through the barrier without any hesitation.

"This is the Herald, my heartmate, Cloudbrother, and his Companion, Abilard," Sparrow said. "He is the official from Haven who is here on business."

The *tyrill* tilted his head in curiosity. "And the child?"

How did he know? How could he know?

Sparrow half-turned to show Thistle asleep in the pack on her back. "There he is, my little man. We call him Tis."

Lord Ivinchi bowed low, his ornate robes trailing in the dusty path. "Lord Herald, Delegation, welcome, a most humble welcome. I am here to escort you to the

Temple of Honored Memory. We are a rustic people, and we have no grand court to receive you. Besides, the Vykaendys-First believes that you will help us most by going straight to the Temple and consulting with the priests there."

Sparrow turned to look at her heartmate, sitting tall and slim in the saddle. If Ivinchi had registered the fact of Cloudbrother's blindness, he gave no indication of it.

"Thank you," Cloudbrother said, his voice steady. "It is our honor. How far is the travel to the Temple?"

"Three days, Lord Herald. And I will travel with you there and ensure you will have good provisions." He paused. "And . . . water."

Sparrow's heart tugged at the pain in the great *tyrill* lord's voice. "We are grateful."

And that was the end of the ceremony between them. Lord Ivinchi turned and wiggled his claws in the air. "Terrific. Good, good, wonderful. Let us go until we must rest in the heat of the day. Come, children."

From then on, they traveled together, one band with a single mission. To bring water to the thirsty land of Iftel.

That night, the little band of emissaries made camp deep in the Vineyards of Glory, on the road to the capital city. The inhabitants of the region had abandoned it in the search for water, but Ivinchi had arranged for two small sealed drums of water to be brought to one of the low-ceilinged temples in the valley where they rested for the night.

Sparrow gratefully drank. The water was sweet and pure, with only a faint tang of wood resin from the container. Thistle was understandably cranky from a long day of travel on a hot and unforgiving pathway. He needed time to wind down and go to sleep, and by then the moon was high in the sky, and the stifling heat of the day had receded somewhat.

They made no fire . . . the danger of it spreading to the tinder-dry grapevines was too high. Instead, they huddled outside, where they could catch the breeze and sleep more restfully before taking up the trail before first light the next morning.

"How sad, all the dead orchards," she said, hearing the rustle of the dead leaves in the listless wind that blew around the entrance to the Temple.

"They are not dead, my love Sparrow," Ivinchi said. "No, no, not dead. They are still alive. They are waiting for water."

"How do you know me, Lord?" she asked. She had been wondering all day, but their journey was long, dusty, and hot, and not much talking had taken place on the trail. Now that they rested before sleep, Sparrow could indulge her curiosity.

"I know many things," he replied, his flat eyes sparkling in the moonlight. "I know you like scones, and you sleep late if the chance appears, but the chance does not come too much these days. I know as much from your friend in the Vale, the one who saw to you when your little was born. Brother mine."

Sparrow gasped. "Rork!" she replied with a growing sense of wonder. Suddenly she felt much more at home in these strange surroundings. "You know Rork! Only he knows these little things about me."

"Little things that matter most," Ivinchi replied. "Little things are not little. Look at your little nestling, he is little. And he is everything. But Rork. He wanted to make sure I looked after you here, and your littleling as well. He is not so little as I had thought! He is a boy, now. The seed of a man."

"Yes, they grow fast," she said. "Too fast, some say."

Lord Ivinchi studied her face, his eyes unblinking in the starlight. "Better to grow than not to grow."

"Yes, growing means change, and where would we be if things didn't change? We'd be no better than stone statues."

"Even the stone statues will change, in the rain, blasted in war, over time."

Sparrow considered this. "Did Iftel change very much, since the Mage Storms? To open, to let people to come in . . . that is a pretty big change, I'd say."

Ivinchi's head lowered, his shoulders slumped, and he sighed. "Yes, it is a change. Some, some of those who fear, they say it is a change that is bad. A change that brought the Thirsty Times to our peaceful land."

Despite the heat, a chill worked its way into Sparrow's bones. "I hope not."

"I think it not so, my love Sparrow. For we were once strangers here in the land as well. The land is not so frail as this. But something is ailing here. We must find a healing. Because with drought comes disease, comes death. Too many little ones already suffer."

And with that sober thought, Sparrow bade her host good night and rejoined Cloudbrother to sleep.

That night, she and her heartmate flew. In their travels until now, they had stayed earthbound, tethered to Valdemar and its familiar and not-so-familiar contours.

But now, here in Iftel, they flew together on the plane of dreams, searching for the source of the drought and the disturbances in the Forest of Sorrows, to see if they were linked.

The hills unrolled below them, blasted by dryness. Sparrow clutched Cloudbrother's hand, wondering at the scope of the devastation. "How could it get this bad this fast? I thought it took months, years even, for a drought to cause this kind of damage."

She glanced at Cloudbrother's face. He was studying the landscape below them, his face thoughtful, his eyes, open only here in the emanation of spirit, luminous and a little sad. "This is not an ordinary drought. This is the same thing choking the forest up north. It's not a drought at all, I don't think. Not the way we think of it."

He was scaring her a little, but Sparrow kept her voice steady. "Then what is it?"

"It's some kind of malign magic. Not something . . . but somebody . . . sucking the life out of these regions. And after what happened with the Forest of Sorrows, we know it has something to do with . . . well, it also went after me."

Sparrow winced. As a five-year-old, her heartmate, then called Brock, had been lured out of their home village by a mist wraith and sickened by a mysterious, deadly fever that robbed him of his sight and almost killed him. Only the swift intervention of the Cloudwalker clan had saved him.

But this, what was happening here in Iftel, was on a much larger scale than what had attacked one young boy all those years ago. "You think," Sparrow asked, "that this is your fever, writ large?"

"There is nothing little, not in matters of magery. What seems small to the ordinary eye can be massively important when it comes to the balance. And I think that something happened all those years ago. The forest became uniquely vulnerable to a threat it hadn't faced in many hundreds of years . . . and it became vulnerable once again. To a sentient threat."

Sparrow stopped her forward motion, hovering uncertainly in the sky. Cloudbrother stayed his flight to hover alongside her, helping her to fly by holding her hand in his.

"You're not saying . . ." she forced out, "that there is some kind of evil Mage, looking to invade Valdemar again? Don't tell me this is happening again!"

"No," Cloudbrother said slowly. "But I think a malevolent being from this cloud level of emanation—a demon of some kind—is looking for a portal to slip into the ordinary world. Looking for me. My elders in the Cloudwalkers tried to teach me as much of my illness as they could, so that I could be ready to defend myself in case the sickness returned. I don't need to tell you that it was no ordinary fever that almost killed me. No fever silvers your hair and gives you an inner sight in exchange for your regular old eyes."

Sparrow wanted to stop him, but she knew this information was crucial to protecting not only Iftel but also her own sweet son. This was not change of the kind that frightened the people of Iftel. This was something buried deeply within the man she loved, a burden he had borne nearly all his life. She bit her lip and tried not to interrupt as he went on.

"The fever drew my soul out of my body, almost all the way to death and the final separation. My shaman elders stopped it, but at a terrible cost. The malady withdrew, for a while anyway, but once I became a Herald and my own strength grew, I only became a more attractive portal."

"I really, really don't like this."

Cloudbrother drew her close to him, and she tucked her head under his chin and looked down over the moonlit, drought-blasted vines. It was so beautiful, and so awful, and her job was to stay steady and not run. She didn't know how this tangle would comb free, but as long as she stood fast, the chance to set things right remained.

But she was so afraid for Cloudbrother that her heart clenched into a fist.

They reached the Temple of Honored Memory after another two days on the road, hidden near the shores of Lake Usho. The priests there had prepared a room in the Temple for Cloudbrother to engage in contemplation.

These priests did not sacrifice or summon. They sat, and listened, and in the silence sought wisdom. And they assumed that to find the way to a solution for Iftel, Cloudbrother had come to do the same.

Cloudbrother welcomed the opportunity.

The travelers carefully washed the dust from off their feet and out of their eyes, and they changed into the robes that the priests provided to them. And Sparrow took Thistle to play in the meditation garden of the Temple, while Cloudbrother withdrew into the room the priests had prepared.

And there he sat, cross-legged, while Abilard fidgeted uneasily in the gravel garden outside. *:I do not like this, I cannot reach him; there is a barrier set around the Temple blocking my mind from him,:* Abilard said into her thoughts. *:Go to him, Sparrow. I will stay with Thistle. Strengthen him.:*

Soundlessly, Sparrow wound her way through the labyrinthine hallways that led to the chamber in the center of the Temple. The priests did not block her way as she went, but neither did they try to tell her what was happening.

Cloudbrother was hidden in the center, like a pearl nestled inside a lotus. His skin was ashy gray, and his spine was twisted as if by a great, heavy weight borne on his shoulders.

Sparrow restrained a cry and instead crept down to where he sat. She touched his fingertips, and they were icy cold. Her palms reached to his face, and his forehead and temples were on fire with fever.

She closed her eyes, knelt before him. Leaned her forehead against his.

And she was swept into a plain of fire.

A wing of war gryphons flew in formation above their heads, brown and speckled, flying very fast on the tempest wind. In this place, Cloudbrother stood tall, blazing with light, a lightning rod for the force that sought to claim him.

"I am going to open to him," he said, looking directly at Sparrow. "That's the only way. There's no water in this land to spare; the sunken lake is barely enough to keep the people alive. There is no magic secret that is going to save us. There is only us. I am going to have to do this thing myself."

He pointed up. "The water is going to have to come from the clouds from where I was born. This is how my Cloudwalker brothers saved me, and this is how I am going to save the forest. If I open to him, the demon, the energy will flow, and balance will return. A closed system is a dead one, my love."

"But it almost killed you last time! It did kill Silver Cloud, the adept who saved you."

Cloudbrother smiled sadly. "My brothers named me after the fever did its work. I'm called Cloudbrother because I can walk in the clouds easier than on earth. I was Brock until then. Brock died that day, and I was Cloud born. I need to call the clouds down to break the hold of the one who claims me. Goodbye, Sparrow. I love you. Best thing you could do is hold the line here and just let the rain pour down."

Before she could reply, he raised his arms to the sky and lifted his face to the clouds. A rending shriek emanated from the roiling storm above their heads, and the rain began to fall.

First a drop, then a drizzle, then a downpour.

Cloudbrother was engulfed in the storm, became part of it. The rain swirled as it fell out of the sky, the clouds darkened.

Lightning clawed across the face of the storm—a face of evil flashed in the sky—

And Sparrow slammed back into her body.

Cloudbrother was sprawled on the prayer mat, terribly still. And the roaring rain pounded on the roof of the Temple, all but drowning out the cries of gratitude of the priests in the garden outside.

Sparrow sat on the mat next to the body of her heartmate, stunned, unable to move, afraid to speak or cry or fling herself over Cloudbrother's body. He had called down the clouds, but she was terrified to find that he had paid the ultimate price.

A rustling by the door and Sparrow turned her head. It was Thistle, his face dark and set, a warrior going into battle.

:PAPA: he commanded. *:PAPA, you belong to me, not to him!: His name is Zeth, and he is already gone. Papa!:*

Ah, her uncanny child. How could he so easily fetch the name of the demon? He had not been Chosen by Abilard, but maybe growing up in the shadow of a Companion drew out a child's Gifts young. And Thistle, from a young age, had shown the art of summoning. Now he summoned his father's soul from the clouds, back into his broken body, to serve the most demanding duty of all—to live.

They had sought a secret weapon the length and breadth of Valdemar. And it turned out, the key to their salvation had been traveling on Sparrow's back all along.

With a groan, Cloudbrother returned. Thistle did not cry, he did not laugh. He walked to his father's side, knelt beside him, and stroked the long silver hair that tangled onto his sealed eyelids.

Cloudbrother breathed. Thistle stood guard beside him. And Sparrow listened as the healing rain poured down over them all. The affliction was broken.

It took three days for Cloudbrother to recover his strength. The Temple priests still said nothing, but their gratitude was plain. It rained and rained.

After three days, Lord Ivinchi returned to the Temple.

In the peaceful, drizzly afternoon, Sparrow and Tis rested with Cloudbrother in the meditation garden. Cloudbrother, exhausted, mostly slept, while Sparrow and Tis sat next to him on a long, splintery bench woven of willow switches. Abilard stood with them, clearly enjoying the gentle showers, and together they listened to the soft music of the rain.

The priests brought Ivinchi to where they sat, and he bowed low before them in the drizzle, his unblinking eyes glittering. "My love Sparrow, I come to you and the magnificent Delegation, bearing a great gift from the Vykaendys-First. In gratitude, and recognition."

The raindrops stung like tears in Sparrow's eyes. "Oh, Ivinchi, thank you. We're the lucky ones, just to be here. You know we don't need a gift."

"But, you do. A little thing, not so little." Ivinchi reached into a fold of his voluminous silken robe, and his clawed fingers retrieved a small, intricately embroidered turquoise silk drawstring bag.

Sparrow reached for the bag with trembling fingers, her breath choked inside her throat. She tugged at the drawstring, opened the bag . . .

And, inside, she found a perfect jade-and-silver fish-creature, serpentine and winged. Brilliant emerald jewel-eyes glinted up at her, twinkling sardonically as if the little amulet were laughing. Intricately scaled, the little figure twined around her fingers, and its drooping silver mustache whiskers brushed against her palm.

Her boy Thistle laughed to see it. "Is it alive?" he asked.

"It is most cunningly wrought, is it not? We believe Urtho himself crafted this little thing, imbued it with power. Have you seen such a creature in life, or is it truly only myth? It is called Dragon, and it calls Water to Earth."

Sparrow watched the little silver sculpture dance in her hand, speechless with awe.

"You seek the spirit of water, dear Sparrow love. Dragon calls to dragon, in the depths of Evendim."

Lake Evendim.

Sparrow couldn't restrain a gasp.

Ivinchi's attention turned to Cloudbrother. "You seek water for your own suffering land, Lord Herald.

My master, Vykaendys-First, earnestly wishes to aid you in your quest. Our balladmakers already sing of the Cloud Born, the Land Healer. May you heal your own land, silent one, great one."

Abilard spoke, his words warm as sunshine inside Sparrow's heart. *:Deepest gratitude, Lord Tyrill. Truly our fates are linked. The Council of Valdemar was wise to send us here. In your healing, we are blessed.:*

Cloudbrother stirred beside Sparrow, and his arm wrapped gently, featherlight around her waist. "Lord Ivinchi, we depart for Valdemar tomorrow. We will present your gift to the Council and seek healing for our land."

Into Sparrow's mind, Cloudbrother whispered, *:I called the water down to Iftel, I can do it for the Forest of Sorrows, too. I must. I still think the answer to how to defeat my demon lies in Evendim. But maybe there is another way. No true way, right? Only the way that works . . . :*

And Cloudbrother's gentle, patient whisper, the pain hidden in his words, tore at Sparrow's heart.

They rode for Valdemar the next morning. As before, Ivinchi joined them. The rain had stopped the night before, and a brilliant rainbow arched over their heads, a promise of peace after the storm.

Reaching down like open arms, from the realms of the Star-Eyed, to embrace the land of her Beloved.

Letters from Home

Brigid Collins

The Collegium bell chimed, signaling the end of the day's lessons. By the time the metallic ring faded, the chatter of students heading for dinner had risen to fill the warm air of a late summer evening. The kitchen had made something that smelled of hickory and grease, which mingled nicely with the aroma of cut grass from the Companion's Field.

Not every student followed the delicious smells to the dining hall, though.

Holding a hand against her forehead, Herald Trainee Marli headed toward the wood-paneled hallway that led to her room. Her Companion, Taren, continued lecturing her as he'd been from the moment the bell rang.

:How do you expect to become a proper Herald if you won't exert yourself in your studies? And you shouldn't skip dinner again,: he said.

The pain behind Marli's eyes spiked, and she winced. She loved her Companion dearly, as she had ever since he had appeared on the outskirts of Fairbend and Chose her, but when he got like this, his voice scoured the inside of her skull like a stiff currying brush.

Added to the pounding headache from another fruitless lesson with her Farsight instructor—another afternoon of trying and failing to look back at the place she used to call home—Taren's nagging could do a number on her already sluggish appetite. He'd gotten worse about it lately, too. These days, the closer she came to mastering her Fetching gift, or the more praise she got when she practiced with the weapons in the Salle, the more discontented Taren got with her struggles in this one area.

The worst part was, she used to love using her Farsight back home in Fairbend, back before she'd been Chosen, back when she'd happily been the girl who would make the miller's son a good wife. She'd looked after her little farming village, seeking out small problems brewing amongst her neighbors and mediating solutions before the situations grew out of control. In fact, her use of her gift had probably helped Fairbend avoid the need of a proper Herald for a long time, which, in hindsight, mightn't have helped the village's trust issues when it came to Heralds. *That* problem had already grown wild and tangled beyond Marli's ability to sort out by the time she understood her power to see what was happening in other people's houses.

But Taren had Chosen her, and that meant she had to become a Herald herself. It meant her sweet Barret would instead marry another. It meant she no longer belonged at the place she'd always known as home.

Apparently, it also meant she had to put up with daily headaches and a Companion's constant needling. She scrubbed her hand against the bridge of her nose, willing the pain to dissipate. Her boots thunked dully against the hardwood of the hallway as she approached her own door.

:I'm doing the best I can,: she said. *:Maybe my Farsight just wasn't meant for long distance.:*

Taren's mental snort sent uncomfortable twinges across her scalp. *:I've never heard so unfounded a claim. You may be able to fool your teachers, but I know your mind, beloved. You have simply got to get over this ridiculous phobia you've developed.:*

:I'm not afraid.:

:In that case, why don't you open one of those letters? You must have a fair pile of them by now.:

The admonition came right as Marli pushed her door open, and she bit back a grunt at the sight of her cluttered room. She did, in fact, have a fair pile of letters, all unopened, stacked on her writing desk. It appeared their accumulated weight had caused an avalanche while she was away, and a few of the brown envelopes lay scattered across her floor. They were all addressed from Yerra, the Fairbend girl she'd befriended the night she left home with Taren—the girl most likely to have been given Marli's spot at Barret's side now that Marli herself was . . . unsuitable.

Scowling at the mess, Marli left the door standing open, kicked aside a growing pile of dirty laundry, and went to drop her class materials on her bed. She gave her still-rumpled bedclothes a cursory pat before dropping herself on top of them, too. The pain in her head throbbed a little less.

This wasn't like her, she knew. She'd always been a homemaker at heart, and she normally couldn't tolerate the kinds of odors thickening the air in here. The sight of clutter usually spurred her into an almost reflexive spree of neatening up.

But those letters . . . she couldn't bear to read them. Scanning their contents would make everything back home painfully real. The simple fact that she'd received nothing from anyone *but* Yerra hurt quite enough. But she couldn't bring herself to throw her friend's correspondence away unopened, either. Marli hadn't been the only one to lose her longed-for future that night. Both of them had promised to support each other as they took on the other's desired role. Yerra had kept her end up.

Marli had . . . wallowed. And the letters piling up had bled into everything else piling up, too.

At least the mail carrier hadn't slid another brown envelope under her door today. Her stomach writhed with guilt at that relief, but from a practical point of view, the lack of an extra letter would keep the clutter from spreading. Without one more letter added to the mountain, Marli could make a start at working through the ones she already had.

:The sooner you read them, the sooner you can stretch your Farsight past this absurd block you've built up,: Taren said.

The writhing in Marli's stomach gave a hard twist. A bitter taste flooded her mouth. "I haven't *blocked* anything, I just can't see that far!"

Her voice bounced off the paneled ceiling, ricocheted back to bring her headache to full force. A few more letters slid from the pile to land on the floor with a fluttery *flump*.

Marli closed her eyes. She hadn't meant to shout. She preferred to keep these conversations with Taren purely mental, even when nobody was around to overhear them.

And of course, in her single-minded haste toward her bed, she'd left her door open, which meant she'd eschewed any semblance of privacy the thin dormitory walls provided.

A soft cough from the hallway told her that her outburst had indeed been overheard.

Marli opened her eyes to find a Bardic student shuffling into view. He was a little older than her—perhaps Barret's age?—and sported a mop of brown curls. His rust-red clothes flowed loosely around his sticklike body, except across his torso, where they bunched and folded under the strap of the mailbag over his shoulder. His cheeks were flushed, and from the light whistle of his breath, Marli could tell it was more because he'd been rushing to finish his work than due to his untimely interruption of her argument with Taren.

He held a brown envelope.

Shame mingled with annoyance, driving Marli up to her feet. "Sorry about that," she said as she stumbled over a set of soiled Grays. "Companion's making a nuisance of himself. Nothing to worry about."

The Bardic student glanced past her to the mess of unopened letters, then down at the yet-to-be-delivered addition in his hand. When he lifted his eyes back to Marli's, the look of betrayal made him appear much younger than she'd originally guessed.

"You haven't opened any of them?"

The guilt churned again, but Marli forced herself to smile and hold a hand out for the letter. "Haven't had time. Life's busy at the Collegium, you know."

But the young Bard didn't hand the letter over. He drew it closer against himself, his fingers clenching enough to crumple the edges.

"You're just going to forget about her, then. Is it really so easy? She's sent you so many letters. I delivered all of those, you know, just about one every day. Don't you get how lucky you are to have someone writing you like this? Doesn't knowing she still cares about you even though you're far apart mean anything to you?"

The envelope was all but crushed by the time he finished. Though his cheeks had darkened through the tirade, his eyes had grown alarmingly bright.

Marli was no Empath, but she hadn't escaped years mediating the myriad problems of Fairbend without picking up a skill for reading people. Not that she needed any great skill to tell this young man was hurting. The guilt twisted again with the knowledge that, however unintentional, she'd been the trigger of this current bout of pain.

She could barely resist the urge to reach out to him, but she managed to keep her hands as they were: one at her side and one held out, patient.

The silence between them stretched and stretched, until finally the young man sniffed.

"Sorry," he said. His shoulders slumped, and the still-heavy bag of undelivered mail slipped forward to sway in front of his hips. "It's none of my business what you do with your mail. I just . . . sorry."

"I'm sorry, too," Marli said. "I've let my personal problems affect my manners." *Not to mention my hygiene.*

Fumbling for the doorknob, she stepped out into the hallway and shut the door behind her. Maybe if she couldn't see the effects of her moping, she'd be less inclined to continue such behavior. The smell certainly improved with the door closed.

Drawing a lungful of fresher air, she managed a genuine smile. "I'm Marli, by the way."

The Bardic student waved the brown envelope. "I know."

"Of course you do. I'm sorry. I just find it easier to be companionable with someone once you've introduced yourself. Might be that's from my country village upbringing. Some of the other Trainees say I'm hopelessly rural."

She'd fallen into the cadence of speech she used most often when solving other people's problems. The others might tease her, but not a one of them had yet proven immune to the calming effect of her country talk.

The high color faded some from the young man's cheeks, though his eyes still shone just as bright. He cleared his throat twice, shuffled his feet. Squeezed that envelope a hair tighter.

Marli let her tone grow softer. "I reckon you'd like to talk about what's eating you?"

"I'm running late already. Have to finish my rounds before I can go to dinner."

Both their stomachs grumbled discordantly. Marli couldn't help smiling, and it seemed neither could the young Bard, though he bit at his lip.

"Seems I'll have missed my dinner, too," Marli said. "Why don't we finish your round together? The kitchen's usually got some after-dinner scraps late diners can beg, and they're used to seeing me late, anyway. I know I always feel better once I've had a decent meal."

The young man relaxed a little. "Okay. I'm Simen."

"I'm happy to know you, Simen." And she was happier to have the promise of his problem to focus on. Maybe if she could help sort him out, she'd feel more ready to tackle her own malodorous mountain of issues.

Maybe. Eventually.

:You can't avoid looking back at the stables of your youth forever, beloved. What's past and done can't hurt you, you know.:

Taren was wrong, but instead of telling him so, Marli gave her full attention to her new friend. Soon enough, Taren's voice slipped from her mind, done with his lectures for today.

With everyone still gone to dinner, the dormitory hall rang with emptiness. A thin breeze flowed through windows thrown open earlier, scattering the growing chorus of cricket song and the aroma of night blooms along the corridor. But beyond Marli and Simen, no signs of human or Companion life emerged. It was a rare moment of peace in a place usually alive with activity.

Simen had yet to deliver Yerra's most recent letter, having put it back in his mailbag as they walked along his route through the Collegium.

"I'm not sure why I feel so comfortable with the idea of talking to you about this. You won't even open your girlfriend's letters."

He stooped to slide a white envelope under the door of one of Marli's neighbors.

"Yerra isn't my girlfriend. She's someone I met the night Taren Chose me. Just a friend." *Just the woman who may have already married the mate of my soul.*

Simen straightened up and blinked his surprise.

"Oh. I just assumed . . . there were so many letters. Usually that means, you know." His blinking grew more rapid, and the brightness in his eyes intensified.

"Tell me," Marli said, though she was beginning to suspect the silhouette of his story.

Simen let out a rattling breath and marched forward as if the motion of his legs would help him form the words.

"It's like this. There's a boy at home, Dreyvin, who's special to me. We've been inseparable since we were children learning the sword together. He's much better at it than me, of course." A brief smile touched his lips. "I came to Haven a year ago when I showed the Bardic talent. We've been having a lot of trouble with local bandits back home, and it's not exactly safe at the keep anymore. Mother was ecstatic to learn that I could leave. But I couldn't convince anyone to let me bring Dreyvin along with me, not the Collegium, not Mother, not even Dreyvin. Mother said she needed him to stay and help protect everyone, and Dreyvin agreed with her. We promised to keep in touch."

He bent to slide another envelope under another door. Marli noticed the way his hand trembled.

"You've heard nothing from him, I gather?"

"Not a single line. I've sent him hundreds of notes. He gets all of my best work, you know? Every time I come up with a witty lyric or write a poem that really captures the way I feel, I send it to him. But he—"

Simen clamped his jaw shut. Marched onward.

Marli followed, drifting behind like a watchful ghost. What should she say? What would give comfort without being an empty reassurance?

"Perhaps he simply hasn't had a chance to respond," she finally said.

"Like you haven't had a chance to read your friend's correspondence?" Simen laughed without humor. "I just want to know at this point. Has he moved on to someone new, or has he merely decided he's done with me now that I'm out of sight? If it's over, I want to get it over with, yeah?"

He sketched a grim smile. It lay flat across his face.

A shadow of Marli's earlier guilt moved in her belly again, but she pushed that aside. "I've the gift of Farsight. It's not so good at distance, but might be I could try to have a look?"

Now, why had she done that? *It's not so good at distance* was an understatement at best, a blatant falsehood at worst. But she couldn't help herself when someone was hurting; Barret had always said she offered more of herself in these cases than she ought.

Hopeful surprise tugged Simen's grim expression into something softer. It made him look a bit more like her Barret, but luckily the effect flickered away before she could draw the breath to gasp.

"You'd do that for me? I thought all you Heralds would be too busy to help with something so unimportant."

"It's important to you, though." Marli said. "I'm willing to try. But I'm serious when I say my gift isn't much use beyond, oh, the bounds of Haven. I fear my specialty is turning out to be a little more local."

But Simen grabbed the last three letters from his mailbag and moved to make the deliveries with renewed fervor. "Any help is much appreciated, I assure you. Even a blurry look at home will be more than what I've got right now, after all."

His mood improved so rapidly Marli worried she'd promised more than she could achieve, despite her attempts to clarify her abilities. The remnants of her earlier headache stirred back to life, reminding her in no uncertain terms of her inability to stretch her Farsight. But it'd break her heart if she couldn't manage to glean some answers for Simen now.

Tentatively, she reached for Taren. His presence was

usually a great source of strength for her, and she always managed to look farthest when he helped her, but in the aftermath of one of their tiffs, his support was iffy.

:Dearest? Are you busy?:

:Not yet,: came the grumbled reply.

Marli smiled. *:Could you lend me a bit of a hand? My new friend here has got a personal problem I'd like to try to help him with.:*

:You're always finding personal problems to help with,: Taren said, but his tone was affectionate. *:Or maybe they're always finding you. What's the crisis tonight?:*

:The lover he left at home hasn't sent him a single note in a year's time.:

:Hmph. Not that you'd know a thing about that.:

:I haven't left a lover behind! Barret and I parted ways as friends.: Friends in name if not in function. A piece of Marli's heart would always live in Barret's, no matter how far apart they were.

:Friends who don't write to one another, I suppose. Does your letter carrier friend have anything to say on the matter of your mountain from Yerra? I can't imagine the sight of it was much of a balm for his *aching heart.:*

Marli made a noise, something between a grunt and a gulp, and Simen quirked an eyebrow. She waved his concern away, muttering, "Companion."

:Haven't you lectured me enough today? I'm trying to help someone who can't do for himself. Will you lend me support when I try my Farsight for him, or not?:

Taren hesitated a long moment, and Marli imagined him swaying side to side with indecision in the Companion's Field. *:If you manage to see something of use for him, will you promise to follow his brave example and look back at Fairbend?:*

:Why would I do that? I already know what I'd see, and there's nothing I can do about any problems hap-

pening there, anyway. Fairbend is Yerra's to care for now.: She'd swallowed that bitter pill once already, forced it down her dry throat that night on the outskirts of her home, and reaped what benefit it had to offer in the form of her life here at the Collegium. Taking another dose would spoil what good that unwanted medicine had done her.

Taren's voice gained a dull edge, an unhidden disappointment. *:I can't help you if you won't help yourself. Ask for my aid when you're ready to face this thing you've built up of your old home.:*

His words faded at the end, as though he'd turned his back on her. Marli saw him cantering across the Field, heading for a cluster of other white horselike figures.

She pressed her lips together and willed herself not to scream. She had no pillow handy to catch a scream leastways. Instead, she banished the images—she'd been using her Farsight without intending to, curse it—and put a smile on before turning to Simen.

The boy was watching her, his curly head tilted to the left, the brown envelope from Yerra held in both hands. The crinkles of his earlier abuse still stood stark on the paper, but no trace of the anger that had led to their creation remained in Simen's face.

Unaware of how Marli's Companion had just walked away from her, he smiled. "Why don't we head to the kitchen now? You can try your Farsight for me, and I'll sit with you while you read this letter, okay?"

Marli nodded, though her mouth went dry. She'd not eaten since breakfast, but she doubted she'd be able to get anything down, least of all another dose of that old medicine.

The tables in the kitchen were smooth, solid, and sturdy in a way the dining hall tables weren't. Though they were built of the same wood, Marli thought—nice reliable oak with dark knots and dusky whorls—the kitchen tables showed their use for good, honest work. They lacked varnish, and thus showed the stains of a hundred spills despite clearly having been wiped clean with vigor twice as often. Knives and scouring sand had left grooves along the surface, easy for a late-dining Trainee to run a fingernail along absently while listening to the clatter and clangs of the kitchen staff cleaning up for the evening.

Most of the staff had left by now, and they'd banked all the fires but one stove. Marli and Simen were told to clean their own dishes once they were finished.

It felt as though the two of them were alone in the world, stranded within a single, flickering patch of light in the darkness.

Simen sat across from her, and the brown envelope lay propped against a plate of sliced bread between them.

Marli did her best to pretend the letter wasn't there, focusing instead on the spiced barley and pork the cooks had rescued for them. She managed, despite her worries, to take in a good amount of her late dinner. The food felt heavy and warm in her belly, not uncomfortable, and her earlier headache had faded away to a mere whisper of discomfort. A readiness uncurled in her, a willingness to try her Farsight at distance once again today. She felt she'd achieve a little something, at least. She had a real reason to look this time, someone who needed what information she could find. It was more motivation than her lessons gave her.

Curling her fingers around Simen's, she smiled. "Let's try it, shall we? If I manage to see anything, then you'll know, once and for all. Get it over with, right?"

All the excitement Simen had displayed as they finished his deliveries together had disappeared over the course of their meal. The shadows draped over his face made him look haggard. His voice, when it came, was very small.

"Maybe this is a bad idea."

Marli sat back. "We don't have to if you don't want."

Simen blew air out his nose and turned his face towards the stove. "It's just, now that we come to it . . . what will I do if he really *doesn't* love me anymore? He's all I've ever wanted, but if he doesn't . . ."

"We can do it some other time, when you're ready."

"I thought I *was* ready." His gaze grew harder, as if the stove had done him wrong. "What if I'm never ready? Or worse, what if I'm ready just in time for it to be too late?"

"You'll look when the time is right for you to look."

Finally, Simen turned his furrowed brow on her. "How am I supposed to know when that is? You can't tell me. You don't know yourself."

He flicked at the brown envelope, sending it skittering across the table. The corner jabbed into the skin of Marli's forearm and bounced back.

Marli worked to keep her tone even. "I know exactly what I'll read in these letters. Looking won't change it or make it hurt any less. But even if I didn't have my own problems to sort through, I couldn't tell you when the time is right for you. Only you can know. That's what I keep trying to tell Taren, my Companion, but he won't stop pushing. It makes me so—so—well," she huffed, blinking a sudden blurriness from her vision. Was it truly so difficult for Taren to understand that she needed his support no matter her decision? Didn't he trust her to know what the right step was for herself?

For a few agonizing heartbeats, she ached to feel—just one more time!—Barret's strong arm around her shoulders, his breath against her cheek, his fingers twined with hers as he sat silent but so comfortingly *there* with her while she grappled with the problems of Fairbend.

The urge to reach back to the piece of herself that still lingered within Barret's heart grew unbearable for the space of a few ragged breaths.

No one would *ever* love her the way he did.

Marli closed her eyes and filled her lungs. Then she emptied them slowly, focusing herself, grounding herself as her instructors had taught her. She was here, now, with Simen's problem to deal with.

She opened her eyes. Simen was looking at the brown envelope and biting his lip again.

Marli reached for his hand once more. "I simply don't push people when they're not ready."

A log in the stove fell, and the fire popped and brightened. For a moment, their little island of light expanded, and the shadows around them recoiled. Then the spray of embers drifted down to join the ash. The circle of light closed in once more.

Simen lifted his eyes to meet Marli's, and he turned his hand so his palm was flush with hers. He licked his lips, opened his mouth. Closed it. Opened it again. Moisture trickled between their hands.

And as he teetered on the precipice of his indecision, Marli remained solid, still, *there,* the deep-rooted tree that would support him whichever way he tumbled.

Midmorning the next day found Marli emerging from the Salle, her muscles singing and a sheen of sweat making her Grays stick to her skin. A cool breeze ran across the path from the Salle to the Companion's Field, and Marli turned her face to catch it. She thought she detected a hint of oncoming rain under the warm, horsey smells of the Companions, though she was no weather reader. The sky was a washed-out gray overhead.

She felt a bit washed-out gray herself.

She had some time before her next Farsight lesson. Time enough to visit Taren. They might be on the rocks at the moment, but Marli had never shirked her time with him.

The crunch of gravel under her boots became the swish of long grass as she stepped from the path to lean her elbows on the rough plank of the fence surrounding the Companion's Field. When she closed her eyes and looked out with her Farsight, she found Taren already cantering toward her.

:Good morning, beloved,: he said, reserved.

Marli returned his greeting, and then they lapsed into silence. It wasn't uncommon for them, and, Marli remembered, it hadn't been uncommon between herself and Barret, either. Sometimes when two people knew each other better than they knew anyone else, a few quiet seconds spent together reflected that bond better than a thousand words spoken aloud.

Taren broke the silence first. *:I am sorry I chose not to help you last night. I hope you were able to find something of comfort for your Bard friend?:*

Marli tapped the toe of her boot against the fence post. *:He decided not to look back. He wasn't ready.:*

:Truly?: Taren bobbed his head in surprise. *:But I thought he was set upon it. I thought the only reason he hadn't already was, as you said, he couldn't do for himself.:*

Marli kept up her tapping, the dull thump resonating through her tired body. *:We humans are good at telling ourselves things are one way if saying it will save ourselves from a bit of pain. We say "I would if only I could" until the moment we suddenly can. It might not make sense to you, since you've never really left your home . . . :*

She nodded in the direction of the stables, where other Companions frolicked or lounged together.

:Leaving home—truly leaving it with no intention to return—it has an effect on the people we leave behind. Sometimes it changes the way people think about us. Sometimes—:

She gasped as the thought hit her. Barret hadn't been the most vocal on the subject of Heralds in Fairbend, but he had agreed, at least in part, with the general distrust.

What if he thought those awful, hateful things about *her* now?

All this time she'd thought the thing that had held her back from reading Yerra's letters was the confirmation of Barret's marriage to Yerra in her place, but if that were true, she would have been able to brace herself and get it over with, as Taren had begged her to do for so long now. Her once-betrothed could marry another and still hold that piece of her in his heart, after all.

No, in truth, her fear was no different from Simen's. It was the unknown factor: what would Marli do if Barret, the sweet, romantic, supportive partner of her old life, no longer found her worthy of his love? How could she handle it if she had been banished from him the same as she likely had been from her home, her family?

After all, not a single one of the mountain of letters she'd received had been from him.

The pain of such a possibility washed over her and left her struggling to get air into her lungs. She clenched both hands around the fence railing. Rough splinters dug into her palm, but she didn't care.

Taren stepped forward and nuzzled her hair. The touch of his warm, hay-and-honey breath on Marli's skin felt so much like Barret's embrace. *:I'm sorry. You're right. I have never . . . lost anyone that way. I don't know how much it hurts.:*

Marli tangled her fingers in his mane as her eyes burned.

The moment stretched on, silent but for the whisper of the wind and the distant whicker of the other Companions. Then the Collegium bell rang, and the chatter and laughter of students shifting between classes filled the air.

Taren pulled back and fixed his blue eyes on hers. *:If you don't want to do your Farsight lesson today . . . :*

Marli chewed her lip. She could use a break. Even a single day without attempting to make her Farsight do what it didn't want to would help. The idea of lounging here with Taren held a whole cartload of appeal. Or she could use her Farsight to find someone nearby who needed her help. If she had a few hours to bury her revelation under someone else's problems—

"Marli!"

Marli turned to see Simen running up the gravel path. His face was flushed with the effort, and when he reached her, he had to put his hands on his knees for a few moments while he caught his breath. Finally, he straightened, adjusted his rust-red uniform, and nodded.

"Do you have a minute? I'm ready. To look back, I mean. I'm ready."

Marli blinked. "Already? But last night you were so—"

Simen scowled. "You said we could do it anytime, so long as I was ready. I'm ready now. If you have class here, I can wait until you have time, but I don't want to wait longer than that."

"Of course," Marli said, "I'm just surprised is all. It's—it's a big thing you're wanting to find out. I expected you would need more time."

"I thought I would, too. But something you said last night really stuck with me. You said you knew what you'd find if you read any of your friend's letters, and that looking won't change it or make it hurt any less. Well, I'm in the same place, but opposite, you see? I don't know what's going on at home, and so I'm imagining a thousand scenarios, each worse than the last. But my not looking won't change whatever it is that's truly happening, right? So I might as well look, and know, and then I can find a way to deal with the situation instead of being angry at something that's only in my imagination."

Marli knew she was staring, but she couldn't help it. Simen's eyes were bright again, but the light wasn't due to barely constrained tears this time. He really was ready.

Marli's throat tightened, and she swallowed painfully. A small part of her wanted to convince Simen that he really ought to take a little more time to think carefully about his decision. She couldn't deny the idea of having a partner in putting off the moment of pain had been comforting.

But she simply wasn't that selfish. If the power to help him was in her, she had to try to use it. The boy was ready, he said, and she believed him.

He looked *so much* like Barret, standing there with that firm look in his eyes, that hard set to his jaw.

Somehow, she said, "I might not be able to see that far, remember."

But Taren stretched his neck over the fence and pressed his nose against her shoulder. *:I will help you focus, beloved, so you can help your friend. I believe in you.:*

A warmth washed over her, as if the summer rain she'd wondered about had indeed begun to fall. It felt . . . *like* Barret's support, but different. It was solidity of another kind.

It wasn't the kind to hold her if she fell, but instead the kind to lift her closer to the height she wanted to reach.

Letting out a breath, Marli relaxed and grounded herself in the here and now. Then she held a hand out to Simen.

"Okay," she said. "Let's look back."

Exhausted, but pleasantly full from a proper dinner time, Marli entered her dormitory and waded into the swamp of dirty laundry and clutter. The weighty air tugged at her limbs, beckoning her to lie down. The day had been too long to do any more work tonight, after all. She'd gotten a lot done.

She'd even managed to look beyond the borders of Haven, *far* beyond, to a little keep beset by bandits. With Taren's help, she'd wielded her Farsight with enough control to see a young man as clearly as if he stood right beside her, and she'd watched him struggle to perform a slightly different dance of protection than the one he'd originally stayed behind to perform. He'd used a shield in the clash against the bandits but no sword, and he wore his homespun shirt with the right sleeve pinned beneath his armor. She'd watched him return to his quarters after the fight, had seen him read a poem written on a well-worn and oft-folded leaf of paper before grappling with the new envelope he'd received that day, and had held her breath as he tried in vain to craft a legible response left-handed.

She'd held Simen up as he'd clung to her and cried out his equal grief and happiness.

All of that was worthy of a rest, right?

But Marli's heart still hummed with Taren's love and her pride at Simen's show of bravery. In the face of those highs, the heavy miasma she'd lived with for weeks suddenly took on an unbearable stench.

She strode to her window and threw it open, letting the fresh evening breeze sweep in. Her curtains fluttered, and the papers on her desk rasped against one another.

With steady hands, Marli gathered every brown envelope from where they'd spilled and stacked them in neat piles on her desk. She couldn't open any yet, but she let her gaze linger on them a moment before turning her attention to the rest of her cluttered workspace.

Simen's bravery was inspiring. He'd gone into the endeavor knowing that he must accept whatever outcome he got, understanding that ignoring a source of pain wouldn't make it melt away. His examination had yielded a bittersweet result, but already his spirit was rising to the occasion. He'd abandoned dinner after an idea for a new song to send to his wounded lover drove him to distraction.

Marli was beyond happy for him.

She didn't think she was quite so brave as him yet,

but somewhere in her heart she felt she'd make it there eventually. One day, with Taren behind her, she'd be strong enough to turn her full-range Farsight back toward the place she'd once called home.

One day she'd be ready to see if Barret still held her in his heart, or if he did not.

The pile of papers yielded to her flurry of neatening up, and beneath a sheaf of completed history reports, she found a few blank sheets. Her ink well and pen had rolled behind a stack of textbooks on the floor, but once Marli rescued them they took up their proper home.

With a blank sheet, a full pen, and an open desk before her, Marli sank into her chair.

Might be she was ready to do one thing, at least.

She picked up the pen.

Dear Yerra . . .

Friendship's Gift

Anthea Sharp

"Will I be all right?" asked the young Herald Trainee sitting on the examining table.

His Grays were smudged with mud, and he looked rather sheepish about losing his balance while trying to show off by walking atop the fence rails of Companion's Field. Luckily, his friends had hurried him to the House of Healing the moment it was clear he'd hurt himself.

Healer Trainee Tarek Strand examined the injured young man, his fingers tracing a gentle line over the Trainee's broken arm. Orange-tinged light pulsed faintly in Tarek's vision, but the fracture wasn't a bad one.

"This should heal up just fine," he said. "Now, take a deep breath—I'm going to work on mending the bone."

The young man complied, and Tarek concentrated, sending healing energy from his hands into the injured area. The orange light faded to yellow, the pulsing smoothing to a steadier glow.

"Good," Master Adrun said from his place behind Tarek. "Your touch is getting more precise every week."

The young man grinned. "My arm feels better already."

Tarek smiled back. He was glad the break had been a simple one, especially as Master Adrun had started observing his work during his Tuesday morning volunteer shift at the House of Healing. Last week, he'd treated an older woman with a persistent cough, and he'd had a difficult time diagnosing what was wrong. He still wasn't certain he'd done everything he could for her, though Master Adrun had seemed to approve of the yarrow tea and additional rest he'd prescribed.

Still, Tarek preferred more straightforward problems—like this young man's broken arm.

"Make sure you have plenty to eat and drink over the next few days," he told the Trainee. "You need to replace the energy your body is using to heal. Also, I'll give you a sling to wear."

Suiting action to words, he went to the supply cupboard in the small examining room and pulled out a sling, swiftly helping the young man into it. A few quick adjustments, and Tarek was satisfied with the fit.

"Come back tomorrow so the Healers can check your progress," Tarek told his patient.

"And no more walking the fence rails," the Master Healer added, his voice dry.

"Yes, Master." The Trainee hopped down from the table, his arm clearly no longer paining him. "Thank you."

As soon as he was gone, Master Adrun turned to Tarek.

"Good work," he said. "Don't forget to write up your notes before you forget the details. Perhaps next week will hold some more interesting medical challenges."

Tarek hoped not. While he was gaining confidence in his Healing Gift, he was still a Trainee, and a fairly new one at that, even though he was the oldest student in the Healer's Collegium by several years. He'd come to terms with the fact that his Gift had chosen to manifest much later than was normal. Although, he had to admit, it was a bit annoying to tower over most of his younger classmates. At least he'd moved up a few class levels and was finally no longer among the absolute beginners.

Master Adrun paused at the door. "I'd like to see you in my office later this week. Will Friday afternoon suit?"

"Have I . . ." Tarek swallowed sudden anxiety. "Have I done anything wrong?"

"No," the Master Healer said, although his expression was unsmiling. "It's more along the lines of an evaluation. You might want to take a look at your textbooks beforehand—especially your herbal."

"I will," Tarek said, his ribcage squeezing with worry.

Was he falling behind? Had the Healers Collegium decided they'd moved him up too quickly? Perhaps Master Adrun was concerned he wasn't prepared for the examinations later that year, when the fifth-year class would be tested on their knowledge of Healing.

The day-long exam sounded grueling, but Tarek had plenty of time left to study. He wanted to do well.

Secretly, he hoped to do well enough to move up another class rank and be one step closer to earning his Greens and becoming a full-fledged Healer.

Then what? The question loomed.

He'd been expected to return to Strand Keep at the end of his schooling—which had *not* been supposed to include additional years due to his inconveniently late-blooming Healing Gift. Now, though, his world had broadened. Being the lord of a border keep seemed more of a tedious duty than the path he wanted his life to take.

Besides, he'd made friends at the Collegium. One, in particular, he hated the thought of leaving . . .

Whatever his feelings for Bard Shandara Tem, however, she never treated him as anything more than a friend. Tarek was—mostly—content with this situation. With an inaudible sigh, he finished up his notes, then left the House of Healing and headed to the Common Room for lunch.

On his way across the courtyard, he paused to take a breath of the smoke-scented fall air. The sun felt good on his face, though frost lingered in the north-facing shadows.

"Hello, Tarek!" The bright voice made him smile as he turned to greet the girl he affectionately thought of as his new little sister.

"Lyssa, good day." He nodded to the lunch basket she was carrying. "Where are you headed with your picnic?"

"I'm joining Shandara." She glanced at him, then back down at the cobblestones.

He gave her a close look. "Is everything all right?"

It was a little strange that she hadn't invited him to join them. Since the events of the summer, he and Lyssa often shared meals with Shandara. In fact, spending time with them was often the high point of his day.

"Oh, yes, everything's fine." Lyssa blinked up at him. "Well—I'll see you later."

She hurried off, and Tarek watched her go, his chest unaccountably tight.

Don't be silly, he told himself. Probably they hadn't invited him because they wanted to indulge in girl talk. He shouldn't read anything into it.

Still, his cheese roll was dry and tasteless as he sat alone in the Common Room. A number of his classmates waved to him, but they had friends of their own, and nobody moved over to join him.

A few Herald Trainees nodded as they passed, but the ones his age were either close to getting their Whites, or were already out on their first-year Circuits. The Masters generally didn't fraternize with the students, which made sense. And the friends Tarek had made among the Blues had all graduated the prior year and returned to their noble families.

He still corresponded regularly with his former classmate Ro, but their paths had diverged so much, Tarek wasn't sure how much longer that would continue. Especially as Ro was now courting a young woman and seemed quite content to settle down and manage the lesser estate his father had gifted him—surprising, given what a troublemaker he'd been at the Collegium.

Tarek ran his hands through his brownish-red hair. Sometimes he wished for those simpler days when he'd scoffed at the Gifts and had known that returning to govern Strand Keep was his destiny.

Now, though, his life had become increasingly complex. Plus, he had a test to study for. And a mysterious evaluation with Master Adrun in two days.

With a grimace, he drank the last bit of tea in his mug, then headed for his room. His herbalism textbook awaited.

"Are you sure Tarek doesn't suspect anything?" Shandara Tem asked Lyssa as the two shared lunch in her rooms.

The younger girl grinned up at her. "Master Adrun said Tarek thinks he's being called in for an evaluation. Though I did feel bad just leaving him standing there in the courtyard. He looked so glum."

Shandara frowned, her Empathy pricking. She didn't like excluding Tarek, but how else were they going to plan?

"We'll make it up to him, later," she said. "Now, tell me about your progress . . ."

Tarek didn't see Shandara at dinner or before class the next morning. He tried to shake off the notion she was avoiding him. Still, it was difficult to silence the voices of worry in his head. Especially when he saw her across the courtyard and, despite the fact he was sure she'd spotted him, she quickly hurried off in the opposite direction.

Finally, at lunch, he caught her leaving the Common Room.

"Shan," he said, determined to connect with her. "I haven't seen you much the past few days. How are you doing?"

She gave him a distracted smile. "I'm well, Tarek—but I don't have time to chat right now."

"Oh?" He tried to keep his tone nonchalant, even as his spirits fell.

Her expression softened. "I'm late for rehearsal—but we'll talk soon. I promise."

"Do you have a performance coming up?" In the past, she'd always invited him to her concerts, no matter how informal. Was she tired of his friendship? The question was like a weighted stone in his belly.

"It's for a . . . private party." She gave him an apologetic look. "I'd invite you if I could, but . . ."

"I understand." He pulled in a breath, his mood easing somewhat. "You can tell me about it after."

"I will, I promise. See you later, Tarek."

He nodded and watched her go, still unsettled but not as fretful as he'd been.

A small hand slipped into his, and he glanced down to see Lyssa beside him.

"I'm starving," she announced. "Do you plan on standing there all day, or are we going to get some lunch?"

"Lunch, definitely." He resisted the urge to tousle her hair.

They collected their food, and Tarek was glad to see that, along with a hearty potato stew, pocket pies were on offer. He wasn't a lad of ten any longer, but he loved the sweet pastries all the same.

Winking, Lyssa grabbed two off the tray.

"One for later," she said, stuffing the extra away.

He practiced restraint, mindful of his role-model status as an older student, and followed her to the nearby table.

"Are you worried about tomorrow?" she asked, between slurps of stew.

"A little," he admitted. Truthfully, the meeting with Master Adrun loomed, a storm cloud on the horizon, growing larger and more troubling by the hour.

"I'm sure it will be fine," she said with the confidence of a child. "He probably just wants to see how you're doing, being the oldest student and all."

"Ah yes, I'm practically an old man now." Tarek shook his head at her. "Look at how white my hair is turning."

Lyssa stuck her tongue out at him. "I'll start calling you grandfather, if you like."

"Ah, no. Wait until next year at least, sprout. Now, tell me how your tutorials are going."

Lyssa had an unusual Gift—one that nobody had suspected until Tarek and Shandara had helped uncover the truth that she was a Mindhealer. As a result, in addition to her normal classes at the Healer's Collegium, she had special lessons with the Heralds, who were better equipped to teach her certain aspects of her Gift.

"They work me hard," she said. "The Heralds are so serious."

"What, and Healers aren't? If you wanted fun, you should have been a Bard."

"As if we have any choice in our Gifts." She rolled her eyes. "Speaking of which, I need to go study for my next tutorial."

She picked up her dishes, gave him a quick kiss on the cheek, and dashed off before he could thank her for her company at lunch.

And speaking of studying, he'd best take a look at his books himself. Despite Lyssa's blithe assurances, he couldn't believe that the evaluation with Master Adrun was going to be easy.

The next day at breakfast, Tarek couldn't manage more than a few bites of porridge before losing his appetite entirely. He settled for a mug of strong, sweet tea, and plodded to his morning class, a lecture on treating wounds in the field.

As he stepped into the classroom, he caught the tail end of a question.

"—at the party tonight?" one of his classmates asked.

"Oh!" another exclaimed. "There's Tarek. Hello. Did you have a nice breakfast?"

Conversations stopped around the room, and everyone looked at him.

Tarek blinked, pausing in the doorway. He felt like a plant being evaluated for its medicinal properties. "What?" he asked.

"Nothing," the first student said. Everyone around him nodded in vigorous agreement.

The awkward moment was broken by the arrival of Master Healer Swindon, who briskly began the class with a series of questions on bone fractures. Tarek was glad to draw on his recent experience, and he felt as though, in that aspect of his life at least, he was on solid ground.

Everything else, though . . . It seemed as though the entire Collegium was set on making him lose his balance.

When the class broke for lunch, he trudged to his rooms. He didn't want to have to see Shan avoid him or Lyssa dart off somewhere. And besides, he wasn't hungry. Maybe after his meeting with Master Adrun, he could nip down to the kitchens and beg some bread and cheese.

That wasn't for a good two hours yet. In the meantime, he might as well crack open his books . . .

Tarek awoke with a start, heartbeat thudding. He'd fallen asleep while studying, the weight of his herbalism tome heavy on his chest. What time was it?

He glanced at the guttering candle on his shelves, his panic receding a bit when he realized he wasn't late for his evaluation. There was enough time to splash water on his face and drag a comb through his hair. He pulled at his tunic, the olive-colored fabric slightly wrinkled, and decided it would do.

Then, an anxious knot in his chest, he headed for Master Adrun's study.

The sky had darkened, drizzle spitting against the windows, which matched Tarek's mood perfectly. The sconces along the hallway to the Master's study weren't bright enough to erase the gray smudges of shadow filling the air. Tarek felt as though he were breathing that dimness, charcoal weighting his lungs. His steps slowed.

Finally, he stood before Master Adrun's door. He knocked, the wood unyielding under his knuckles.

"Come in," the Master Healer called.

Tarek entered the study.

A cozy fire burned on the hearth, though it did nothing to erase the chill inside him. Master Adrun sat at his desk, frowning intently at some paperwork.

"Sit," the Master said, indicating the chair. "I just need a moment."

Throat dry, Tarek perched on the cushionless chair. He waited while the Healer shuffled through the pages on his desk. After a solid minute had ticked by, Master Adrun nodded and pushed the papers to one side. Steepling his fingers, he gave Tarek a considering look.

"I'm sure you're aware your position in the Healer's Collegium is unique," he said. "You seem to be handling it well, but I'd like to hear your perspective on being the oldest student we currently have enrolled."

"Ah." Tarek leaned forward, trying to muster his thoughts. He'd come prepared to answer questions about the properties of herbs and plants, to discuss the manipulation of Healing energies. Not to be quizzed on the particularities of his situation.

But still, he was a lord's son, as well as a student at the Healer's Collegium, and his early lessons in diplomacy had not entirely deserted him.

"It's not, perhaps, the easiest," he finally said. "But I can't argue with the fact that my Gift manifested so late. And, in a way, I think it's probably inspiring for the younger students to see that even someone several years older struggles with the lessons and with mastering their Gift. I also hope that, having a bit more life experience, I bring some additional insight into the classes."

Master Adrun nodded. "I'm not certain any of her other classmates could have helped Lyssa with her problem. Your perception and thoughtfulness has not gone unnoticed."

Tarek breathed a silent sigh of relief and felt his shoulders relax. So far, it didn't seem as though they were planning to kick him out of the Collegium.

Master Adrun glanced at the window, where rain streaked the glass, and frowned.

"Very well—I suppose I'll quiz you on your herbal studies now." He sounded resigned, as though he'd been hoping to avoid doing so.

The questions started out easy enough, but they soon moved to more advanced properties of medicinal plants. Tarek was sweating over a query concerning the toxicity of pain-killing barks when a knock sounded on the study door.

Master Adrun leaned back in his chair, a slight smile tugging at his lips. "Yes?" he called.

"It's Shandara. May I come in?"

"By all means."

The door opened, and Shan stepped inside. Her hair was damp from the rain, and moisture darkened her shoulders, turning her formal Scarlets a deep red.

"Hello, Tarek." She grinned at him. "How are you surviving the evaluation?"

"Er, well enough." Confused, he glanced from her to Master Adrun. Instead of being an annoyance, it seemed as though the teacher had been expecting her interruption.

"It took you long enough," the Master Healer said,

confirming Tarek's suspicions. "Poor Tarek had to answer over two dozen questions."

"I'm sorry—the rain delayed me." Shandara gestured to the window. "Along with everything else that could go wrong, of course. But we're finally ready."

"Ready for what?" Tarek said, his confusion mingling with a sudden, irrational hope. His heartbeat sped, and the room suddenly felt much warmer. Could it be? No. Certainly not.

"For *this*." Master Adrun reached beneath his desk and brought forth a stack of emerald-dyed cloth. "Tarek Strand, it's my great pleasure to present you with your first set of Greens. Welcome to the ranks of Healer. You are now an official graduate of the Collegium."

With a whoop of delight, Shandara bent and gave Tarek a warm hug. He returned it, blinking back the moisture pricking his eyelids.

"High time!" she said.

"I . . ." Tarek swallowed, still trying to believe it. He glanced at the pile of folded Greens in his lap. "I don't know what to say. Thank you."

"Thank *you*, Healer Tarek," the Master said. "You have faced a difficult path with grace and maturity, and the Healer's Collegium is richer for it. Now go change. I believe the party is waiting on your presence to begin."

"The party?" Tarek turned to Shandara.

"Of course." She smiled him. "The planning was a bit complicated, but we managed to get everything together, despite one thing after another."

"Ending with the rain," Master Adrun said. "I didn't mean to test you quite so thoroughly on your herbal knowledge, Tarek, but Shandara needed time to move the preparations from outside into the Herald's Collegium. I understand it was rather an undertaking."

"Just how big is this party?" Tarek asked, his suspicions prickling. At last, everything was starting to make sense—Shandara and Lyssa's preoccupation, the other students' strange behavior, Master Adrun's surprise "evaluation."

"Originally, we were going to have a small gathering here in Master Adrun's office," Shandara said. "But then some of your classmates got wind of it, as did your old instructors when you were a Blue, and, well, it turned out that practically the entire Collegium wanted to come and celebrate with you. We'd planned to set up tents in Companion's Field to accommodate everyone."

"That's . . . quite an event." Tarek was stunned. *That* many people wanted to congratulate him?

"There is one more thing," the Master Healer said. "Although you are now a full Healer, we'd like you to remain at the Collegium for a few more years, to make sure we fill in any knowledge gaps. However, myself and the rest of the Healer's Collegium agree that, at this point, experience is by far your best teacher. Is that acceptable?"

Unable to keep from smiling, Tarek glanced at Shandara. She grinned back at him, her eyes twinkling.

Stay at the Collegium, as her peer and friend? His heart expanded at the thought.

"Absolutely," he said.

Master Adrun let out a cough that sounded suspiciously like a laugh. "Excellent. Now, you'd best go don your new Greens, Healer Tarek. You have a celebration to attend."

Attired in his emerald-green finery, Tarek strode into the Herald's Hall to cheers and applause. Part of him wanted to blush and stammer, but his border-lord blood kept his chin high, his smile wide. Besides, Shandara walked at his side. The knowledge of her support made him feel as though he could tackle any challenge, solve any problem that life threw in his path.

His surprise and delight doubled when his old friend Ro stepped forward, his fiancée on his arm.

And it tripled when he saw his mother and little sister waiting. Shandara pressed his arm.

"Go make your greetings," she said softly. "I have music to provide. I'll find you later."

She hurried off to where two other Bards waited on a small stage. Soon the sound of harp and vielle and hand drum swirled through the room, brightening the already festive atmosphere. Long tables lined the walls, piled with food and drink, and it seemed that everyone Tarek had ever met at the Collegium was there.

He joined his mother and sister, not surprised to find that his father had elected to stay home at Strand Keep. Although Lord Strand had come to grudgingly accept Tarek's new skill, he did not entirely approve of the Gifts. Not that the Gifts needed a curmudgeonly lord to accept their existence—as Tarek's own Healing Gift had more than demonstrated.

Ro thumped him on the back and told everyone within earshot the tale of how Tarek had saved his life. Toasts were drunk, much food was consumed, and part of the hall was cleared for dancing.

Through it all, Tarek was aware of Shandara, playing her harp and singing. Every time he glanced her way, she was looking at him, a smile on her face.

Lyssa grabbed his hand and pulled him into a lively reel.

"You would not believe it," she said. "Everything that could go wrong in planning your party, did. Word barely reached your family in time, and then *so* many people were invited, we were worried someone would let it slip. Then the kitchens made the pocket pies one day too early, and then the rain. Plus, we both felt terrible about keeping secrets from you."

"I forgive you," he said.

"Shan was afraid you'd think we didn't like you anymore." Lyssa made a face. "Wasn't that silly of her?"

"My feelings were a little hurt," he admitted.

"They were?" She looked at him in surprise. "But we're family. We wouldn't stop liking you, no matter what happened. Now *you're* the one being silly."

"I suppose I am." Tarek shook his head. In retrospect, he'd let fear and worry get the better of him. "It just shows there's always another side to the story, doesn't it?"

"You'd better remember that." Lyssa narrowed her eyes in a mock scolding. "Now that you're a big Healer and all grown up."

That made him laugh, and he lifted her off her feet, spinning her around twice before setting her down.

To no one's surprise, the party lasted well into the evening. Tarek was certain Lyssa consumed at least a quarter of the pocket pies herself—though he did contribute to the effort. The group of musicians on the stage changed. True to her word, Shandara found him, and extracted him from the circle of Healers telling stories of their travels.

"Let's go outside," he said to her. "This a grand party, but I wouldn't mind a moment to catch my breath."

"Of course," she said. "Maybe it's even stopped raining."

They stepped out of the Herald's Collegium to discover that, indeed, the sky had cleared. Twilight softened the air, and the golden curve of the full moon was just rising over the rooftops of Haven. He looked at it, and the shining silver river winding beyond, and sighed.

"Are you sorry you're confined to the Collegium for a few years yet?" Shandara asked, a solemn note in her voice.

"Sorry?" He turned to face her. "Never. I have more to learn, the Masters are right about that. But even more . . ." His nerve failed him. "I was hoping that we can continue to be friends."

Her lips tilted up, the bright moon reflected in her eyes. "More than friends, perhaps?"

"Yes." Heart pounding, he reached out and took her hands. "If you'd like."

"I would." She took a step forward, closing the space between them.

Their lips met in a soft kiss, and Tarek's pulse thumped, hard. Then settled into a new rhythm. This was where he belonged—in Haven, in the Collegium, his fingers entwined with Shandara Tem's.

"Hooray!" Lyssa barreled out the door. "I thought you two would never kiss."

Laughing, Tarek and Shandara opened their embrace and pulled her into their circle.

"You don't mind?" Shan asked. "I was worried it might make you feel left out."

Lyssa snorted. "Silly. The both of you. It's obvious you've had feelings for each other for *ages* now."

"There's a code of conduct between student and instructor," Shandara said, somewhat primly. "I couldn't break that."

"And I wouldn't have wanted you to." Tarek smiled at her. Her honor was one of the things that drew him to Shan. And her empathy, and her smile—

"Come on." Lyssa tugged at their hands. "You don't want to miss the rest of your party, Tarek."

"This has been the best part." His eyes met Shandara's, and the warmth in her gaze made him feel ten feet tall.

"Yes," she said.

"But there's still dancing," Lyssa said. "And pocket pies."

"Well then. Pies," Tarek said. "We can't let those go to waste."

Wearing his new Greens, his friends at his side, Tarek strode back into the light and music, back into the shining current of his life.

Whatever happened next, he was ready.

Confounding, Enduring, Perfect, and Strong

Ron Collins

A strange rustle of branches woke Nwah that next night, a sound that was clearly not the wind scratching through dry leaves but, instead, the hint of fabric scrubbing against bark.

Her feline ears rotated to catch the sigh of human breath. *:Kade?:* she whispered through a groggy haze.

She was haggard from the effort of calling forward the animal horde the day before. Her body ached, and her thoughts were fading almost before she had them. The ley line she searched for was buried in the remains of a ghostlike dream.

Without moving, she opened her eyes.

Kade's bedroll was across the clearing, the blanket now raised with two lumps rather than one—Kade with Winnie, his new bedmate who had left her military father behind in Tau and who, despite Nwah's natural distrust, seemed sincere in her desire to learn Kade's healing arts.

The rasp of their breathing came from under the blanket. Nwah imagined them spooned together, Kade's arm over Winnie's midriff, and felt a jealousy she didn't want to admit. It made her feel separate and alone.

The rustling came again.

Was it a marauder?

She flared her nostrils in hopes of sensing something, but the odor of the fire at the clearing's center was still overpowering, despite the coals having faded to embers hours earlier. Her lips pressed against the sharpness of her teeth. Muscles around her eyes grew tight, and she flexed her claws. Her shoulders and hindquarters ached with the strain of recent abuse.

She should have known better than to send the pack away.

Maakdal and the rest of the *kyree* had answered her call to save Kade. They would have stayed for as long as she needed them, but she was embarrassed at her helplessness, and Maakdal, the pack's alpha male, had been preening and presenting in the ways alpha males do when they have things in mind beyond purely protecting their dens.

The memory of his maleness made fur raise around her neck.

She imagined the flat weight of his body on top of hers, the hardness of his fangs against the back of her neck. For a moment she forgot how much it would hurt to move.

Even before sending them away, she felt the sway she held over Maakdal—the power she held over them all, really. Was she their queen? Their prophet, perhaps? No. Neither of those seemed right, but Nwah couldn't pretend the animal horde had not treated her like some sort of royalty—and she couldn't pretend that the idea made her uncomfortable.

When she sent them away, she had explained to Kade that the power of the nearby ley line would protect them, that even as empty as she was, Nwah could use it against any danger that might come from the woods.

She could manage, she told him as the horde retreated.

Now she knew better.

The truth was that she had sent them away simply because the weight of expectation had been too great. The pressure of a thousand eyes had made her feel exposed, and the strength of Maakdal's desire had felt dangerous in ways she didn't like, and in ways she didn't trust herself to deal with.

Now, while her body was weak, her mind was apparently worse.

Try as she might, Nwah couldn't find a handle strong enough to grapple the ley line.

More rustling came, and again she sensed nothing beyond odor of the campfire. Damnation.

:Kade?: she said too softly.

She looked to the bedroll again.

Her heart pounded.

She would never forgive herself if her stupid pride caused them trouble, but waking Kade for no reason would be embarrassing, too.

From five points around the clearing, the woods erupted.

:Kade!: she screamed, yowling against pain as she rose up.

Kade woke, groggily flinging his blanket to the side, but tangling himself in a mass of legs and feet and elbows.

Voices rose as dark figures burst into the clearing.

Hawkbrothers?

Brigands?

At first Nwah couldn't say, but then it registered that these raiders wore a sigil—crossed swords and a boar's head. They were no rogue raiders.

She growled from deep inside as she flung herself at the dark silhouette of a man preparing to club Kade over the head. Sinking her claws into his shoulder, she bit the fleshy back part of the man's arm. He cried out, and, as his blow missed, the two of them fell into the woods with an impact that knocked Nwah's breath away.

Bootsteps thudded around the clearing. Heavy blows landed.

The man elbowed Nwah in the ribs as he stood to run. Her lungs ached as she drew an empty breath and tried to get her body to work.

Her vision watered, and she sucked in harder as she willed herself to stand, but instead she stumbled and crashed headfirst into a rough mound of dry peat.

Harsh grunts and the clamoring of struggle rang in her ears.

Winnie screamed in a manner that made Nwah imagine her defending Kade.

The sound of the fight grew more rugged.

Nwah steadied herself, whining in pain and blinking her wavering vision away, still trying to breathe.

"Here!" a muffled voice called.

"Got her," said another.

"Go!" called a third.

Hurried boot fall echoed through the woods.

Finally, she could draw a full breath. A moment later she could stand without her knees buckling too much. A careful series of strides brought her back to the camp to find Kade standing alone in the now silent clearing, the side of his face running with blood that glistened in the darkness, his arm held at an angle.

:Winnie,: he said, his eyes wide in the darkness. *:They took Winnie.:*

Still shaken, Nwah stepped gingerly to the edge of the firepit. Embers warmed her as she shook the taste of dry peat from her maw.

She was as confused as she was startled.

Her senses were up, though, her hackles engaged in full.

The woods around her tingled with the nighttime, and now that her blood was pumping, her body seemed to be stronger.

The ley line was stronger too.

It seemed to taunt her from a distance.

Something about that bothered her. She wished her magic was something more than instinctive. She wished she understood it better. But her learning was self-taught, her gains all based on trial and error. The gap in her understanding made her unhappy.

:Did you hear me?: Kade said. *:They took Winnie.:*

:I heard you. Are you all right?:

:I'll be fine. Just bruises and a cut. We've got to go back to Tau.:

:No, we don't,: Nwah replied.

:Yes, we do. They were obviously here on orders from her father. I should have known better. I should have gotten us farther away.:

:Those men weren't from Tau, nor were they simple raiders.:

:What do you mean?:

:They wore a sigil: She imagined the crossed swords and boar's head, and opened her link to Kade. *:That's not Tau's livery.:*

:You're right. It's not.:

He looked at her then, his expression carrying a deep sense of betrayal.

:You let it happen,: he said. *:You sent the pack away because you had your magic. But you didn't do anything to stop them.:*

:I wouldn't do that,: Nwah said.

:Really?:

Nwah began to answer, but stopped.

That's what had bothered her about the ley line.

She had been able to touch it before she dozed off—had, in fact, used the line's power to scan the area before leaving Kade and Winnie to whatever bedtime activities they were going to engage in. But when the marauders came the connection was dead. Or, if not quite dead, it was at least distant and cold.

Now it was firm again.

It took only the barest of her thoughts to bring its presence to fill her.

The ache in her shoulders as magic filled her made her feel worse.

:I wouldn't set Winnie up like that, Kade.: she finally replied. *:You know that's true. But your question has me wondering how I missed sensing them. Even more, it has me wondering why I can't feel them now.:*

Kade's expression fell. *:We have to get her back.:*

:You're not listening.:

Kade turned away, and even in the dark Nwah's vision was good enough to see muscles bunching in his neck.

Nwah wanted to explain, but she'd been with him long enough to know better. Now was not the time to engage in conversation about the meaning of a dead ley line. Waiting was annoying, yes, but he was human and therefore so much more complex than a *kyree*, or at least so much easier to enrage with the wrong word at the wrong time. Everything was so personal with him.

:I know you don't like Winnie, but I can't believe you're being so petty around her. I saw how you were with Maakdal, after all.:

Insect call rose in the time she waited before replying.

:I recognized the sigil,: she finally said.

Kade turned to her. *:Why didn't you say that in the first place?:*

She bit back a sarcastic response.

:Tell me what it is, then,: he said, coming quickly to the firepit, then kneeling beside her, his eyes again wide, his forehead beading with sweat that smelled like brine.

:The markings are from a barony somewhere nearby. I saw it long before you and I ever met—on a traveling trunk Rayn had with her. She said it was from a place she lived in for several years.:

Rayn, a female warrior from Oris, was the first human Nwah had been pair-linked with. She had been murdered, though, killed defending a friend against bandits in the Pelagirs. The rending of that link had been so traumatic that Nwah had nearly despaired herself to death. Kade's healing was all that had saved her.

After these years together, Nwah and Kade had traveled to the land of Oris as a pilgrimage of sorts, specifically so she could visit Rayn's homeland.

She remembered Rayn's trunk, saw its worn and weathered sides of wood that smelled of liniment from the inside. The workings were cast-iron that squeaked when they opened.

:Can you find this place?: he said.

The loss in his voice cut through her.

Almost as if by itself, magic from the ley line flooded her heart.

Maakdal's presence in the distance was strong, but the swirled jumble of Kade's confusion and fear was stronger.

He was frantic, his anger a churning ball of fire. He was bitter, too. He wanted Winnie back, but Nwah couldn't tell if that desire was from pure longing, or because of the humiliation he felt at his failure to protect her.

She didn't like seeing him this way.

Nwah stretched herself into the line of power with a revitalized sense of purpose. A current of magic crashed over her as if she werea rock at the bottom of a waterfall. Her pelt tingled all the way to her tail, which she thumped across her flank. She stood steady, then drew a lungful of fresh air as she reached through the woods, feeling living creatures as if they were each a part of her—a dozing woodchuck, an owl perched on its branch, deer and ferrets foraging, the massive elk to the eastern way. And, in the valley below not so far away, Maakdal and his pack of *kyree*.

Maakdal's maleness was overpowering as he stood

against the backdrop of the moon. The outline of his dark shoulders made her proud in a tribal way that she realized should have always existed within her, but had not.

She belonged with him in a way she didn't with Kade.

:Have you seen this?: she spoke to Maakdal through her magic, showing him the crossed swords and boar sigil.

He was a *kyree* with no magic, but the ley line was strong. Nwah reached her magic out and felt his thoughts. His eyes grew slitted and cold, and his huge head gave a nod that said *yes* before leaving to rouse the *kyree* around him.

Nwah turned to Kade, knowing her kin would be here soon.

:Yes,: she said. *:I can find the homelands of that sigil. Or rather, Maakdal can.:*

Maakdal spoke of the barony as he, Kade, Nwah, and twelve more of the *kyree* clan struggled to pick their way through the nighttime forest.

The woods were heavy and the land uneven, so the work was difficult even for the *kyree.* Nwah wondered how Kade, with his limited eyesight managed, then realized he really wasn't managing at all—he was stumbling and falling at nearly every step, branches and sharp fronds cutting him along the way—but he was constantly healing himself, willing himself to go forward despite the danger and pain.

Nwah tried to focus as Maakdal explained how the barony's ruling family had come to its post in the earliest and wildest days of the Eastern Empire, and how it had passed its reign down through many generations despite the turmoil around it. *:In the elder days they hunted this forest heavily,:* Maakdal said. *:Hence the wild boar under crossed swords.:*

Today its ruler was Baron Xavier Donit, a man of at least seventy.

The baroness had passed years before, so now the baron lived mostly with the aid of his two sons and one daughter—each were said to have ways with magic, as did so many in the Eastern Empire. The days when this land was as deep in magic as the Salten Sea was in water were long past, but Nwah had heard Rayn's tales. She knew magic was still here for the taking, and the strength of the ley lines that were so prevalent here did nothing to dispel those stories.

This barony was a small land, though, limited in power.

:It remains unconquered only because it's too inconsequential to matter to anyone else,: Maakdal said.

:Or,: Nwah replied, slipping around the hundredth thicket patch of the night, *:because it's too hard to get to?:*

That brought a chuff of laughter from the pack leader. She liked how Maakdal's voice sounded in the darkness. Deep and comfortable.

Nwah had regained her composure before the pack arrived well enough that his presence didn't buckle her knees as it had earlier—in fact, the essence of magic she was drawing from the ley lines allowed her to feel the wave of intimidation she was creating within him. *Strange,* she thought, *to feel this kind of influence over another.* She was just a *kyree* from the Pelagirs, wasn't she? And Maakdal was no cowering pup. The idea that he would yield to her made her anxious in a strange way, and the fact that he was traveling just a stride from her while Kade walked a few paces behind made her feel equally uneasy.

So much was changing.

She glanced at Kade. He was nervous, talking to himself at times, and clearly affected by the loss of Winnie.

:Why would they take her?: he said at one point. *:She's so early in her learning—not powerful at all . . . it must have been a mistake . . . maybe they meant to*

take me. Someone needed a healer and they came for me. Just got her by accident . . . :

The intensity of his focus on Winnie was intense.

She was about to comment on it, but then stopped short as she thought about the question she had been most avoiding.

Was their link a mistake?

At one point, Nwah was certain this link was everything either of them would need. But now Kade was entranced with Winnie, and if Nwah was honest with herself, she had been admiring Maakdal's sleek flanks and strong strides as he cut through the woods.

Were Nwah and Kade doomed to break apart?

She had already suffered one fracture. She couldn't imagine another.

:But, why not just ask me?: Kade continued to ramble. *:I would have come straight away. No need for abduction. Unless, of course, they wanted me to do something horrible. Heal a murderer? Bind a thief? Keep a man alive so they could hang him? I've heard of that happening.:*

It didn't help that Kade was almost certainly wrong.

If the kidnappers took Winnie, then this was about Winnie.

Was the baron planning to ransom her?

Would Winnie's father pay? Or maybe even the Monarch of Oris? If so, what was it that made Winnie so valuable?

Normally, she would have been debating these questions with Kade, but Kade didn't seem to be of a proper frame of mind right now so it seemed better that he not consider this angle.

Kade yammered on.

Nwah ignored him, but she pondered another question: If the Kingdom of Tau would pay a ransom to retrieve a young woman who had left her father behind, what price would Winnie pay in return?

* * *

Nwah sent an owl ahead to scout.

It returned as daylight was breaking, swooping silently over the treetops and appearing almost as if by magic out of the dusky skies. She took a perch on the thickest branch of a huge birch tree, her motion made dramatic by a cascade of brown and white feathers as she settled.

In the thin light, Nwah could see Klethas Castle in the distance: home to Baron Xavier Donit.

The small manor made of mortared stone nestled on a barely consequential plot of land south of Tau, bordered mostly by the steep side of a valley and a long and winding creek. Despite the earliness of the day, the little tillable land around it was already being worked by farmers. By its scent, the rest would soon be home to cattle and sheep.

Nwah touched the ley line and molded the magic that came to her.

The power was strong here.

She felt a sense of intoxication as it played in her mind.

:Tell me what you saw,: she finally said to the owl.

Behind unblinking eyes, the bird of prey described the situation. When she was finished, the owl shifted her perch and groomed her wing.

Nwah thanked her, then turned to find both Kade and Maakdal studying the castle, each clearly plotting separate advances.

:She's not there,: Nwah said. *:The owl reports Winnie is being held a distance from the castle.:*

Kade grimaced. *:That makes no sense.:*

:And yet, it's true.:

Nwah described the shelter, which the owl said was barely large enough to be called a cottage and was built into a limestone crevasse in the valley wall.

Winnie was restrained nearby, each hand lashed to a separate tree.

:I don't understand,: Kade said. *:Why would the baron keep her outside the manor proper?:*

:I'm only reporting what the owl said.:

The distrust in Kade's response bothered her, but to be honest the question was good. If the baron had taken Winnie for ransom, lashing her to trees outside the castle proper seemed a strange way to reap any benefit. It felt more like a blood sacrifice out of a child's tale than any castle intrigue.

:The clan can distract the guards,: Maakdal said.

Nwah rucked up her shoulder fur to show her pleasure. That he had commanded the full force of his twelve *kyree* to join them without her asking had barely surprised her, but Maakdal's unconditional acceptance of her report felt different, more important.

:If they occupy the guards, we would be free to retrieve Winnie,: Kade said to Nwah after she passed him Maakdal's proposal.

:I can cover our steps,: she said, knowing it wasn't her steps she was worried about. *:Then we would be silent.:*

:That's the plan, then. The kyree *draw attention, and we save Winnie.:*

She agreed.

Suddenly Kade's expression changed.

He nodded with sagely depth, his face grim.

:I see it now,: he said to himself. *:This is exactly what the baron would do if he wanted me to chase her. He didn't net me in his raid, so now he's dangling Winnie before us like a worm to a fish.:*

Nwah chuffed, but said nothing.

Perhaps Kade was right after all. Maybe this was all about him.

From a position behind a thick clot of brush, the shelter appeared to be just as the owl described, small and built of rocks and thatch. It was perhaps four strides of a grown man deep and an equal length wide, built into the rough crook of a cliff-like face of the valley wall. It had a window and a door, both closed and both showing darkness behind panes of glass.

Though the day had fully broken, the area was shaded by trees. A steady breeze rattled through the upper canopy, and the smell of water came from below. The land around the cottage was a flat mound for some distance before falling again toward a basin wherein a brook gurgled somewhere lower.

There were five guards nearby, each one positioned exactly where the owl said they would be. Nwah felt the *kyree* nearing each post. The rush of the hunt made her blood surge. The idea of Maakdal leading the pack gave her a strength she didn't know she had. Kade's sense of urgency as he crouched beside her served to double that strength.

The plan called for Nwah to scan the area with her ley magic and report problems as they approached the clearing where Winnie had been tied. She didn't feel anything out of the ordinary, but that didn't make her feel better.

She wished again that she understood more about what she was doing. The gambit's dependency on her magic made her uncertainty taste like bile.

The place was silent, though.

Clean.

With her magical tendrils spread, Nwah got a read on the life around her. Once again she felt creatures of the wood stirring, and—even better—she felt the guards. If she could sense the guards, it was reasonable to think she could feel other people—and the house itself felt cold and empty to her.

She wondered how much time they had before the baron was due to arrive.

:Everything looks in order,: she said to Kade. *:Almost too much in order.:*

His face grew even more grim as his gaze went to where Winnie was slumped over, her arms straining against the ropes as she leaned forward on her knees. The green fabric of her nightclothes draped from her shoulders to pool on the dirt below her. Her dark hair, thrown over her forehead, covered much of her face. She was motionless, seemingly sleeping.

:She probably fought all night,: Kade said.

He gripped his hunting knife, an act that brought Nwah memories of times he'd used that knife to aid in healing people they'd met on the road.

She began to warn him again, but he turned to her.

:I understand,: he said. *:Maybe this is a trick. Maybe they're expecting me to come get her. But what they aren't expecting is you. Just like back in Tau, right? You're our secret weapon. So follow the plan. Keep my back while I cut her down, and we'll have Winnie with us in no time.:*

Nwah tweaked a whisker but said nothing. Jealousy or not, she owed him this. The power of his conviction was strong.

She gave the clearing one more scan.

:All right,: Nwah said. *:It's time.:*

She gave a sharp bark, the signal for her *kyree* kin, and the forest erupted with yips and crashes. Human voices called out amid the thrashing of leaves and forest underbrush.

Kade was already on the run.

Nwah took off across the grassy mound right behind.

Winnie raised her head, her eyes tired and dull.

Kade grabbed a rope.

As the knife blade bit into cord, Nwah felt a pain like something tearing in her gut. The ley line ripped away from her.

Gasping.

Nearly falling as a blanket of magic seemed to enfold her. Her senses fading.

:Kade!: she tried to yell, but it came out as a strangled yip.

Kade turned, his eyes sharp with surprise.

Where Winnie had been was now only a heavy anvil of iron dangling between two cords, dancing and swaying in discordance, one rope deeply frayed, the other still intact.

The door to the cottage opened, and a dark-robed figure stepped into the clearing. "You didn't think you'd get her back that easily, did you?" The voice was feminine, as was the face she revealed by pulling the hood back from her head.

Nwah struggled as hard as she could, but couldn't move.

The woman chuckled with too much satisfaction. "That's the beauty of this magic," she said. "The harder you fight, the more it entangles."

She was a wizard, clearly, tall and graceful in stature, a user of magic much more refined than Nwah, as attested to by the fact that she could pull the magic of the ley line from the *kyree*'s grasp with such ease. Her skin was smooth despite her age—ten years past Kade, maybe fifteen. Her robes were the burgundy and flax colors of the barony.

What she said about her magic was true. Nwah's limbs sank into an invisible mire around her. The air seemed suddenly stale and clotted.

Kade gripped his knife, and, as he took a step toward them, Maakdal, too, emerged from the forest from the other side of the clearing.

"If either of you come near," the woman said to the pair, "your beloved Nwah will die."

The Mage raised both hands, and the fabric of the clearing stretched in ways that made Nwah's mind boggle. Where Nwah's magic was raw and wild, this woman's was ordered and showed attention to detail. This Mage had been prepared while they had merely blundered into her trap like so many newborn pups.

Pressure came across Nwah's ribcage, and she gave an involuntary squeak. She was fully trapped. Completely unable to move. She glanced to Kade, then

Maakdal, unable to keep fear from her eyes, yet also unable to miss the fact that while both were willing to die for her, neither was willing to risk her life in doing so.

The woman strode forward and ran a gentle finger over Nwah's flank. Her touch made Nwah's pelt quiver.

:So,: her voice came through the ley line, *:this is the notorious Nwah, ruler of the* kyree *my spies said caused such a commotion in Tau? The wonderous Nwah that my Rayn gave me up for?:*

A chill crossed Nwah's spine. *:You knew Rayn?:*

:Knew her?: The woman's smile grew playful. She bent to one knee, running her hand in an overly intimate way down from Nwah's forehead to scratch under one ear. *:Yes, you could say I knew her, if by that, you meant we were together.:*

Nwah's narrowed eyes asked her next question.

:Oh, silly kyree. *Where should I start? That we were lovers back when we could afford to be young and carefree? That we were going to conquer the world—or at least the doleful Eastern Empire—me with my magic, she with her sword? The two of us together, ruling side by side, both day . . . and night?:* She rose with a predacious smile on her lips, then stepped around Nwah, glaring menacingly at Kade and Maakdal to keep them in their places.

Nwah saw her two males exchange glances.

She wanted them to run, but she knew them better. Even now, they both edged closer.

What would they do?

The scuffling in the wood was quieting. Would Maakdal command the *kyree* in a new plan? Would Kade twist his healing in the darker directions for her?

:We could have done it, too,: the woman continued. *:The Empire is weak now, ruled by a dunce and his dolts no more capable of making big decisions than my father. Is that where I should start then, my lovely Nwah? That it could have been so easy?:*

Nwah swallowed, suddenly understanding who this woman was.

:You're the baron's daughter.:

:Lady Venitha.: She gave a mock curtsy as she completed her circle of Nwah. *:At your service.:*

Nwah's brain looped on itself as she tried to remember stories Rayn told about her life before. She told so many, but Nwah was young and so enthralled with her new pair-mate that she missed most of the details.

She remembered one moment, though. A night sharp with autumn chill when Nwah was in a curious mood and Rayn was feeling reflective. They had been nuzzled together for warmth against their open-air camp.

:What is love?: Nwah had asked. Her back was against Rayn's belly, her front paw covering her nose, her tail looped between her legs.

Rayn rubbed Nwah's shoulder.

:That's a big question for a little kyree,*:* she finally said.

:That's not an answer,: Nwah pressed.

:Love is difficult because it can be so many things,: Rayn said. *:It can be earned or not, requited or not, unconditional or not.:*

:I don't understand.:

She laughed. Soft and warm. *:I wish I could explain it better.:*

:If you can't tell me what love is, can you tell me what it is not?:

Rayn shuffled around, adjusting her position to engulf Nwah, cupping her against her chest tightly enough that Nwah could still remember the warmth of Rayn's breathing and the strength of her embrace.

:Commanded,: Rayn finally said. *:The one thing love cannot be is commanded.:*

Standing enthralled in the clearing, Nwah understood the truth.

Venitha had tried to force Rayn to love her.

:Eventually, though, Rayn left me,: the Mage said.

:You knew that part, though, didn't you? I'm sure Rayn told you all sorts of stories about me. Some of them might even have been true. She loved my "lunatic ideas" so much when we were simple hooligans. But she never believed me when I said we were going to rule together. She didn't have what it took. Thought my weak-kneed father would shut me down, and when he didn't, she left and found you instead. I've been looking for you ever since I heard news of Rayn's untimely end.:

The portent of that statement started to sink in.

:Are you saying . . . all this . . . : She glanced to Kade and Maakdal, then to the now deathly still anvil, before taking in the Mage. *:You're saying you captured Winnie just to bring* me *here?:*

Lady Venitha scoffed. *:If only. The guard was meant to capture you straight away, but as they're as dense as most of their type, they brought me the healer's strumpet instead.:*

:You're insane.:

:Perhaps,: Venitha said. *:But with you by my side, we can lead the Empire even more firmly than I could have with Rayn. You see that, right? You controlling the animal kingdom, me dictating the human side. What a lovely pair of Monarchs we could make!:*

Suddenly it made sense.

Venitha wanted Nwah to join her.

Something else fell into place, too, or perhaps it was just an idea that felt right: Could Venitha have been behind the raid that killed Rayn? Per her own word, she had been tracking her ex-lover. She knew of their pairing. She was clearly jealous, and just as clearly vindictive. Was it possible Lady Venitha had ordered Rayn killed?

:I won't do it,: Nwah said.

:Oh, but I think you will.: Venitha pulled energy from the line, and both Kade and Maakdal, who had been slowly advancing, staggered, clawing at their necks and struggling to breathe. *:Because if you don't, both of these strapping young men will die.:*

Nwah's cry turned to a whine as she watched, helpless as Kade's face gasped toward blue and as Maakdal bucked and twisted in a macabre dance before falling to the ground, his jaw clacking and smacking as he tried to draw breath.

:Stop it!: she called, looking up to take in the hard-set features of Lady Venitha, who stared at her victims with an expression of ecstasy. *:Stop it,:* Nwah yelled, but she knew it was too late . . . that she had only one recourse . . .

Then came the dark outline of something round, heavy, and iron, swinging in the shadowed light behind the Lady, looping with perfect geometry to crash into the Mage's head with a deep *thunk*.

Venitha collapsed in a single movement.

Her impact with the ground came with a heavy *thud*.

Standing in her place was Winnie, her nightclothes dirty and torn, her hair loose and tangled from the bed. Her feet were spread, her hands, wrapped around the handle of a frying skillet, were still tied at the wrist.

"Who's the strumpet now?" Winnie said as she looked down at the Lady's comatose form.

The restraints fell from Nwah's sides. The ley line came flooding back.

Behind them, Kade and Maakdal took deep breaths of clean air.

Nwah lay on her side, resting against the stone wall of the shelter, watching as Kade tended to Lady Venitha, amazed at how easily he gave up his previous resentment to heal her. That trait spoke truth to his calling and gave a depth to his power that Nwah took an odd sort of pride from.

He was her pair-mate, after all.

He was going to be a well-admired man of the Gift.

But she loved him for more than that, though she couldn't say exactly how.

She was tired again, though.

Drained in a way different from overexertion.

She watched also as Maakdal brought his *kyree* together again, personally seeing to the status of each, commenting on cuts and bruises, praising each act of heroism. They had lost no members, and Nwah saw how that result was as much due to Maakdal's preparations as it was to each of her kin's skills.

She loved him, too. Differently, yes, but just as deeply and with a passion just as impossible to describe.

:She's a sad case,: Winnie said through Nwah's magic as she sat beside Nwah and began to pet her. Nwah had used her magic to get Winnie's story straight from her lips.

The Lady Venitha had restrained Winnie's hands and feet, then left her tied to a cot in the shelter. During the commotion, Winnie had slipped to the floor and dragged the cot to the makeshift kitchen, where she used a knife to cut the bonds from her feet. There hadn't been time to deal with her hands, so she grabbed the only thing she had at her disposal—the cast-iron skillet.

:Yes, she is a sad case,: Nwah replied.

:Obsessive.:

Nwah gave a half-purr to agree. *:Love is like that sometimes.:*

:Yes, it is,: Winnie replied.

They sat there, resting against the hard rock of the shelter wall, watching the men do their work. For the first time, Nwah felt the strength that came from the young woman, strength that had always been there but that Nwah had missed, mostly because she hadn't wanted to see it.

Hadn't wanted to think Kade might find it attractive.

Nwah stared at Winnie, feeling fingers run over her pelt with care.

As she watched Kade work, her expression was a mix of many things. Calm. Curious. Wondrous. Interested.

The cool breeze moved the tangle of hair that fell over Winnie's forehead.

:You're lucky,: Winnie said to her as she pushed it back in place. *:You've got them both.:*

Yes, Nwah thought. *I am lucky.*

As was Kade.

Love is hard, after all. Difficult to define.

She was right to say love can be obsessive. But it can be kind, too. And strong. It can be enduring and perfect and confounding.

Love can be many things, Rayn had once told her, and that was the truest thing of all.

The Once and Future Box

Fiona Patton

The roof of Haven's Iron Street Watch House had been in a dreadful state for as long as Sergeant Hektor Dann could remember, with broken and missing tiles allowing rain, snow, and, once, fist-sized hail, to work their way inside. Although not the oldest nor, by any means, the poorest Watch House in Valdemar's capital city, each successive captain had insisted that they did not have the money for repairs, expecting each successive sergeant to send as many sweepers, runners, and junior constables as necessary into the attics with mops, buckets, and oiled tarpaulins to temporarily stem the tide of destruction. It wasn't until its most recent commander, Captain Travin Torell, late of the Breakneedle Street Watch House, had discovered a river of water running down the inside wall of his office, that the funds had been found.

The very next day an army of workmen descended on the old building, sending clouds of dust and dirt showering into the street below. The crash of tiles was nearly deafening, and almost immediately, Sam, the Watch House cat, made his displeasure known with such strident outrage that the cook scooped him up and ran for her mother's house. Hektor doubted they'd see him again.

The Messenger Bird Master and his apprentice,

Hektor's sister, Kasiath, had relocated their pigeons to the roof of his cousin's tavern, the Iron Penny, the night before, and, as the coop landed on the growing pile of discarded slate in the street below, a fine mist of dried bird dung joined the mantle of grime already coating every surface both inside and out. The main hall immediately filled with angry shopkeepers and smiths, then emptied just as quickly as another wave of dust and dirt drove them away.

"That's how to keep complaints down," Hektor's older brother, Corporal Aiden Dann noted with grim satisfaction as the cacophony of smashing tiles, pounding feet, and shouted orders drowned out the rising murmur of anger from across the street. "They can't make 'em if we can't hear 'em."

"We'll pay for it later," Hektor replied, raising his hands in a helpless gesture toward an old woman who was pointing her finger at him in a deeply disturbing gesture of coming retribution.

By noon, the few prisoners in the basement cells had to be evacuated to the Water Street Watch House, along with the two semiretired watchmen who guarded them, and most of the young sweepers who kept the place—more or less—clean, were pulled from the site by their mothers, fearing for their health. The captain lasted another hour before he and the new Watch House dog, Spotters, fled to the reading room of the nearby Marian Temple. Glaring at the plaster dust covering the duty officer's desk, Corporal Hydd Thacker wondered in a sour tone if the mice and the spiders would be next to desert.

The following day, the street was jammed with wagons hauling the wreckage away and sending new clouds of debris billowing into the air. Then it rained. For three days. The workmen covered the gaping roof in tarpaulins and abandoned the site.

When the sun finally reemerged, Corporal Kiel

Wright glanced around in disgust as he and the two eldest Dann brothers slogged through rivulets of sodden construction debris to reach the front door.

"Whole place looks like a den of drowned rats," he noted.

"A den of drowned, angry rats," Aiden added as Night Sergeant Jons greeted their arrival with a thunderous expression.

"I can't walk into my own home without draggin' half the Watch House in on my boots," he growled, "which irks my dear, sweet wife and her mother to no end, so you do somethin' about this. I don't care what, just somethin', before I arrest the whole lot of 'em for causin' a domestic disturbance."

"The Cap'n . . ." Hektor began, then glanced down as their youngest brother Padreic, recently promoted to the position of Chief Runner, shook his head dolefully.

"What, Paddy?"

"Cap'n's run off . . . I mean gone off," he amended as Hektor frowned at him, "to Restinn."

"When?"

"First thing this mornin'."

"S'on you then, Hek," Aiden pointed out.

Hektor looked from Hydd's expectant glare to Aiden and Kiel's equally expectant smirks and, closing his teeth on the profanity that sprang to his lips, went in search of the foreman.

"As I tol' yer Cap'n at beginin'," the older man said, tapping his pipe against the wall, "t'aint unusual wi' a buildin' o' this age. Tis hard ta see full damage 'til tiles be off, but I was sure we'd find rot in the sheetin', what with that leakage pattern an' all. An' we did, so it all has ta go. An' if that rot's got down into trusses, they'll hav'ta go, too. No sense puttin' new sheetin' an' tiles over rotten trusses; the whole thing'll collapse sooner'r later. In meantime, my oldest boy, Eban's, been checkin' attics. He says damp musta been workin' up there for years. Walls be in a right shockin' state."

"Walls?"

"No sense puttin' in . . ."

Hektor held up one hand in a weary gesture. "How much longer do you think you'll be?"

"Can't say for sure."

"Estimate then."

The foreman rubbed at the back of his neck, his expression finally apologetic. "A month maybe."

The month passed. Piles of rotten wood added a layer of muck to the already filthy street, and the wagons brought in to haul the larger pieces away only served to churn it into soggy ruts. When the new timber and slate finally arrived, Hektor's younger brothers, Night Constables Jakon and Raik, had their hands full trying to keep the local children, who seemed determined to get themselves killed, off the stacks. It wasn't until they appealed to the local knitting circle, made up entirely of these children's grandmothers, that peace was restored.

"Maybe you should have a whole troop of little ol' lady watchmen patrollin' for you."

Master Smith Linton's comment drew a loud guffaw from the crowd of blacksmiths watching the proceedings from the front of the Awl and Tongs tavern across the street. "'Course, if this mess keeps interruptin' trade, they'll be comin' after you with needles at the ready."

Neither the watchmen nor the grandmothers could disagree.

A week later, a shortage of nails stalled the work yet again, and Hektor finally abandoned his office, spending most of his time trying to avoid his neighbors. As the first heat of summer chased spring from the city, he and Aiden made their careful way through the debris field toward the Iron Lily, where most of the Watch had taken up shop, only to see five local youths kicking something they at first thought was a ball until they took a closer look.

"What are you doin'?"

All five started guiltily; three made to run until Aiden shot them a warning glare, then subsided with sullen expressions as the other two tried to look innocent. The largest of the youths squirmed under the watchmen's scrutiny, then raised one shoulder in a brief shrug. "Uh . . ."

Hektor glanced down, his eyes widening slightly. "Is that cheese?"

"Uh . . ."

"Why are you kickin' cheese in the street?"

"Uh . . ."

"Words, Brandin, words."

"'Cause it's . . . uh . . . round?"

Aiden snorted. "Not any more," he observed in a dry tone while Hektor gave another youth trying to hide behind Brandin a raised eyebrow. "Does your father know what you're doin' to his prize-winnin' blue cheese, Mazin?"

The youth started as if he was surprised that Hektor had seen him.

"Uh . . ."

"Never mind. Just clean it up." Hektor glanced down. "And why are you barefoot?"

Mazin pointed mutely to where a pair of soft leather shoes, tied by the laces, were draped over a shop sign. The others snickered.

"They're new, see," Mazin explained, "so I didn't wanna get 'em dirty, so I took 'em off an . . . Brandin kinda . . ."

"Put 'em somewhere safe," the larger boy stated with a disarming smile both men knew was patently false.

Hektor closed his eyes briefly. "Just get 'em down and get all this cheese cleaned up."

"And then get gone," Aiden added. "You all have work to be doin', so get doin' it before I set you to cleanin' the rest of the street."

As they carried on their way, Hektor ignored his brother's nostalgic smirk. "Don't," he warned.

"Wasn't gonna."

"Liar."

An hour later, Paddy burst into the Iron Lily's back room where Hektor was trying to tackle a mountain of dusty paperwork.

"Hek, we found treasure! That is, the workmen found treasure! You gotta come!"

"A treasure chest, see!"

Two of the laborers were muscling a large strongbox onto the duty officer's desk. Workmen, watchmen, and bystanders crowded around it excitedly, and Hektor used his elbows to clear a path.

Although covered in cobwebs and spotted with rust, the box looked both solid and sturdy; made of heavy, cast iron, banded with studded metal, and sporting two odd-looking locks. The top was engraved with a simple crest Hektor had never seen before: two unfamiliar crossed objects, one twisted, the other L-shaped, superimposed over a cityscape that might have been Haven.

"T'were tucked behind concealed door in attic wall," the foreman announced. "My youngest boy, Jazper, found it."

Beside him, a man of at least thirty beamed happily. "Musta been there for decades, what with all the junk piled in front," he supplied.

"Did you try to open it?"

"Sure, but it be locked, see, an' no keys. Eban an' me wanted ta smash it open, but Da reckoned it prob'ly belonged ta Watch House, what with it being in Watch House, so we should bring it down to ye."

"What about finder's fee, tho'?" one of the carpenters piped up.

"Finder's fee don't apply, Mertin," Hydd shot back before the foreman or his sons could answer. "Jazper dug it outta our wall. Might as well say a finder's fee applies to the kettle since you found it in our cupboard this mornin'. And by the way, we'll be wantin' that back."

Mertin made to answer, then, after a glance at Hydd's face, thought the better of it.

"Kettle aside," Eban said thoughtfully, running his fingers along the metal banding, "Watch Houses don't use strongboxes like this."

"How would you know?" one of the junior constables demanded.

"'Cause our cousin has the contract, that's how!"

The two men squared off until a cough from Aiden reminded them where they were; then they subsided, muttering.

"If Watch Houses don't use them kinda strongboxes, then it aint Watch House property," one of the tilers persisted. "Leastways what's inside aint. Up for grabs, I'd say."

"Up for passin' about to the folk whose trade has suffered while you lazy gits have been muckin' about pullin' boxes out of walls instead of cleanin' up that street out there," Linton growled.

No one had the courage to gainsay the much larger man except Aiden, who shot him a warning look.

"It was in our wall, it's our property 'til we open it an' see if there's anythin' that identifies the original owner inside," he said bluntly.

"So, can we open it then, please?" Paddy asked, hopping from one foot to the other with impatience.

"No keys," the foreman reminded him.

"There's plenty of keys hangin' about. Maybe hundreds."

"We should probably wait 'til the Cap'n gets back," Hektor suggested, much to the dismay of the gathered. He glanced about, allowing himself a moment to enjoy the sudden, tense silence. "Still . . ." he mused. Everyone held their breath. "There's no tellin' how long he'll be gone for . . ."

"Likely until the work's done . . ." Kiel supplied.

"Which'll be at least another couple of weeks . . ." the foreman added.

"You said it would be a month six weeks ago," Aiden growled.

"No sense . . ."

"So, are we gonna open it, Hek—I mean Sarge?" Paddy demanded, refusing to be distracted by another pointless argument.

Hektor smiled. "'Course we are. I want to know what's in it same as you do. Get your runners together and search out every key in the place."

With a whoop of delight, Paddy took off, the younger members of the Watch tight on his heels.

But several hours and dozens of keys later, the box remained stubbornly locked.

"I had no idea we had that many keys lyin' about," Aiden noted, poking at the pile with one finger. "Now what?"

"A locksmith?" Hektor suggested.

His older brother barked in derision. "You got authorization for that kinda money? They're the most expensive trade in the city."

"You could sell them keys," Mertin suggested.

"Don't you have a roof to fix?" Hektor shot back.

"Shift's over," he replied with a grin. "We was just waitin' to see if you could get it open a'fore we left."

"Well, obviously we can't, so clear off," Hydd snapped.

"For that matter, our shift's over too," Aiden noted.

"What do you want to do with it, Hek?" He jerked his thumb at the strongbox.

"Leave it on the duty desk."

"You figure it'll be safe there?"

"If it isn't, we don't deserve it to be."

"Good point."

The next morning, the main hall was once again filled with people come to watch and make suggestions ranging from the dangerous to the ridiculous.

"You could toss it off the roof."

"Or let a cart run over it."

"Or smash them locks with a hammer."

"How 'bouts I hold it for you 'til you find a way in."

By midday, no more than half the crowd had wandered off. Hektor looked over their heads to see Aiden opening the door for their mother, come with their noon meal. Once again using his elbows to clear a path, he joined them just as Hydd greeted her with a huge smile.

"Anything in that big basket for me, Cousin Jemmee?"

She raised an eyebrow at him. "Well, there were enough currant buns for those on duty," she answered, "but not for this many."

"Half a minute. I'll arrest the lot."

"Hey, Ma."

As Hektor caught the basket up and moved it out of Hydd's reach, she kissed him on the cheek.

"So where's this mystery box of yours?" she asked.

"Through here."

A stern glance was all Jemmee needed to clear a path for her and her sons to the duty officer's desk.

"Looks like we may have to call for a locksmith," he said gloomily.

Jemmee laughed.

"A whole house of watchmen, and no one remembers

that we have one of the most infamous lock-pickin' family livin' a stone's throw away from here in Littlewell Court."

Hydd smacked his forehead. "A course, the Tyvers!"

The Dann brothers exchanged an equally puzzled look.

"Tyvers? Ol' Jeb's brood? Aren't they brewers?" Hektor asked.

"They are now," their mother answered with a knowing smile. "But in your great-granther's day, there wasn't a home nor a shop they couldn't get into. He never could bring 'em to justice."

"No one could," Hydd agreed grudgingly. "There was some talk they was protected."

"Protected? By who?" Hektor asked.

The older man shrugged. "Dunno. Some said the Crown."

"Talk sense," Aiden scoffed as the crowd gave a collective gasp. "Why would the Crown protect a family of lock-picks?"

"No idea," Hydd shot back. "T'was a different world back then. All I know is what my granther tol' me, that Jeb's da, Connon Tyver, suddenly had enough brass to go into legit business with his wife's brother, who was a brewer by trade, an' the whole clan pulled up stakes from down by Exile's Gate an' moved up to Littlewell Court."

"If they're legit now, how can one of 'em help us?"

Jemmee smiled. "Because Connon Tyver's little sister, Morag, was the best charm-dubber in Haven, and I wouldn't say she went too strictly legit."

"Charm what?"

"'Twas the old word for lock-picks," Hydd explained.

"Who you callin' old, Hydd Thacker?" Jemmee demanded.

"Uh . . ."

"She married Albert Vinney of Littlecotte Lane," she continued, chuckling at the panicked look on her cousin's face.

"Yeah, but is she even still alive, Ma?" Aiden asked.

"I wouldn't be tellin' you about her if she were dead, son."

He reddened, much to the general amusement of those listening. "Right. Uh . . . we can send Paddy to ask her to come if she's up to it."

"Oh, she'll be up to it. She never could resist a challenge. And there's no need for you to go anywhere, young man," she added sternly toward her youngest son as Paddy made for the door. "You just step outside and send Brandin. He's her great-grandson," she added for Hektor and Aiden's benefit. "He's kickin' a cottage loaf about in the street for some reason."

Once he understood that he hadn't been dragged into the Watch House because of the bread, and that his errand would net him a pennybit but no more, so he was to stop asking or he'd get nothing, Brandin ambled off. Half an hour later, the gathered hushed as he returned with one of the best charm-dubbers in Haven on his arm.

Morag Vinney was a slight, stooped woman in her eighties with wisps of gray hair peeking out of a brown knit cap and a black shawl wrapped tightly about her shoulders. The hand that clutched Brandin's wrist was dark with liver spots, but her eyes were clear and she gave Hektor a shrewd look as her great-grandson muttered his name in her ear.

"Dann, huh?" she said with a snort. "Figures. You lot've never been able to do nought else but interfere in the doin's of other folk. You one of Thomar's brood? He married Tansy Wright as I recall."

"His grandson," Hektor answered, used to such interrogations by the elderly citizens of Haven.

She nodded. "I knew yer great-granther, Dolan. He were a proper gentleman him. Not like Thomar. A right little bastard, he was. He still with us?"

"No, ma'am."

"Pity. He were a fine fella."

Also used to such changes of opinion in the elderly, Hektor just nodded.

"And this is the *mystery* box?"

Something in the way she said it caused him to give her a shrewd glance of his own, but she ignored him.

"We found it in attic wall," Jazper piped up.

"No doubt."

"Can you get into it, ma'am?" Paddy asked eagerly.

"What's it worth to you, boy?" she snapped back. "I don't come cheap. Never did."

Brandin leaned down and whispered something in her ear.

"Cousin Kidda's Rosie, huh?" Morag turned a look on Paddy that made him blush right up to his ears. "He good to her?"

Brandin shot his friend an evil grin before nodding. "Yeah, Granny, he is."

"Well, all right then. That makes him close enough to family for a reduced rate. I'll have a look."

They set the strongbox on a small table and fetched her a chair. She peered at the double locks for a long time, lost in thought.

"Watch Houses don't use them kind of boxes," Eban pointed out to her.

She sniffed at him but didn't bother to answer.

"An' we couldn't find any keys that fit the locks," Paddy added.

"That's 'cause the one on the left's a screw lock," she replied.

"A what?"

"Takes a key fashioned like a screw. I haven't seen one of them in a donkey's age. Brings back a pile of memories, I must say."

"Do you recognize the crest as well, ma'am?" Hektor asked.

She ignored him, her gaze turned inward. "So long ago it was," she said. "Long before the rheumatism made it all a thing of the past. Connon an' me had such a time, we did. Could dance on a ridge pole in a wind storm, us two. Da always said we were the most talented of the whole family until that blasted girl, what was her name . . . Sara, Sonya, something like that; yup, 'til she got involved."

"Ma'am?"

Again, she ignored him. "That's when everythin' changed. They say for the better, but I don't know. That blasted girl did what no watchman, nor guardsman alive could ever do. She neutered the entire Tyver family. Turned us soft. All in the name of Valdemar." She gave a snort. "All in the name of easy livin' an' no adventure. What kind of life is that?" She glanced at Brandin. "You have no idea what your daddy coulda been, boy. What you coulda been. What you coulda done an' you coulda seen."

"The inside of a cell, Morag?" Hydd asked gently.

"Ha. For a few minutes maybe. You lot never could keep a Tyver, even overnight. We were that good."

"So, you do recognize the box, ma'am?" Hektor asked again.

"Oh, aye, I recognize it, Dolan. But I ain't seen it for years. It was so long ago, an' everyone else involved is long dead now."

"Can you open it?"

"I can open anything, boy." Her voice held a flash of temper as she glared up at him. Fishing into her sweater, she pulled out a small, silver key on a fine chain around her neck. "Brandin, go home and pull the wooden box out from under my bed; not the little one, the big one. Here's the key." She passed it over to him. "Fetch the black leather bag from it. And my sweets." She fixed him with a stern glare. "Touch nothin' else in that box, an' I'll leave you the contents when I pass. Touch anythin' else, an' you get nothin', understand?"

"Sure, Granny." He grinned at her.

"Good boy. Go."

As Brandin passed Paddy, he smiled at his expression, then jerked his head. "C'mon. I might need yer help to get past Granny's dogs."

Paddy glanced at Hektor, who nodded distractedly, and the two boys took off like a shot.

Aiden watched them go. "Might want to bring him on as a runner," he mused.

"Might as well," Morag growled. "He's already ruined, hanging out with watchmen as he is. Not good for anythin' else now."

Hektor chuckled. "It's settled then. I'll speak to the Cap'n when he gets back."

"You do that. And you," she pointed at Kiel. "Fetch me a cup of tea an' a biscuit or two. Not those hard, nasty ones from the kitchen, mind, the nice ones Cap'n Fernlow keeps in his desk drawer."

"Uh . . ."

"Bottom drawer on the left. Bang it in the center with yer palm. That'll spring the lock. Cheap piece of junk."

"Uh . . . Hek?"

"Cap'n Fernlow retired, ma'am," Hektor explained. "It's Cap'n Torell now."

"Still the same desk?"

"I . . . maybe."

"Bottom drawer on the left."

Hektor gave Kiel a tiny shake of his head. "Kriss?"

One of the younger runners pushed his way to Hektor's side. "Yeah, Sarge?"

He handed him a penny. "Go to Nanny Agga's bake shop an' get some nice biscuits."

Kriss gave the coin in his palm a dubious look. "How many, Sarge?"

"Two."

"But she sells a dozen for five pennies an' two dozen for ten. That'd be enough for all of us."

"You got ten pennies?"

"No, Sarge."

"Neither do I. Two."

Morag gave Hektor an amused look as Kriss left, his shoulders slumped in misery. "Better not be thinkin' of payin' me with two measly biscuits, Thomar Dann," she said sternly. "I expect to be paid with proper coin of the realm. Petty cashbox is in the Cap'n's top middle drawer. Takes no more'n a hatpin to get into it, even for a watchman."

"Thank you, ma'am, but we have operatin' money on hand."

"Then you coulda sprung for more biscuits."

He sighed. "I'll send him out again."

"You do that."

Brandin and Paddy returned, their faces flushed with both excitement and mischief, just as Kriss headed out with the ten pennies clutched triumphantly in his fist. Morag snatched the bag of sweets from her great-grandson and counted them suspiciously.

"Thought I tol' you not to touch nothin' else?"

"I didn't," he protested. "Ever'thin' in the box is still there."

"An' these sweets?"

"Were on yer dresser. An' we only had one each." When she continued to stare at him, he grinned. "Mebbe two each."

"Yer a little . . ." she began, and then smiled. "Tyver. Give me my bag."

He handed it over.

She rifled through it, muttering to herself, while the crowd leaned forward in hushed anticipation. Finally she drew out a small wooden key, the shaft twisted to resemble a screw. She stroked it lovingly with one finger, then held it up.

"Looks a bit small," Hydd noted. "You sure it'll fit?"

Morag turned an ice-cold stare on him, and he fell back a step. "You tellin' me my business, boy?" she demanded.

"Uh . . . no ma'am."

"Good thing." She returned her attention to the key. "So many years," she murmured. "Used to wear this little treasure around my neck. Never took it off 'til years later. Not 'til after Albie passed. He was a good man, a bit wild, but I liked 'em wild in them days. Must say, I still do." She made to say something else, but after a glance at Paddy and Brandin, snapped her teeth shut in annoyance. "Anyway, in you go, little one." She fit the key into the left-hand lock and turned it gently. The lock opened with an extra loud *crack* in the silence and, as one, the gathered gave an involuntary gasp.

"Well, that's mine." She sat back, her expression turned inward again.

After a moment, Hektor coughed. "Ma'am?"

"Hm?"

"Were you going to open the right-hand lock?"

"I would if I had the key, but I don't. Connon always carried that one." She smiled a little sadly. "He was a fine musician, my big brother was. Not Bard fine, of course, but fine enough to suit me. He played the gittern. I used to get him to play for me when I was a little. He knew all kinds of songs."

Her smile grew sly as she ran her fingers along the crest. "An' that's why no one coulda ever got into that right-hand lock. No one ever knew the secret of it 'cept us. An' Sara, a' course. Or Sonya. Damn, I wish I could remember that blasted girl's name." She sighed. "She got involved when our brother Iffan died. That's when it started; for us, anyway;,wantin' justice for Iffan. Or maybe revenge. Prob'ly revenge."

She shook herself. "But that's the past. The present's about to run up an' bite us on the ass if I know that lot up there, so we'd best be quick. You, boy." She gestured Paddy over. "Go find a Bardic student, not a Bard, they're too . . ." Paddy leaned forward, a gleam in his eye. "Just too," she finished. "Long as they play the gittern an' as long as they've got their tools with 'em, get 'em to come with you. Tell 'em there's a story in it for 'em. That's all the motivation they'll need. And hurry up," she called after him as he headed through the crowd. "Time's short. We don't wanna miss openin' this thing after all the fuss it's caused."

Hektor frowned. "Why would we miss openin' it?"

She waved a dismissive hand at him. "Why isn't my tea ready?" she retorted. "A body could die of thirst around here."

"It's comin'."

"Good boy. Egan, isn't it?"

"No, ma'am. Hektor. Egan was my Da."

"Hmff. There's too damn many of you to keep track of."

"Yes, ma'am."

It only took Paddy a few minutes to return with two young women in tow, each toting instruments that Hektor assumed were gitterns in soft, leather carriers on their backs. Before he could introduce them, one of them smiled.

"Hey, Auntie Morag. You wantin' a concert?"

"Later, Peggi dear. Who's this?"

"My friend Sally."

"Either one of you have your tools with you?"

"Always," Sally answered promptly.

"I need a string winder."

Both women immediately produced small L-shaped cylinders and Morag smiled as the gathered crowd murmured their sudden understanding of the crest.

"In plain sight," she chuckled as she slid Peggi's into the right-hand lock and spun it counterclockwise. The lock opened with another extra loud *crack*, and Morag reached for the lid as everyone leaned forward.

Inside was a small, leather notebook, a tiny pencil

attached to the spine by a short length of wool, and two large piles of papers and letters tied together with faded ribbons.

Brandin rocked back on his heels, his expression deeply disappointed. "S'at all?"

Morag snorted. "What'd you expect?"

"Well, gold an' jewels an' stuff like that."

She chuckled again and, reaching in, pried a piece the lid's inner lining free to reveal a leather bag that chinked when she held it up. "You mean like this, maybe?"

The assembled murmured excitedly, but before she could reveal the contents, a commotion at the front door made her straighten.

"That you, Seran?"

Watchmen, smiths, and workmen alike parted to reveal a tall woman in her early forties, dressed all in white.

"Seran passed away some years ago," she answered, moving through the hushed crowd with consummate grace. "But I trained under her in my first year. My name is Ivy."

"Herald Ivy, you mean."

"Just so."

"Yer late."

"Too late, I see. You probably shouldn't have opened that so publicly."

Morag snorted. "It were public the moment it came outta that wall. This way everyone's curiosity's been sated." She glanced at Paddy who was eyeing the papers with a gleam in his eye. "Well, nearly everyone's. What do you think, boy, should we read 'em out loud?"

"Morag, they carry the state seal," Herald Ivy admonished gently.

"Ah, so they do. But this don't," Morag held up the notebook. "This carries Connon Tyver's name, his life, and Iffan's death . . . and so long ago that what went on won't matter to anyone anymore 'cept his family. We got a right to claim it, after all we did."

"The Tyvers were invaluable," Ivy agreed. "The world is a safer place now thanks to all the people who stepped up in Valdemar's hour of need. We have to examine the notebook; you know that, but I can promise you I'll do everything in my power to get it back to you."

"What about them gold and jewels?" Mertin now demanded, pushing forward. "There should be a finder's fee."

"And there may be," Ivy said, a hint of steel finally entering her voice. "But that's for the Crown to decide."

"Mystery's solved," Morag added, cutting off the murmur of dissent. "You all know who the box belongs to now and what's in it." She slapped the lid closed. "So get to your own business, all of you, it's near dinner time."

"Who's gonna clean up that street out there?" Linton demanded, refusing to wilt under her cold stare.

"Well, it ain't gonna be me and it ain't gonna be you, Linton Kray," she shot back. "So, you just leave it to those whose job it is." Waving Brandin forward, she stood with his help.

"I'll let you know how much my services cost," she told Hektor as Herald Ivy took charge of the box. "Send the boy there with my payment." She gestured at Paddy, then leaned toward him. "When you come, bring some of them biscuits and there may be a story in it for you." She winked at him, and he grinned.

"Morag," Ivy warned.

"Oh, hush, Seran. There're some things that need to remain secret and some things that need to be passed on. The younger generations have to be prepared to step up if that world ever comes back again. You can trust the Tyvers to know which is which. For that matter, you can trust the Danns too, for all they are interferin' little busybodies."

She turned. "That was fun, Hektor. You can call on me anytime. Give my love to Tansy."

"I will, ma'am."

The crowd parted as Morag Vinney, the best charm-dubber in Haven, left the Watch House, then slowly broke up, heading for their own homes through the layers of construction debris still littering the street.

Jazper turned to Eban. "We gonna check other walls?" he asked.

His older brother grinned. "'Course, we are. But tomorrow. Ol' lady's right. It's near dinner time. Ma'll be waitin'."

He tipped his hat toward Jemmee, then headed out.

Hektor glanced at the dust still covering every surface, then followed, the rest of his family falling into step behind him.

Acceptable Losses

Stephanie Shaver

The Quarry

There should be more blood.

Wetness spread across Wil's face, but when the Herald reached up to touch it, he found only water from the puddle he'd landed in. He sprawled across scree and rubble, gravel biting into his palms.

There should be more blood.

Whose, exactly?

Smoke poured out of the mine entrance and filled the quarry with a pewter-gray haze. His nostrils stung with a mix of smells. Some unidentifiable—the acrid chemical that mixed with the explosion when it tore open the shaft. Some hideously familiar—the smell of burning bodies.

Wil staggered to his feet, reassembling the moments of the last candlemark. Death on both sides. The heat and chaos of something like Griffon's Firestarting Gift, but not. And when he tried to reach his Companion—

:*Vehs?:* he thought.

No answer.

:*Vehs?:*

The bond remained unbroken, but the silence yawned between them.

:VEHS!:

The Waystation

:*Stop yelling, Chosen, I'm right here!*: Vehs said.

Wil bolted up in his bed, gasping from his vision. Turning, he looked to see if he'd woken Ivy, but thankfully, his daughter slept soundly in her own boxbed. Or maybe she didn't. He knew sometimes she faked it.

:*Aubryn thinks she's sleeping,*: Vehs informed him as Wil stumbled out of the Waystation and into the bright morning light. It took a few grinding thumps to get clear water running from the pump instead of rust brown. He made a mental note to let Cyril know.

Assuming we ever see each other again . . .

He shoved the thought aside.

They were in the foothills of southern Valdemar, amid hardwoods that had been part of the Pelagirs centuries ago. They'd since been tamed thanks to the Hawkbrothers and simple farming. The Waystation sat between villages, a sturdy, well-provisioned structure that stood against the seasons and wandering critters, artfully hidden by foliage.

:*Is Aubryn eavesdropping on my daughter's dreams?*: Wil asked, splashing cold water on his brow.

:*They . . . talk.*:

Wil paused. Aubryn watched over his daughter while he rode Circuit, but they were not bonded in the way of a Herald and her Companion.

Yet.

:*Is there something I should know?*: Wil asked.

:*Is there something* I *should know?*: Vehs shot back. :*How many more times will you wake up like this? Some things you can't shield from me. Your Gift is careening off the trail again. What's going on?*:

Wil grimaced. They had left Cortsberth a month ago, riding southwest toward the Baireschild holdings. They were closing in on Madra, Lord Dark, and their weapons cache.

And, as always seemed to happen, his Gift of Foresight had caught on to the impending threat that entailed.

Danger! it screamed. It roiled in his gut and woke him up with visions both insanely detailed and maddeningly light on details. The only place it didn't find him was . . .

A Waystation, but not to be found in Velgarth.

:*Chosen?*:

Wil exhaled slowly. :*I'm tired, Vehs.*:

He felt a surge of comfort travel down the bond between them. :*It's been a long road.*:

:*This is not a kind Gift to have. When Lelia was alive, she could—*:

Wil stopped before he could relitigate this line of thought. Lelia's Bardic Gift hadn't been able to lull him to sleep for over half a decade.

:*I'm sorry, Chosen.*:

Wil shook his head. :*Anyway. We have visitors coming today.*:

A note of surprise. :*We do?*:

:*It'll be Lyle and Rivan.*:

:*That's—! Wait. How long have you known?*:

:*A couple of days. I expected them to contact us sooner, but Lyle's Mindspeech isn't very good, and Rivan's probably focused on riding. If the visions are right, they're not alone—I'm just not sure who's with them.*:

The Queen knew he needed support and, after what happened in Highjorune, that the Guards couldn't be wholly trusted. Lord Dark and Madra's false Bards could be anywhere, infiltrating anything.

An army of Heralds would be ideal. He also knew that to be about as likely as Vkandis Sunlord showing up for tea.

A sick stone of intuition tumbled in his belly whenever he thought about Lyle's arrival. With every oscillation, the worry grew.

Like picking at scabs. It never heals.

:*Chosen?*: Vehs's worry didn't help, either.

:I'm just tired. Weeks of this. My sleep hasn't been good. I'm ground down.:

:But Lyle will help, yes?:

:Sure.: Lyle had been Wil's intern. They'd ridden Circuit together, fought wars together. And not for nothing, Lelia had been his twin sister. Ivy loved her uncle.

And it will be good for Ivy to have family to take care of her if—

Another thought Wil closed down before it could grow roots.

The Waystation door popped open, and Ivy emerged, her dark hair sticking out in a marvelous display of bedhead.

"Good morning, *liebshahl*," Wil said to his daughter.

Ivy yawned. "Morning."

Out at the clearing's edge, the Companions whinnied. Ivy waved back.

"What's for breakfast?" she asked.

"Butter on a stick," he replied, not missing a beat.

"Dada."

"Baked horse apples."

"Ewww!"

"Stale bread and cheese rinds," he said at last, which earned him a groan. She was growing up far too fast for his comfort.

"That's the joy of life on Circuit, *liebshahl*." Being around his father in Cortsberth had brought back words from his childhood. He remembered how his sister Daryann had smiled on the rare occasions their father lavished praise on them in the form of Karsite terms of endearment.

Daryann. She'd been gone since before even Lelia's time—an older ache, that one.

Wil walked over and put one arm around Ivy, kissing the top of her head. For a moment he held her, and she grew a little still—a small miracle, at this age.

At least we had this time. Please let her remember it with happiness, someday.

She laughed and squirmed away, running off to collect the morning's bouquet of sourflowers.

"Come back inside for a reading lesson," he called. "And a rubbish breakfast."

"Okay!"

Maybe that'll take my mind off things, Wil thought.

But he knew better.

The Quarry

Wil staggered around the quarry, trying in vain to reach his Companion.

:Vehs?:

Now he pinpointed what was wrong. It wasn't a *:Thought:*, just a regular *thought*. He could still *sense* his Companion, but the steady background hum of connection between them—a channel he associated with his Mindvoice—had been supplanted by perfect silence.

Wil wiped tears out of his eyes. The odd, acrid perfume clung to the back of his throat. His head swam, and his eyes and skin stung.

A figure emerged from the smoke, face concealed behind a beaked leather mask.

"Hey—" he started to say.

The figure pushed up her mask, and Madra's icy eyes glowered at him.

"You," she said, spitting the words with a mix of hate and confusion. "Why aren't you *dead?*"

The crossbow cradled in her arms hummed.

There should have been more blood.

The Waystation

"'Bat' and 'rat.' They rhyme. Why?"

"Hmm . . ." Ivy squinted at the words on the page. "They have the same buh-buh-buh sound."

Wil rubbed his shoulder, as if by doing so he could

ease a pain it had yet to earn. The stone in his belly had grown roots and spread across his back and into the back of his skull. He would be its marionette soon enough, a creature driven by fear and worry, and he needed to do *something,* but he didn't know what. Trying to teach Ivy to read hadn't helped.

:*She's not ready.*:

Aubryn's voice. Unlike Vehs, the Companion wasn't a joker; she exhibited a steady calm and grew easily irritated by tomfoolery.

:*Sometimes I wonder why you volunteered to watch a child,*: Wil replied.

Her response came back measured and solemn. :*Because we needed each other, Herald.*:

And he remembered the terrible loss she'd endured—the kind that usually killed Companions.

:*Aubryn—I'm sorry—I—*:

:*Jaylay and I were destined. And a Chosen destiny is a broad stroke, as broad as birth. Little brush strokes, like the unfortunate patch of ice that took his life—that can escape even one who is Gifted with Foresight, such as you. Companions can and do survive loss and go on to Choose again. Perhaps I will, too.*:

Wil glanced at his daughter as she said that.

:*Just not yet,*: Aubryn concluded, and pointedly withdrew.

Wil grimaced. *Stupid,* he thought to himself. But before he could beat himself up, a *third* Companion's voice said, :*Knock knock!*:

Some days I liked it better when it was just my *voice in here,* Wil thought, but Ivy jumped up and bolted out of the Waystation, shrieking, "*Uncle Lyle!*"

Wil followed.

Ivy ran straight at Lyle, who scooped up his niece in a hug. Behind the dismounted Herald came brightly painted wagons, with men and women on horseback. They all looked akin to Lyle—the black hair, the creamy tea skin.

But of course they did—because they *were* Lyle's kin.

"Hellfires," Wil muttered.

"Is there a problem, Herald Wil?"

The question came from his side. He hadn't heard the woman come up next to him, yet there she stood, a curiosity in subdued midnight blue, a curved sword on her hip. She looked the same and yet different from the others. He didn't immediately recognize her, yet he couldn't shake the sense that he *knew* her.

"No," he said flatly. "Sorry. Lelia and Lyle's family is prolific, to say the least. You are . . . ?"

She inclined her head. "Khaari."

Wil fumbled through his memory for what Lelia had taught him of her family's language. "*Zha*—um—*hall*—"

"Wind to your wings, too, Herald," Khaari said, clearly amused by his attempt.

From there, Wil waded in amidst the cousins, enduring handshakes and hugs as he sized up what had been brought to the Waystation's doorstep. He counted two dozen. Their weapons consisted of knives, compact bows, and a few short, curved swords. Little to no armor, but they did all have good mounts. A handful had participated in the last war with Ancar or skirmished with brigands, but most had only heard tales.

Wil withdrew into the Waystation. The stone in his belly tumbled and spun. He couldn't spot Ivy, but he could hear her laughter. When he'd last seen her, they'd put bright clothes on her and threaded flowers through her hair. She now blended in seamlessly with the family, just one cousin among the many. Outside of a Companion, he couldn't ask for better caretakers.

:*Vehs,*: he thought, :*this is a good time for us to do some scouting.*:

:*Oh. You . . . don't want to wait for the cover of night?*:

:*It will take us a candlemark to get to the quarry, then back again. We don't know what's waiting for us, and we don't have anyone with a Gift to survey the terrain. Cover of night would not be advised.*:

A heavy sigh. :*Okay. Look. I was enjoying handpies.*:

Wil rolled his eyes skyward. :*I'm sure Aubryn would be happy to—*:

:*You will do no such thing!*:

:*Then get your shiny tail over here.*:

As Wil ducked out of the tack shed with Vehs's gear in his arms, he found Lyle waiting for him.

"Heading out?" he asked.

"Thought I'd take a chance to survey the quarry," Wil replied.

"What quarry?"

"I'll explain when I return. Sorry, Lyle. No time to waste. If you want to talk, do it while I'm saddling Vehs."

:*You're not being nice, Wil.*:

:*Hunh. So, if I'm nice, will Madra think twice before killing another Companion?*:

Vehs recoiled mentally from the retort.

"So . . . what do you think?" Lyle gestured to the rapidly emerging camp of his kin.

"There's . . . certainly a lot of them," Wil said.

Lyle grinned. "Well, plenty of room for them here. These southern Waystations sure are something."

"Vehs says this one used to be part of Solmark before they moved the village."

"Yeah?"

Wil shrugged. "Companion wisdom. Just have to trust it."

:*Would I lie to you, Chosen?*:

:*Lie? No. Omit. . . .* :

:*Well. That cuts both ways, doesn't it?*:

Wil flinched and swung into the saddle.

"No bridle?" Lyle said.

"On a Companion? Waste of time." *And I have so little time left,* Wil thought. "Keep an eye on Ivy, okay? I should be back by dinner."

"Okay." Lyle's brow furrowed. "Wil—are you—"

"I'm fine, Lyle."

:*No. You're not.*:

Oddly enough the comment came not from Vehs but from Aubryn, the perennial eavesdropper. Wil glanced around and found her lurking a distance away—across the clearing, where Ivy played a game of tag with the cousins. Khaari stood beside the Companion, an odd duck in her midnight-blue leathers.

:*Out of my head,*: Wil thought at Aubryn.

"Set up your camp, Lyle," he said. "We'll talk later. Someplace private." He indicated the Waystation pointedly—with Madra near and Lyle's limited Mindspeech, it would be the best place for them to talk.

"All right." Lyle sketched a salute. "Herald."

"Herald."

Wil placed his hand on Vehs's neck. :*Let's go.*:

The Quarry

The bolt fired and pain striped Wil's shoulder. Madra's face twisted as he spun, but they both knew the truth: She'd missed.

"Damn—it—" Madra fumbled with the device, trying desperately to reload it.

Wil charged at her.

There'd been a time when she'd been Androa Baireschild, an agent of peace. When she'd lived to help others, to *Heal*. He'd known that person, once.

Wil drew his long-knife and slashed at Madra and the monster she'd become.

The Waystation

A Waystation, but not of Velgarth.

Wil wandered down a path in a starry place, toward a small building with warmly lit windows. Someone played a gittern, singing a song he hadn't heard in ages.

Just one more loss in his life, but one he felt the keenest.

You uncovered the false Bards and Madra's plans, Lelia, he thought. *But I'm the one who'll put an end to them, if it's the last thing I do.*

And it probably will *be the last thing I do. . . .*

Every step he took made his worries sink into the ground, the stone in his belly whittling down to a pebble. A few more steps and it would vanish to nothing at all.

His hand reached for the door—

:*Chosen.*:

Wil started awake, gasping. He'd fallen asleep, lulled by the gentle summer heat and his Companion's rolling gait—and true, Vehs would protect him—but given what they'd found at the quarry, the fact that he'd dozed at all made him sick all over.

:*But you're tired, and I am glad to shoulder this load. You need your rest so you can plan.*:

Vehs's reassurance washed over him, tamping down on his racing heart and the flood of anxiety. Wil took several deep breaths, pressing his face into his Companion's mane.

:*Another vision?*:

He shook his head. Not the starry place Waystation. He didn't know quite *what* it was, but it didn't *feel* like it came from his Gift. It felt . . . different.

:*Are you okay?*:

"I'm okay," he whispered.

:*Really?*:

The stone in his belly turned. *No.*

But to his Companion, he said, "Yes."

Vehs sighed. :*Very well.*:

The cousins had a full meal waiting for Wil—a welcoming stew of pulses and minced meat, with plenty of charcoal-baked bread to scoop it up with. The fiery spices made his eyes water, but he had become accustomed to the pain of eating their food over the years, and he now welcomed it.

"It's good?" one of the cousins, Megyn, asked.

"Amazing," he said, guzzling water.

Lyle sat down next to him as he finished.

"How'd it go?" he asked.

"I went unnoticed," Wil replied.

"Was there a danger you'd be caught?"

Wil shrugged. "Madra could have had an army waiting. She's surprised me more than once."

"But you're still here."

"I daresay I've surprised her, too." *Foresight has to have* some *advantages other than making me crazy.*

Ivy came out of nowhere and pounced on him, giving him a fierce hug that nearly upended his plate of food.

So much for that Foresight advantage, he thought.

"Can-I-sleep-in-a-tent-tonight-ple-e-e-ease?" she asked.

"Uh—yes?" he said.

"Yay!" She kissed his cheek. "Love you!" And she vanished again, running off to rejoin the horde.

Wil furrowed his brow. "What just happened?"

"You were visited by a rare but powerful chaos spirit," a soft voice said from the side where Lyle wasn't. Wil started, turning to find that Khaari had—once again—materialized out of nowhere. "Herald, we should talk."

Wil set the plate aside. "'We?'"

"Khaari's an elder among my people, Wil," Lyle said. "You can trust her."

"Lyle, can we please go talk about this in the Waystation?"

"Yeah, but Khaari—"

"No. Heralds only."

"She—she's *like* a Herald?"

The seed of doom growing inside Wil thrashed angrily. "Lyle—"

"Wil, do you know what Kal'enedral are?"

"No."

"What if I told you the Herald Captain trusts her?"

"What if I told you that I asked the Herald Captain to send an army to stop an insurrection, not a bunch of gleemen who've barely seen a battlefield?" Wil snapped.

Lyle recoiled, and even Khaari's calm mask broke momentarily, her eyebrows knitting together.

"Wil," Lyle said weakly, "you asked the Queen for help. You specifically said: *no Guards*. She did the best she could. My kinsmen aren't your typical gleemen. We are descended from Shin'a'in warriors."

Wil leaned in close. "Your kinsmen could be descended from northern berserkers. It doesn't matter. They're all going to die," he said. "And it's going to be because of me."

:*Chosen—*:

Wil slammed his shields up, cutting out Vehs's commentary.

Then he retreated from all of them, into the Waystation's gloom.

The Quarry

Wil slashed once, twice. Madra collapsed in blood, screaming. He took a single step forward, driven by a mix of rage and bloodlust.

Something large and shadowy moved off to his right, an indistinct blur in his vision. *Curious.*

The distraction pulled his focus—

Madra surged upward, a dagger in her hand.

"*Give Lelia my regards,*" she whispered, driving the knife through his ribcage, up through his lungs, and toward his heart.

With his dying breath, Wil cried his Companion's name.

The Waystation

Wil unrolled a map and used spare teacups and Lelia's old gittern, Bloom, to weigh it down. From a pouch that hung around his neck he removed a small quarrel head and set it down next to the map. He arranged a handful of small river stones across the map. Eight in a pinkish quartz for the ones he knew, and eight whitish-gray—the ones he didn't.

Someone knocked on the door.

"Go away," Wil said.

"Your Companion is about to splinter the door," came the reply.

Wil sighed and dropped his shields.

:*Vehs, don't break the Waystation.*:

:*Then LET THEM IN.*:

"Fine." Wil walked over and lifted the bar up.

Lyle peeked inside. A moment later, Khaari pushed past him. She glanced down at the map.

"I'll put on tea," she said.

Lyle barred the door before taking in the table display, touching the rocks with what remained of his left hand. An unfortunate encounter with a Hardorn axman had relieved him of two of his fingers. "This doesn't look so bad."

"And you'd be wrong," Wil replied acidly.

"Do you want to berate me or enlighten me?"

Wil bit back a retort. *That's fair,* he thought. *He doesn't know what he doesn't know.*

He pointed to the spot representing the quarry. "Madra's been importing outKingdom weapons. Nothing you've ever seen before. Crossbows the size of your forearm that cave in a man's chest. Flasks of oil that incinerate Companions. She could have ten men and still wipe out your whole clan."

"Wil—"

"I *wish* I were exaggerating, Lyle. *I'm* the one with

Foresight. Do you think I'm running around with a big frown on my face because it's telling me everything's going to go perfectly? Do you have any concept of how deep in the muck we are? Because *I do*. I begged Selenay to send me an army of Heralds *for a reason*." His voice took on a keening tremor. He stopped to take a steadying breath. "I've been tracking Madra and this—*Lord Dark* person for two seasons now. I've *finally* found them, and I'm pretty sure it's not good enough. But if we don't do something now, she's either going to escape—with a load of weapons that seem to be designed to destroy the country we've spent our lives defending—or *she's* going to find *us*. It's not like Waystations are hard to find."

"And Lord Dark?" Khaari asked.

Wil shook his head. "Who knows. He seems more than content to let others do his work for him and to speak through his servants—*literally*." His skin crawled at a memory from Cortsberth. He shook himself out of it. "We can assume he's either Gifted or has access to Gifted. He has access to Madra, at least. Though I wouldn't call her a Healer anymore. Not after all she's done."

"Wait," Lyle said. "She's a Healer?"

"*She's* Androa Baireschild. Madra's not her real name." Wil gestured at the map. "That's why we're so close to the Baireschild Estates. She put everything where she knew the land. Have to wonder if Lord Grier Baireschild knew about any of this."

"Her brother. Isn't he a Healer, too?"

"He is."

"They've got a brother who's a Herald, too."

"Plus a million scheming cousins." Wil spread his hands. "Who knows who in this family's involved in this?"

"So what twists a Healer?" Khaari asked, softly.

Wil shrugged. "I mean, we have lots of stories of Bards going rogue because . . . well, they're Bards.

Heralds? Tylendel. One legend who shut himself off from his Companion and made a terrible choice. But what causes a Healer to twist?"

"Pain," Khaari said into the yawning quiet. "Crippling pain."

Wil curled his fingers into fists. "Regardless. She made a choice. She'll answer for it."

Khaari went to fetch the tea, returning with the steaming kettle. "What's your plan, Herald?"

"Lyle and I have been on the front lines. Your family and their willingness to sacrifice . . . don't mistake me. I appreciate it, I do. But I'm tired of loss in this family."

Khaari raised her brows. "So when it's someone else's family you don't know, the loss is acceptable?"

Wil frowned at her. "That's not the point."

"What is the point, Herald? How do you intend to stop Madra and Lord Dark without losses?"

Wil gazed into the gathering gloom.

"Wil?" Lyle said.

"There's loss," Wil said. "And then there's acceptable loss. I think . . . I think Vehs and I can do this ourselves."

"Wil, no."

:*Chosen* . . . :

"Herald," Khaari said, "that is suicide."

Wil let their protests washed over him, but he turned his ears instead to the distant sound of the cousins—laughing, singing, and clapping.

Shift the octaves just a bit, and all those happy noises transmuted into cries of terror and pain.

In his visions, he smelled burning bodies.

There should be more blood.

Wil cast his mind back to a memory of a dream. To a Waystation not in Velgarth. To a doorway and a voice he missed.

I'm so tired, Lelia, he thought.

"And what's it called when I lead others to die with me, Khaari?" Wil asked.

Khaari began to answer; Lyle got there first.

"So you'll just leave Ivy," he said.

"Excuse me?"

Lyle's hands curled into fists. "You heard me," he said through clenched teeth. "Your daughter needs you. Just because everyone's left *you* doesn't mean you leave *her*."

Wil's face flushed. "I—"

"No." Lyle slammed his fist down on the table. "*No*. You listen, *Herald*. I get it. The people you loved died. Selenay didn't send you a gift-wrapped Midsummer present of a perfect army of Chosen warriors. As if anyone ever gets what they want. But you know what? *Lelia gave you something*." He pointed toward the door. "She gave you *her*." Lyle shook with anger. "And you're going to throw your life away because you think this is about *taking turns* and you're too tragically *noble* to remember that the point of Foresight is to *change what you've been shown*."

Khaari sipped her tea. Outside, one of the Companions whickered.

"Sixteen against nearly double that number," Lyle said. "I'm no master strategist, and I know nothing about Madra's weapons, but if she's down in a quarry with one exit, it seems like we have the upper hand."

"Have you considered collapsing the mine entrance and letting the oathbreakers starve to death?" Khaari asked.

Both the Heralds stared at her.

"Or . . . a siege?" she asked.

"Maybe we could divert a river into the quarry?" Lyle asked.

"Or lure in a nest of colddrakes," Khaari said.

"That seems . . . dangerous," Wil said. "And impossible."

She shrugged. "While we're wishing, why not wish big?"

"Let's not go down this path," Wil said. "Can I have some time to think? Again?"

"Certainly," Khaari said. "I need a stroll to clear my head, myself."

"I wonder if dessert is ready," Lyle said, following her out.

Alone once more, Wil put his head in his hands. He could *feel* Vehs tiptoeing around his thoughts, a subtle query in waiting.

:*Yes?*: he asked.

:*Is this what's been bothering you?*:

:*Our imminent demise? Yes.*:

:*You didn't tell me?*:

His throat knotted up. :*My visions aren't exactly crystal clear. They start and leave off at random points. Parts are maddeningly blurry. The only certainty was that I'd die. And that . . . how do I tell you that?*:

:*Oh, Chosen. This . . . is always the bargain. A bargain I put upon you, if you really stop and think about it.*:

:*I don't, thanks.*:

:*I appreciate it.*:

Wil spun the quarrel. :*Can I trust Khaari?*:

:*Mostly.*:

:*Mostly?*:

:*Yes, mostly. Aubryn thinks she's reserving something, but . . . it's like Alberich-level reserve. She needs to get to know you and learn what she thinks you're capable of, and then she'll let you in. Do you know what I mean?*:

Wil ran his hands over the gittern. :*Yeah. I think I do. Okay. Let's try trusting.*:

He exhaled slowly, emptying his mind.

The gittern hummed. The quarrel flashed. Wil's focus slipped—

—outward—

—and forward.

The Quarry

Madra emerged from the mouth of the mine, cradling the crossbow in her arms.

Angry gray thunderheads massed in the sky over Wil's head. No blood, no acrid smell, no burning bodies. The air stifled them with a growing humidity.

A different *then* this time. The same quarry, but a different time. A changed future.

"You think you've won," she said.

"I have," he said.

She smiled. Her arm dropped to her side in a deliberate gesture.

Something blurred out of the mouth of the mine, but his vision couldn't seem to focus on it. He heard Madra scream-laughing a familiar refrain as something tremendous rushed toward him.

"*Give Lelia my regards.*"

Then the vision turned to white.

The Waystation

A Waystation in the forest. . . .

He walked toward it. Had always been walking toward it, in a way, since the day he'd been born. Vehs passed silently nearby. Wil couldn't see him, just felt his presence.

Flowers nodded in the night breeze, perfuming the air. A million stars winked overhead, a million fireflies flashed back in answer. Gittern music welcomed him through the door, and a dear voice sang a welcome.

Wil reached for the handle—

—and dropped his hand.

"Not yet," he said.

With a click, the door sprung open all on its own. Khaari leaned in the entryway.

"Well met, Herald," she said. "Do you walk the Moonpaths, too?"

Wil woke up with a start.

The *real* Waystation. Where the quarrel still spun, and Bloom hummed softly.

"Give Lelia my regards—"

"No," Wil said, scooping up the quarrel and shoving it back in the pouch.

:*Vehs*,: he said. :*Get Lyle and Khaari. We have a siege to plan.*:

Deep in his belly, Wil could feel the seed of the stone starting to dissolve.

The Quarry

Nothing had gone right.

Heralds.

Madra tried not to let her annoyance show, but she couldn't help picking at the scab on her arm. For a week now they'd festered in this dank hole, waiting. They'd run out of water, and no one knew how to work the old pumps. Their options, like their cups, had run dry.

She'd had a plan, once. A fantastic one, years in the making. But no plan survived first contact with the enemy, and hers had barely survived first contact with the Bard Lelia, much less a determined Herald. She'd known the cache had been compromised, but Wil's pursuit and a lack of competent help to move it had put everything into disarray. And by the time she'd rallied that help. . . .

Too late.

She glanced out the mouth of the mine entrance. The Herald's guards patrolled the ridge above the quarry, just out of range. They made no effort to hide, and at night they drummed and made so much racket no one could sleep. They'd clogged the exits with boulders and killed or captured her sentries on the first day. She'd prepared for an assault. She'd gotten a siege instead.

Gods damn them all to the deepest, coldest, harshest

hell. The one with the demons that flayed you alive and used you as a hand-puppet after.

Madra licked her lips, cracked and dry. Lack of water would kill them before scurvy and starvation, a miserable way to go. What then of the fabled Heraldic "mercy"?

Oh, they offered it. Daily. One of the Heralds would ride out and call out terms of surrender. Sweet promises of "justice" and a "fair trial."

Ha! Her mouth twisted at the thought. None for her. She had the blood of a Companion on her hands, to say nothing of Ferrin. And that twice-traitor Carris should have been added to the tally, but Wil had won *that* battle—Madra's spies had informed her the little bitch was already back to Haven. Probably singing whatever song Selenay desired.

:*Bond with me.*:

The voice wound its way through her mind, wrapped her spine, and settled like oil in her belly. Madra shuddered and shook it off. The call came every day, and every day it got a little harder to resist. Especially when she was just . . . so . . . *tired.*

"Hey, Madra," a voice said.

She turned to look at Galos, among the last of *her* Bards.

What good they've done me, she thought.

"So, ah, we've been talking," he said, not meeting her gaze.

"You have," she said flatly.

"We . . . we think it's time," he said.

:*Bond with me, Madra,*: the voice purred. :*We'll get out, together.*:

"Time for what?" she asked.

"To . . . surrender. You know. Like th-the Heralds have offered—"

She touched his forehead, shutting down his mind with her Gift. He collapsed instantly.

In a way, she did him a mercy.

In the shadows of the cave, something groaned as it rose.

"If you eat them all, could you Gate?" she asked.

:*No, no,*: it replied. :*Not here. No.*:

"Well, eat them anyway. I'm done with them. You and I can rebuild and live to fight another day. Carris is the last traitor I'll suffer." She hoisted her crossbow and turned back toward the mine entrance, touching a pouch that hung from a belt on her hip.

Behind her, she heard the wet crunching of bones, and then the screams started.

For Galos, she did a mercy.

Judging by the screams of the others, no such mercy was allotted.

The Waystation

Wil knew before Rivan's mindcall that today would be the day.

They'd turned the Old Solmark Waystation into a makeshift basecamp, rotating day and night shifts at the quarry. Khaari kept them outfitted by going to Solmark for food and supplies, and the cousins kept Ivy occupied with reading and knife-throwing lessons.

That morning he'd woken up to an oppressive air and the hot, sticky promise of an impending thunderstorm. Even though his shift wasn't until evening, he'd paced restlessly all morning, waiting and waiting, until—

:*Wil, something's wrong at the mine.*:

He saddled Vehs in record time, gave Ivy a quick kiss and hug, and then galloped off to the quarry.

He heard the screams as they rode up. They pulled alongside Rivan and Lyle on the ridge above the mine.

Is she killing them? An accident? He didn't remember this in his visions, but his visions tended to start with her emerging from the cave mouth. He glanced up at the sky. Thunderclouds. It looked right.

The screams stopped.

And then Madra stepped out, smiling, crossbow cradled in her arms.

"Surrendering?" Wil yelled down at her.

She laughed. "There's no one left to surrender, Herald. I took care of that. Like I'll take care of you."

"So you're surrendering?"

She shook her head. "You think you've—" she started to say.

"*Now!*" Wil yelled.

Above the mine entrance, Khaari and the cousins triggered the rockslide.

Madra dove forward, crossbow flying out of her arms as she avoided the thunderous rain of scree and boulders. Dust flooded the quarry below. With a week at their disposal, they'd had enough time and hands to engineer the trap per Wil's design and the ingenuity of the cousins.

Not exactly a river or a colddrake, but the next best thing they could manage.

Wil waited, holding his breath. This was the part of his vision where things went unstable, the part he couldn't predict. But—

I think . . . it worked? Wil thought, a smile daring to spread across his face.

Something pushed the rocks aside.

Not easily. It didn't burst through them like in a Bard's tale, instead digging away with purposeful sweeps.

From the overlook above the mine, Khaari gave a high-pitched howl, drew her sword, and leaped down the escarpment as if she were half-mountain goat.

"*Scatter!*" Wil bellowed, and the cousins broke for the treeline, until only the Heralds, their Companions, and Khaari remained.

Wil and Lyle began nocking arrows.

The thing inside the mine emerged, poking its head through the debris. It had a serpentine body, an enormous beak, feathery wings, and hooked talons. Gore splashed its chest. It looked like something mashed together from spare pieces, a monstrous grab bag of parts that filled the quarry. It glared balefully at them as it perched on the boulders.

I take it back, Wil thought. *This didn't work at all.*

The construct looked up at Khaari curiously, then bent its head and reached for something, picking it up before launching into the sky. Khaari slashed at the creature, but it ignored her, beating its wings lazily before circling once, gliding past, then crossing again. It angled toward the Heralds as if commanded.

The arrows largely bounced off the creature's body. One sank into its neck, but it glided on, undeterred. In the second before it banked up, Wil saw Madra clutched in its talons.

She met his gaze as she flung a powder in his face.

"Give Lelia my regards," she hissed.

Wil's world filled with an acrid perfume. His eyes and skin burned. His head exploded in red fire.

:*Chosen—!*: he heard Vehs cry.

And then silence.

Between

The morning started with quiet and an internal stillness.

Wil opened his eyes and wondered if he'd gone deaf. But sound hadn't abandoned him. He sat up to the shush of sheets and muffled birdsong coming through the unfamiliar shutters. He didn't know where he was, but a moment later he heard soft footfalls, and then Ivy was standing beside him, looking up worriedly.

They shared a long moment.

She wrinkled her nose.

"Your breath stinks, Dada," she said.

"Good to see you, too, *liebshahl,*" he croaked.

She flung her arms around him. The doors opened, and Khaari and Lyle entered. They looked equal parts relieved and dour.

"Don't get too close," he warned them. "My breath is atrocious."

Khaari snorted. "To be expected. You've been out a few days, and the Healer's been forcing all manner of potions down your throat."

"Oh, good. Potions." He rubbed his head. "What did Madra throw at me? I can't hear Vehs."

Lyle and Khaari exchanged a look.

Out of decades of habit, Wil tried—*:Vehs?:*—but to no avail. The bond hadn't broken, but the disconcerting silence between them echoed dully, like when his ears got stuffed up from a cold, but a million times worse.

The acrid powder. What was it?

Was it . . . permanent?

"Where did you find a Healer?" he asked. "Where are we?"

Again that exchanged look. Wil felt fragments of his memory starting to return.

"What . . . was that . . . *thing* . . . with Madra . . . ," he asked.

"That," Khaari said, "was what I came here for."

Wil stared at her.

"I have not been completely forthcoming. To be honest, Herald, you had every right to not trust me completely when we first met, though not for the reasons you think. The Shin'a'in are sworn to certain duties. And your Madra unearthed something she should not have. She calls it Lord Dark. I had a suspicion it was in the mine with her, but. . . ." Khaari bowed her head. "Trust . . . may have been hard for me to grant you, as well. I'm sorry. I truly believed the cave-in would work."

"Did anyone of our number die?" he asked.

Khaari and Lyle shook their heads "no."

"Acceptable losses, then," Wil said.

The door opened again, and a man in lush green entered, his robes trimmed in gold. Attire that suited both a Healer and a lord.

Lord Grier Baireschild inclined his head. "I'm glad to see my patient is doing well," he said. "The Kal'enedral got you here just in time for me to save you. When you are recuperated, Herald, we should talk about what we're going to do about my so-called sister."

Wil's Quarry

The wind snapped at Madra's face, and her ankle and wrist sang with a distant agony; she'd broken both evading falling rocks.

The presence coiled around her spine and the base of her neck no longer felt alien, and she wondered why she'd fought it for so long. It siphoned off the pain, she knew not to where. It used it for something. She didn't care what, so long as things hurt less.

:*We were always meant to be,*: it crooned to her. :*Always, my chosen.*:

:*Yes,*: she thought back at it, wearily. :*Of course.*:

At least the Herald would bother her no more. She'd thrown enough of the *erakk*-fungus in his face to ensure that.

Lord Dark's talons pressed into her sides, the tips drawing just a little blood. But no matter. Blood had drawn her to it, blood bound them together. What was a little more now?

They flew together toward the Pelagirs, and new plans.

Weight of a Hundred Eyes

Dylan Birtolo

"Help!"

The voice called from inside the granary, a panicked shout that jerked Paxia's attention like the crack of a whip. She dropped her water bucket, the liquid spilling over and soaking into the dirt road as the young girl stared at the building. She blinked once and rushed forward, investigating the source.

The door to the sturdy wooden building stood open, illuminating the front room with shelves warping under the weight of the bagged supplies they carried. The smell of fresh-milled grain made the air heavy.

Paxia weaved around the barrels, heading to the large rolling door leading to the grain storage area. She grunting with the effort to move the slab of wood standing over twice her height; the wheels squealed in protest as it opened.

A pile of grain sacks blocked the entrance, tall enough to prevent Paxia from seeing farther into the room. Between the edge of the door and the sacks, she saw Jindar, his legs pinned. His face tightened in pain, and his skin flushed red as he reached up with both hands to wedge the grain high enough to slide out from underneath. His arms shook with the strain, but he couldn't escape. He gasped as his arms collapsed to his side, and he winced as the burden shifted.

When he opened his eyes, he saw the girl standing in the doorway and smiled with relief despite the tear streaks running down the sides of his face.

"Paxia, go get help! Please!" He sucked in breath through his teeth and arched his back as much as his compromised position allowed him to.

Paxia started to turn when she heard a horrible groaning sound, like trees in the forest during a windstorm. The long chutes stretching through the empty space near the top of the granary shifted, the supports holding them in place bending to their limits. A *crack* sounded, and a large splinter flew across the room as it burst free from one of the pillars. Jindar looked up at the chute over his exposed body, his eyes wide as the rest of him froze like a fish stuck in ice.

As the support buckled under the strain, shards of wood flew through the room, a sharpened hailstorm. Jindar covered his face with his arms, shielding his impending death from sight but doing little to protect against the crushing impact.

A strong wind summoned from the doorway burst through the room, toppling the top couple of sacks from the pile and blowing the falling structure away from Jindar. It crashed a few feet from him, kicking up a cloud of dust and dirt that made him cough before the lingering wisps of the wind cleared the air.

Paxia stood in the doorway, both hands held in front of her, fingers extended and palms facing out as if she was pushing against an invisible wall. Sweat made her light hair stick to her face, and her breath came in ragged gasps that made her shake with each inhalation.

A handful of people rushed into the granary, the first one easing Paxia to the side so they could lift the sacks off Jindar. The young girl stood in the corner, trembling as she stared ahead, not seeing anything. Even though no one looked in her direction, she felt the eyes following her, watching as if they were boring through her soul. She turned to look over her shoulder, but she saw only the wall. She heard the others speaking as they pulled Jindar free, the voices coming from a distance as if she sat at the bottom of a well.

"What happened?"

"I was moving some of the stores around, and one of the shelves collapsed. Been saying we needed to replace those for months now! It crushed my leg, and I got trapped. Got lucky when the grain chute collapsed. Just missed me."

Paxia looked up as he told the story, opening her mouth to say something but stopping herself before any words came out. Hadn't she helped? She could've sworn she had. But what could she have done? Her eyebrows scrunched together as she tried to piece the memory of events back together, but they felt indistinct. She looked down and curled a fist as she tried to force her mind to remember.

"Paxia, are you alright?"

"Must've been scary, seeing someone almost die."

"She just stood there, didn't do anything."

"Probably was terrified."

The voices closed around her, making her feel crowded, and she sank back further into the corner. They distracted her focus and made it harder to think. But through it all, nothing diminished the feeling of being studied and judged.

Paxia stood up straight and let the blacksmith hammer drop from her fingers to thud into the dirt. She closed her eyes and began to shake, clenching her hands into fists to try to block the sensation. She knew if she looked back, no one would be there, but that did little to quell the sensation of someone watching her. Most days, the notion was a mild scratching at the back of her mind that she ignored thanks to the rhythmic hammer.

"What's wrong?" Reynaud asked as he walked into

the room, carrying a yoke laden down with buckets of water that sloshed with each step. He put them down near the forge.

Paxia reached up and pinched the bridge of her nose while taking a deep breath, taking comfort in the odor of coal smoke and heat. She shook her head, trying to clear it to no avail.

"Let me guess, we've got a visiting Herald?"

Reynaud stopped as he reached for one of the buckets and looked at the smith. He mouthed the single word "how" before continuing with his chores. Paxia reached up and rubbed the back of her neck, glad that the heat of the forge kept her skin red. She hoped it would hide some of her discomfort. She always knew when the Heralds came, ever since she was a girl. It heightened the sensation of the hidden watchers.

After dumping the water into the reservoir, Reynaud came back around, tossing the empty buckets near the wall. Paxia bent down to pick up the hammer and tossed it in his direction. He caught it against his chest and looked at her with a single raised eyebrow.

"Finish up these horseshoes. I'm going to take a break and will come back to check on your work."

She walked out of the forge, listening to the steady ring of hammer on metal behind her. On her way, she scooped up a handful of water and splashed it against the back of her neck, appreciating the cool drips that ran down on either side of her spine as she stood up and stretched her back. Once outside, she untied her hair, letting it drop down and feeling the weight of it tug against her scalp. She scooped up the light strands and tossed them over a shoulder, keeping her neck open to the air.

Across the street, she saw a pure white horse staring at her in a way that reminded her of the pressure she never escaped from. Even if the legend of Companions wasn't known throughout Valdemar, she would have recognized that the creature was far from normal. It wasn't just its appearance, or its bright blue eyes that could enchant with a single glance. To her eyes, the horse had an aura of light surrounding it. She turned away, heading down the road and moving away from the creature. Her hand strayed up once again to the back of her neck as her steps quickened.

As she came around the corner of her forge, she knocked a young girl to the ground as her stride carried her through the child. Paxia slid to a stop and crouched down, reaching out to the girl. "Are you okay, Tessa? I'm so sorry."

Paxia took the girl's arm in her hand and helped her to stand back up. The youngster smiled and nodded. "I'm okay. I'm gonna go skip rocks on the ferry!"

The last part was said with such a tone of confident authority that Paxia couldn't keep the grin from her face. "Well, then you better find the good ones." She tousled Tessa's hair before reaching down and picking up a rock from the ground. Brushing it off with her fingers, she handed it over. "Flat enough to just shoot across the water."

The girl took the rock and looked it over before scampering on her way with the urgency of a focused child. Paxia watched her go, her vision trailing across the Companion staring in her direction. The smile faded, and Paxia turned away, glad to be have the corner of the building between her and the watcher.

The Herald left later that night, but the sense of being watched still clawed at Paxia's awareness. She sat at one of the tables in her forge, enjoying the lingering heat of the day's efforts as she cradled a cup of mead.

Reynaud sat across from her, his own mug resting in his lap as he propped his ankles on the corner of the table. "Why don't you like Heralds?" he asked, cutting to the question without any preamble.

Paxia sighed and moved her hand in a circle, watching the waves of amber liquid climb the sides as they circled around. "It's not that I don't like them. I don't have anything against them. I just feel uneasy when they're around."

"Why? I mean, they just come around, ask some questions, and then they go on their way after taking care of a dispute or something."

He paused to offer Paxia a chance to respond, but when she didn't, he continued. "If you ask me, their Companions are the amazing ones. Have you ever been lucky enough to spend time with one when they come by? They're smart, smarter than a horse, and that's saying something."

Paxia's hand shook, disturbing her rhythm, and a few drops of mead splashed over the side of her cup, soaking into the wood of the table. She put her drink down and pulled her hands back, resting them under the table.

"Do you ever get the feeling that—they're watching you?" Paxia asked, her voice softer than normal as she posed the question to her apprentice.

"Nah, not really. I mean, they watch everything I guess, and they're smart, like I said. But I don't think so." He looked at her and tilted his head to the side as he noticed her discomfort. "You're not worried they're keeping an eye on you, are you? Why would they? You haven't done nothing wrong, and you're just a smith. I mean, a good smith, but you're always helping folks. Why would they scare you?"

"I'm not scared, just uneasy. There's a difference."

Paxia crossed her arms in front of her chest, lifting her eyes to stare at Reynaud as if daring him to challenge her statement. He raised his hands to either side to signal his surrender. They continued their drinks in silence until Reynaud finished his and left to return to his family's home. Paxia remained at the table, playing with her mug and trying in vain to avoid the sensation that someone was lurking in the shadows of her forge, watching her. Always watching . . .

Standing up, she hurled her wooden cup behind her. It struck the wall, and the vessel cracked from the force of the impact. But no one was there, just as she knew there wouldn't be.

Reaching up, she ran her fingers through her hair and dug into her scalp along the way. Every time a Herald visited, the hidden eyes grew in strength. Knowing that sleep would elude her for the next few days, she fired up the forge. Until the sensation dulled, the only sleep she'd get was from collapsing in exhaustion.

Her hammer rang out through the night, the steady clang of metal on metal echoing through the village.

The weather cooled, and the breeze felt refreshing as it danced through the open sides of Paxia's forge. She caught the earthy smells of dirt and grass that warned of a forthcoming storm. She kept her attention focused on her work as the wind picked up, only aware of the intensity of the storm when her shop descended into darkness usually reserved for sunset. Putting down her tools, Paxia stepped outside.

As she did so, the wind whipped around her, hard enough to make her take a step with its intensity. It tugged at her hair, yanking it free and snapping it out to her side. The dark clouds looked like coals cooled beyond the point of being useful. A storm this intense hadn't assaulted their village since before Paxia had started her apprenticeship.

Several people rushed past her, running down the road toward the river. Reynaud saw her, and she gestured for him to come close, fearing her call would be lost on the wind.

"What's going on?" she shouted in his ear to be heard over the howling.

"Some of the children were playing in the river and are stuck on the other side. We're trying to get a crew to rescue them."

Paxia didn't wait for him to finish explaining before she ran off to join the others in their rescue attempt. The wind made the surface of the river froth with whitecaps. On the far side, three children sat huddled around a fourth who lay on his back unmoving. The rope connecting the two sides snapped in the wind and rain, but the ferry the children used to cross was torn apart. Pieces of it lay scattered on the shore downstream from the crossing.

As Paxia ran up, a couple of villagers tried to get to the far side, using the rope to move hand-over-hand. But the river slapped at their bodies and tore them free. Only the lifeline around their waists kept them from being washed downstream or pulled underwater.

The people stood around the rope support, screaming at each other as they tried to brainstorm a way across. Paxia stood far enough away that their words were lost long before they reached her. She stared at the surging waters, shaking her head.

"What is it?" Reynaud asked, coming up behind her.

"We'll never get across with the storm this strong."

"Are you saying we should leave them? Cayl could be hurt!" Reynaud gestured at the boy in the mud.

"No. We need to do something . . ." Paxia's words died as she felt herself grow distant, and the entire world seemed to lose distinction. She no longer felt the needles of rain stabbing into her flesh. The howling wind mixed with the voices to form one continuous song that bore no meaning.

Paxia dropped to her knees and closed her eyes, reaching out with her hands and feeling something that wasn't there. The smith felt the eyes behind her, boring into her soul and growing in number. It felt as though they existed right behind her neck, but she tried to push them away and focus on . . .

Paxia wasn't sure what she focused on. She only knew she needed to help the children. There was no way they'd get across the river with the storm raging.

As she focused, the wind slowed down. The continuous gale weakened to strong gusts, until those too became pale imitations of their earlier intensity. Paxia felt a different current, something other than the wind and the water, what she could only describe as a pulsing lifeline under the ground itself. In her mind's eye, she dared to touch it, letting the energy of it flow up through her arms and into the sky above. She didn't know why, but it felt right on a level she could never explain.

The stares in her back became painful daggers that made her shiver and want to scream, but she continued to focus.

"Paxia, get up! The storm is weakening!" Reynaud reached out and grabbed her shoulder, shaking it.

The smith snapped her eyes open and pushed his arm away. Her other hand came around and her palm slammed into his chest, shoving him away hard enough that he slipped and fell into the mud.

"Don't touch me!" she screamed.

She jumped to her feet and bolted, running in the direction of her forge. The weight of the stare followed her. People stopped and watched as she ran past, people she'd known her entire life, people who had helped raise her or she had helped raise. They whispered questions, and Paxia knew she had to be the subject of their secret conversations.

When she reached the forge, the smith grabbed the wall to pull herself around and flatten her back against the treated wood as she panted for air. But she still felt watched. Measured. Judged.

Snagging her hammer from the ground, she attacked the wall, swinging her weapon into it several times and making pieces fracture off and lance through her flesh. She continued attacking the structure until she collapsed to her knees, eyes shut tight, gulping down air. The weight of the stares continued pressing down on her, and she curled up over her knees, fingers digging into her shins hard enough to bruise.

Time bore no meaning, and Paxia couldn't say how long she lay in that position. At some point, Reynaud entered the forge and eased down to place a hand on her shoulder. She looked at him and blinked several times as if banishing sleep from her eyes. Looking past him, she saw the sky was dark, and stars sparkled in the dark canvas.

"Are you okay?" he whispered.

When she moved to sit up, he winced, pulling his hand back. The motion was subtle, but enough to make Paxia realize the damage that had been done.

"I think so," she lied. The skin at the back of her neck still crawled, and she reached up to rub it, trying to chase away the insects that weren't there. "How are the children?"

Reynaud sat back on his heels and offered a light smile. "Good. The storm cleared up just in time. As soon as it did, a few people got across and carried them back." His smile faded and he took a quick breath. "Cayl hit his head on a rock when the ferry got ripped apart and hasn't woken up. They sent for a Healer."

"I'm glad." She paused. "Sorry about pushing you away. I don't know what happened."

"Don't worry about it. If you're sure you're okay, I'll see you tomorrow?"

Paxia nodded and pushed herself up. Reynaud offered her a hand to help her stand and then turned away, taking long strides to get out of the forge. With a sigh, the smith snagged the bottle of mead standing on the table. She hoped it might chase away the ghosts clawing at her mind.

After an hour, she realized the futility of that approach and went to work. As she attacked the metal, she had no image in her mind, no goal she worked toward. She brought the hammer down over and over, using the motion to tire herself out. As time wore on, she used more force, knowing those eyes continued to judge her behavior. With a scream, she slammed down hard enough to snap the haft of her hammer with a solid *crack*.

Paxia collapsed to a knee, draping her arm over the anvil. She looked up and saw Tessa standing at the entrance to her forge, staring with wide eyes.

"Get out," Paxia snarled. "Stop staring!"

She hurled the broken handle in the child's direction. The girl ran off, and the smith collapsed to the ground in front of the anvil, falling into the blissful ignorance of exhausted sleep.

The Healer came two days later, and Paxia knew he arrived before the news spread. Her watchers had started to become uninterested only to spark in intensity, which made her snap again at Reynaud, chasing him from her forge. After he left, her shoulders slumped and she collapsed in a chair, draping her arms in front of her across the table. She regretted the words as soon as they flew from her mouth, but that was too late.

When she heard a shuffle in the dirt behind her, she jumped up and turned around.

"I'm sorry, Reynaud . . ." her sentence died as she saw the stranger in her forge.

He was about her height, dressed in fine traveling clothes that far exceeded anything she saw in her village. His head was shaved smooth, with only a bare hint of stubble showing. He carried a sword on his hip and managed to look comfortable and graceful without being ostentatious or lording his wealth and position. Some part of her wanted to like him as soon as her eyes fell upon him.

"Greetings. I am Herald Adouin. I came here to heal the young boy, Cayl."

Paxia felt her hand twitch as it tried to reach up to

the back of her neck, but she willed it to stay in place. Her desire to like the man fled as soon as he revealed his title.

"How is he?" she asked, keeping her voice even.

"He is well. There was some swelling under his skull from striking the rocks, but I've managed to bring it down. He should be fine within a day or so. The advantage of youth."

He offered a smile that Paxia imagined worked well on ladies—and possibly lords as well. However, she couldn't chase the feeling of the lurkers just beyond her ability to see. His presence agitated them, made them feel more pressing, as though the sound went from a dull pulse to a sharp buzzing. It served as a potent antidote to his charms.

"That's good," Paxia said in a clipped voice as she went back to the anvil and picked up her hammer. She worked on her latest commission, ignoring him.

Despite the brusque interaction, he stepped closer. He kept his hands behind his back, whether to hide them or as some sort of formality, she couldn't tell.

"Would you be willing to accompany me on a walk?"

"What for?" Paxia asked, continuing to ring her hammer against the metal.

"There's something I wish to discuss with you." He paused. "It concerns the safety of your village, of the children like Cayl."

Those words made the smith stop with her hammer held above her head. After a moment, she tucked it into her belt and nodded, gesturing for the Herald to lead on.

She fell into step behind him as they took a route that led them to the nearest border of the village. The Companion walked up beside Adouin, lowering her head so that she could rub her face against his arm. She looked at Paxia, and the human glanced away.

"Nia says that there's something important you need to do."

Paxia stopped and raised an eyebrow.

"My Companion," Adouin explained, gesturing the magnificent animal beside him. "Her name is Nia, and she told me that we needed to speak. She has something you need to see."

This time when Paxia looked over at the Companion, she was surprised to see Nia drop her gaze and look to the side, as if the animal was ashamed. The smith knew the Companions were more than they seemed, but that reaction seemed oddly human.

"What does she need to show me?" Paxia asked. "What is it she wants of me?"

"She says you won't believe words. We need to show you. It involves your watchers."

Paxia's eyes widened, and she took a step back. Adouin's eyebrows squeezed together as he offered a shrug and held out his hands in front of him with the palms up. But the Companion kept her head turned away. The mere mention of the watchers magnified their intensity, and Paxia had to take a few quick breaths as her skin crawled.

"Please?" Adouin asked. "If not for you, for the children?"

Afraid to trust her voice, Paxia nodded, walking along beside the Herald, his Companion on the far side of them. Their path took them to another horse, this one brown and tethered to a stake in the ground.

"Nia didn't think you would trust her to carry you," Adouin offered as way of explanation.

The group set off at a fast pace to the east, crossing over the plains at a steady rate. The entire time, Paxia's mind rolled over the possibilities, but she couldn't come up with any idea of what the Companion wanted to show her. The smith's legs squeezed the mount harder, and her fists squeezed the reins until her knuckles whitened from the strain.

After a few minutes, Paxia realized the strain that had followed her for years lightened as if brushed away by the wind of their travel. With each successive stride it grew lighter until it vanished, and no trace remained. She pulled back on her reins, pulling to a stop that left her mount's hooves sliding through the grass.

Paxia sat for a moment, feeling a freedom she'd never experienced since she was a child. The world burst into life in a way that she had never imagined possible. The aura around the Companion increased in intensity, but even beyond that, the ground itself seemed alive. The smith saw a current of power running under their feet, something she knew she could touch.

"What . . . ?" she managed to say.

Adouin and Nia came close, just an arm's reach away. The Herald reached out and placed one of his hands on the smith's shoulder. She twitched at the touch, but turned her head to look at Adouin out of the corner of her vision.

"Nia says this can be your life. That you will be happier here."

"How?" Paxia asked. Her shoulders tensed in anticipation of the cost for such a future.

"You can never return to Valdemar. Nia says you're special, like a Herald, but you can't live in Valdemar any longer. You're a threat to others . . . and yourself."

Paxia froze, not blinking as she stared at Adouin. He continued, talking faster to try to soothe the pain. "You'll be happier here. You won't have to worry about the watchers, whatever they are. Nia says—"

"You knew about this?" Paxia growled, cutting him off. Her eyes shifted to the Companion, who twisted her neck to look away.

Adouin opened his mouth to offer an explanation, but Paxia roared and grabbed the Herald's arm, yanking hard and pulling him out of the saddle to slam against the ground with a grunt. Before Nia could react, Paxia launched herself out of the saddle, wrapping her arms around the Companion's neck and pulling her to the ground with her sheer weight.

The Companion scrambled, kicking up dirt and making the other horse panic, driving it off a short distance. Paxia rolled over her shoulder up to her feet and yanked her hammer free from her belt. The sheer level of betrayal running through her powered her motions beyond any rational thought.

"You *knew*," she growled. "All these years you *knew* and did *nothing*. You just let me suffer. Do you have any idea what it's like to be a child and watched all the time and have others think you're crazy every day?"

Mad with rage, she swung her hammer at Nia. The Companion got her feet under her enough to dance away before the weapon came close to connecting.

Adouin recovered and lunged at Paxia with his sword, moving between the smith and his Companion. She jumped back and swatted at his blade with her hammer, making it ring as it cut through empty air.

"What are you doing?" he screamed.

"How many others have you left behind?" Paxia screamed back as she charged. She whipped her hammer back and forth with a strength and speed only possible through years of working a forge and using the pounding of steel to hide from the feeling of being scrutinized.

Adouin tried to keep up, but he lacked the skills to match her power. The best he managed was to retreat while trying to deflect any blows that came too close. He stumbled, falling back and lifting his sword up to try and stave off her blow.

She brought her hammer down and shattered his sword, sending the broken end into his shoulder. He cried out and she lifted her hammer once again, holding it high above her head. As she started to bring it down, two thousand pounds of horseflesh slammed into her shoulder, driving her across the ground and sending her weapon flying from her hand.

Nia charged forward, the ground shaking under the

impact of her hooves as she ran at the smith again. Paxia rose up to her knees and lifted her arms in front of her, pulling on the energy she felt beneath her. The Companion rose up on her back legs and brought her front hooves down. They struck an invisible barrier, making her bounce and slide off to the side. She tried again, but met with the same resistance, unable to get closer to her target.

"Nia . . ." The weak call pulled the Companion from her defensive rage, and she turned to her Herald. Adouin stood with one hand pressed against his shoulder, blood seeping into his clothes around his fingers. "Please . . . stop."

The Companion snorted and walked back to Adouin, keeping Paxia within view of one of her blue eyes the entire time. She nuzzled the Herald with a light touch in his uninjured shoulder.

The smith stood up, hands clenched in fists, but not yet advancing.

"I don't know what's going on, and I don't know why you have such hatred for Nia, but I promise, she did nothing to hurt you." He paused, and his mouth hung open a small amount. He glanced at his Companion before shaking his head and turning back to Paxia. "Nothing intentional. There was nothing she could do."

With a wince, he climbed up on Nia's back. Paxia lowered her head and glared at them through her eyebrows.

"You should not return to Valdemar," Adouin said.

"So now you banish me after torturing me and driving me to madness?" Paxia barked a laugh without warmth. "I will return home, and I'll make sure you're paid your due."

The Herald opened his mouth to say something but stopped and swallowed, wavering a bit in his saddle. "I'm sorry," he offered before Nia turned and they galloped back to Valdemar.

Paxia spit on the ground as they left and watched

them disappear into the distance. Walking over to her hammer, she snatched it up and went to retrieve the mount left behind.

She would return to Valdemar, but first she needed to learn what she was capable of—and how she could use that to find her justice.

Woman's Need Calls Me

Mercedes Lackey

Woman's need calls me as woman's need made me.
Her need will I answer as my maker bade me.

—INSCRIPTION ON THE BLADE OF
THE MAGE-FORGED SWORD, "NEED"

"Why is it that whenever the great powers fight, it's always the little people that get screwed?" asked Melysatra.

Since she was riding on a tiny, dusty track over rolling hills covered in grass and scrub, with the only sign of life an occasional wild goat peering at her as she passed, and the horse was not going to answer, this question might have seemed rhetorical.

However . . .

:Because avalanches don't take votes from the pebbles before they fall,: said the familiar voice that sounded as if it were coming from somewhere in between her ears.

Mel cocked her head to the side. "That—sounds really good," she said admiringly. "You ought to have it embroidered as a motto or something."

:Cute. Where would I hang it?:

"I could have it tooled into your sheath?"

:Huh. Not an altogether bad idea. By the way, did you just pick a direction at random when we left the Temple-hostel, or have you an idea of where we're going?:

"Well . . . you're the one that picked the Temple as a destination in the first place, if you'll recall. Not that I objected." Mel chuckled. "The looks on those bastards' faces when we carved them into tiny giblets when they thought I was just a single, simple Mage, easily overpowered? Priceless. That would have been worth the trip alone. But to answer your question . . . I sort of picked a direction at random. We're headed *away* from what used to be Ma'ar's Tower, which is all I really care about." She shuddered. "We're going to need to put a lot of distance between us and that particular disaster if we're going to get someplace where the Mage Storms are weak enough to survive."

:We're that far now,: Need informed her.

She looked down at the sword at her side and patted the hilt.

"I'd like to get a lot farther," she replied. "And yes, I know you can warn me in time to get into shelter, but those things are officially not what I consider to be a good time."

The sword was quiet for a moment. *:We're about to get into forest. And there's running water crossing the path ahead of us when we get there.:*

"You're making me soft, lazy, and forgetful of my foraging and scouting skills, sister."

:No, I'm not. I'm just saving you time.:

The conversation, half aloud and half silent, continued until the pair approached the predicted forest. It was idle banter more than actual conversation; Mel had been Need's bearer for four decades now and was well into a fifth. She'd been a low-level Mage in Urtho's army, valuable as much for the fighting skills Need gave her as for her magic—although she used the little she had very cleverly. They'd survived the war between Urtho and Ma'ar, they'd survived the frantic exodus of Urtho's people by jumping through a Gate that dumped them in the middle of the wilderness alone, and so far, they had survived the wilderness and the Mage Storms.

But truth to tell, Mel was getting tired of it all. Given her druthers, she'd "druther" settle down somewhere, start a nice little inn, experiment with some of those beer and wine recipes she'd collected over the years, do a little healing magic, a little hedge wizardry. There was just one small problem with that plan.

The sword, Need. Need had been created, back before the Mage Wars, as an instrument of justice, specifically for women. She was exceptionally special, even among magic swords. If you were a magician, she gave you all the skills of an expert swordswoman. If you were a swordswoman, she served as a magician. But the key to all this was that you had to be a *woman*. Need could only be used by a woman. And she was *very* picky about whom she selected. After decades of Need saving her pert ass, Mel felt an obligation to find someone Need really, really wanted to partner with, because there was a price to be paid for the partnership. When Need sensed women in trouble, she *had* to go there and either she, her partner, or both would have to solve the situation. So far, a woman Need approved of had not crossed their paths.

Then again, if Mel created that inn, maybe such a woman would come to *them*. It was worth considering and putting to her partner as an option.

But first they had to find a town that had figured out how to survive the Storms. They hadn't been very lucky in that, so far. The nearest they had come had been that Temple they'd just left. Which . . . was a nice place, but they were an Order of teetotalers, and an inn that serves no beer or wine never survives for long. Mel wasn't a bad cook . . . but she wasn't good enough to make up for the lack of liquor.

All this went through her mind as she set up a secure, defensible camp, set out subtle alarm traps, and picketed the horse with grass and water in reach and a small pile of oats. Then she got water, started the fire, got one pot of what would be oat porridge started to cook overnight in the coals, and a second of what would be supper with jerky and dried vegetables over the fire. The good thing about being in a forest tomorrow would be that she'd be able to actually *see* any game that got scared up, and hopefully she would shoot something. Out on the grasslands, rabbits were just movement in the tall grass. And, of course, there would be plenty of fuel. The bad thing was that it would be a lot easier for things to sneak up on her at night.

:Mel, I'm getting a vague feeling of wrong ahead of us,: Need finally said as she was waiting for the jerky to turn back into meat and the water to turn into broth.

"Like calling you?" Mel asked.

:More like a whole village is in trouble,: the sword replied. *:I'm hearing the females, but it's a sense that everyone is involved.:*

Mel perked up at that. A village endangered would mean a lot of grateful people if she and Need solved their problem. A lot of grateful people meant a lot of spare beds—or at least, beds by the fire, in a cottage—and a lot of cooked meals before she wore out her welcome. *And maybe I can convince Need about settling, starting that inn, and letting her next bearer come to us . . .*

"Well, that sounds like an opportunity to me," she replied. "Obviously it's more than a day's ride?"

:Three or four at a guess, depending on how straight and clear that track is.: Need definitely sounded all right with them going in that direction. *:It's a level of urgent concern but not panic at the moment.:*

"So we don't have to ride hell-for-leather. Good, I'm not sure old Sam is up to that." Sam had been a gift from the Temple, and a princely one at that. He was a genuine warhorse, full stallion and all; he was past middle age, but his breed was good in service until they were thirty, occasionally older. She'd happily left the mule she'd ridden in on with the Temple. The mule had happily stayed. Combat had not suited her; mules are, after all, pacifists by nature.

By this time, the sky was dark and full of stars, and the sunset was just a lingering red line on the western horizon. Mel tasted her soup, decided it was done enough, and polished it off, burying the pot of oats and water in the coals and ashes and covering it to keep any unwanted visitors out. Her bedroll was ready; all she had to do was get into it. She'd done a quick wash when fetching the water. And one thing she never needed to do was set a watch. Need never needed to sleep.

"Good night, partner," she murmured, patting the sword laid ready beside the bedroll.

:Sleep well, partner.:

This is some incredibly old forest, Mel thought, for about the hundredth time since they had entered its outskirts. From the outside, she had not realized just how huge and ancient the trees were, because the margins were first new-growth, then what she would have normally considered "mature" trees. But then . . . then the trees had gotten bigger, and bigger, until most of them had trunks it would take ten or more men, arms completely outstretched, to circle. The trunks went straight up and up, only spreading out into a canopy when they were so high above her that the thought of climbing them made her dizzy.

It seemed impossible that a forest this old could have survived the war, but it had. And now there was no one to ask *why* it had survived . . . but some of the people who had scouted the first escape Gates had reported back "huge forest," before they grabbed supplies and started ushering people through, so maybe some of Urtho's folk were to be found in here.

:Village should be coming into view about now,: Need warned her. Despite the size of the tree trunks, Mel could still see a reasonable distance down the track. A bright spot between the trunks appeared.

That's probably the sunlight on the cleared spot

where the village is. Need didn't seem to think there was any more urgency than there had been before, so she kept a Sam to a steady pace—

Or rather, she tried . . . because as that bright area got wider, his ears perked up, he arched his crest, flagged his tail, flared his nostrils, and broke into a trot. Not the most comfortable of paces, but Mel couldn't blame him. He must have smelled other horses, and he knew that where there were horses, there was hay and oats and maybe mares.

So she rode into the village looking to the untutored eye like a triumphant warrior. As long as you looked at Sam and not too closely at her.

Sam stopped at the dead center of the village and struck a pose, looking around for the other horses. And since everyone in the entire village had just been alerted by the sound of his heavy hooves pounding the track, the curious gathered.

:That's a good sign,: Need observed, and indeed, it was. In plenty of the villages that Mel had ridden into, the sound of a warhorse drove people into hiding, it didn't lure them out to see who it was.

While Mel waited for someone nominally in charge to turn up, she got a good look at the village and was both surprised and pleased. There must have been at least thirty to forty substantial buildings, from wooden-shingled cottages to a couple of three-story houses that a relatively wealthy merchant or farmer would not have been ashamed to own. Not surprising in a forest like this, they were all made of wood, although unlike any other house she had ever seen, they were black. After a moment, she figured out that the black was tar that had been used to waterproof them instead of paint. And the very oldest of these buildings looked as though they had been here for at least a couple of centuries.

At a second glance, there was something else different about these houses. All of them were, either in whole or in part, built on top of a foundation of what must have been the stumps of the huge trees, planed flat to the ground. It made her head whirl to think how much work that must have taken.

People around here dressed absolutely alike, which was interesting: leather trews and fabric shirt and supple leather tunic for both sexes, in a limited palette of browns, yellows, and dull reds. But again, that was smart if your resources for fabric were limited. If everyone in the family wore the same outfits, they could be handed down regardless of which sex the child was. *Not a lot of sheep or flax in a forest.* Fabric obviously had to come from outside.

Finally someone—she guessed it was a blacksmith from his leather apron—approached her stirrup. He opened his mouth, and she prayed he would utter something she understood, or she'd have to burn some precious magical energy to learn the local language in a hurry.

"Well coom, leddy," he said, and she let out her breath in a sigh of relief. "Who be ye?"

"Melysatra of Silence Tower," she said, "Formerly in service to the Mage Urtho."

Truth to tell, she expected incomprehension at best. Instead, the man's face lit up. "Och, well!" he said. "There be more of setch peoples some tenday down rood. Good folk and all. T'kind as he'ps at need. Got tree here a-now, t'he'p wi tha Beast. Be ye here for same?"

"I am," she replied, with a little prodding from Need.

"Then I be take ye to 'em, if ye'll foller, leddy," he said. She gave Sam a little nudge to get him going as the blacksmith walked off, the crowd parting for him.

Pretty much everyone was smiling at this point, so Mel judged she'd said all the right things.

But where he brought her was . . . unexpected.

Right at the edge of the village was a perfect circle of perfect meadow. She judged it to be between ten and fifteen acres worth. It had absolutely no right to be here, and the edges were cut off as precisely as if they had been laid out by a surveyor.

In fact . . . now that she looked closer, the edges were cut right through the center of the trunks of many of the trees. Whatever had happened had occurred about the time when the magic around Urtho's Tower imploded, because while the trees with parts cut off were dead, they weren't shedding limbs yet.

What in the Seven Hells. . . . She had a good idea what she was looking at: some sort of epic displacement magic. The meadow had no right to be here because it wasn't *from* here. And probably somewhere in some far off meadowland, there was a fifteen acre circle of these enormous trees, planted where they had no right to be either. It had to be an effect of the Mage Storms that had followed the fall of Urtho's and Ma'ar's strongholds.

Sam was very happy to see all that lush grass, however, and just as happy to see the three other horses, since he was a very sociable animal.

The three horses, she was pleased to see, were out on a standard and familiar picket line, and she was even happier to see that the three young men—who had made a very respectable and neat camp—were wearing faded blue tunics with a familiar design.

"Warrik's Wolves?" she called, as she got within easy speaking distance.

All three heads came up, and all three faces wore smiles. "Aye, lady. Another refugee from Mage Urtho's forces?"

"That I am, and damned glad to see a familiar uniform. I got dropped by my lonesome in the back of nowhere." The blacksmith grinned as if he were responsible for the four of them finding each other. Mel patted him on the shoulder. "Thanks, friend. I'll find out what this Beast of yours is all about and see what I can do to help."

"Tenkee, leddy," he replied. "Us'll tell ta wives tis one more at table."

"They bring us meals," one of the lads said as the blacksmith ambled off. "Beats my cooking any day."

She made a face. "Mine too. Let me picket Sam and get settled, and then we can introduce ourselves and you can explain things to me."

Shortly she had her own shelter pitched, her bedroll laid out on a nice soft pile of cut grass, and had learned that the three young men were named Harl, Kerd, and Pol, that they were the only three of their mercenary company to have come through with a big group of tribesfolk, and that when this village had sent that group a plea for help with an unspecified "Beast," they had volunteered.

"They're good people and all, Mel," said Pol, who seemed to be the one most inclined to do the talking. "But they're very keep-to-their-own-kindish."

"They are that," Mel agreed, who'd had a few interactions with the tribesfolk.

She also learned that the circle of displaced village and forest had been the location of the village's inn and tavern. "They don't seem all that—upset—about losing the tavern and whoever was in it," she observed cautiously.

Harl laughed. "It seems the owner of the tavern was generally disliked. Since this happened in the middle of the night, he was the only one in it. All that I hear is, 'We bain't miss 'im. Miss his mead, though.'"

She also learned that the Beast had appeared shortly after the tavern and forest vanished and the meadow appeared. "Mage Storm, then," said Mel. The lads nodded. "Might have dropped another plot of land around here with something in it. Could be some monster of Maar's. We never saw everything he'd made. Has anyone actually seen it?"

"Oh, yes," Pol said. "They may seem relaxed about it, but they're not. It's not an immediate threat to this village, but they know it's moving toward us, and they know it's already destroyed a village west of here, because the survivors made it this far. They have an expert hunter tracking it."

Harl added shyly, "He comes back here every few days to see if help came, they say. He should be back any day now."

"And let me tell you, we're damned glad to see a Mage," Pol went on. "This is some sort of creature of a sort they've never seen before. If it's something of Ma'ar's, well, we're going to need you. And if it's not something of Ma'ar's . . . we might need you even more."

"Nice to be needed," she said dryly and winked. "An old bitch like me doesn't hear that very often from a lot of young bucks like you."

She managed to surprise a laugh out of them, which made them all friends, and shortly after that, two boys, a girl, and an older woman approached them carrying buckets.

She discovered that the buckets were an extremely clever way of carrying a whole dinner without spilling. Three nested dishes were inside. The top held something that looked like a loaf of bread and turned out to be a very large mushroom. The middle held braised meat. The bottom held sliced fruit drizzled with honey. And immediately, she noticed the lack of bread. Which made sense—there were no grain fields around here, after all.

And that . . . made her rethink the vague plans that had started in her mind for rebuilding their tavern here. No grain meant no beer . . .

But wait, there was fruit. And honey. So, wine and mead at least. *I can work with that.* There might be something else she could ferment and distill. A starchy tuber or root, for instance.

The mushroom was shockingly good; she was expecting something tasteless and woody for its size, but no, it was roasted to perfection, dense, and with a meaty taste. One thing she did sorely miss with it was butter. But then . . . no cows in a forest.

Would this meadow be enough to support some cows?

She paid only half an ear to the three young fellows chatting away, but enough of one to be able to respond appropriately and pleasantly. Night came quickly to this towering forest, and before too very long it was full dark.

The horses dozed on their picket; one of the young men spread nuts of some sort on a flat stone he dug out of the fire and shared the toasted result. They were bigger than she expected, but they were definitely pine nuts and tasted grand with a sprinkling of salt. *So I'll have bar snacks.*

:You're already planning on settling here, aren't you?: Need asked, amusement in her voice.

:I guess I am,: she replied.

:Oh, it's a good idea. The place doesn't have a tavern anymore, and you're due for a chance to settle down.:

She blinked. Well, that was interesting. She'd expected to get an argument from the sword, but . . . well, maybe Need had been thinking the same thing—why go hunting for a new bearer when you could let the new bearer come to you?

Need didn't seem inclined to say anything more, so she took to her bed while the lads were still talking around the fire. Maybe *they* were still young enough to stay up half the night, but she was an old campaigner at this point, and the first lesson of campaigning was eat and sleep when you can.

The hunter did indeed show up at just about mid-morning. A slim, middle-aged, extremely fit man named Lemuel, he had a very worn bow, a quiver full of expertly crafted arrows at his belt, and a beard. Otherwise he looked like another of the villagers. He also looked relieved to see them.

"Tha Beast looketh naught like ony crathur I ever saw afore," he said once they'd all introduced themselves. He shook his head. "Lethal, 'tis. An it be only a day away. Seems t'not want t'wander too far from a uncanny place."

"Uncanny place?" That got Mel's attention and Need's too. "What kind of 'uncanny place' are you talking about?"

But Lemuel just shook his head. "I canna rightly say, only 'tis uncanny," and Mel had to be satisfied with that. She looked to the three fighters, and as usual, Pol took the lead. "Can you bring us there on tracks the horses can use?" he asked.

"Oh, aye," Lemuel replied, and brightened. "I see where this's goin'. A-horse we can be there just arter noon, an' we start now."

"Then let's start now," Pol decreed. "Harl, you and I and Mel will pack up our kit and get the horses saddled, bridled, and loaded. Kerd, you get provisions for three days for all five of us. We should be ready to go by the time you get back." When Kerd ran off to the village, Pol turned to Mel. "Can your horse carry double?"

She snorted, as she turned to pack up her bedroll. "Triple. Quadruple, even. He's built for a man in full armor, and he barely notices me."

Pol cast a glance full of envy at Sam, then laughed. "And I bet he eats enough for three horses too."

She shrugged and laughed. "Within every silver lining, there's a dark cloud."

Pol had timed things well; they were just tightening down all the straps and cinches when Kerd came running up with small leather packs. "The blacksmith says this is what they carry with them on long trips—"

The pack seemed awfully small for three days' worth of provisions, but the hunter nodded with approval. "Aye," he assured them, digging into the bags and coming up with flat tan squares wrapped in paper, and a dark brown block that looked like nothing she'd ever seen before. "These be nut-flour cakes," he said, holding up the tan stuff. "And this be dried meat pounded wi' berries."

Now she understood. That was very concentrated food. "How hard is it to gnaw some off?" she asked.

"Still got all m'teeth, leddy," Lemuel replied, grinning.

Packs tied to the top of their gear on the horses, they all mounted up. Lemuel looked up very doubtfully at her. Sam was a tall horse, and if he wasn't used to riding—which, of course, he probably wasn't, since she hadn't seen any other horses in this village—he was probably pretty uncertain about how to get up there.

"Follow me," she told him, and led him to a stump that stood about as tall as his waist. "Put your left foot on top of mine and give me your left hand," she ordered, and hoisted him up to the makeshift riding pad she'd rigged behind her saddle. He grunted with surprise, probably at how far he had to spread his legs. Sam was *not* a thin horse.

"Eh, leddy, this'un feels unchancy," he said uneasily.

"Just hold onto that loop of rope I rigged behind my saddle," she told him. "Sam has a surprisingly easy pace; you won't fall off."

She took the lead as Lemuel directed them down a series of game trails—and indeed, even at Sam's fast walk, a pace the others had to trot to keep up with, he didn't fall off.

With Sam setting the pace, shortly after noon, they reached an area where Lemuel indicated they should stop and leave the horses behind. "Lessen ye want tha horses t'be bait," he added soberly.

"How big is this Beast?" Mel asked as she helped Lemuel slide off, grimacing with sympathy at his groan as he touched the ground again.

"Big," he said. "Tall as tallest housen i' village."

They looked at each other, then looked at his arrows. "Lemuel, how do you feel about staying here to guard the horses?" Pol asked. He pulled an arrow out of his quiver and showed it to the hunter. His was a proper war arrow with a *makaar*-killing point on it. Lemuel's was . . . a hunting arrow with a deer point. The pull on Pol's bow was probably twice, or even three times, that of Lemuel's.

The hunter took the hint. "Aye, that," he said. "Ye're aright. I'll do nobbut tickle 'im." He pointed at a game trail that wound through the smaller trees and brush that somehow found enough light to thrive beneath these giants. "Foller that. 'Twill take ye to tha uncanny place. He'll be not far from't. On'y time he strayed was when he et Waybrook."

Mel made them all hold still long enough to cast "Featherfoot" on them. She wasn't powerful enough for a full Silence spell, but this would muffle their footsteps and prevent any breaking twigs from making a sound. Then they all crept down the game trail at a crouch, with her bringing up the rear, ready with the handful of combat spells she had at her disposal.

They heard the "uncanny place" before they saw it. A sound like a nest of angry wasps—and when they finally got to a place they could see it, well, it was uncanny, all right.

What looked like a column of pale lavender light, barely visible, began at the ground at the end of the trail, and continued up as far as Mel could see. The area it covered was roughly house-sized, and inside it, the vegetation was just . . . wrong. Plants and grasses were in bloom, bearing fruit, and dropping autumn leaves, all at the same time. Bushes had two or three kinds of leaves on them, some shapes she didn't recognize. One bush didn't have leaves or branches at all; it seemed to be a cluster of spiky insect legs, which moved restlessly.

"Change Circle," she hissed under her breath. She'd

never seen one, only heard of them—places where magic went wild, distorting and twisting the unfortunate creatures that got caught or stumbled into them.

:I haven't seen one of those in a very long time,: Need replied. *:Must have been caused by the Mage Storms.:*

Before any of the lads could ask her what she meant, the Beast slunk into view, and she smothered a gasp of dismay. Well, now she knew why the Beast lingered around the Change Circle. It probably was trying, in its dim way, to figure out how to get changed *back*.

It had two heads on the end of the long, sinuous neck of a cold-drake. One was the cold-drake head you'd expect to find there. The other was the head of a *makaar* and most closely resembled that of a horned vulture, just as the gryphon's head resembled that of an eagle. Black feathers sprouted in channels between the scales, all down the cold-drake neck, ending in a six-legged body. The body was all cold-drake, complete with the heavy, thrashing tail, though it too had black feathers sprouting from between the scales. Four of the legs were the cold-drake's, and two were the *makaar*'s forelegs, growing from the shoulder, and looking absurdly small on the cold-drake's massive body. And the black wings of a *makaar* sprouted from its back, much too small to allow the thing to fly.

As they watched, the thing walked up to the Change Circle and tried to get inside, but it threw up both heads and sent out a roar and a scream when it touched the lavender light. Cries of agony, it sounded like to Mel. Something about the Change Circle obviously caused it great pain. It backed up, tail thrashing the brush unmercifully, and screamed again.

:I think we ought to back up and try to come up with some kind of—: Need began.

The Beast whipped its neck around as if it had *heard* her, and both pairs of eyes stared right where they were hiding.

Then it charged.

Mel got off a light-flash right into its eyes, which was the only thing that saved them. Blinded, it continued its charge anyway, but at least they were able to fling themselves out of the way as it blundered on in a straight line, bouncing off tree trunks and tearing up the ground with its talons.

They regrouped immediately as it bounced off a last trunk, then stood its ground, shaking its head to clear its vision. It pivoted and peered in every direction, shaking its heads. And then it spotted them, uttered its twin cries of rage, and charged again.

They barely made it away from the thing, and two of them were unconscious. Pol had Harl draped over his shoulder, and Mel managed to get a spell off to lighten Kerd enough that she could manage him with one hand—because her arm was broken. She'd blinded the Beast a second time, but it had swept the three of them with its tail, and Pol was the only one who'd dashed away unscathed. They'd managed to get away before it got its sight back again, but they could still hear it in the distance, thrashing around and screeching.

"I think we might be far enough away," Mel panted. "And I need to do something about my arm right this minute, or I'm not going to be able to cast another spell."

"It's so fast . . . how can something that big move so fast?" Pol gasped, lowing Harl to the ground. He knelt beside his fellow mercenary and felt him all over. "No broken bones, just a concussion, I think."

Mel had already dropped Kerd, and fumbled in her belt pouch for the numbing talisman. She pressed it into her arm and sighed with relief, then pulled on it until she felt the bone ends click into place, "Can you get a splint on this?" she asked Pol, who'd just checked Kerd.

While the Beast continued screaming in the distance, Pol got her arm splinted, then laid his two unconscious fellows out and covered them with leaves to keep them warmish. Mel bound the numbing talisman into the bandages around her arm, but she wasn't going to be using that limb any time soon. "It's too fast," she groaned, sitting on the ground beside Kerd. "We need a better Mage than I am. I wish to *hell* I was a fighter, not a Mage!"

:So give me to Pol,: Need said.

"Why?" Pol asked.

:Give me to Pol!:

"Because this's a magic sword. If you're a Mage, she can turn you into a trained fighter. If you're a fighter—she turns you into a *major* magician. But only if—"

:GIVE ME TO POL, YOU BLITHERING IDIOT!:

Mel stopped in midsentence, briefly "deafened" by Need. *:But I thought—:*

:Just give me to Pol!:

Mel gulped, and fumbled off the belt holding Need, wordlessly handing belt and sword to the mercenary. "She says to give her to you."

Pol stared. "What?"

"Just put her on. She'll explain for herself, I guess." At this point, Mel was so confused and exhausted she couldn't think clearly. Pol got up off his knees and strapped the sword on, and for a moment, Mel wondered—was Pol a woman disguised as a man?

But . . . no. No, there was no doubt Pol was male. Not from this angle. And besides, why would Pol have bothered? The Wolves had both men and women in their ranks. There was no reason for a disguise. Pol stood there with a "listening" look on his face, and his expression changed literally from moment to moment. At one point he looked as though he was going to cry. But mostly, he listened, and nodded, and finally he offered his hand to Mel, who took it, and he pulled her to her feet.

"Let's finish this," he said with determination. "I

want you to hit that thing with—Need says, that blinding spell on the *makaar* head, followed with something she calls a—a stink spell? On the cold-drake head. She says she thinks those two together will shock it long enough for it to stop moving, and that's when she'll hit it."

"We sure as the seven hells can't leave it running loose," Mel agreed. "It's only a matter of time before it goes hunting for food again, and *makaar* prefer humans to anything else, so they'll go straight for the next village. Let's do this."

Once again, she cast Featherfoot on them both, and they slowly made their way back to the Change Circle. The Beast was still rampaging and raving, so at least they knew where it was.

It had torn up everything there was to tear up around the Change Circle in its futile search for them. Perhaps because at the moment the *makaar* head seemed to be in charge. The cold-drake head shook every so often, and its pupils were dilated so much there seemed to be no iris to them. It seemed to be letting the *makaar* head do what it wanted while it got its vision back.

Now Mel understood why Need had been so specific about which spell to put on which head. The *makaar* had no sense of smell; the cold-drake did. If she got them reversed, the cold-drake would still be able to track them by scent, and the *makaar* by vision. Right now, the *makaar* head was in control, the cold-drake still concentrating on getting its sight back, which was why it hadn't detected them yet.

But its sense of hearing made up for its lack of sense of smell. She barely breathed, "Signal when ready."

Pol raised his hand slightly. She kept one eye on it, one eye on the Beast, and both spells ready in her mind. Pol dropped his hand, and she let off the blinding spell on the makaar's head, then the "stink" smell on the cold-drake.

The second smell didn't just smell "bad" . . . it was so awful it was literally a weapon. It brought on uncontrolled coughing, tearing, and gagging in humans, and was devastatingly effective on entire groups of soldiers. It could literally stop any monstrous beast she'd tried it on in its tracks.

And it absolutely stopped the Beast. It flung up both heads in pain and confusion, howling, and not only freezing in place, but digging the claws of all four walking feet into the earth to brace itself against attack. But attack didn't come from them.

It came from the Change Circle.

A bolt of lightning as thick as a man flashed out from somewhere at the top of the Change Circle and struck the Beast in the middle of the back. It was eye-wateringly bright, and the simultaneous crack of thunder nearly knocked her over with its concussive force.

And still the Beast stood, though she could see through dazzled eyes that Need had definitely hurt it. She couldn't *hear* the shriek of pain, but since both heads tossed wildly with mouths open, she assumed they were shrieking. She had a little warning before Need and Pol hit the Beast with a second lightning bolt; she clapped her hands over her ears and ducked her head, only looking again when it was safe. Need had *definitely* hurt it this time. One more—

Again, she ducked her head and protected her ears. This time her hearing had recovered enough that she heard the thunderclap again—and heard Pol shout *"Now!"*

She stood up and saw that the Beast was down, and she used the one good offensive combat spell she had—a fire-arrow—and cast it again and again at the makaar head's eyes, while Pol and Need rushed in and plunged Need's blade through the cold-drake's eye into its brain. Then, they turned to do the same to the *makaar.*

But there was no need. She'd already killed the *makaar* head. And Pol jumped back as the body thrashed in its death throes.

And right at that moment her mind finally put two together with a puzzling two and came up with four. She went to Pol's side, and they both watched the Beast die, and her hearing finally got back to normal. And that was when she turned to him.

"All your life you've felt as if you were born into the wrong body, haven't you?" she said, quietly, as he looked at her, his pupils widening at her words. "You've known you were a girl, and yet you were somehow stuck in this—"

She stopped, because his eyes were glistening, and she was afraid he was about to cry. "Oh, my poor dear," she said instead. "That's why Need could go to you."

He took a deep, shuddering breath. "Need . . . wants you to put your hand on her so she can talk to both of us."

She did.

:I can fix that—maybe,: Need said, as soon as Mel had her hand on the sword's hilt.

"Define 'maybe,'" Mel replied.

:I know how to do a complete physical transformation. It takes a lot of power, which I normally don't have access to, but there is *that much power in the Change Circle. And that will have the advantage of draining the Change Circle, so it can't hurt anyone anymore. But . . . the odds are 50–50 whether I can control the magic, because it's chaotic and unpredictable.:*

"And what happens if you fail?" Mel asked steadily, since Pol seemed to be having trouble speaking.

:Best case is Pol dies. Worst case is Pol will wish he'd died.:

"I . . . there are already days I wish I was dead," Pol blurted. "Being a monster wouldn't be worse than this. Being *dead* wouldn't be worse than this!"

Mel thought about forbidding this. Just taking Need away from Pol, right now, and saying it was not going to happen.

But this wasn't *her* life. It wasn't *her* right to forbid another person something that did no harm to her or anyone else.

"Life's not a bowl of roses as a girl, you know," she cautioned, giving Pol one more chance to back out. "There's breasts—they're fun, but damned inconvenient, too. And all the monthly garbage. And men will always treat you differently than they do now—some as something to conquer and dominate, some as something to protect, some as someone beneath contempt. Even the ones that treat you as an equal will treat you differently than they would have as an equal *man*. Sometimes that will be great. Sometimes, not so great."

Pol's eyes were very, very bright now, and he was having a hard time getting the words out. "I'll take that chance. I'll take all those chances. Please. . . ."

She shook her head. "Don't ask me for permission. It's not my life, it's yours. All I'm doing is giving you information. Take your life, Pol, and make it what you want to make it."

He took a very deep breath.

:Ready?: asked Need.

"I've been ready all my life."

Together they stepped into the Change Circle.

Mel got Lemuel and the horses, and together they collected Kerd and Harl and got them to the Change Circle, where she worked Healing magic on them. When they finally came to, she explained to them that Pol had volunteered to take her magic sword into the Change Circle to close it down, knowing it might kill or change him forever. And then they had all settled in to wait.

By nightfall she could tell that the power in the Change Circle had diminished somewhat. "This is going to go on through the night," she said. "We might as well eat and bed down." So they made a campfire and gnawed their way through the trail food, she worked a little more Healing magic on the lads, and then Lemuel volunteered to take the first watch.

But she couldn't sleep, of course. Her arm throbbed, but more than that, she hoped and was afraid to hope. She stared at the Change Circle, at the vague form inside it, and hoped, and was afraid to hope. She knew she could never truly understand the agony of someone who felt—who *knew*—she had been born into the wrong body. It was so much more painful than merely wanting something. This was *necessary.* Necessary as breathing.

But what if she came out a monster? Worse, still male? All she could do was pray, which she didn't do often . . . but pray she did, and to a goddess: Agnetha, who, surely, surely would heed the prayers of a woman to help a woman.

Finally, at dawn, as she continued to keep a bleary-eyed vigil, the Change Circle suddenly flared, crackled all over with lightning—and died.

And she peeled herself out of her bedroll and ran, full of dread.

Well, the vague, shadowy form that knelt with Need across its knees wasn't obviously monstrous—or dead—

"Pol?" she called.

And Pol looked up, lip quivering, eyes too bright.

"It worked," she whispered, and burst into tears.

And Mel gathered the girl into her arms and let her sob with relief and joy and a hundred other emotions until she was exhausted.

"Dunno what to say," Harl said, looking bewildered.

They had all traveled back to the village to deliver the good news. The villagers were somewhat in awe of Pol's "sacrifice" and entirely unsure of how to respond except by deciding to throw a feast in their honor. That at least gave everyone something to do, but in the morning, the warhorse was still in the room, and Pol's two companions just didn't know what to do about it.

"It's all right," Pol told Harl, patting him on the shoulder. Pol didn't look *that* much different from her old self, aside from the breasts and the curves, and the softening of her face. As if the old Pol had had a twin sister, perhaps.

"You lads do me a favor. Go ask the blacksmith how he'd feel about building me a new tavern, hmm? I think I'm going to settle here if they will," Mel interrupted. Happy for any excuse to get away from an increasingly uncomfortable situation, they left.

Mel put her good hand on Need's hilt. "Obviously you've chosen Pol," she said.

:Obviously. But . . . this . . . took a lot out of me. I think I am going to sleep for a while.: The sword's thoughts came slowly, as if they were swimming through honey.

"What does that mean?" Pol asked, uncertainly.

"It means she won't be talking to you directly, I think," Mel replied.

"For how long?"

She shrugged. "Maybe not again in your lifetime. That was *major* magic, young one. It drained her. Look, you useless piece of iron, tell Pol how to use you before you doze off on us!" She'd suspected this was going to happen and was not entirely unhappy that it had. Pol was going to have enough on her hands adjusting to her new life without having Need yammering at her.

:When there's a woman in trouble . . . that you can help . . . you'll feel it. Feel bad . . . when you move away. Feel better . . . as you get closer. Then, when . . . you need magic . . . will what you want. I . . . have . . . to . . . sleep.: And then . . . there was silence.

"I understand the first part, but what—"

Mel patted her shoulder. "Settle down. Just think of what you've seen Mages do in the past. Will it to happen.

The stronger your will and imagination, the better the spell will be. Try small things, like moving silently, at first. Work your way up. You'll figure it out. And when Need's ready to go to someone else, you'll know that, too." She laughed a little. "Trust me, you'll be ready to settle down *long* before she's ready to move to a new bearer."

"I—" Pol began. And then, her mouth gave an odd twitch.

"Already?" Mel asked, knowingly.

"I—I think so." Pol's mouth twitched again. "It feels like something tugging at my gut. East and south."

Mel sighed. She didn't envy the girl. But then again, Pol was now both a highly trained fighter *and* a Mage more powerful than she had ever dreamed of being. It was all up to her now. "Get your gear, and take Sam. I don't need him, and you will. Go before your friends come back."

Her eyes flickered in the direction Harl and Kerd had gone. Her mouth took on a wry twist. "Aye, they don't really know what to do with me, do they?"

"And neither do you know what to do with them. Go."

She watched Pol and Sam and Need ride off into the forest, east and south, with a little sadness, a little relief, and a great deal of wonder. How would they fare out there? Well, she hoped. Pol had all the tools she needed to, well, become something of a legend, if that was what she wanted. And if she didn't, all the tools to carve herself a good and useful life. It would be up to her, and her alone, to see if she could be happy. *And that's more than many can say,* she thought, as they vanished into the distance. *And as for me—I've helped plenty, hurt few, and here I am, with a small miracle I assisted along. That's more than many can say, too.*

From where she stood beside the picket line, she saw Harl and Kerd approaching with the blacksmith, the three of them yammering away and making building-like gestures at the circle of meadow. And she started to grin. It looked as if she wasn't the only one who found the idea of settling here a good one. With two strong lads to help, making that tavern a reality was going to take less time than she thought.

Pol's not the only one with a new life, it seems, she thought, and began walking to meet them. "Have you got someone that makes barrels?" she called. "You need the right barrels to make good mead and wine."

Just like you need the right people to make a good life.

About the Authors

Dylan Birtolo resides in the Pacific Northwest, where he spends his time as a writer, a game designer, and a professional sword-swinger. He's published a few fantasy novels and several short stories. On the game side, he contributed to Dragonfire and designed both Henchman and Shadowrun Sprawl Ops. He trains in Systema and with the Seattle Knights, an acting troop that focuses on stage combat. He jousts, and yes, the armor is real—it weighs over 100 pounds. You can read more about him and his works at www.dylanbirtolo.com or follow his Twitter @DylanBirtolo.

Jennifer Brozek is a multitalented, award-winning author, editor, and tie-in writer. She is the author of *Never Let Me Sleep* and *The Last Days of Salton Academy*, both of which were finalists for the Bram Stoker Award. Her *BattleTech* tie-in novel, *The Nellus Academy Incident*, won a Scribe Award. Her editing work has netted her a Hugo Award nomination as well as an Australian Shadows Award for *Grants Pass*. Jennifer's short-form work has appeared in Apex Publications and in anthologies set in the worlds of *Valdemar*, *Shadowrun*, *V-Wars*, and *Predator*. Jennifer is also the Creative Director of Apocalypse Ink Productions and was the managing editor of Evil Girlfriend Media and assistant editor for Apex Book Company. She has been a freelance author, editor, tie-in writer for over ten years after leaving her high-paying tech job, and she's never been happier. She keeps a tight schedule on her writing and editing projects and somehow manages to find time to volunteer for several professional writing organizations such as SFWA, HWA, and IAMTW. She shares her husband, Jeff, with several cats and often uses him as a sounding board for her story ideas. Visit Jennifer's worlds at jenniferbrozek.com.

Brigid Collins is a fantasy and science fiction writer living in Michigan. Her short stories have appeared in *Fiction River, The Young Explorer's Adventure Guide*, and *Chronicle Worlds: Feyland*. Books 1 through 3 of her fantasy series, *Songbird River Chronicles*, and her dark fairy tale novella, *Thorn and Thimble*, are available in print and electronic versions on Amazon and Kobo. You can sign up for her newsletter at tinyletter.com/HarmonicStories or follow her on twitter @purellian.

Ron Collins is the bestselling Amazon Dark Fantasy author of *Saga of the God-Touched Mage* and *Stealing the Sun,* a series of space-based SF books. He has contributed 100 or so stories to premier science fiction and fantasy publications, including *Analog*, *Asimov's*, and several volumes of the Valdemar anthology series. His work has garnered a *Writers of the Future* prize, and a CompuServe HOMer award. His short story "The White Game" was nominated for the Short Mystery Fiction Society's 2016 Derringer Award. Find current information about Ron at typosphere.com.

Hailed as "one of the best writers working today" by bestselling author Dean Wesley Smith, **Dayle A. Dermatis** is the author or coauthor of many novels and more than a hundred short stories in multiple genres, including urban fantasy novels *Ghosted* and *Shaded*. She is the mastermind behind the Uncollected Anthology project; her short fiction has been lauded in year's best anthologies in erotica, mystery, and horror; and in her spare time she's taken up editing anthologies. She lives in a book- and cat-filled historic English-style cottage in the wild greenscapes of the Pacific Northwest. In her spare time she follows Styx around the country and travels the world, which inspires her writing. To find out where she's wandered off to (and to get free fiction!), check out DayleDermatis.com and sign up for her newsletter.

Michele Lang grew up in deepest suburbia, the daughter of a Hungarian mystic and a fast-talking used-car salesman. Now she writes tales of magic, crime, and adventure. Author of the *Lady Lazarus* historical urban fantasy series, Michele also writes urban fantasy for the Uncollected Anthology series.

Fiona Patton lives in rural Ontario, where she can practice bagpipes without bothering the neighbors. Her partner Tanya Huff, their two dogs and many cats have taken some time to get used to them but no longer run when she gets the pipes out. She has written seven fantasy novels for DAW Books as well as over forty short stories. "The Once and Future Box" is her eleventh Valdemar story, the ninth involving the Dann family.

Diana L. Paxson is the author of 29 novels, including the Westria series and the Avalon novels, numerous short stories, and nonfiction on goddesses, trance work, and the runes, and more than 90 short stories. Many of her novels have historical settings, a good preparation for writing about Valdemar. She also writes nonfiction on topics from mythology to trance work. Her next book will be a study of the Norse god

Odin. She also engages in occasional craftwork, costuming, and playing the harp She lives in the multigenerational, multitalented household called Greyhaven in Berkeley.

Angela Penrose lives in Seattle with her husband, seven computers, and about ten thousand books. She's been a Valdemar fan for decades and wrote her first Valdemar story for the "Modems of the Queen" area on the old GEnie network, back in the 1980s. In addition to fantasy, she also writes SF and mysteries, sometimes in combination. She's had stories published in *Loosed Upon the World, Fiction River, The Year's Best Crime and Mystery Stories 2016,* and of course *Pathways,* the last Valdemar anthology.

Growing up on fairy tales and computer games, *USA Today* bestselling author **Anthea Sharp** has melded the two in her award-winning, bestselling *Feyland* series, which has sold over 200k copies worldwide. In addition to the fae fantasy/cyberpunk mashup of Feyland, she also writes Victorian Spacepunk and fantasy romance. Her books have won awards, topped bestseller lists, and garnered over a million reads at Wattpad. She's frequently found hanging out on Amazon's Top 100 Fantasy/SF author list. Her short fiction has appeared in Fiction River, DAW anthologies, *The Future Chronicles*, and *Beyond the Stars: At Galaxy's Edge*, as well as many other publications. Her newest novel, *Star Compass*, is now available at all online retailers.

Stephanie Shaver lives in Southern California with a prepositional phrase-crushing spouse, two rambunctious children, and a very patient cat. By day she works for Blizzard as a program manager; by night she's probably trying to catch up on sleep. You can find her full bibliography at sdshaver.com, along with occasional ramblings when she isn't sleeping or chasing the kids off the cat.

Kristin Schwengel lives near Milwaukee, Wisconsin, with her husband, the obligatory writer's cat (named Gandalf, of course), a Darwinian garden in which only the strong survive, and a growing collection of knitting and spinning supplies. Her writing has appeared in several previous Valdemar anthologies, among others. After finding a YouTube documentary of unknown origin on the supposed strategies of Harald Hardrada during his time in the Byzantine Varangian Guard, she immediately decided to make use of those tactics in a Valdemar story.

Growing up in the wilds of the Sierra Nevada mountains, surrounded by deer and beaver, muskrat and bear, **Louisa Swann** found ample fodder for her equally wild imagination. As an adult, she spins both experiences and imagination into tales that span multiple genres, including fantasy, science fiction, mystery, and her newest love—steampunk. Her short stories have appeared in Mercedes Lackey's Elementary Magic and Valdemar anthologies (which she's thrilled to participate in!); Esther Friesner's *Chicks and Balances*; and several Fiction River anthologies, including *No Humans Allowed* and *Reader's Choice*. Her new steampunk/weird west series, Abby Crumb, debuted this summer. Find out more at www.louisaswann.com.

Elizabeth A. Vaughan is the *USA Today*-bestselling author of fantasy romance novels. She has always loved fantasy and has been a fantasy role-player since 1981. You can learn more about her books at www.writeandrepeat.com.

Elisabeth Waters sold her first short story in 1980 to Marion Zimmer Bradley for *The Keeper's Price*, the first of the Darkover anthologies. She then went on to sell short stories to a variety of anthologies. Her first novel, a fantasy called *Changing Fate*, was awarded the 1989 Gryphon Award. Its sequel, *Mending Fate*, was published in 2016. She is now concentrating more on short stories. She has also worked as a supernumerary with the San Francisco Opera, where she appeared in *La Gioconda, Manon Lescaut, Madama Butterfly, Khovanschina, Das Rheingold, Werther*, and *Idomeneo.*

Phaedra Weldon grew up in the thick, atmospheric land of South Georgia. Most nights, especially those in October, were spent on the back of pickup trucks in the center of cornfields, telling ghost stories, or in friends' homes playing RPGs. She got her start writing in shared worlds (*Eureka!*, *Star Trek*, *Battletech*, *Shadowrun*), selling original stories to DAW anthologies, and she has sold her first urban fantasy series to traditional publishing. Currently she writes three series (The Eldritch Files, the Grimoire Chronicles, and the Zoe Martinique novels) as well as busting out the occasional *Shadowrun* novel (her most recent one is *Identity Crisis*).

Through her combined career as an author and cover artist, **Janny Wurts** has written nineteen novels, a collection of short stories once nominated for the British Fantasy Award, and thirty-five contributions to fantasy and science fiction anthologies. *Destiny's Conflict* is her current release in the War of Light and Shadow series. Other titles include standalones *To Ride Hell's Chasm*, *Master of Whitestorm*, and *Sorcerer's Legacy*; the *Cycle of Fire* trilogy; and the Empire trilogy written in collaboration with Raymond E. Feist. Her paintings have appeared in exhibitions including the NASA 25th Anniversary exhibit, Delaware Art Museum, Canton Art Museum, Hayden Planetarium in New York, and have been recognized by two Chesley Awards and three times Best of Show at the World Fantasy Convention. She lives in Florida with three cats and two horses and rides with a mounted team for search and rescue. Her life experience as an offshore sailor, wilderness enthusiast, and musician is reflected in her creative work.

About the Editor

Mercedes Lackey is a full-time writer and has published numerous novels and works of short fiction, including the bestselling *Heralds of Valdemar* series. She is also a professional lyricist and a licensed wild bird rehabilitator. She lives in Oklahoma with her husband and collaborator, artist Larry Dixon, and their flock of parrots.